I0654899

Minsk Rises

A Cove Rock Book

Published by Cove Rock
A Division of Cove Rock Media
Clearwater, Florida

MINSK RISES

MINSK RISES

ERIC ALMEIDA

Published by Cove Rock
First released in digital format in 2011

ISBN-13: 9780692730270
ISBN-10: 0692730273

Cover photo by Tatyana Yablonskaya
Cover design by Diane Whiddon

www.ericalmeida.com

PROLOGUE

25 March 2007

For this round the regime had cordoned off more than just Oktyabraska Square; they'd sealed off nine surrounding blocks. Russell Piper knew because he'd reconnoitered the entire periphery on foot, from Internatsionalnaya and Lenin Streets to GUM department store, from the Presidential Palace down to the Svisloch River. Militiamen arrayed along every sidewalk and interior courtyard. Shops, restaurants and cafes closed---a contrived *sanitarni dien*, or "cleaning day", according to blunt, government-issued door-signs. Almost noon on a mild and sparkling March Sunday, and the heart of Minsk was locked down and void of pedestrians.

He climbed onto an elevated corner at the Belarussian National Circus, where several thousand displaced demonstrators were coalescing on the plaza and opposite sidewalk. Prohibited red-and-white banners of the Belarussian opposition waved overhead among them, together with the blue-and-gold standard of the European Union. Numbers grew to five or six thousand as additional people flowed in from other directions. Soon they erupted with chants: "Zhivye Belarus! Zhivye Belarus!" *Long live Belarus! Long live Belarus!*

Piper released a disappointed exhalation. The slogan wasn't his favorite; he preferred those he'd heard on video from the previous March 25th--- more animating and powerful ones, in his view. *Truth. Freedom.* Most important, though, was that demonstrators weren't capitulating.

Before the crowd could grow much further, a line of buses pulled up on Yanka Kupala Street and disgorged hundreds of black-helmeted, baton-wielding riot police. One column ran straight up onto the terrace where Piper was standing and forced him and others off in a moving ring, also giving him the chance to view the policemen up-close. Young faces behind the plexiglass face-shields. Malleable eighteen and nineteen-year-old boys from the villages. Willing to take orders. Ready to do combat.

They began pushing the crowd up the Prospekt, in an involuntary procession. Caught in the flow, Piper heard his cell-phone ring and pulled it from his inside pocket. The caller was another U.S. observer, a Russia hand sent over from Langley; the situation on the other side of Oktyabraska Square had taken an equally adverse turn. The principal opposition leader and former presidential candidate had scuffled with militia in front of GUM and been diverted south with several thousand other demonstrators, all now detached from the main procession.

Thus far, an inauspicious start.

Upon disconnecting he took closer look at the demonstrators around him, however, and found new basis for encouragement. There was a preponderance of students, as usual, largely male. But also a healthy turnout of females---at least twenty percent of the total, he reckoned, perhaps more. He knew Minsk contained a plethora of modern-thinking, ambitious young women, just as Kiev did during the tumultuous weeks of November-December 2004. Then, at the historic epicenter on the *Maydan*, the proportion had been even higher. Closer ratios generated more energy and impetus. In Minsk, he believed, the higher the female share, the better.

His attention swung to the opposite side of the Prospekt, where five or six male students, in a burst of defiance, tried to stand their ground around a flag. There was a whir of batons, smacks against bone and flesh. Several stumbled to the ground with blood on their faces, flecking scarlet on a snow-bank before they were promptly hustled away to waiting paddy-wagons.

Other marchers rippled with outrage, but didn't falter, even if the message was clear. The regime was ready to inflict severe violence, if challenged. To crush mass movements and stray individuals alike.

Just ahead on the bridge over the Svisloch, municipal police already lined both curbs, preventing protesters from spilling onto the asphalt, while additional riot detachments kept channeling the protesters forward. This procession would be forced all the way up the Academy of Sciences and beyond, until it was spent.

Piper thought of reaction from Washington and shook his head.

For now the Kiev scenario didn't apply. There were certain promising signs. But Minsk still had considerable distance to go.

There would be no Orange Revolution here, at least not this year.

*   *   *

The chirping phone roused Lena Antonova out of deep concentration. She put down her pen and marked her place in the article she was notating: *Looking beyond Social Commentary in Dreiser.* Natasha was known to call at importune moments. She was now speaking over background noise from a television and sounded excited, almost out of breath. "I had the volume up for a reason," she said, when Lena asked her to lower it.

"What are you doing?" Natasha asked.

"Preparing for my lecture tomorrow."

"Turn on *Euronews.* There's a live report coming on soon from Minsk, about the demonstration. Quick!"

With a sigh Lena rose, crossed the living room and grabbed the remote. She clicked on the TV and found the channel. A report was in progress on the European Union's 50th-Anniversary celebration in Berlin.

"What's the big deal? I already knew about it…."

"Wait…There it is. That's just one block from your apartment!"

Back on-screen a live transmission issued from the Prospekt, just past the intersection with Masherova. Flags, streams of youthful faces under shaggy hair. A contingent of demonstrators, not much younger than Lena herself, shouted and pumped fists as they moved cross-camera. The frame shifted to a reporter, standing next to a lamp-post as marchers filed behind. The demonstration had been scheduled for noon on Oktyabraska Square…Stymied by militia, he said…. Leaders harassed…Protesters now marching toward the Academy of Sciences, numbering six to seven thousand. He held his microphone with a slumped posture, as if he'd yearned for more.

Video images from Iran replaced those from Minsk. Other tales of frustration and woe, further from home. Lena wasn't surprised. She returned the phone to her ear.

"What I expected," she said. "It's not even a lead story this year. By tomorrow it will be forgotten."

Natasha didn't relinquish her enthusiasm.

"Why don't you go out and have a closer look? Descend from your ivory tower?"

"And do what? Get videotaped by the militia? Cause complications for myself at the Institute? Who needs it?"

"You might at least check it out from your balcony. You have a great view."

"I'll think about it. By the way…Why aren't you out there?"

Silence fell on Natasha's end of the connection. When she spoke again her enthusiasm had ebbed.

"I thought about it. But I was worried about beatings by the militia."

Lena sighed again. Just as she'd thought. Most people still weren't ready to cross those lines.

She admitted. She was among them.

*   *   *

Piper tucked his scarf inside his overcoat and lowered the edge of his beret as he watched the protesters regroup in front of the Academy of Sciences. Video cameras proliferated across the stepped plaza: half a dozen from Russian and Ukrainian television stations, several from Western news organizations, the rest wielded by plainclothesmen from the Belarussian KGB. A gray militia van pulled up with curtained windows and big loudspeakers on top. "Gatherings are prohibited at the Academy of Sciences," it boomed. "You must proceed to Bangalore, to Freedom Park."

Freedom Park was a tract of un-manicured grass and trees on the outskirts of the city, muted and out-of-sight. None of the protesters budged.

The injunction was repeated. Same result. Instead, the protesters seized on the name and revived a chant from the previous year:

Svoboda! Svoboda! Svoboda!

Freedom. Piper adjusted his outlook. If he was reassigned to Minsk---if Langley overruled his objections and discounted the stress to his marriage, due to insistence from the White House---he might really have something to build upon.

Sensing attention from his side, he turned to meet the gazes of two female protesters: early-to-mid 20s, probably university students, totemic marvels who could energize any setting---especially ones like this where politics amplified their sway. Disposed, just now, to share expanding possibilities. Visceral urges rushed to the fore.

For all the disparities with Kiev he recognized them. Freedom was a rousing idea. Capable of producing big changes---the kind he believed in and sought to advance.

This time round, he'd just have to curb some of its accompanying defilements.

Revolutions and sex, he knew from Kiev, often marched in tandem. And sex could be the most powerful change agent of all.

CHAPTER 1

Saturday, 19 July 2008

Back in better days---more prosperous, ascendant, confident days---Evan Morris had never envisioned himself in Belarus. He'd known little of the country, and held little desire to learn more. On this particular afternoon, moreover, out in the countryside, he felt even more displaced than usual.

Across the clearing several programmers tramped out of the woods with bundles of branches, chopped with hand axes. From inside the *dacha* came kitchen sounds: women preparing skewers and other barbecue fare. *Shashlik.* One of the few Russian words that he'd retained through seven months of lessons.

The fault didn't reside with Lena. He couldn't have asked for a more conscientious tutor. The language just wasn't sticking, and he had had no one but himself to blame.

Deciding he couldn't stand idle, he walked toward the barbecue pit and intersected with Yuri. One-time member of the Soviet scientific elite. Head scientist in the lab. Diligent host. The dacha was his.

"Would you like another beer?" Yuri asked in English, with his usual tobacco-cured bass.

There would be vodka toasts later on, Morris presumed. He needed to save himself.

"No thanks. Not quite finished with this one."

Yuri squinted at him, taking a drag from his cigarette. In addition to being the only foreigner present, Morris was also the boss. Envoy from corporate back in Santa Clara. Therefore subject to special attention, which had both pluses and minuses.

"Then I have another idea," Yuri declared after a moment.

Morris looked back. He hoped it didn't involve breaking a sweat.

"Would you like to pick berries with me?"

"Wild berries?"

"Yes, raspberries. Mid-July is perfect season. We can eat them for breakfast tomorrow. There's a very good place nearby...what do you call it in English?"

"A patch."

"Yes, a patch. Anyway, it's less than two kilometers away. Right along a trail that runs near here."

Morris wasn't fond of traipsing through brush, due in part to numerous childhood bouts with poison ivy. Then he recalled there was no poison ivy in the European sub-continent. And the trail was a bonus, which made him more receptive to the idea.

"I suppose so," he said. "Why not?"

"Good. As I say, this patch is an excellent one. We can fill two buckets each in no time."

Yuri ground out his cigarette, disappeared into a shed and re-emerged with four plastic buckets, handing two over. They set out, traversing the clearing and entering a path into the woods. Greenery enveloped them, with tall pines and birches creating a speckled canopy overhead. Belarus wasn't over-hot---even in mid summer---and the scented air made the walk pleasant. Their dirt footpath soon converged onto asphalt: a trail about two meters across, painted white along its borders, in fine condition. Yuri noted Morris's surprise.

"Our president has a dacha near here," he explained. "Actually more like a compound. I've never seen it. It's behind walls…He uses this trail for skiing in the winter."

Morris took that to mean cross-country skiing. "Is it okay to walk here?"

"Yes, Yes. It's okay. His house is quite far. Probably three kilometers."

Morris looked at him. Yuri sensed his concern.

"I wouldn't worry," he added. "He doesn't even come here in the summer, as far as I know."

Yuri increased his pace and Morris angled out his buckets as he followed suit. For a man in his early 60s with a sedentary career and a two-pack-a-day habit, Yuri had aged amazingly well, with a trim physique, full gray hair, and considerable stamina. Something to do with the Russian's childhood in Siberia, Morris figured.

Though he himself didn't exercise much, he was lean and could keep up without much exertion. Around a bend, asphalt slightly banked with the terrain. The asphalt pathway continued to impress him.

"How far does this trail go?" he asked.

"It goes in a loop, about five kilometers. There are a couple of others connected to it… a small network."

"No one uses it in the summer?"

"Occasionally the national ski team trains here…on those roller skies."

Morris glanced back over his shoulder, then forward again. Observing this, Yuri assured him.

"Don't worry, you'll hear them coming, if they're here."

Minutes later Yuri gestured off the trail down a wooded embankment.

"This way," he said. "Follow me."

They veered down a faint footpath, only slightly matted. Otherwise there was little evidence of human visitation. Thirty meters further down, full sun broke overhead. A tangle of brush and vines came into view, covering a sizable ravine. Ground under Morris' feet became a little damper. Yuri stopped and Morris drew up beside him.

"It's the best picking I've ever found," Yuri proclaimed, nodding and squinting over the area. "And no bears, either."

Morris' reaction prompted a smile from the Russian.

"They're a worry around berries in Siberia," he elaborated. "They like the sweetness. But not here. There are no bears left in Belarus."

Morris smiled back. "What about people? Do many others know about it?"

"I don't think so. I discovered it on my own, by accident. In fact I've never met anyone else here."

Morris gazed back over the ravine and realized he hadn't mulled his troubles since setting out from the dacha. Agonies he'd left behind in the States, back in the Bay Area, in the high-intensity environs of Silicon Valley, were more distant than twenty minutes earlier. Money troubles most of all.

"Where do we start?" he asked, smiling and shifting his buckets forward.

"Anywhere you want," Yuri answered. "There are berries everywhere."

CHAPTER 2

Truth was, certain aspects of life in Belarus had started growing on Morris. This was just the latest example. Still standing at the edge of the patch, he plucked several raspberries off the closest bush and tasted them. Yuri was correct: juicy but not overripe. They soon diverged: Morris moving along at random and plucking berries almost by handful. Seeking freer movement, he set his empty bucket on a rock, stood at full height for a moment to plot its location, and continued. Yuri's rustled off out of sight through the brush.

Overhead sun created a soothing sensation on his face and arms. His shirt became damp, while violet juice colored his fingers. So what if Belarus was the only sizable, industrialized country in the Western world without a golf course? Where Soviet-era bureaucracy still held sway and customer service remained a novel concept?

That mattered less this afternoon. Belarus had other merits which balanced out the drawbacks.

Vines grew denser as he roamed more deeply. In 20 minutes his first bucket was full, with more than enough berries to satisfy a half-dozen people. He re-traced his steps to the first bucket, and set the full container down on the rock. He straightened again and looked around.

Faint rustlings emanated from the interior of the ravine, though the coordinates were unclear.

"Yuri, you still out there?" he said, raising his voice.

"Out here," Yuri's shouted back, deep from another tangent.

While Morris gravitated toward another cluster of berries and resumed picking, additional murmured voices issued from a different quarter. He stopped and listened. His view was concealed by overgrowth but it sounded like two or three people.

Perhaps this berry patch wasn't as unknown as Yuri imagined.

The voices---all male---got closer and louder, perhaps 20 meters away. Morris couldn't discern what they were saying; his Russian wasn't even close to the task. He contemplated going back to retrieve his first bucket. However, that seemed overdone. Why would anyone steal berries when there were so many available?

When the group veered off in a different direction, he resumed picking and filled his second bucket within five minutes, then stretched and slapped his palms together in a crossways motion, attempting to clean them but only spreading juice from right to left. Upon re-tracing his path to the rock he found the first bucket where he'd left it, undisturbed. Yuri was nowhere to be seen, and he realized they'd neglected to establish a timetable for rendezvous. His best bet, he reckoned, was simply to wait. He sat down, careful not to stain his trousers with his hands.

Once he was seated, sounds emerged nearby. No voices: just rustling. He stood again and peered over the tops of the bushes, on tiptoes.

He expected to see Yuri. He was wrong.

CHAPTER 3

Tops of two heads became visible: one a blond buzz-cut, the other capped by light-gray homburg. To Morris' surprise English passed between the two men, in non-native-speaking accents. Blond buzz-cut emerged from behind a cluster of vines: broad-shouldered and muscular, with a ripped neck and wrap-around sunglasses. He halted abruptly and fixed on Morris' hands. Morris assumed, at first, that this was due to his stained fingers. Then he realized the man's attention arose from other reasons.

To discern if he was armed.

"Schto vi delaete zdes?"

Even under ordinary circumstance Morris would have labored in vain to understand the question. He kept his hands by his sides, staying non-confrontational.

"I don't speak Russian," he answered.

An instant later the man wearing the gray homburg emerged: mustachioed and older, somewhat olive-skinned, holding a pail full of berries. Morris took him in. The man did likewise.

This didn't please blond buzz-cut. His face hardened further, and he interposed himself with several quick steps, his fingers splayed for attack. Morris sensed the man was capable of breaking his neck with a single, lightning-fast movement. A pistol grip also protruded under his lightweight jacket. In what now sounded like a Russian accent, he switched to English.

"What are you doing here?"

Morris deduced that he'd ventured too close to the presidential compound and run afoul of security. He tried to stay calm. "Just picking berries," he answered, gesturing toward his two overflowing buckets, still resting on the rock.

Blond buzz-cut held his stare. "Are you here alone?"

"No, I'm with a colleague...I'm visiting his dacha..." A shout from Yuri interrupted Morris, coming somewhere from the middle of the patch.

"Evan, where are you?"

Blond buzz-cut reached inside his jacket and pulled out an automatic pistol. When Morris saw the weapon on full display he stiffened.

"That him?" blond buzz-cut said, lowering his voice.

Morris nodded. Yuri's rustling grew closer.

"Okhrana!" blond buzz-cut barked. *"Ostavaetes tam!"*

Yuri's progress came to sudden stop. Silence fell over the ravine for several seconds. Blond buzz-cut pulled up his walkie-talkie and barked in a Russian command, concluding with, *"Bistro!"* Ruckus ensued from the direction of the trail: snapping twigs, sliding dirt, frenetic displacement of brush. A second security man materialized, close-cropped and muscular like the first, with brown hair. Blond buzz-cut spoke to him in hurried tones and gestured in the direction of Yuri. The latter drew a pistol and scrambled off.

Morris let his gaze wander again to the older man with the homburg and mustache. Blond buzz-cut took angry note.

"Attention here!" he commanded. "Your documents!"

Morris turned his gaze back and slowly extracted his wallet. With further deliberate movements he pulled out a copy of the main page of his passport and handed it over, trying his best not to leave juice stains on the paper.

Lately he'd tried to avoid unpredictable situations. He'd gotten pounded by too many already, especially of his own making.

This looked like another one.

CHAPTER 4

Outside his apartment building Piper made his usual quick survey of the courtyard, and noticing no one unusual, proceeded to circular inspection of his Mercedes. Satisfied that no tampering had occurred, he de-activated the locking system and threw his laptop in the backseat.

If there was ever a Saturday afternoon when he would have preferred to avoid the office, this was it. But Caroline had assured him she'd be packing anyway for the next couple of hours and their two teenagers would be out with friends until dinnertime.

Her departure was closing fast and they were determined to take this in stride.

While backing out into a three-point turn, he thought ahead to his upcoming video conference. It was not a pleasant prospect. He'd supposed he'd have to get used to the pattern. There would be plenty more Saturdays in Minsk like this in the coming weeks.

At least for today, Caroline would be waiting for him when he got home. That buttressed him somewhat.

* * *

Faces in the mirror burned with self-improvement. The women pumped their knees and swung their elbows in exaggerated arcs, exhorted by an instructor over a pulsing tune from Madonna:

If you want my body
You need to prove your love
Prove your love to me...

The instructor cut into the refrain:

Ras, dva, tri, chetiri, i nazad
One, two, three, four and back

Lena followed along, even though she still found it a little ridiculous. These aerobics sessions at *Bagira* served certain purposes. Health, slimming. Perhaps a boosted mood. But did they really deserve this kind of seriousness?

Ras, dva, tri, chetiri, i nazad..

For all her diligence, she didn't push herself to extremes. This stood her in contrast to other women in the class, many of whom aimed to enhance their figures before August beach vacations in Turkey, Cyprus or the Crimea--as if a kilogram or two or some extra firmness around the behind would make a difference. Which also implied these agonies were for men.

These women considered themselves modern and independent. What kind of self-determination was that? Energies like these were better directed toward sublime pursuits. Though Lena had to admit, even knowledge seemed elusive lately...Escape rather than genuine enlightenment...Maybe the specific outlet didn't matter...

Prove your love to me
Prove your love to me...

In the mirror she confirmed that she was one of few class members with a carefree look. Detachment was key...Adoption of the right perspective...Still, she'd accepted that some of these trends from the West were hard to contravene, particularly if you were just one year short of 30...

When the dance component ran its course members of the class broke ranks to gather rubber/foam mats from along the wall, then re-spread to original positions, assuming positions on hands and knees. As if on cue, two male trainers abandoned their customary post at the vitamin/juice bar and entered the training hall. They reclined against stationary bicycles, which afforded an unimpeded side view of the aerobics floor. The adjacent weightlifting area was empty of other men.

Next target: the gluteus muscles.

Posteriors jutted up; arms stretched out; the women initiated backward leg-raises. Lena sensed eyes of the trainers sweeping across the group. The two were both around 25 in age. Amiable enough, perhaps. Still...empty-headed *kachki*---pumpers---who inflated themselves with protein shakes and steroids.

In any case their attention soon settled on one of the younger members of the class: a medical student. Lena couldn't say why, but that irritated her somewhat.

Perhaps because they were the only men present.

All the same she kept at it. Nowadays, there seemed to be little choice.

*　　*　　*

The secure communication facility of the U.S. Embassy in Minsk was a room within a room: a windowless compartment constructed of lead, vinyl and polyurethane, stuffed with electronics and capable of holding four people at the most. Almost every U.S. embassy had one. Piper, who suffered mild claustrophobia, had long disliked them.

Especially lately. In Minsk he was the man on the spot.

Over the video link, from a secure conference room in the West Wing---7:30 a.m. East Coast time---were Jim Stapleton, the Deputy Director and Head of Operations at the CIA, and Vice President Wade Gallstone. Gallstone, overfed and balding, hunched over one corner of the conference table, a permanent half-scowl under his wire-rimmed glasses. Stapleton sat at the other corner: lean and cerebral, with a thatch of gray hair and bags under his eyes that had gotten worse in recent months. It was no secret in Washington that Gallstone wanted to get rid of the Deputy Director. In typical fashion Gallstone was now doing most of the talking.

"I'll be blunt, Russell," he said, looking hard at Piper over the feed. "Just because the government there forced us to practically close our Embassy doesn't mean we should back down. The President wants to keep up the pressure."

Piper tried to stay even.

"Even with our reduced staffing, Mr. Vice President," he said, "We've increased our involvement with the opposition parties. Just since April we've doubled their funding prior to September's parliamentary elections, renting additional office space and paying for seminars in Vilnius and Warsaw."

"Double it or triple it again," Gallstone fired back.

Despite half-trillion-dollar budget deficits and looming fiscal implosion, the White House was throwing millions into Belarus. Far more than Piper really needed.

"How do you propose to spend it?" Stapleton interjected, his voice as drained of emotion as he looked of energy.

Gallstone shot him a caustic stare. "Russell's report yesterday said that Western funds are not the key to change in Belarus."

"Correct."

"I don't accept that. We're spending more money in Iraq now, aren't we? And we're starting to see some progress. Why should Belarus be any different?"

Despite the absurdity of the claim Piper and Stapleton kept their even expressions. Stapleton responded.

"With all due respect, Mr. Vice President, Belarus is quite a bit different. And I should note that thanks to Russell's efforts, we are making strides in our intelligence gathering there."

"*Intelligence?* Don't give me that goddamn crap, Jim. I've read plenty of intelligence reports in my day and know they're often worthless. Belarus has been stalled out for long enough. I've determined we've got to whip things up a little bit. Just repeat the Orange Revolution, further north. Why the hell not?"

Silence fell over the link; Gallstone had never been so raw. For him as much as anyone, Iraq had become an interminable, slow-motion nightmare. Meanwhile the American economy was teetering. Presidential poll numbers were dreadful, as the Administration wound down its second term. In Belarus, the White House was looking for some kind of salvation. Or, at minimum, diversion. To Piper they were looking in the wrong place, and he knew that Stapleton agreed. He directed his gaze straight onto the video camera.

"What happened in Ukraine was indigenous and essentially peaceful," he said. "Success came through numbers, not open agitation. Sure, we helped with money and organization, but on the margins. Change arose from within. And despite all that---and despite my own involvement---I should add that the Orange Revolution has not fulfilled its original promise. Ukraine hasn't exactly become the sort of well-functioning democracy we'd hoped for."

Gallstone locked his fingers and crushed them together. He appeared about to detonate.

"I'm tired of these endless dissections," he scowled. "That's all in the past. Right now we've got to be pro-active. Assert our interests more aggressively. *Incite change.* Not just promote it."

The harsh ring alarmed Piper. A diplomatic offensive was already underway against Belarus from both the U.S. and Europe. Strains were resulting with Russia. Much more, and there might be unintended consequences.

"Incite change?" he asked. "Do you have any specific measures in mind?"

"That's your job, Russell. *Find a goddamn way.*"

When Stapleton and Gallstone signed off the video screen went gray. Piper reached over, turned off the equipment console, and leaned back, arms folded across his chest.

Incitement was not the best approach for Belarus just now. It was the last thing he needed as well.

CHAPTER 5

Independence Prospekt flowed past outside: ordered and leafy, with large-proportioned Soviet-classical architecture, its broad sidewalks mostly devoid of pedestrians, reflecting the customary exodus of a summer weekend. Under normal circumstances, a benign and agreeable tableau.

Morris' perspective was altered from the backseat of a state-security vehicle. This one---a dark gray BMW---happened to resemble his Five-Series, now in storage back in Palo Alto. Except for the dark-tinted windows. And blond buzz-cut, sitting in front with the driver.

Wordless. Threatening. Free of legal constraints.

Morris held no illusions. Belarus was a dictatorship, all its other pluses aside.

His cell-phone remained in his back pocket. One of his pre-programmed numbers was the U.S. Embassy. He considered making the call, but decided to hold off. Not provoke the situation any further.

Just before Lenin Street, McDonald's slipped by on the right. An outpost of normalcy. The effect dissolved when the car slowed down just after GUM department store. Hulking up on the right was the dull yellow, columned facade of the Belarussian KGB headquarters. Blond buzz-cut spoke into his walkie-talkie. Massive two-story steel-and-wood doors opened near the next corner. Morris had noticed these before. Always closed. Until now.

The BMW turned off the Prospekt, crossed the sidewalk and entered the complex. Morris looked back in disbelief as the doors re-closed. He wheedled his phone from his pocket, unworried now about juice stains.

"I'll take that," blond buzz-cut said, holding out his hand.

"I believe I have the right to call my Embassy."

Blond buzz-cut's eyes narrowed. They pulled into an interior courtyard. Norms from outside seemed to fall away. Choices as well.

"You'll get it back later."

Morris handed the device over. Another stern-faced guard appeared, this one wearing a uniform. He and blond buzz-cut escorted Morris inside and ushered him straight into a receiving room, with a tripod-mounted camera and a counter for fingerprinting.

"Stand over there," blond buzz-cut said, pointing to a white back-screen.

Morris asked if he could visit a restroom, in part to wash his hands.

"Later. We'll take pictures first."

*   *   *

Flanked by two uniformed minders, Morris climbed two flights of stairs and marched down a long, high-ceilinged corridor, with office doors closed on both sides. There was little sign of activity; the environment was even calm. He also drew some encouragement from the fact that he'd been allowed to clean up. His unsettlement lifted further when they passed an empty secretary's desk entered a spacious, well-appointed office. Two large windows faced the Prospekt, permeated with natural light. This was no interrogation chamber.

A middle-aged man stepped forward, a different class than blond buzz-cut and the other security muscle. Civil in manner, dressed in cotton shirt and summer slacks. He gave Morris an appraising look. "My name is Dimitri Shinkevich," he said, extending his hand. The two minders withdrew and closed the door. Shinkevich ushered Morris over to a cluster of four chairs around a low table, gestured toward one, and seated himself opposite.

"First, let me express my regrets…that this was necessary," he said. His English was good: only a slight accent.

Morris nodded, figuring he'd fare best if he stayed polite.

"We dragged you away from a shashlik."

"Yes."

"Would you like some coffee or tea?"

"Tea, I suppose."

The Russian picked up a phone, and while he was speaking Morris took further stock of the large office. Whomever he'd seen in the woods northwest of Minsk had been consequential. Enough to drag an apparently high-ranking official like Shinkevich into the office on a Saturday afternoon. Shinkevich promptly resumed.

"I've consulted our file on you, Mr. Morris…"

Morris was jarred by this revelation but didn't react.

"…As far as we know, everything you're doing here is legal."

"It is. I've obeyed all laws and regulations since I got here. The same holds for my company."

Next, at Shinkevich's prompting, he recounted the episode from start to finish: the berry-picking expedition with Yuri, the spontaneous encounter with blond-buzz-cut and the mustachioed man with a homburg hat, and subsequent transport back to Minsk. Tea came in the interim, served by a young male functionary.

However the official's focus was quite specific.

"Describe the man you saw in more detail…the one with the hat."

"He had a dark mustache. Relatively tall. Olive skin. He was carrying a pail full of raspberries."

"Did you hear him speak?"

"No." Morris was being honest. At least in strict sense.

"Could you guess where he was from?"

"Not Russian, I guess. More southern....Turkish, maybe. It was hard to say."

Shinkevich considered this answer.

"Would you be able to recognize him again?"

"Possibly. Though the hat sort of shaded his face."

Subsequent questions were perfunctory and factual. Verification of Morris' home and office addresses in Minsk. Confirmation of his marital status. Work hours. Identities of Yuri and other employees. His private Russian lessons with Lena. Leisure pursuits or lack thereof. Travel patterns and interactions with Morris' parent company back in Santa Clara.

At last Shinkevich stood and handed Morris a business card. It contained just the KGB emblem, "Ministry of State Security" in Russian and English, and Shinkevich's name and telephone number.

"I wish to help you avoid more trouble, Mr. Morris."

Morris opened his mouth to speak. Shinkevich paused and studied him.

"What about my colleague, Yuri Pavlov?"

"Don't worry. He's been questioned and released."

Morris nodded, somewhat relieved.

"We're going to take you home, and give you back your phone. My advice...my firm request...is that you not discuss this episode with anyone. Not your employees...not even with Yuri. Nor..." Shinkevich's eyes flitted back down his folder, "...with Lena Antonova, your Russian tutor. It will be simpler for you that way. And for all those you're associated with."

"Understood."

"And there's no purpose in involving the U.S. Embassy in this. That would only create new complications for you."

Morris didn't respond. This induced a hard squint from Shinkevich.

"Do you have any immediate plans to leave the country?"

"No...not in the next few weeks."

"If your plans change, will you inform me in advance?"

Morris considered for a moment.

"Yes. I can do that."

"Good."

Shinkevich let some long seconds pass, and added, "I sincerely hope this matter doesn't develop any further."

"I don't see why it should."

.

CHAPTER 6

As occasional rituals went, this one was innocuous enough: a promenade up and down the Boulevard of Victors, shop-browsing around Nemiga, idle commentary and occasional commiseration. Lena and Natasha rounded the river path below the Old Town, each bearing a shopping bag: body lotion for Natasha, sandals for Lena. Zhurvavinka materialized on the bend ahead, with bright umbrellas, babbling voices, and low-volume music. Lena knew what was coming next.

"In the mood, I hope?" Natasha asked.

"Again, Natasha? We just went there two weeks ago…How about a change?"

"What do you propose?"

Two groups of 18 or 19-year-olds passed them from behind. The boys were smoking; the girls, in separate contingent, eating ice cream. Too young even for Lena's fourth and fifth-year classes at the Institute. Lena looked ahead again at *Zhuravinka*.

"The second-floor patio looks pretty active," Natasha observed.

Lena sighed. The appeal to Natasha was obvious. Foreigners occasionally showed up there, at least in warmer months. And foreigners were scarce in Minsk these days. Natasha's latest focus: Italians, connected with her study of the Italian language.

"You know my attitude toward meeting men in cafes, Natasha."

"Who says we're there to meet men? We'll just have a drink and enjoy the scene."

Lena sighed again.

"All right."

Cigarette smoke hit her nostrils as they closed the distance. A threesome of close-cropped Russian men in tight t-shirts and sunglasses loitered near the entrance, and gave them lingering appraisal as they passed inside, according Lena primary attention, which was typical. Natasha ignored the men in any case. She had other objectives in mind.

They continued through a lobby, up stairs, and found the second-floor terrace packed. However Natasha's hopes for a more plentiful and higher-grade assortment of male prospects went unrealized. It was the usual scene---an overwhelming preponderance of females, mostly in their 20s and early 30s---a veritable expanse of girls-only tables.

Which made Lena wonder, once again, why Natasha remained so intent.

After several minutes wait, they secured a table by the railing, with a wide, unbroken view of the river and the glassed Exposition Hall on the opposite bank, and ordered glasses of Martini and Rossi. Ignoring panoramas, Natasha angled her chair inward and made a quick scan of the limited number of male groupings, trying to appear nonchalant.

"I spotted three guys back in the corner," she said. "I think they might be Italian." Through dedicated independent study and several visits to Italy, Natasha had become fluent in Italian. Lena shifted in her chair and shot back an exasperated expression. Natasha showed mild exasperation of her own. "Why are you always so indifferent? You can't bury yourself in books all summer. Who is it lately…Sartre and Camus?"

"That's just recreation…also a way to improve my French. Anyway, I'm not against foreigners, you know that. It's just that I doubt the motives of the ones that come here."

Natasha suddenly brightened. "Then maybe you'll like this…I'd almost forgotten. So happens the U.S. Embassy is having an outdoor reception, a cocktail party…here at Zhuravinka, in honor of two of our writers. It's Thursday, July 31ˢᵗ, less than two weeks away. I think I might be able to finagle a couple of invitations."

"They're still putting on parties, even with their reduced staff?"

"Apparently they haven't shut down entirely."

Lena considered for a moment.

"What do you say?" Natasha persisted. "I thought you would be enthusiastic!"

"I am. I'm just thinking about my schedule." Natasha gave her a teasing look, ready with what had become a recurring theme. Lena cut her off. "…It doesn't concern Evan Morris," she said. "I'm thinking of joining my mother in Ukraine. Maybe for just a week. It would be nice to get out of the city. On the other hand, there's the issue of our cat… And I am enjoying the quiet in the apartment."

"By the way…I think those guys toward the wall are trying to make eye contact."

Playing along, Lena allowed herself a prolonged glance. Two of them, well across the terrace. From a distance, they looked Russian. Prosperous and well-dressed: perhaps more refined than the three-some down below. Though older and heavier. Divorced, Lena guessed, or even married. Too old for serious interest in any case. And definitely not Italian, which mitigated Natasha's curiosity.

One of them seemed to contemplate an approach, and Lena prepared herself for what was bound to follow. Polite but inane banter. The inevitable brush-off.

Another late Saturday afternoon in Minsk. The U.S. Embassy reception was gaining appeal.

A break from routine, if nothing else.

*　　*　　*

Four stories below, seven or eight parked cars lined the opposite side of Communisticheskaya Street, lead vehicles adorned by ribbons and balloons and drivers standing at-the-ready. While Morris looked on, the associated wedding party milled in front of the municipal marriage bureau directly below his apartment, posing for photographs. There had been a flurry of ceremonies there in May and early June, but lately the number had dwindled, so he guessed this one was the last of the day. The bride, easy to spot with her flowing white dress, was the center of attention, and like most he'd observed there earlier, looked young, no more than twenty or twenty-one. At the behest of the photographer she and the groom crossed over into the adjacent park to shoot another round of images, leaving their guests to smoke and converse. Ten minutes later the assemblage piled into their waiting vehicles and formed a moving convoy down the street, windows open and horns blaring, and disappeared down around the corner, bound for further celebrations.

In their wake the neighborhood became mostly quiet and empty again: several young mothers pushing strollers on the river promenade, a few others walking dogs or clustered around benches in the park.

Neither the festivity nor the ordinariness of the ensuing scene did anything to improve Morris' outlook. He faced away from the window into his living room, crossed his arms and mulled the previous hours. Shinkevich's admonishments were unambiguous. This wasn't over.

Pacing through to his bedroom, he opened the glass door onto his rear balcony. The courtyard below presented another standard picture. Around the stairwell: four young men in their late teens drinking beer from bottles; in the playground, two children playing on a swing, attended by their mothers. No security sentinels or strange vehicles---at least none that caught his attention. Still, he presumed his home phone was now tapped. Same for his cell-phone, which the KGB had had in their possession for almost an hour, and which they could also use to monitor his location.

All of which precluded voice contact with the U.S. Embassy.

He considered turning off his phone and simply walking over; the compound was only 10 minutes away by foot. Despite their reduced staff, the Consular Department was supposedly still able to help American citizens in emergency situations. In short order he decided against it. His best bet for now seemed to adhere to Shinkevich's instructions. Vacating the balcony, he walked back inside and glimpsed his image in the hallway mirror. Rattled---but just a little. As he reached the kitchen, he remembered Yuri and called him on his cell-phone. The Russian answered at once, his bass voice plucked with uncharacteristic stress.

"*Bozhe moi,* Evan. Are you okay?"

"I'm fine Yuri."

"Where are you?"

"Home."

Yuri's voice relaxed a little. He related that he was back at his dacha. Morris gave a brief encapsulation of his ride into the city and visit to KGB Headquarters, leaving out sensitive elements. The situation was disquieting enough already.

"Back to you, Yuri...what happened after I got taken away?"

"An okhranik kept me standing in the berry patch until you'd gone. Another one met us on the trail. They brought me back to my dacha, in an electric cart. They questioned me...especially about you and our work together at the lab. They also took down the identities of everyone at the shashlik...our programmers, wives, everyone...Then after about an hour, they left."

"No one else was detained?"

"No."

"Well, that's something positive."

Yuri paused again. His next words were even more careful. "I myself have an appointment to visit KGB headquarters...On Monday morning, just before work. I may be a little late."

"Anything I can do to help?"

"I don't think so, Evan."

Silence fell over the connection. Morris stuck to the conventional.

"By the way...Are you continuing with the shashlik?"

Yuri grunted, his bass deepening. He was innately incapable of contrived enthusiasm, under any circumstances. "Some of the people went home early. They lost the mood. The rest of us are eating the food, though."

"On Monday, will you stop by and see me as soon as you arrive at the lab?"

"Of course."

After they signed off Morris stared at his cell-phone for a moment. When he'd accepted this job assignment in Minsk, he hadn't sought contentment. Just two years of stability and retrenchment. Relative reprieve.

Now, even that looked far-fetched.

CHAPTER 7

When Piper crossed the threshold Caroline emerged from the living room, marking her place in a book. She looked down at the plastic bags in his hands, with a slight smile. Most of his afternoon tensions ebbed away.

"Really, Russell, I could have done the shopping today," she said.

"Wasn't much trouble."

Despite her disappointment about his posting to Minsk, she hadn't allowed the issue to dent their domestic interactions. It had always been that way through his career.

"Find some decent salmon?" she asked.

"Think so. Seems fresh."

"Just drop the bags on the counters. I'll put everything away and get started."

"Okay, I'll re-join you in a few minutes."

After swinging by the kitchen Piper dropped his laptop off in the study, which also served as guest bedroom. Their apartment---once a prize for membership in the Soviet nomenklatura, most recently rented by the Swiss Ambassador---was relatively rare for central Minsk by virtue of its dimensions, consisting of five rooms plus kitchen. Passing further he heard his daughter Melanie through the closed door of her bedroom. He washed his face and hands in the bathroom, re-joined Caroline and opened a beer, with an inquiring nod back toward the corridor.

"One of her friends from Exeter, I gather," Caroline responded. "On Skype."

Piper reached for the peanut jar. He knew Melanie's attitude didn't differ much. After Kiev, both mother and daughter had counted on two or three years in Washington, which would have coincided with Melanie's final year of prep school and first year or two at college. Nick also hadn't yet shown himself. Caroline glanced at the wall clock.

"He left after lunch," she noted. "Said he'd be home by seven."

"Opposite problem. He doesn't want to leave."

"The girls, it seems."

"That's become clear."

Piper punctuated the remark with a slight laugh, a mouthful of peanuts and a swill of beer. While Caroline prepared a salad, he spread the salmon fillets onto a skillet, marinating them with olive oil, and sprinkling them with black pepper, oregano, basil, minced onions. Next he filled a pot of water for the rice and placed it one the stove. As he extinguished the match he beheld her again across the kitchen.

Many of their evening routines hadn't changed since his second year of graduate school, when they'd first moved in together. Same went for Caroline herself. With her long-limbed proportions and luminous complexion she still thrilled him across a room.

"I put a bottle of Sancerre in the fridge to chill before I left," he said. "Can I pour you a glass?"

She smiled, aware that he already knew her answer.

"Sure."

Piper uncorked the bottle, laid out two glasses, and sampled the wine from one of them. Confident that the vintage was acceptable, he filled her glass and crossed the kitchen, handing it to her. She beheld him as she accepted it.

"You weren't thinking about the wine just now, though, were you?" she said.

"No."

He examined her face. She looked back and took a sip.

"Five weeks is a long time, Russell. We've never spent so much time apart."

"I was thinking the same on my way home. But we'll manage, right?"

He adopted a light expression. She did likewise.

"Why wouldn't we?" she answered. "I think we're capable by now."

Piper reached out and placed his hand on her waist. The signal was sufficient; after almost twenty years together, and eighteen years of marriage, they were habituated to subtle gestures, particularly when the kids weren't around. Later on they'd have some hours alone, which would have to sustain him for a while.

He'd drawn appropriate lessons. Resolved in advance.

Politics apart, there would be no repetitions of Kiev.

* * *

For Morris, the encroaching sensations were all too familiar. Shell-shock and hopelessness, mingled with self-recrimination. After a moment, he stopped himself. What mistakes had he really made, in this instance? Deciding to pick berries?

He forced himself to think pragmatically.

His next idea----almost a reflex---was short in coming. He walked to his kitchen, extracted a can of Coke from the refrigerator and proceeded into the spare bedroom, where his laptop computer was set up on a desk near the window. He cracked open the can and grabbed his mouse.

The Internet was not as easy to monitor as his phones, he knew, particularly a high-speed DSL connection. Even capable programmers required some time to tap into a given link. And because this was

Saturday, there was a good chance that the KGB hadn't yet addressed this component of their surveillance; he might have an evening to surf and search.

Determine what risks he was facing. Maybe even ascertain the identity of the mustachioed man he had seen in the woods. He opened a browser and accessed Google.

The man was probably not Russian. Darker. Southern. But from where? Turkey? An Arab country? Or just some region in the eastern Mediterranean? He decided that was too speculative.

Instead, in the search bar, he typed: *Foreign*. Broad enough not to bias the results ...In addition the man was under guard---the apparent responsibility of the KGB. A politician of some sort, here on vacation? That didn't account for the alarm. Perhaps in Belarus incognito. *Criminal?* He added it. A fugitive? Both were good words. He added those as well and stopped typing.

Foreign criminal fugitive Belarus. Then hit enter.

The number of hits startled him. His throat tightened as he scanned the headlines. He started right at the top.

CHAPTER 8

The first link was to the *London Daily Express,* dated 16ᵗʰ April 2003. The headline read:

IRAQI GROUP CLAIMS HUSSEIN IN BELARUS

Saddam Hussein, Morris presumed. This was confirmed by several lines of description that followed. He vaguely recalled such reports, but then, as now, he'd paid minimal attention to international news. He did know Saddam Hussein had been captured long ago---in Iraq, not Belarus. That he'd gone to trial some months later and ultimately been convicted and executed. On the other hand, the mustachioed man in the woods had looked Arab. He clicked onward. The story read:

> *LONDON, April 16th – An Iraqi exile group claimed today that former Iraqi dictator Saddam Hussein, whose whereabouts have been uncertain since the U.S. and British-led invasion of Iraq last month, has taken refuge in Belarus.*
>
> *The group, the Iraqi Freedom Alliance, citing "credible sources within Iraq", asserts that Hussein secretly fled Iraq aboard a chartered*

civilian airliner in the week prior to the initiation of hostilities by U.S.-
British coalition forces on March 20th "accompanied by numerous
family members, perhaps including sons Odai and Qusai, and several
representatives of his governing inner circle."

…Reports have circulated this week that Hussein is no longer in
Iraq, and has taken refuge in a third country. Speculation has cen-
tered on Belarus because of previous links between's Hussein and the
Belarussian president Alexei Lukashenko…

Morris read on. The claims, as he knew, proved invalid. He went back
to his Google search list.

Dozens of news items continued to connect Hussein with Belarus
through the spring and summer of 2003, many of them dating from
late June, when a cache of blank Belarus passports were discovered at
the hideout of one of Hussein's top aides. One read that "U.S. officials
have confirmed a news report by a British journalist in Baghdad saying a chief aide to Saddam Hussein obtained Belarusian passports for
himself and other officials in Hussein's regime…Belarusian Foreign
Ministry spokesman Konstantin Savinykh has dismissed the reports
and said the passports most likely are forgeries." There was a picture
of Hussein's aide: bald and fat. Not the man Morris had seen.

He scanned through several more pages of hits, most intent on
those with **Belarus** in bold letters.

On the third page a new cluster of hits caught his attention.
Along with **Belarus** these contained **card deck** and **Iraq's 55 Most
Wanted**. Cards: Morris remembered such a gimmick by U.S. occupa-
tion authorities.

At last he found a site that showed the cards, laid out in miniature on the site of the U.S. Defense Department. Hussein was number one: the ace of spades, with a reward of $25 million. Then his two
sons, also with ace rankings: $15 million each. Other faces followed-
-with descending reward levels---and were mostly similar: dark and

mustachioed, like Hussein himself. But not the slightly more cerebral type Morris had glimpsed that afternoon.

Until he noticed a group photo, taken at some sort of parade. Morris straightened and clicked the image to enlarge it.

Hussein was front and center, flanked by his two sons. Just behind Saddam's right shoulder stood a man wearing a suit and tie, in contrast to the green fatigues and berets worn by others. Detached, more refined-looking. His face was distinct, though Morris stared some seconds to be sure.

There was no mistake. It was the man in the woods.

As Morris moved his mouse over individuals on the podium, captions appeared, showing names. He stopped on the man in the suit. Name: Amoud al-Tikriti. When he clicked on the caption a pop-window opened:

*Amoud al-Tikriti – Private investment counselor to Saddam Hussein, age 56. Also Hussein's first cousin. Manages money secreted in Hussein's private accounts in Europe and elsewhere, which likely total in tens of billions of dollars. Has spent considerable time outside Iraq since the early 80s. Last spotted in Geneva, January 2005. No record of violence, though of considerable financial importance to Hussein, his extended family, and key members of his Baathist inner circle.. Reward level: **not yet established**.*

Morris' hand froze on the mouse-pad. The apartment grew suddenly quieter.

Different sensations spread through him. Familiar ones. Sensations he was used to feeling in front of a computer screen. He took a big swallow of Coke, and swung his head in several circles to loosen his neck. Then after a deep breath, he clicked back to *Google* and opened another link.

The sensations drained away just as quickly as they had risen up.

The **55 Most Wanted** program had wound down as the occupation progressed. It had eventually been shut down in early 2006.

He leaned back in his chair and closed his eyes for a moment. When he opened them, he determined that the closure was for the better. Amoud al-Tikriti was obviously an important figure. The current situation was complicated enough already.

Money would only impair his judgment.

CHAPTER 9

Lena parted the palm fronds with one hand, leaned over, and poured exactly a quarter-liter of water into the ceramic pot. By now she had memorized the hydration requirements, in both quantity and frequency, for some 23 house plants, all of which her aunt had specified before departing in June.

Next came two cacti, one large and one miniature; followed by a Japanese Newgold; three ferns; a Cissus; a Humata; and another palm---interspersed with trips to the kitchen to refill her plastic watering container. She then stood in the center of the living-room, rotated in place, and performed visual inventory, running through her embedded mental checklist.

Satisfied that the interior portion was complete, she returned promptly to the kitchen for another refill, then retraced onto the balcony, jutting over Krasnaya Street. Long trays were aligned against both ends, filled with marigolds, violets, and late-blooming lilies, while two pots hanging from the railing formed dual complements of wisteria. Their various allotments of water necessitated another trip to the kitchen.

Only when she was done did she put down the container, rest her hands on the railing, and survey the street below.

A mostly-empty tram car scraped against curving rails below, a few plaintive faces visible through the windows. Otherwise only half-a-dozen souls and a few cars circulated up and down the street---somnolent and static, as usual on a summer Sunday. Little had changed from the previous weekend, or the weekend before that, or the weekend before that...

Worse: each recent summer in Minsk---indeed, each full rotation of seasons---was already starting to look a lot like the last, with minor permutations. Tidy, for a large metropolis. And tranquil, now that political disturbances were receding into the past. But also isolated, monotonous and inert. Much like the country at large.

Not really participating in the wider world. An attribute, she worried, that applied to her as well.

Many friends from her student years---at least the most talented, ambitious ones---had fled abroad in search of more dynamism and opportunity. Those who had remained had come to terms with limited horizons, or even sunk into apathy. She therefore understood why her aunt, a divorced musician with no children, found diversion in house-plants. And why she'd nevertheless decided to flee to Ukraine for most of the summer, along with her mother, leaving the plants behind.

The essential human yearning for advancement, rejuvenation and growth.

And here she was, still in Minsk, conscientiously fulfilling her duties while global changes raced ahead without her.

She released a quiet sigh, went back inside, and closed the balcony door. From the living room she performed one last survey, then checked to make sure the *fortochki* were open on the upper windows, so the indoor plants could receive adequate ventilation. On her way out of the apartment she was careful to double-lock the door.

She pressed the elevator button and thought ahead to the reading she'd planned for afternoon. She still had her intellectual pursuits. That was one domain where she could keep moving forward.

Or at least create the sensation of movement.

*   *   *

Few cars occupied the long, straight highway out to Minsk-II Airport, which was consistent with typical patterns. During a lull in conversation, Piper moved both hands to the wheel of their Mercedes S550 and reflected for a moment, relishing the controlled, air-conditioned comfort. Caroline examined him from the supple station of her passenger seat.

"My main worry is that you'll feel isolated, Russell…With the staff reductions, you won't have much company."

"My schedule won't be that demanding. I'll be fine."

They'd covered this a few times already. He gave her a sideways glance.

"…As I've said, whatever I lack in socializing, I'll make up for with extra training. Especially my runs."

"That's my other worry. That you'll push yourself too hard in this summer heat."

"Really…I'll be fine. Call it my way of coping."

He reached over and lightly squeezed her knee, a gesture he often employed when behind the wheel. Separation issues aside, he knew she was looking forward to two-and-a-half weeks at her parents' ocean-front home in Rhode Island. The other component of their journey was unavoidable but vitally important: she, Melanie and Nick planned a tour of seven universities and colleges in the Northeast, a precursor to Melanie's applications and to her senior year at Phillips Exeter. Nick, for his part, was to interview at the same prep school for possible junior-year enrollment.

"This still doesn't feel right, Dad," Melanie observed from the back seat. "Any chance your plans will change…so you could join us for at least a week in Rhode Island?"

"I'll try, Melanie. But as I said last night, I doubt it."

"I would have stayed here with you, Dad," Nick said.

There was a sarcastic cut to his voice.

Piper caught his son's face in the rear-view mirror, before he turned a dissatisfied gaze toward undulating farmland and green forests outside. To this point Exeter had been a hard sell, and Piper understood why. Nick stood out at his gymnasium in Minsk: the only foreigner. He'd already invited several female classmates home: lanky, light-hued stunners nearly equal to him in height. The girls had startled Piper, not least because they were only fifteen or sixteen years old. Thanks to previous schooling in Kiev, as well as a high degree of motivation, Nick's Russian was already fluent and even surpassed Piper's.

"It makes sense for you to see these colleges at the same time as Melanie, Nick," Caroline noted from the front seat. "We've been through this."

Nick didn't answer her.

"And it's already late July," she continued. "Aren't most of your friends leaving the city on vacation?"

"Not all of them."

"You'll be back by September," Piper reminded him. "It's not that long."

Nick's expression lightened somewhat in the mirror.

No one broached details of Piper's summer undertakings. Both Nick and Melanie understood his official job at the Embassy was just a cover, astute enough to trace the vectors. Caroline was somewhat more informed. She'd also understood---although Piper had never told her explicitly---that the current crux lay in unwelcome initiatives from the White House.

"You won't let these work demands get to you...will you?" she said.

"I'll try not to. And I'll have my way of blowing off frustration, when necessary. If nothing else, you'll come back and find me in fine health."

Piper smiled and gave her another glance. The curving, modern-istic Soviet-era behemoth of Minsk II International Airport loomed ahead.

"Here we are already."

Ten minutes later, after he'd parked the car and returned to the Lufthansa gate, he watched through glass barriers as his family checked in for the flight to Frankfurt, and proceeded into short lines at passport control. Especially in threesome, they presented an ideal picture---one he knew he would be a fool to jeopardize again.

Belarus remained quiescent for now. Maybe that would help.

His plans were also more multi-faceted than he'd let on.

Thus far, results were encouraging.

CHAPTER 10

Just after half-past seven on Monday morning, Morris bended along the underground passage to the Victory Square metro station, resisting the urge to glance over his shoulder. Past the turnstiles on the broad steps down to the platform, he encountered an upsurge of disembarking passengers, which he avoided by hewing right. He stopped in his usual position halfway down the platform's northbound side, and looked around. An assortment of office workers and young people waited opposite, most exhibiting the bland expressions typical of big-city commuters. He'd always sensed unbreachable divides between himself and the Russians, particularly because of language. However he also saw them as fellow sufferers on the planet. Just as consigned to torment and arbitrary fates as he was, even more so.

Today was different. He beheld them with more vigilance.

A few glanced in his direction, perhaps sensing he was a foreigner because of his laptop case and general comportment. No particular face stood out.

When the subway train pulled up, only two other passengers boarded his car. He remained standing, gripping the overhead rail. Doors closed and he stared at his reflection in the window. On the gaunt side, as usual. Otherwise: conventional. Shirt pressed and hair in place.

Inside he felt different. His esophagus constricted, splaying a jangle through his thorax.

He reached the Academy of Sciences without incident.

*   *   *

The lab consisted of an outer room with bookshelves and a conference table, and two spacious inner chambers with large windows facing onto Surganova Street. In the latter, desks and computers were scattered in several clusters according to code-writing activity. Sergei was the only programmer already present at his computer; the rest tended to be later risers. His head pivoted up when Morris entered and went over to shake his hand: a Russian custom at the start of each workday.

Pale and lanky, Sergei was just two years out of University, was continuing graduate studies part-time, and still had the look of a student about him. He appraised Morris' face, but kept his initial inquisitiveness on hold; like the other programmers he was chary of direct queries, particularly to the boss. Minutes later, though, he made deliberate intersection at the coffee maker. While Morris filled his mug and stirred in some sugar, the Russian took the pot and poured coffee for himself.

"Yuri told us what he observed at the berry patch."

"An unfortunate episode. Not just for me, but for everyone at the shashlik."

"I heard you were taken away."

"Yes. To KGB headquarters here in Minsk."

Sergei's eyes widened slightly. Even in post-Soviet times, the initials induced alarm. Morris took a sip of coffee. The programmer remained fixated and didn't raise his own mug.

"...I was questioned and released. I'm hopeful nothing more will come of it."

The door opened to the outer office. Gentle footfalls indicated Anna, the lab's lone female, and administrator-translator. After Sergei, usually the first to arrive.

Her expression provided further confirmation of what Morris knew already. This was not going to be a routine work-day.

CHAPTER 11

Remaining programmers materialized in short order---nine total, all in their 20s and 30s---and stopped by Morris' desk with morning handshakes, All were stiff; a few looked downright gloomy. In order to pre-empt further inquiries, Morris said he would make an announcement at their customary 10 a.m. meeting.

In the interim he heard several hushed exchanges in the other half of the lab. Otherwise, just spare, incidental tapping of keyboards. Everyone was waiting. At 9:57 he glanced at his watch. To get attention, he rose to his feet and cleared his throat, just as the outer door opened.

It was Yuri. The scientist's posture was tense and his blond/gray hair hung limp, as if he'd been perspiring. He drew up and locked eye contact with Morris.

"I rushed back to make our meeting," he said.

Everyone stared at the elder Russian, trying to discern what had happened. There were no obvious clues.

"I'd like to meet you in your office first, Yuri," Morris told him.

"As you wish."

Next he swept his eyes across everyone else. He already had their full attention.

"Our meeting is postponed to 10:30," he announced.

*   *   *

Yuri retained a private office separate from the rented lab space---a perk issuing from his official standing at the Institute. He led Morris wordlessly to his door halfway down the corridor, inserted the key, and gestured inside toward one of the two couches. The Russian's stoicism held as he exited the room briefly to fill a coffee pot with water, then returned and started the coffee machine. Only his stilted hand movements gave away his tension---and something else.

Caution. The same sort Morris detected over the phone on Saturday. The senior scientist sat down opposite while the coffee was brewing, and lit a cigarette.

"I had my meeting," he said simply.

Morris eyed him. The Russian squinted back through wafting smoke. A curtain seemed to have slid down.

"Can you tell me how it went?"

"I went in at the appointed time. They brought me to an office upstairs, to meet an officer."

"Shinkevich?"

"Yes. He said he spoke to you on Saturday."

Morris nodded.

"...He didn't really discuss his talk with you. What he most wanted to know was what you'd told me. About what happened to you during our berry picking."

"What did you tell him?"

"The truth. The fact is you didn't tell me much."

"On purpose."

"I know. And your attitude is the right one."

Yuri took another drag and scrutinized him for a long downbeat. Smoke escaped his mouth by increments before he continued.

"...Next he was interested in general information about you, as well as our laboratory. How you came over from the U.S. for *Cognition*

Software, finalized your contract with me, and started things up. How we hired the programmers and so on. Also how you got settled here… your life outside work, things like that."

"And?"

"What could I say? You seem to live pretty quietly. I said that you stayed in the city, as far as I understood, except for our *shashliki*."

Morris nodded. The only exception to this pattern was a weekend golf excursion to Vilnius in May with Jeff Esposito, a colleague---something he'd previously mentioned to Yuri.

"Anything else?" Morris asked him.

After a flash of hesitation, Yuri's eyes traveled sideways to the coffee maker. He rose, laid out cups and saucers, and filled them near the rims. Finally he re-seated himself on the couch and responded.

"He also wanted to know about your politics."

"Hmmm…That didn't come up in my meeting with him."

"…Whether you ever criticized the government here…what you thought of the official American attitude toward Belarus. I told him you never mentioned such matters. That they didn't seem to interest you that much."

"Good. That's true."

It was. Management had instructed him to steer scrupulously clear during his stint in Belarus. The directive hadn't been hard to follow.

"How did it end, Yuri? Did Shinkevich say he'd be in further contact?"

"He gave me his card. But that was it."

"Do you think anything more will come of this?"

"Hard to say, I suppose it depends on you."

"That is, on how I behave?"

"Yes. I think as long as you do what Shinkevich says, everything should be fine."

Vague disharmony cut through Yuri's bass-line pronouncement. As if he didn't believe it himself.

CHAPTER 12

L ena un-folded the table's side-leaves and laid out instruction materials. Her cat---really her mother's more than hers---noted the re-
configuration, quite aware what it portended. After six months these
preparations had become ritual, for human and feline alike.

So had the sessions themselves. She would coax Morris along,
speaking slowly and encouraging him to express himself in new ways.
There had been increments of progress over the past several months.
Very small ones. Lack of intelligence wasn't the issue; in English Morris
came across as perceptive and analytical. Neither was discipline; at
home he did the written exercises she prescribed. Perhaps Americans
just had congenital obstructions to foreign languages. Or more simply: Russian was complicated. The Cyrillic alphabet presented the first
hurdle, and it just got more vexing from there.

Aware that air in the apartment remained stale from afternoon
heat, she walked to the kitchen, her cat trailing behind, and verified
there were several cold cans of Coke for him in the refrigerator. On
the way back she inspected her appearance in the hallway mirror.
Moderate makeup, professional-looking blouse and skirt...

At the beginning, she admitted...She'd been intrigued. Not
attracted, really; that would be overstatement. After all, she'd had

plenty of respectable suitors in recent years, including a visiting, rather older Swedish academic and a young local banker. All of whom she'd rejected, for one specific reason or another, due more broadly to what Natasha called her "impossibly high standards"---a charge she thought a little unfair. Nonetheless Morris was well-mannered and consider-ate, given to meticulous grooming, didn't smoke, apparently drank little, and was only six years older than she was. Which already consti-tuted a decent foundation. In addition he was a manager in a large, established foreign company, which by itself made him an automatic candidate for most other unattached girls in Belarus. Skinnier than she preferred, perhaps. And rather inhibited, in general...which she supposed stemmed from his recent life events. Divorce, apparently initiated by his wife. Financial reversal, to which he alluded occasion-ally with pained expression, which also puzzled her somewhat...How could a guy his age, who owned a BMW and a condo on a golf-course in California---whatever he'd just been through---be dissatisfied with his material situation? That was one facet she'd probably never under-stand about Western men.

Bottom line: decent guy. Though in emotional shutdown. An apparent non-starter on the romantic front.

The doorbell rang as Morris arrived for his lesson. On time as usual. He diligently took off his shoes just inside the door. A little preoccupied-looking, but otherwise the same. Out of politeness he reached down and stroked her cat. Lena knew what proceeded from that.

"Feel free to wash your hands, Evan."

"Thanks."

To Lena soft drinks were unhealthy and wasteful. But Morris' com-pany paid her well for these lessons, in cash---enough to make her feel relatively comfortable when combined with her sinecure at the Institute. She and her mother owned the apartment. Fixed expenses were minimal.

She retrieved a glass and can and retraced her steps to the living room. Before Morris re-appeared she filled his glass, watching the fizz rise to the top. The effervescence struck her as incongruous with what lay ahead for the evening.

She released another quiet sigh.

*   *   *

Today's theme was one they'd begun the previous week. She'd given Morris a typed dialogue to study and memorize.

"*Shto vhi sdelaete dlya raboti?*" Lena asked. What do you do for work?

Morris looked at her intently across the table. With delayed reaction, as usual.

"*Ya zanimat upravelenie.*" I work in management. He'd studied. Words were correct, though again with botched endings.

"*Nyet, Evan,*" Lena responded patiently. "*Ya zanimious upravleniem.*"

"*Ya zanimous upravleniem.*" His repetition was more mimicry than understanding. Study notwithstanding, Morris didn't really understand the endings or why he was using them.

"*Upravlenie kovo?*" she asked. Management of whom?

"*Programmisti computers.*"

"*Nyet, Evan. Computernix programmistov.*"

This prompted another robotic repetition. Lena continued:

"*Na kakoi firme?*" For what company?

There was no ending required here. Morris understood and answered correctly.

"Cognition Software."

"*Horosho, Evan.*" Good, Evan. "*Vam nravitsya vasha rabota?*" Do you like your work?

Morris put down his Coke but didn't answer. Lena repeated the question in Russian, very slowly. Finally the meaning registered. Morris' eyes burdened. His response was weary.

"*Da.*"

Lena still didn't entirely understand. Why did he lack enthusiasm for his job? He was a top manager for an American high-tech company. From her perspective he had every reason to be content.

Linguistic obstacles prevented him from elaborating in any event.

"Povtorim etot dialog, s pravilenimi okochoniemi etot ras," she said. Let's repeat this dialog, with correct endings this time.

A blank, almost beseeching expression came back across the table. She relented and repeated the sentence in English.

Morris nodded. At least he was cooperative.

That counted for a lot. All the same, she suppressed another sigh. Her life felt stuck in place. Just like Morris and his Russian.

CHAPTER 13

The scene often revisited Morris, perhaps because it exemplified a phase, even an apex of sorts. Early evening in San Francisco, late spring, the kind of gathering he'd started to attend over previous months with Nora. Cocktails on the rooftop terrace of a private art museum, about 50 people, subtle vibes of exclusiveness. Rain had withdrawn hours earlier and clouds around the Golden Gate Bridge had dissipated, opening sweeping vistas of the Bay. Sunlight angled in from the Pacific over western hillcrests, still direct enough to warm the skin. Pacific breezes were sweet and fresh, permeating his nostrils.

Mingled with other scents, there'd also been the distinct tang of money.

For Nora the milieu wasn't quite so novel as it was for him. Her development work at Stanford had acclimatized her, and since she'd left her job she hadn't abandoned fundraising, exactly, just shifted from one side of the equation to another. Indeed, the transition had seemed smooth and easy.

Price of admission to this particular event: ten thousand dollars per couple.

Ties were few on the men---in keeping with Bay Area norms---though expensive suits and ultra-tended female bodies predominated, along with cohorts of Swiss watches and designer shoes. All of which yielded quick glances and instant appraisals: the kind of acute physical awareness that had typically made Morris uncomfortable. In his self-perception he was still a decidedly un-cool geek from northern New Jersey, whose main aptitudes had been math and computer science, rather than making money.

Still, he and Nora were among the youngest present. Many of the 20 and 30-something dot-com millionaires who had recently colonized this sort of affair, he'd noticed, had faded away since the tech crash.

He was not among them. Today, after markets had closed in New York and Chicago, he'd squeezed in 18 holes of golf back in San Mateo, then driven into the city in his BMW Five-Series, straight to this event. From the bar he collected two chilled Chardonnays and turned back to re-locate Nora. She'd already breached a small circle of middle-aged financial types. He sidled up and handed her the wine. Others made space, shifting their attentions. Conversation dwindled.

It was time for another introduction.

"This is my husband Evan," Nora said, with posture that suggested a meaningful moment.

Morris rounded the bases while Nora orchestrated nods and handshakes. He was adept at names and had no trouble keeping them all straight: one of his few strong suits when it came to socializing. One in the group was a man in his late 40s named Barry Palmer. He was soft and overweight by California standards, though his well-cut suit compensated somewhat. So did his wife, who looked like she spent half her week at the health club. He supplied the segue:

"Your wife produced superb results co-chairing this fund-raising drive, Evan."

"It fits with her experience."

Palmer sized him up. "We know what she does, at least in her spare time..." He shot a twinkling glance at Nora, who had made brief remarks at the beginning of the party. "...What do you do?"

Morris still wasn't at ease answering this question. He didn't wish to sound pretentious. Nora intervened.

"Evan is an investor," she said.

Curiosity heightened a little around the circle. Morris guessed a few of the men on the prowl for either new contacts or clients. Palmer's gaze pivoted downward for an instant, then bored back up. "Oh really? Are you attached to a firm?"

"No. I just manage my own investments...or mine and Nora's, I should say."

"Impressive, especially these days." Palmer sounded intrigued. "How, if I may ask, did you reach that enviable position?"

Quick glances outside the circle ceased. Nora stiffened slightly, waiting to see how this played out.

"Well, back in the mid-90s I went to work as a programmer at Cognition Software, down in Santa Clara." He paused and observed that the name provoked instant flashes of recognition, as usual. "... Soon I moved up to manage a team and got some stock options. Also invested in other tech stocks. Timing was good. I left the company in January 2000. Two months later I married Nora."

"We settled in Palo Alto because of my job at Stanford at the time," Nora was quick to add. "Evan could choose. He had the freedom."

The group took several seconds to digest this information. Then gazes drew back. Palmer appeared to reach immediate conclusions, looking less impressed. This was 2003. Wreckage from the NASDAQ still smoldering. Portfolios decimated. Jim Berenson, whom Morris took for a broker, was the first to break the short silence. "Ah yes, the tech boom. The 90s. What a time. Did you get hit like everyone else?"

Morris had fielded this question before. Modesty was his natural suit, so he didn't swell up. "Luckily, no," he answered. "I didn't like the fundamentals...and became worried about a sell-off. I shifted to cash in the spring and summer that year."

"You're kidding," Berenson said, mouth opening. "Entirely?"

"Ninety-five percent."

Eyelids rose around the circle.

"Wow...not bad," Berenson observed. "Get away unscathed, then?"

"Yes. Partly because I avoided the dot-coms."

Assessments re-calibrated. Gazes re-fixed. At last Nora smiled. She couldn't resist an addendum.

"Evan even shorted the market that fall," she said. "Right, Evan?"

"Well..." Morris just smiled with closed lips and nodded.

Palmer's skepticism appeared to ebb. He re-engaged with a new attitude, holding his drink forward. "My compliments, Evan. And what are you into now, if I may ask?"

Attentions became different. Not just curious. Also self-interested.

Morris answered honestly. "Bonds, some dividend plays. I've also gotten more involved in options, lately. I try to stay diverse."

Nora could see that he was still a little uncomfortable. "Meanwhile we're moving into the city," she interjected. "We've bought a place over on Nob Hill. We're renovating it now."

Nods ringed the circle. Nora smiled again, more broadly.

Their qualifications were in order.

CHAPTER 14

Some agents still expected live interactions, even if no words were exchanged. Bits and bytes were not enough. Two of Piper's current informants fit this category, including Konstantin Mironov, senior official in the Interior Ministry.

Piper had just begun warming up on his *Lifecycle* when Mironov walked in to the main training area, wearing sweat pants and t-shirt. As usual the Russian refrained from direct eye contact, and looked down to turn on his iPod. Transmission by modified Bluetooth took less than five seconds, straight to the receiver implanted in Piper's sport watch---stored there in flash memory for later transfer to his computer.

Mironov took position on a treadmill several machines away and began a slow and lumbering jog. By now the sensitive data had already been erased and scrubbed from hard storage inside the Russian's iPod, thanks to artful coding by programmers at Langley. Most important: his intelligence to date---presidential security directives, tactical police plans, advance warning of opposition crackdowns, and the like---had proven quite worth the trouble. Piper checked his watch face: a small digital icon next to the date confirmed another successful data transfer.

Once back at his office, he'd look over the material and distill it into an intelligence report.

First, though, he had to complete his workout.

On the bike's control panel, he selected a random hill profile, the highest difficulty level, and a 30-minute session. Then hit *Enter*. As the program kicked in he re-gripped the handlebars, roused by the throbbing aerobics music, and through half-closed eyes his gaze out onto the floor.

A high-impact class was in full progress, with seven or eight participants, including a strawberry blonde in the middle of the group---twenty-one or twenty-two, he guessed, conspicuous because of her contours and clinging spandex workout briefs. She bore an intent expression and shimmers of dampness around her neck, perhaps seeking to trim a few pounds for a summer bikini.

To Piper the effort was unnecessary. Those curves suited him fine.

Sensing his attention, the girl flicked over a spontaneous glance, with quick eye contact and a frisson of interest, which was all he needed. Once she'd turned back toward the instructor he hung his gaze for about five seconds longer: sufficient to make a full-length visual imprint before he closed his eyes...She was back in his apartment now, leaning forward, bracing her elbows on the backrest of the couch, arching her back. He hooked his fingers into her waist-band and peeled back her spandex...

His imagination kicked in full. So did his energy level.

With a primal exhalation, he ratcheted up his RPMs. On the bike's console---through his half-blurred vision---he noted a burn-reading of 1250 calories per hour. Even at his advanced fitness level, he figured his pulse rate was climbing toward 150.

The first 12-14 minutes were invariably the hardest. Soon after that, he knew, endorphins and endocannabinoids would pervade his bloodstream, offset some of the pain, and conduct him into ambits of subliminal ecstasy. Mironov's intelligence material, at least for the remainder of his workout, had slipped to the margins. This had become the main event.

His means of release and re-calibration during Caroline's absence.

*   *   *

Lena referred back to a page that she'd bookmarked, and copied another quotation into her notebook. She then placed the original text aside and leafed through passages and commentary she'd assembled thus far, primarily in French. These she'd organized by category: *Life/Death, Work, Ethics, Love, Religion, Politics and Miscellaneous.* Most transcriptions were from Sartre and Camus, including some from the work she'd just completed: a French edition of Sartre's *Transcendence of the Ego*.

Pages were starting to fill up. With one exception.

The section on *Love* remained mostly blank.

Existentialists had plenty to say on life and death---"being and nothingness," as Sartre preferred---on work and achievement, questions of right and wrong, and especially politics. On love, by contrast---and even on the broader question of male-female relations---Lena found just a meager assortment of platitudes or commonplace idealizations. For example, this trivial observation from Sartre:

> *"Neither sex, without some fertilization of the complimentary characters of the other, is capable of the highest reaches of human endeavor."*

These were supposed to be among the most daring and original minds of Twentieth Century Western culture. Was this all they had to offer on the subject?

Sartre's own relationship with Simone de Beauvoir was confounding and ambiguous, seemingly beyond his own powers of comprehension. And Camus had a similarly jumbled record with women. She reflected for a moment. In love, could the two philosophers have been handicapped by their abstraction?

She'd worried lately that she was prone to the same mistake.

Her cell-phone rang from across the room, where she'd left it on a bookshelf, breaking her continuum of thought. Marta, her cat, roused from the sofa and jumped to the floor as Lena got up to answer. The caller, again, was Natasha.

The catalyst this time was an e-mail she'd just received from an on-again, off-again suitor in Italy, named Fabrizio. His passion had revived, according to his latest declaration and plethora of Italian superlatives. He'd proposed a 10-day beach rendezvous in Rimini in late August. Lena listened patiently. As usual she was skeptical. Sensing this, Natasha emitted a contrived sigh. "Well...*I'm* excited. And I'm going to give it some serious thought."

"I'm not saying you shouldn't, Natasha."

"You have no opinion?"

"How can I? This has occurred rather suddenly."

As Natasha rambled on, Marta began brushing against Lena's calves: signaling a desire to be fed. Lena glanced at the clock on the piano; time was almost six-thirty. She and Natasha would probably dissect and comment upon this development for another 15-20 minutes, with no real result. Meanwhile, Marta was right. The feline, in fact, displayed more clarity and direction than they did.

It was almost time for dinner.

CHAPTER 15

To Morris McDonald's constituted a sanctuary: one of the few establishments in Minsk where he felt automatically at home, even if he seldom encountered other foreigners there. The familiar menu and motifs, together with the prompt and courteous customer service, gave him a welcome quotient of Americana during his midday escape from the lab. His favorite outlet was the flagship near Oktyabraska Square---the same one he'd passed en route to KGB Headquarters---where he knew that the majority of staff, almost all of them young, spoke some level of English. He tended to lunch there two or three times per week.

All the same he tried to mix in some Russian when ordering. Numbers, if nothing else. He was a long-term regular, after all; he reckoned he should at least make an effort.

"*Adin* Big Mac, *pozhalista*," he said.

The girl behind the counter, probably about 17 years old, registered his accent at once and smiled. Morris suspected he'd ordered from her before.

"Yes?" she said, defaulting to English.

"*Adin* medium French fries…"

She keyed in the further entry and smiled again.

"…and a large chocolate milkshake."

"Here or to go?"

"Here, please."

She punched up the total, and instead of telling him the amount---in either English or Russian---extended her hand to the front of the cash register and pointed to the display screen. Morris nodded back with a beleaguered smile and handed over a 20,000 ruble note. After she made change, he navigated back through other customers toward his habitual destination on the second floor, already looking forward to his first delectable mouthful of fries.

Blond buzz-cut came suddenly into view: near the entrance, feet apart and arms crossed. Morris pulled up short and stopped.

The security man's impassive stare made clear that that outdoor tables were off-limits---and by extension, any attempt at exit. He then shifted his gaze toward his right left, prompting Morris to do likewise.

Less than two meters away, Shinkevich leaned against one of the high eating counters, this time wearing suit and tie. He measured Morris' reaction with a sharp gaze, evidently pleased that they had caught him unawares. His hands were free of serving tray or takeout bag. The KGB officer was not here to have lunch.

"I thought we might have another talk," he said.

Morris looked back at him.

"I'm about to eat."

"I can see that."

"I was heading to the second floor."

"Good. I'll follow you up."

*   *   *

Morris preferred the second level of McDonald's for its ample space and relative separation from the bustle and traffic of the main floor. Moreover in summer the addition of two street-side seating areas usually yielded an abundance of empty places. Today Shinkevich seemed to find it suitable for the same reasons. At his direction they settled at a table near an arched window, blocked from outside view by a vividly colored photographic mural, while blond buzz-cut took up new position near the top of the stairwell, keeping them in view. Morris stuck his straw in his milkshake and spread his fries on the tray. His appetite had already abated.

"Have I done something wrong since our meeting on Saturday?" he asked.

"So far, no. Not to our knowledge, at least."

Morris looked back and placed several fries in his mouth. He concluded that he'd been triangulated and tracked by his cell-phone signal, which didn't surprise him. In addition KGB Headquarters was just a block-and-a-half down the Prospekt; for Shinkevich, McDonald's had the advantage of convenience.

And perhaps symbolism. To show that no venue was off limits.

He clasped several more fries between his fingers, put them in his mouth and swallowed. Then ventured another question.

"What's the purpose of this encounter, then?"

"Just call this a show of our seriousness…That we're in this for the long-term."

This last phrase carried an extra chill, beyond what had transpired on Saturday. Before Morris could pose another question, the KGB man abruptly stood.

"I'll be in further contact," he said, then turned and walked away.

CHAPTER 16

Morris jerked awake with his heart pounding, overrun by the same images and pronouncements that had bedeviled him before going to sleep. When these didn't recede he raised his eye-shades, found his room suffused with the dull light of early-morning, and looked over at the digital clock on his nightstand. Time was 4:33 a.m.

Still lying on his back, he tried to relax. It was futile; his entire body buzzed with anxiety. His last recollection of waking in such agitation was during his financial bust-up: a several-week period when all his options positions seemed to be moving against him at once. When one trading day after another had yielded ever-more staggering losses...

Shinkevich's interception at McDonald's had shaken him more than he'd realized.

Seeing little purpose in lingering in bed, he got up, walked to the kitchen and made a pot of coffee. The first mug and a bowl of cornflakes cleared his head somewhat, and he reflected on his position. He'd obviously stumbled into an issue of importance. Amoud el-Tikriti---whatever the Iraqi had been doing since 2003---mattered a great deal to Belarussian authorities. His presence in Belarus was evidently secret, and also controversial. But why?

He wished he could do further research on the Internet. By now, though, he was fairly certain that both his home and office connections were compromised.

That left him guessing. And therefore vulnerable.

One core lesson he'd drawn from his options travesty was to shun exposure to broad, unpredictable forces. To pre-empt similar degenerations through stop-loss measures and alternative strategies, not just in his financial affairs, but in his life in general.

By his third mug of coffee, however, no alternative strategies had come to mind. Instead of agonizing further he quickly dressed and left for the lab.

The hour was still early. He could at least divert himself with work.

Twenty-five minutes later, after exiting the Academy Metro station, he strode down a still-quiescent Surganova Street, laptop slung over his shoulder. Anxiety re-gripped him when he spotted Yuri waiting for him outside the Institute. The ember in Yuri's cigarette blazed several times as he closed the distance, noting the Russian's pallor and tautness. He checked his watch. Yuri ordinarily arrived an hour-and-a-half hour later.

"It's only 6:45, Yuri. Is something wrong?"

The scientist ground out his cigarette.

"I wanted to talk before you went inside...Shinkevich visited me last night at home. During dinner."

Yuri scrutinized his reaction, swept his gaze up and down Surganova, then glanced back at the Institute, with its dozens of windows looking down on them. "I suggest we take a walk," he said. "Back toward the swimming facility. It's quieter there."

Morris' laptop was already weighing on his shoulder. He considered dropping it off. Instead he repositioned the strap and they continued down the sidewalk, rounding the corner of the Institute.

"I happened to be early today, Yuri. You could have waited a long time."

Yuri squinted as he lit another cigarette.

"That's not important," he answered.

*   *   *

At the rear-side parking lot, they drew incidental, drowsy attention from the attendant in his raised booth. A green soccer field opened up just beyond, still void of activity. Yuri glanced again back at the Institute, and waited until they reached the tree-lined approach to the aquatic complex, before recounting Shinkevich's visit. The KGB man had rung his doorbell a little after seven in the evening, just as he was finishing a pre-dinner drink. To minimize unsettlement for his wife, Yuri had accompanied him down to the courtyard of his building, and talked to him in a children's play area. The message had been menacing and succinct, just like the one to Morris at McDonald's. *This is serious. Have the sense to do what we say.*

As Yuri concluded, they reached the swimming complex and drew up by a fountain. The facility appeared still closed: operating on summer hours. They seemed alone. The Russian paused to light another cigarette. A hand tremor showed---a first.

"Just before Stalin died, my uncle was visited by the KGB and taken away," he said. "We never saw him again."

"Aren't those days over?"

"Don't be so sure. Also don't assume this is going to go away."

He paused for a long drag on his cigarette and squinted back toward the Institute.

"We shouldn't linger here," he said. "Better to return to the lab."

On the walk back, Morris reformulated his plans for the morning. This was no time to lose himself in work.

He really did need to find alternative strategies.

CHAPTER 17

Lena's phone rang as the doors scraped shut. While the elevator began its droning, laborious descent she released a sigh, groped her purse, and consulted the display. She didn't recognize the number, and thought twice about answering.

"*Allo,*" she said.

The caller was Morris, calling from a landline, which he seldom did. Something in his intonation was also off, causing her to press the receiver close to her ear. All she could glean, before the elevator thudded to a stop on the ground floor, was that he wished to alter their lesson plans. She implored him to hang on as she hurried down the half-flight of stairs and out her building entrance. The courtyard was quiet, except for several *babushki* who she recognized, chatting on a bench about ten meters away. She moved to one side, staying in the afternoon shade.

"*I'd like your assistance with a practical matter, Lena. I'd have trouble with it on my own. I'd hoped we could treat it as a lesson.*"

They'd done this before on a few occasions. Fact was, Lena welcomed the variation.

"Should be all right. What do you have in mind?"

"A purchase. I'm still thinking over the details. If you don't mind I'll tell you when we meet."

Tension filtered through his voice again, which was out of character and gave her pause. Curious attentions arose in parallel from the *babushki*, who'd heard her speaking a foreign language. She turned her face away from them.

"Anything unusual, that will require me to make inquiries in advance?"

"No, no...much like what we've done before. I suggest we meet in front of the statue on Jakuba Kolis Square. I'll explain everything there, and we can continue on by taxi or metro." He hesitated for an instant. *"I'd even like to invite you to dinner afterward. Make that part of the lesson plan as well."*

Lena absorbed this.

"I suppose that's okay."

When they signed off she remained in place for a moment, struck by the possibility that Morris might finally be making some sort of romantic overture. She quickly dismissed it.

Though she didn't object to his proposal. If nothing else, it offered a detour from the norm.

*   *   *

Pedestrian traffic around the intersection flowed in multiple streams. Morris surveyed them through the glass panels, particularly alert to loiterers at the Academy Bookstore. He'd last employed a public telephone during his first days in Minsk, before he'd gotten a mobile subscription. Since then he'd retained his calling card in case of emergencies or unforeseen situations.

This fell in both categories.

Trying his best to blend with the crowd, he stepped out of the booth and retreated toward the bookstore, positioning himself in a recessed corner. From there he performed another scan. Passersby gave him the usual quotient of curious glances, but none stood out. Satisfied at last that he'd made his call unobserved, he turned back down Surganova toward the Institute.

His qualms nonetheless persisted. He'd started to involve Lena, even on the margins.

From the beginning, he'd regarded her with a kind of reflexive awe. She was foreign, first of all---with a combination of in-born attractiveness and hard-earned accomplishment that he'd seldom encountered back in the States. Exquisite looks, multiple languages, full professorship in her late 20s...the ensemble was formidable.

To this point, romance had been out of the question. He still wasn't ready to extend himself like that.

This was another kind of initiative. And he'd determined he had little choice.

CHAPTER 18

Piper stayed incognito at public opposition events. At smaller gatherings of leaders and core activists---because his role was understood---he could be more open. Nonetheless he preferred low profile. To provide occasional counsel, not supply initiative. Serve only as enabler.

At least that was the idea. Now he was front and center yet again.

"...We believe the basic conditions for democratic change are still present," he said, speaking Russian to the usual admixture of students and middle-aged academics. "And the U.S. remains committed to help."

Participants numbered about a dozen: assembled in rented office space in Vitebsk, stark and spare despite the considerable expense, funded, like most else, by grants from the United States and the European Union. A question came from the back. The speaker was a pale and scraggly-haired male, early 20s. Either just graduated or still a student. Looking to the U.S. for cues.

"Your Vice President and Secretary of State seem to be mentioning Belarus a lot in the past couple of months, in more aggressive tones."

"I would say that's true," Piper answered.

"Does that signify any change in policy?"

Piper considered his answer.

"Let me put it this way...The U.S. does not want the world to lose interest simply because there are no elections pending."

Insistence rose in the student's voice. "So how do we hold the world's attention...What does the U.S. want us to do?"

Attention crackled up around the room. Piper re-directed it.

"You're asking the wrong question. Creative approaches are required. The kind that have to come from you."

While he paused to let the point sink in, he caught the gaze of a female activist, slender, with long auburn hair, probably also a recent graduate, one of just three females present. In many outward respects, a younger version of Caroline. She'd gone out of her way to exchange greetings with him in English before the meeting.

Another expectant pause ensued. Instead of filling it Piper took a step away from center-floor and directed an open hand toward a bearded professor seated in front, a former presidential candidate for the opposition.

"With that, I'll defer to Dr. Malkovich."

As Piper re-took his chair he glanced back at the girl. She had not taken her eyes off him.

He could redirect political queries. About others he was less sure.

*   *   *

On his way down the Prospekt Morris remained twined in thought, oblivious to the faces of other pedestrians. No matter how he re-appraised recent events, whatever frames of reference he adopted, he kept gravitating to the same comparison---the same essential simi-larities between his ruinous options play two years earlier and his cur-rent predicament with the KGB.

One was that he was exposed to risk. The other was that he had no countervailing positions.

In trading parlance, he was completely unhedged.

By time he reached Jakuba Kolis Square he'd made up his mind. Precautionary measures were in order.

He approached the center of the square concurrently with Lena. Both of them, in keeping with established pattern, were exactly on time. He could see she was slightly guarded, and curious, after his obscuration on the telephone, so he got quickly to the point.

"I'm going to Vilnius again," he said. "To play golf. If possible I'd like your help in buying another ticket."

"When are you going?"

"Friday evening, if we can arrange the train."

Lena paused to take this in. Morris hastened to inject some normalcy.

"...I realize it's sort of sudden. But I decided it's been too long. And I need the relaxation."

"I see. So what's your plan for this evening?"

"I thought we could take a metro straight to the train station. Buy the ticket first, then have dinner afterward. I can tell you more while we eat. And of course try to mix in some Russian."

"As you wish."

As they turned and walked toward the metro entrance, he resolved once again to reveal to her only what was necessary. Full disclosure, he'd determined, would just create additional risks and complications. On this undertaking he was sole decision maker. And would therefore bear sole responsibility. Which highlighted another similarity between this undertaking and his big options play.

He would operate completely on his own.

CHAPTER 19

The meeting got back on track as Malkovich discussed the expansion of grass roots support in the Vitebsk region. Half an hour later he wrapped up the agenda. Chairs were pushed aside, juice and cookies brought out. Intent not to re-assume the limelight, Piper steered past a small group that formed around Malkovich and picked up a bottle of mineral water. He then turned around in unobtrusive manner, ready to engage in further informal discussion on the sidelines.

At once the young female activist filled a place at his elbow, standing very close.

This time she spoke Russian, pleasant to the ear and his other senses. Her interest clearly extended beyond politics. In response to her questions, he remarked that the conclave struck him as worthwhile, after the stilted start.

They promptly veered in a non-political direction.

"Did you drive up from Minsk today?" she asked.

"Yes. This afternoon."

"Long trip."

The girl smiled. Too tactful for direct inquiry.

"Not so bad, really. The highway is good."

While he took a sip of water she sidestepped him and picked up a glass of juice from the table. Her cotton blouse consisted of overlapping flaps that tied together in the back, affording a side-view of cleavage and white skin, a swath of which was also visible above the waistline of her low-cut jeans.

She straightened and raised her glass. Her back was angled to the rest of the room.

"By the way my name's Katya."

"Mine's Russell."

She nodded, with another smile. He'd already announced his name during the meeting. All the same they'd crossed another threshold.

In short order he learned she'd been born and raised in Vitebsk, then gone to Minsk for university, where she'd first gotten involved in the opposition movement. After graduation she'd returned home to stay with her parents, and continued her political activity. In this domain, she lamented, Vitebsk presented meager opportunity. The population was either wary of the opposition, apathetic toward politics in general, or both.

Piper offered several supportive comments. That, in fact, was why he was here. The girl smiled again, partly to herself. She had a second opening.

"Do you like Vitebsk otherwise?" she asked.

"Yes, though I admit I don't know it very well."

"Oh really?"

She waited a suitable downbeat, observing him with her gray eyes.

"...Are you staying a while, if I may ask?"

Her smile spread. Piper couldn't prevent himself from reciprocating. Before answering he took another sip of mineral water.

He'd expected to be tested during Caroline's absence. He just hadn't expected the first one to occur so soon.

* * *

Minsk central station was an expansive modern structure of marble and glass, opened in 2005. In the half-empty third-floor café, Lena and Morris settled at a window table which overlooked the adjoining square. Opposite were the massive, Soviet-classical apartment towers bracketing *Kirov* Street: twin edifices constructed by German prisoners-of-war in the late 40s, as obligatory contributions to Minsk's post-war reconstruction. Morris glanced at them and placed his newly-purchased ticket on the table.

"So, this will be similar to May," she asked. "...Centered on golf?"

"More or less. Same hotel, same golf club."

He paused.

"...However my friend won't be meeting me. This time I'll be golfing alone."

This fact surprised her somewhat.

"Alone? You don't mind?"

"Not really. At the club I'm sure they'll pair me with another player, or include me in a threesome."

Before she could remark further a waitress appeared with fast-serve menus, which contained English translations. After consulting his, Morris ordered sausage on a roll, salad, along with his usual Coke, by indicating desired items with his index finger. His parallel attempt at Russian came out as garbled as ever. For herself Lena ordered a chicken cutlet with cheese, salad, and tea. Meanwhile another worry occurred to her. On this trip, unlike the previous one, Morris would have no one to receive on the other end. When the waitress had gone, she glanced back down at Morris' train ticket, and reiterated a suggestion she'd made in the terminal.

"Evan, I'm quite happy to accompany you here tomorrow evening, to make sure you find the right train. Don't forget none of the departure information is in English. It wouldn't take me more than a half an hour, just like last time."

Morris shifted in his chair and interlocked his fingers on the table.

"Thanks again, Lena. But I really prefer to try this on my own."

He observed her face and saw that she was skeptical.

"...How about this?" he added. "If I run into problems, I'll call you on my cell-phone."

"All right...But I do suggest you get here early...And will you call me from the train later if you run into problems at the border?"

"Okay."

She put her apprehensions aside, reached to her handbag, and pulled out a folder. Despite herself she felt responsible.

"Peresmotrem frasi puteshestvie, togda?"

When he stared back for a moment, she translated.

"Shall we review travel phrases, then?"

He nodded. Before they started he glanced over his shoulder and around the café.

This still seemed out of character to her, until she guessed the source. He was anxious to escape Minsk, even for a weekend.

Much like she was.

* * *

Feet shifted across the room; Malkovich took leave of his supporters and came over, appearing weary but satisfied. After exchanging a few remarks with Piper about the meeting, and confirming their morning appointment, he shook hands and he proceeded out the door, cell-phone to his ear. Others quickly followed. The gathering was winding down. Piper remained standing with Katya near the refreshment table.

"Dr. Malkovich obviously values your advice," she said.

Piper acknowledged the compliment with a nod.

"You're meeting him again tomorrow?"

She'd heard the exchange. There was nothing to hide.

"Over breakfast. We're staying at the same hotel."

"The Eridan?"

"Good guess."

She waited another subtle downbeat.

"...So happens I live in the same direction."

Piper beheld her as he finished his mineral water. Two volunteers started tidying up nearby. He put down his glass and caught another view of the exposed strip around her midsection, followed by another bout of eye contact. His defenses were already falling.

"I'm often followed by security services after these meetings, Katya. I wouldn't want to cause you trouble."

"Let's decide outside. I'll leave first."

"All right....I suppose we can try."

Without further preliminaries she turned and preceded him onto the street. Upon following her and attaining the sidewalk, Piper performed an immediate scan for the KGB sedan that had parked out front before the meeting. It was gone---called off early. Her smile re-formed as he rejoined her. They set off at once across the city's central park.

In motion again after the meeting, he registered the after-effects of his late-morning cardio blowout at *Bagira*, which he'd completed before the drive up. Though his legs were fatigued---in a familiar, pleasant way, free of pain---the rest of his body still coursed with a surfeit of positive juices. He felt both relaxed and mildly euphoric. He took in the languid tableau around them. People idled on benches under the soft light, or watched children playing, enjoying the lull of early evening and inclined toward enjoyment...

The roof of the *Eridan* became visible over the treetops. The scenario was easy to visualize, even if it wasn't foreordained...an invitation to the hotel restaurant ("for the pleasure of conversation")...a shared bottle of wine over dinner...mutual resonations...natural progression to the hotel bar afterward ("why not?")...close contact and slide toward intimacy...

However his workout had also expended surplus energies. That brought clarity.

"Where's your apartment located, Katya?"

"One block to the east of the *Eridan*."

They approached an intersection of several walkways. One pointed toward the hotel; another angled right.

Piper gestured toward the latter.

"Is this the most direct route?"

She flicked a subtle half-glance toward the hotel, then a fuller, more pregnant one upon him.

"Yes. Though I'm in no rush."

"Neither am I."

Piper smiled at her as they veered along the rightward path. He also slowed down, placing his palm deftly on her lower back.

He'd make extra time for conversation. That variety of indulgence was just fine.

He'd also passed his first test.

CHAPTER 20

The lab was quiet except for clicking computer keyboards. Usually the sound soothed Morris. Not this afternoon.

This was his last chance for a gut-check. To make sure his plan made sense.

He rose from his desk and made a discreet exit. Out in the corridor he stopped at a plate-glass end window overlooking a cluster of tall trees. Branches swayed under darkening skies, auguring a downpour. In his search for middle ground he'd come up with just one sound idea---based in part on reflexes he'd acquired during his divorce. What he needed most at this point was someone who could place his recent encounter with al-Tikriti on confidential record, bestow impartial advice, and represent his interests if further complications arose.

In short, he needed a lawyer.

From his earlier involvement in setting up the lab he knew that there were attorneys in Minsk. But these were few in number, and probably no less vulnerable to the KGB than he was. They didn't constitute real protection.

Vilnius was different.

Outside, a finger of lightning traced down over the swimming complex, accompanied by a crack of thunder. First drops splattered the window.

They also served as punctuation. He turned away from the window and pulled out his mobile phone.

Before dialing he reminded himself of his core premise for this undertaking. He would temper his exposure, not add to it. He would avoid extremes.

He would not replay earlier mistakes.

* * *

There was a recording in Russian. Then the translation, in heavily accented English: *The party you are calling is temporarily unavailable.* Another attempt yielded the same result. Morris thought for a moment. This was the first time he'd called Shinkevich. Maybe he'd caught the KGB official at the end of a late lunch, or occupied with other business. To pass several minutes he paced deliberately down to the end of the corridor and back. Then stopped again in his original position and tried again. Same recording: Shinkevich's number remained unavailable.

Still calm, he pulled out his wallet and extracted Shinkevich's business card. Taking care to enter the digits correctly, he called his office number. A female secretary answered in Russian, with a middle-aged voice.

"Dimitri Shinkevich, pozhalizhista."

"Kto govorit?"

"Evan Morris."

"Kto?" Her tone was perplexed and irritated.

"Evan Morris…Vee govorite po angliski?" *Do you speak Russian?*

"Nyet."

He tried to speak slowly and clearly in English. "Once again, my name is Evan Morris. I'm an American citizen in Minsk…I met Mr.

Shinkevich on Saturday." There was a long pause on her end. At last she seemed to give the call some importance, struggling to comprehend what he said. "Please ask him to call me," Morris concluded.

He couldn't tell if he got the point across.

After disconnecting he stared at the floor for a minute. This hadn't figured in his deliberations. Friday was a working day; he'd assumed Shinkevich would be reachable. One feature of his plan was to inform the KGB official only after he'd purchased his train ticket, allowing him little time to respond. What he wished to avoid most was another summons to KGB headquarters prior to his departure---another interrogation that would likely include pointed questions.

And if Shinkevich objected altogether? Simply abort the trip. Cancellation was easy. He had no meetings scheduled yet in Vilnius and hadn't even made a hotel reservation...

The elevator to the lobby opened and Yuri emerged, in the company of the Director of the Institute. Both nodded at Morris as they passed, observing the phone in his hand.

For an instant Morris considered aborting regardless of Shinkevich's availability. Instead he stuck to his plan. One component was to wait and inform the lab until the last minute, so there'd be no time for questions about his trip. Why implicate anyone---Yuri especially---with advance knowledge?

Clouds burst outside as he turned back to the window, splattering heavy drops on the glass. He checked his watch: just after 3:30, about two hours before he had to leave. Still time to contrive another demonstration of good faith. He strode back into the lab and re-seated himself at his desk. The rain started driving down in sheets, coating the glass and blurring the view onto the street. From his wallet he pulled out Shinkevich's card again, found his e-mail address: Shinkevich@kgb.gov.by, and opened a compose-mail screen. He considered himself a mediocre writer, and took care with his wording as he typed:

Mr. Shinkevich,

I just tried reaching you on your mobile phone but was unsuccessful. I also left a message with your secretary.

Due to your request to be notified about foreign travel, I am informing you that I plan to travel to Vilnius for the weekend. I will leave on the evening train to Vilnius today (Friday) and will return to Minsk on Sunday evening.

I am traveling alone, in order to play golf. This is my second trip to Lithuania for this reason. I may assure you I have no plans to contact the U.S. Embassy in Vilnius or any other Western governments about my experience last weekend.

Please excuse the late timing of this message. I made this plan at the last minute, based on a simple desire to escape Minsk for a couple of rounds of golf.

Sincerely,

Evan Morris

* * *

Piper's second-floor office was exceeded in size only by the Ambassador's, with two tall windows overlooking the Embassy courtyard. Just outside, trunks and limbs rocked and swayed. Water smacked the walls and roof, enveloping him in gentle cacophony. He turned back toward his computer screen. On display was a secure transmission from Deputy Director Stapleton. Another one-to-one, written communication, meant to alert Piper in advance. Also to protect against future bureaucratic fallout:

To: Russell Piper, Belarus Station Chief
From: James Stapleton, Deputy Director
Russell,

At the Vice President's request, Belarus was the main theme of my breakfast briefing this morning with the President, Vice President *and National Security Advisor. Accordingly, I provided copies of your latest intelligence summaries and field reports, which I've found both comprehensive and judicious. Following my presentation---and without advance warning---Vice President Gallstone made a formal (verbal) proposal to move Belarus into the category of "Highest Priority: Immediate and further action required."*

Despite my categorical objections, the President agreed to consider the proposal. He will make a final decision by our next breakfast meeting on Tuesday. You're well aware of the implications of such a designation, particularly for your activities as Station Chief.

In advance of Tuesday, the President has instructed me to solicit your reaction, and that you "reconsider and re-weigh all considerations" before rendering your recommendation. I would therefore ask that you submit your specific response to me by Sunday. This will allow us time for discussion on Monday over a secure video feed, in advance of my Tuesday breakfast meeting at the White House.

Regards,

Jim

Piper winced and shook his head. Stapleton's sub-text was clear. Forces were already aligned against them. And his own individual options? He could sign on and score some career points with Gallstone and the current foreign policy cabal. Win a "team-player" label…Maybe set himself up for a political appointment, such as a post with the NSC. Or he could hew to facts and produce some bothersome counter-arguments, quite possibly setting the stage for his own demise….

The White House would probably roll forward in any case.

Svetlana's voice roused him from the doorway to his office. She was a Belarussian administrative assistant from the first floor, one of the few remaining with recent staff reductions, delivering non-urgent mail. He beckoned her inside, and registered her thin summer dress and makeup as she drew up to his desk. With a smile she took a magazine off a small stack of materials in one arm.

On top was the August issue of *Men's Extreme Fitness,* to which he'd just subscribed. A buffed-up actor was on the cover. The tagline read **How to Make Testosterone Work for You**.

When he looked up again, she lingered by his desk, transmitting an immediate vibe with her closeness.

"I wanted to tell you I've decided to postpone my vacation until September, Russell," she said. "Now doesn't seem like the right time, with so many other staffers leaving next week."

"Frankly, I'm relieved to hear it, Svetlana. There's a good chance I'll need you."

"...And if you'd like me to do anything extra, just say so. I'm prepared to work late, if necessary. I really don't mind."

The implications were evident. Caroline's absence had not gone unnoticed.

"Thank you, Svetlana. But let's hope we won't have to."

She prolonged her smile before turning away, revealing intimate outlines beneath her summer dress. There'd been undercurrents for a while. Now they were welling into the open. After she'd gone Piper drew a deep breath, looked back down at the cover of *Men's Extreme Fitness,* and made a mental note to read the feature story that evening at home.

He hadn't quite worked Katya out of his system. Already he sensed Svetlana would be next.

Gallstone was not his only challenge.

CHAPTER 21

Minsk Central Station drew closer on the right, early-evening sun glinting off its steel and brown-glass façade. The driver studied him in the rear-view mirror. "Gde?" he asked. *Where?*

"Tam," Morris answered, pointing ahead.

Just one other taxi stood at the long curb as they pulled up and stopped, creating a somewhat conspicuous entrance. Morris determined it made no difference. He'd offered suitable advance notice to Shinkevich and was hiding nothing. With his laptop slung on one shoulder and wheeling his suitcase, he proceeded straight inside through the sliding doors, into the gaping, sky-lit atrium. It was dense with travelers, milling and crisscrossing in all directions; he navigated through them and stepped onto the up-escalators.

In the central waiting area over the tracks announcements echoed across the public address system. Instead of trying to decipher them he approached the main departure board, which Lena had indicated earlier. He'd studied and re-studied the Russian spelling of "Vilnius" until it was imprinted on his memory, and found it on the board. Departure was 18:35. His train was on schedule.

Down on the platform he quickly found his train-car, exactly where Lena had specified. The plump female train attendant gave him a once-over as she examined his ticket, then invited him to board. To his relief he found his first-class compartment empty. He settled by the window and kept his eye on the platform.

Still no untoward presences. No militiamen.

Most notable: Shinkevich had not responded to his afternoon messages. That, together with the official's absence of contact since McDonald's on Wednesday, perhaps boded well.

Morris reviewed his rationale. His intention here was to circumscribe existing risk. Not assume another one. That was the baseline.

Whistles blew. Brakes unlocked with a shudder and the train began a slow roll out of the station.

This initiative was underway.

CHAPTER 22

Lena wasn't really surprised that Natasha was going to Rimini. However the next part astounded her.

"Are you telling me you *want* to get pregnant?"

"Let me put it this way," Natasha answered. "If it happens, I won't mind. In fact, I'll be pleased."

Lena put down her chopsticks and stared across the table. As the admission took hold she slackened with dismay.

"Natasha. You haven't even seen Fabrizio for seven months. And in the past he hasn't shown himself to be the most reliable guy on the planet."

"So?"

"Doesn't that give you pause?"

"Why should it? He's pretty well-off. And his family seems wealthy besides."

"What if he doesn't marry you?"

From their side table at *Planeta Sushi*, Natasha glanced absently around at surrounding diners, mostly women in their 20s and early 30s. She put down her own chopsticks and evinced a patient, sympathetic expression. The intimation was that Lena was naïve. Lena had seen it before, and found it vaguely irritating.

"For all your academic attainments, Lena, you really are innocent in some matters….Aren't you aware of Western paternity laws these days?"

"Not in detail."

"Well, I am. I've done research on the Internet. If a man gets a woman pregnant, his paternity can be confirmed with DNA testing. After that…at least in Europe and North America…he's obligated by law to support the child, whether he marries the woman or not. And support her too, basically. Up until the child reaches 18. There are some minor differences among countries. But that's the law."

"Even if the man is tricked? For example if the woman falsely tells him she's using contraception?"

"Irrelevant. Biological parentage is all that matters."

Several pieces of Maki sushi remained on Lena's plate; she paused and fixed on these for a moment. Ramifications were troubling, on several levels. One in particular. She looked up again at Natasha across the table.

"Don't tell me you plan to deceive Fabrizio like that…"

"Not exactly."

"What do mean 'not exactly'? Are you going to tell him about your intention, or not?"

"I'll never bring up the subject. You could say I'll simply leave it in a gray area."

"Hold on…Didn't you use birth control last time you met?"

"Yes."

"So he's likely to show up this time thinking the same…"

Natasha raised her eyebrows in a show of nonchalance, nodding slightly. When Lena transmitted an incredulous stare, she re-assumed the manner of sophisticate, instructing the uninitiated.

"Lena, look…Fabrizio has chosen to get involved with me. To have his fun. So he's hardly blameless in this equation. If he makes easy assumptions, or prefers not to use a condom, that's his problem. Okay, if I could, I might choose someone else. But I just turned 30.

My fertility's not going to last forever. If the kind of guy I want hasn't shown up by now, why should I expect him to during the next five or six years? Where am I going to find him? At Zhuravinka? Or in a setting like this?"

She made a gesture around the restaurant, which Lena accommodated with an encompassing glance. Apart from several couples, about eighty percent of the tables were again occupied by young females, in groupings of two, three or five: well-turned out, incontrovertibly attractive, absorbed in each other---a tableau that had become predominant not just at *Zhuravinka*, but in Minsk at large over the previous seven or eight years.

Still, Lena still couldn't believe what she was hearing. She made the same gesture.

"I'm sorry, Natasha, our girls just don't do things like that, regardless of what occurs in the West."

"Well, if they don't maybe they should...Let's face reality, Lena. Society is changing. So are the rules. Women have to fend for themselves nowadays. I've made that recognition. Therefore I've decided to take matters into my own hands."

She paused for effect, awaiting Lena's reaction. Lena obliged.

"And Fabrizio's too?"

This was not the one Natasha wanted.

"...You know, Lena, you're almost thirty yourself. You're impossibly selective, for one, and haven't been thrilled by recent prospects. Maybe it's also time for you to be more realistic. And practical."

Lena released a detached exhalation and leaned back in her chair, reassessing young women at surrounding tables, engrossed in their typical animated conversation. Were they really moving toward the same mentality? If so, this was one facet of Westernization with which she took issue, despite its connotations of freedom.

"What can I say, Natasha? I'm somewhat taken aback. However it's your life. All I can add is that I think differently."

"Are you saying you would never consider something similar?"

Lena hesitated. Natasha seized upon this at once.

"That's what I thought..."

Lena had to be honest. She hadn't really thought that question through, to the end.

CHAPTER 23

Saturday, July 26th

When Morris finished his scrambled eggs, sausage and bacon, he returned to the buffet for three *pain au chocolate*. Back at his table he signaled the waitress for his third mug of coffee.

With his first bite he beheld the view again, across a plaza toward Vilnius' main Cathedral and Belltower. It had become familiar during his last stay at *Hotel Klaipeda* in May. Sunlight brightened the cobble-stoned expanse, empty except for a solitary jogger and several dog-walkers.

The canines prompted him to check his watch and calculate the time in California.

He and Nora had owned a dog. A cocker spaniel named Molly, which they'd often walked together in the evening.

The scene came back to him. As excruciating as ever.

*   *   *

"Evan, I can't stand it any more. It's gotten to the point where I can't even concentrate during my volunteer activities. What's going on?" She scrutinized his profile as they walked. Morris had hoped for a turnaround over the previous several days. A respite. Instead the damage had just gotten worse.

When he didn't answer right away her impatience only mounted.

"You've been sequestered at home all day long lately in front of your computer...for what now? Ten days? Two weeks? No golf...constantly on the phone with your broker. If I'm not home I can hardly reach you by phone during trading hours. I've had to resort to text messages with my own husband."

Morris cleared his throat. "I'm sorry, Nora."

On the leash, Molly slowed her forward progress and twisted her snout.

"...In the evenings you're like a zombie. Our conversations are short and mechanical...I'm not surprised, with how little you've been sleeping. Did you even sleep at all last night?"

"I don't know. Maybe an hour or two."

For reassurance Morris looked down at Molly, who at last forced her head all the way back for direct eye contact. The canine's rueful and worried expression only compounded Nora's alarm.

"I've seen some empty Fedex envelopes in the trash this week," she said. "All from your broker."

"Yes. I didn't see any point...in making you worry."

This didn't go down well.

"Evan, I don't usually delve into your trading activities, but this seems different. I'm your wife. At a certain point I deserve to know."

Morris spread his eyelids to focus. Houses and lawns on their cul-de-sac now appeared surreal.

"Well?"

"Those envelopes you've seen concerned margin calls," he answered. "They've been going on for a while. In fact they started last week."

Nora's back straightened. "But you've used margin before. You've said it's not dangerous if used properly..."

"In principle that's true."

"What's different this time?"

"This time the…scale is larger. Our exposure much more extreme." He paused… Evasion was no longer viable…"About a month ago, both my puts and calls started to move against me. Even on what I thought were my more conservative positions. I determined the trends were anomalies. So I basically redoubled my bets."

"Redoubled? How?"

"With additional margin."

The surreal seemed to take hold of Nora as well and her eyes also sought out Molly. The dog looked uncertain whether to continue along their normal route or double back to the house. After hesitating for an instant she continued plodding forward.

"When the markets continued against me," Morris continued. "I had to liquidate our other long positions in stocks and bonds, in order to maintain the bets I'd made in the options markets."

This took a moment to sink in.

"But you're usually so careful. Basically risk-averse…or so I thought." When Morris' gaze fell to the asphalt, Nora looked at him with disbelief. "Why didn't you tell me earlier?"

"I always thought it would turn around. At least up until this week. After all I'd always been right before."

Her voice strained. "So what exactly has been the result?"

"Three million dollars in margin calls just in the last two days."

"Margin calls…that doesn't tell me enough. What's the bottom line?"

"I've…we've…suffered losses. Big ones. Much more than three million."

"How big?"

When Morris told her she stopped in her tracks and gasped. So did Molly; the leash went slack in his hand.

"Good God," Nora sputtered. "That's eighty percent of our net worth…more." Her assertiveness at last departed her, superseded by shock and disbelief. "Do we have any chance to recover?"

Morris had hesitated before answering. He had avoided this conclusion until there was no other.

"No. I don't think so. Not any more."

"More coffee, sir?"

Morris shook himself out of his reverie as the waitress refilled his
mug. When she was gone he glimpsed another dog being walked in
the square. The dog looked happy and secure. So did its owner.

In the divorce Nora had taken sole possession of Molly. That had
been one blow added to all the others.

CHAPTER 24

Four other breakfast-goers entered the restaurant---both older couples who'd probably stuck together through years of thick and thin. Morris knew that if he lingered in their presence he would probably start brooding again over Nora, so he gulped down the remainder of his mug and made a quick exit. From the lobby he ascended the glass-walled elevator to the fourth floor and returned to his room, where he brewed an additional small pot of coffee and got back behind his computer.

One reason the *Hotel Klaipeda* appealed to him was its free high-speed Internet access. Here he could roam fast and unhindered. And without being monitored by the Belarussian KGB.

First he checked e-mail: no new messages. Then with quick clicks of his mouse he opened six sites he'd bookmarked the previous evening.

He'd found them on the site U.S. Embassy in Vilnius, which maintained a list of attorneys and firms "sufficiently competent in the English language to provide services to English-speaking clients." The Embassy nonetheless disavowed "responsibility for the professional ability or integrity of the individuals or firms listed."

Morris took this to be a standard disclaimer, and didn't dwell on it.

Twelve firms were listed, along with links to their Web sites, all of which had English-language versions. Most were affiliated with blue-chip stalwarts in the U.S., but only five included American-trained lawyers. Of these five only three had lawyers that were U.S.-born. Morris preferred an American lawyer if possible. Also one with a name he could pronounce.

He checked his watch: 7:40. His plan was to send e-mails to potential candidates, and follow up if necessary with phone calls. His goal: a face-to-face meeting later that morning.

Already the gloom that settled over him at breakfast was easing. With constructive direction, he felt more upbeat. He copied over the first e-mail address and got started.

*   *   *

The Agency had long limited White House briefing papers to two pages. However this President had a notoriously short attention span, particularly for written material. Piper therefore endeavored to keep to one page. He re-read his opening paragraphs:

> *The March 2006 presidential election in Belarus was marked by manipulation of the Belarussian constitution, fraudulent balloting, and repression of electoral opponents---all of which enabled President Lukashenko to claim a third term. However these very excesses also engendered new dissatisfaction in the population, particularly among educated and affluent urbanites. Demonstrations in Minsk immediately after the balloting revealed a vital mass of Belarussian citizens who aspire to greater democracy and a freer economy, and who are willing to rally around opposition parties.*
>
> *During the past two years, regrettably---despite concerted political pressure and a range of sanctions by United States and the European Union---the Lukashenko government has succeeded in stifling successor*

demonstrations. And open support for the opposition has waned, even if significant segments of the population remain discontent with the status quo. In an effort to counter this trend the U.S. is already providing critical financial assistance; U.S. covert support for opposition parties this year has amounted to about $5 million per month, more than adequate for our purposes....

He sipped his coffee and remembered Gallstone's angry push for more funding---$15 million per month or higher. Far beyond what was needed. He winced and read on to the close:

...A more urgent, crisis-type approach, one involving even more aggressive public diplomacy, is not only unnecessary, but likely to be counter-productive. My recommendation, therefore, is that the current proposal for re-classification of Belarus be rejected.
*   Signed,*
*   Russell Piper*
*   Station Chief - Minsk*

Piper put down his empty mug and mulled the conclusion. The paper was sure to enrage Gallstone. Simmering conflict would boil into open battle. He stood from his desk and paced across his office. From his small refrigerator he grabbed a bottle of mineral water, and with tensed forearm twisted off the cap and scrunched it in his fist.

His writing also dissatisfied him. Eighteen years of government service had deadened his prose. He needed to prune the bureaucratic phraseology. Perhaps employ simple bullet points for the sake of the President.

He swilled some water; Caroline had now been gone almost a week. Time for his first Saturday workout at *Bagira* in his new rotation: one hour of explosive weight training, with four sets on most exercises, then an obliterating 30-minute cardio blowout on the *Stairmaster.* Afterward he hoped return to the office with a more lucid head.

His gym bag lay on the floor near the door. He scooped it up on his way out.

*   *   *

In the lobby Morris received a cordial "Good morning" from the young female receptionist. She seemed to remember him from May.

That first weekend truly *had been* centered on golf. Jeff Esposito, a former fraternity brother at Cornell and now in the marketing department at Cognition Software, had traveled through Eastern Europe on a nine-day swing. Appointments in Warsaw on Friday and Moscow on Monday, with a free weekend in between. Due to the absence of golf in Belarus, they'd settled on Lithuania, and a course a half-hour outside Vilnius.

Today there was no taxi waiting. And Jeff was likely off in some other corner of the globe.

Outside the sliding glass doors, Morris crossed the adjoining square, and turned left on Gedemino Street, the city's main drag, blocked off into a pedestrian-only zone for the weekend. He walked straight up the empty traffic lanes and at the next intersection took a left onto Totoriu Street. Beside an upscale hotel he re-checked his map, turned right onto Liejyklos Street, then climbed uphill, and veered left. One block further on he sighted a distinctive, curving building which Grinevicius had mentioned: a school. The words over the door read: *"Vilniaus Salomejos Neries Gimnazija."* Vokeiciq Street lay just ahead.

The artery looked at once familiar from May; cut grass and cobblestones, interspersed with seasonal cafes. Grinevicius had told him to look for a prominent *Nokia* store on the left; Number 22 lay directly opposite. Morris found it: a recessed archway with access to second-floor offices. He entered and found only one door inside, dark brown and unprepossessing. Next to it was a push-buttoned directory.

There were only two tenants. Including the one Morris wanted, noted in both English and Lithuanian:

John Grinevicius, Attorney at Law
John Grinevicius, Prokuroras Teisė

Over the phone Grinevicius had described himself as "second genera-
tion on both sides". But American, born in Chicago. With no language
barrier.

Other biographical information on the lawyer's web site also
was also reassuring. Undergraduate degree from Columbia in East
European studies. Boston University Law School. Massachusetts and
New York Bar Exams. Proficiency in both Russian and Lithuanian.
Twenty-eight years old. Founder of his own firm just fourteen months
earlier. There were some voids in Grinevicius' short web resume, but
Morris knew that was typical of anyone just starting off. Moreover the
other six or seven lawyers he'd contacted---all in larger firms---had
either brushed him off or suggested postponement until Monday.

During his divorce he'd experienced numerous frustrations with
attorneys, both his and Nora's. Arrogance. Inadaptability. Slow reaction times.

By contrast Grinevicius had reacted by e-mail at once. Taken his
phone call minutes afterward. Tactful, according to first impressions.
A good listener.

Morris figured he needed that latter quality most of all. Along
with prudent advice.

He pushed the button on the console.

CHAPTER 25

Grinevicius waited on the second-floor landing, recognizable from a photograph on his web site. As he shook hands Morris registered the lawyer's height: a lanky 6'4" or thereabouts. In this respect and others, including his dark hair and pale skin, he resembled many Lithuanians he'd observed around Vilnius. His informality, however, was all-American. Once inside the office, they passed by a secretary's desk with computer and a small adjacent waiting area, both empty.

"I don't have a full-time secretary," the lawyer explained. "Just a law student who helps me out in the afternoons…weekdays, that is. I keep my administration to a minimum by making use of technology. Like e-mail, for example."

"Suits me."

Indeed, Morris' had found his divorce lawyer in San Francisco far too paper-oriented. A small conference room/library became visible through a side doorway. Grinevicius acknowledged it with a relaxed gesture.

"We'll meet in there," he said. "But first I'll complete the tour."

The intention was clear. Grinevicius aimed to reassure. Underline that his practice was well-established, despite its short existence. They proceeded into his medium-sized office, which looked well-inhabited

and worked-in. Law journals and reference books lay scattered on a
coffee table, suggesting intellectual and theoretical bents. Avant-
garde posters added a contemporary edge, along with a large window
overlooking Volklecizt. A plethora of electronic equipment was configured around the lawyer's L-shaped desk. Most prominent: two large
flat-screen monitors, one at the center and the other on a perpendicular side surface.

"I see you've gone with two screens," Morris said.

"I've found dual-screens improve my productivity. I now swear by
them."

For Grinevicius' type of work, Morris could definitely see the
advantage. On the floor nearby were two tower servers, each coupled
to a router an uninterruptible power supply.

"One is my Web server and the other is my office server," the lawyer explained. "I have a high-speed cable connection into the office."

The rest was organized on different shelf levels in a low-slung back
cabinet. These included a scanner; black-white laser printer; color
laser printer; backup storage device; and a sleek, expensive laptop
in a docking station, featuring an ergonomic keyboard and wireless
mouse. Nothing was lacking. Including two rather high-end speakers
a woofer box on the floor.

"For when I need to relax," Grinevicius noted, unembarrassed.

Morris couldn't find fault with that, either. In his programming
days, he'd often listened to music while writing code.

The only non-technology item on the desk-surface was a photograph of an attractive, dark-haired woman, somewhat younger-looking
than Grinevicius. Presumably his wife or girlfriend. Other framed
photographs on the nearest wall, in any case, attracted more attention.
Morris drew closer to take a look. Grinevicius didn't seem to mind.

There were half a dozen shots: five showed Grinevicius in assorted
modes of extreme rock climbing; a sixth showed him standing on a
panoramic peak with two fellow climbers. Colors were vivid, captured
under bright sunshine and apparent warm weather, judging by the

tank tops and other lightweight sports gear. Locations varied, with dry, arid environments in some backdrops and lush greenery in others. Several images showed Grinevicius hanging off small outcroppings of rock by the finger-tips of one hand, sinews rippling in his forearms, his long legs dangling down into space. Picks and ropes were represented in some shots but looked optional.

Some of the heights, even filtered by photography, were unnerving to Morris. Rock-climbing was not the sport for him.

"Looks pretty serious," he said.

"It was, for quite a while..." A wistful expression crossed Grinevicius' face.

Morris glanced back at him: an implied invitation to continue. The lawyer obliged.

"...In college I took up hiking around the Hudson River Valley on weekends. Basically I progressed from there...joined a student club. Soon I was scaling vertical rock faces. Between college and law school it became my main avocation. I began traveling to exotic locations, looking for bigger challenges..."

He paused and came closer, pointing to one of the images.

"That one's in Arizona, not far from the Grand Canyon." He let Morris absorb the downward view into a gaping chasm. "This one was taken at Tuckerman's Ravine in New Hampshire....That one in Colorado...These two in Europe...in the Pyrenees in southern France and Spain. This last one was taken in Turkey."

"Have you kept it up?"

"During law school I cut back a little due to time and financial constraints. But I got back into it more intensively when I graduated. When I moved over to Lithuania a year-and-a-half ago I remained keen on it. Turns out there are some excellent rock formations in southeastern Poland and Slovakia..."

He paused again, revealing another trace of wistfulness.

"Then, about a year ago. I met a woman here in Vilnius who..." he said with a slight shrug. "...changed my priorities. Convinced me to give up climbing because of the danger. To start to think about marriage and family. We got engaged in June. We'll be married next spring."

"Congratulations."

"Thanks. Are you married?"

"Divorced."

Sympathy crossed the lawyer's features.

"Sorry to hear that…Anyway I've got to focus on building my practice," he said. "Let's go into the conference room. We can talk about your case there."

Morris hadn't made up his mind yet about Grinevicius. The rock climbing implied a propensity for risk. But that, in any event, was now part of the past.

And most of his other impressions were favorable. He had just a few other questions before going ahead.

CHAPTER 26

The green-glass table and black, tight-mesh chairs in Grinevicius' conference room held to motif. Reference books on American, EU and Lithuanian law filled two low-slung bookshelves, underneath additional framed posters marking recent East European art shows. A large-paned window was cracked open, allowing sounds to filter in from Voklecicz Street. The lawyer settled opposite and opened a legal pad. Amiable or not, Morris assumed the hourly clock was now ticking. He got right to business.

"I saw your resume on your site," he said. "Your education is obviously very good."

Grinevicius acknowledged the remark with a nod, minus the sort of self-importance Morris had often encountered from other attorneys.

"… I just became curious about some of the years for which you listed no activity…Then how you ended up in Lithuania."

"Sure," the lawyer replied without hesitation. "While I was at Columbia I began waiting tables part-time at a high-end restaurant in Manhattan…Tuxedoed staff, magazine reviews, that sort of place. Helped pay my bills. Tips were great, often three figures for a table. In fact so good…better money than I could have gotten anywhere else at that point…I moved into it full-time for two years after graduation.

Paid off my student loans and funded a big portion of law school. Not to mention four months of climbing in Europe, before I started."

Morris guessed some of Grinevicius' office photographs came from this period.

"…During that trip I also visited Lithuania for the first time since I was a kid. I found I liked it…and not just because of my heritage. I began thinking of practicing law here later on."

The narrative was becoming clearer. The lawyer pressed on.

"…At BU I soon concluded corporate and other traditional legal paths in the U.S. didn't appeal to me…too conventional. Therefore I repeated my earlier pattern from New York. Found weekend work at another gourmet restaurant, in what is now the Langham Hotel. After graduation I worked full-time there for another year, in order to move to Vilnius and finance my own practice."

"Quite an initiative. No practical obstacles?"

"No. I'd passed bar exams in the States, and after a year of coursework passed the equivalent here in the Lithuanian language. So happens there's a special law that allows people who are first or second-generation Lithuanians to come back and establish permanent residency. And with my marriage, in any case, I'll soon get dual citizenship."

Morris glanced down at his own notepad. Grinevicius' site listed specializations in property law, inheritance, private international law, criminal law, and international taxation. Somewhat eclectic---though other firms in Vilnius listed similar assortments. He asked him about it.

"U.S. multinational companies have moved into Lithuania in recent years," the lawyer answered. "But I knew I wouldn't get much work from them. They tend to go with bigger firms. And frankly I prefer to represent individuals."

Grinevicius paused, like a salesman winding a pitch.

"…My specializations are somewhat connected with my family history. My great-grandparents and grandparents…on both sides…were quite prosperous before the war. When the Soviets annexed the country in 1939 most of what they owned was expropriated. They fled to the States before the German occupation in 1941, and didn't come back when the Soviets re-asserted control in 1945. When the Soviet Union came to an end, a lot of what was taken by the Communists remained in government hands, or people who were connected to the Party. Therefore I've tried to establish a specialization in suits by Americans of Lithuanian descent, seeking to reclaim their lost property. So far about half my clients fall in this category. However those cases tend to drag on for years. As it's turned out, most of my day-to-day work is in international taxation."

Morris was a little surprised. The specialization didn't seem to fit Grinevicius' freewheeling past. Grinevicius sensed his reaction, and explained.

"...Not tax returns. I represent American citizens living in Lithuania who experience difficulties with the IRS."

"Like audits?"

"Exactly. They're a common problem for expatriates. Automatic suspicion, you could say..." For an instant Grinevicius' upbeat projection faltered. "...which I know from first-hand experience. After I moved over here I was audited because of my tip income in Boston... after the fact. Got stung with a big penalty, for no good reason. Money I could have invested in my practice."

Morris decided Grinevicius deserved credit for being forthright. And he shared the lawyer's aversion toward the IRS. The Byzantine U.S. tax code had created accounting nightmares during his trading years. He looked down again at his notes.

"Any experience with Belarus?"

Grinevicius got back on pitch. It was now clear; he really wanted this case.

"No, I have to admit. Belarus is still kind of a black hole for the international legal profession---even for Russian speakers like me. But from what you've described, your case intrigues me."

"Why?"

"I distrust governments in general. Particularly their ability to roll over the individual. And Belarus' government is worse than most."

Morris still had to learn Grinevicius' rates. But he had pretty much made up his mind.

CHAPTER 27

Under the heading **Selecting a Lithuanian Lawyer**, the Web site of the U.S. Embassy in Vilnius advised the following:

> *...Ask for a written schedule of fees...specifying currency and exchange rates where feasible. Lithuanian lawyers are not allowed to work on a contingency-fee basis...*

Morris now examined Grinevicius' list:

Attorney services rendered in Lithuania:	*200 Euros/hour*
Attorney services rendered outside Lithuania:	*250 Euros/hour*
Paralegal services:	*90 Euros/hour*
All travel, filing and delivery expenses paid by client	

Somewhat higher than he'd expected in Lithuania. But considerably lower than he'd paid in California.

"These look acceptable," he said. "I'd like to go forward."

A slight smile crossed Grinevicius' features. His salesmanship had worked.

"Good, I'm pleased to represent you."

Morris bent down and extracted a file folder from his canvas brief-case. Grinevicius opened a fresh page on his legal pad and leaned forward.

"I'll start with some basic facts about myself," Morris began. "Then I'll describe what happened last Saturday."

*   *   *

After brief summaries of his employment and residential status in Minsk, Morris proceeded straight to the *shashlik* at Yuri's dacha and the berry-picking expedition. From there he became slow and delib-erate. Accuracy was essential. Grinevicius mostly listened, interject-ing occasional questions for clarification. Lines filled quickly on his notepad.

For sake of chronology Morris withheld the Iraqi's identity until later. When he described his transport into KGB headquarters and subsequent questioning, Grinevicius' questions multiplied. Morris didn't spare detail back in his apartment: his sighting of surveillance at his building entrance, his assumption about his cell-phone, inter-vals of time as he reached various conclusions. Then he got to his Internet research.

"I soon identified the man I'd seen in the berry patch," he said. "...that is, the man in the gray homburg. I found a photograph and description of him on the site of the U.S. Defense Department."

Grinevicius stopped taking notes, fixing his eyes across the table.

"...Turns out he's Iraqi. His name is Amoud al-Tikriti."

"Iraqi...interesting. Some sort of political figure?

"You could say that. Remember the "55 Most Wanted" list at the start of the U.S invasion?"

"Of course."

"Hussein was number one, and his sons numbers two and three?"

The lawyer nodded again.

"Al-Tikriti wasn't on the list. But he may as well have been. Apparently he was the head of Saddam Hussein's financial operations."

"Wow..." At last Grinevicius paused to jot some notes. When he looked up his eyes were intense with new thought. "...Does that list still exist?"

"No. It was shut down several years ago, after Hussein was executed and most of the others had been rounded up."

"And al-Tikriti? Did he become a fugitive?"

"That's where the picture grew complicated. It's also one of the reasons I saw fit to travel to Vilnius and enlist an attorney."

Grinevicius straightened his long frame and repositioned his forearms on the table. What had already been an intriguing case had suddenly become much bigger.

"You were right to come," he said.

CHAPTER 28

The guy on the stair-climber was out of the ordinary. That was for sure.

Lena re-acquired his image in the mirror. She wasn't one to stare. Still, she couldn't keep her eyes away. Not because he was probably a foreigner, and rather good-looking besides. More the torment he was inflicting on himself.

His pumping was so determined and furious that she wondered if he'd bust the machine. Associated oxygen requirements were evidently enormous: his rhythmic breathing was loud enough to compete with the music and even annoy the aerobics instructor. Sweat spilled down his body in volumes, drenching his t-shirt and workout shorts and running from his elbows onto the floor. Occasional swipes from a hand towel sprayed droplets in random directions from his head and arms. He glanced occasionally at the control panel through a veil of salinity and...pain? Bizarre ecstasy? She couldn't tell which. Otherwise his eyes had been mostly closed for over 15 minutes.

This guy was exercising at a level of intensity that she'd never seen before.

RAS! DVA! TRI! CHETIRI!

The shouts came from the instructor---louder than usual and edged with exasperation. Music was blended pop/rap from Gwen Stefani. Half the class was out of sync.

...E NAZAD!

With slight embarrassment Lena pulled her eyes off the mirror and struggled to get back on beat. Others around her did the same. She wasn't the only one distracted by the foreigner.

He hadn't been there during her recent classes; she was sure she would have noticed. Today she'd first spotted him in the weight training area; he'd been alone there except for a trainer, who'd observed from polite distance as he'd performed reverse curls with a bent barbell. His back view alone had been enough to magnetize her attention. Tall---probably around 187 cm---and well-proportioned, with broad shoulders tapering down to a trim waist and muscled legs. Full head of brown hair. Her first guess that he was about her age---somewhere around 30. In men she assigned priority to brains and character, rather than physical traits. Nevertheless...

By means of mirrored angles, additional components came into view. Rather pumped up, but not to the steroid-induced excess of a *kachok*...Then a machine had slid out of frame and she'd gained a free line of sight to his face, in different light.

Mature. Definitely older than 30. Incontrovertible lines around the eyes. Smatterings of gray hair on the sides...

Late 30s? Early 40s? Not a Slavic face. Most definitely not Russian... too square-jawed. She could recognize her compatriots almost without fail...Probably American or British, she reckoned...More likely American. Diplomat? Businessman? There weren't many left in Minsk these days in either category...

Nonetheless she'd avoided reflected eye contact; she simply was not that brazen.

Now, from the aerobics floor, she purloined another glance in the mirror. His furious intensity had not subsided. One effect of his riotous breathing and unpredictable fans of perspiration had been to drive the two trainers away from their gallery position of the previous Saturday. Though voyeurism seemed least on this foreigner's agenda...

RAS! DVA! TRI! CHETIRI!

The instructor remained vigilant. This time Lena was careful not to fall out of step.

...E NAZAD!

Again she caught his image. Narcissism was a possible explanation. But that didn't account for such brutal effort, such self-infliction...It was simply hard to fathom.

She sighed to herself and looked away, swinging her arms with the routine. Maybe existentialist philosophers left male-female relations aside for good reason.

Some gulfs between the sexes seemed too wide to breach.

*   *   *

In conclusion, Morris recounted his failure to reach Shinkevich and his somewhat harried departure from Minsk. Grinevicius didn't fault him for the initiative, given the stakes. The pretext also seemed to please him, for some reason.

"Why golf?" he asked.

"Belarus has no courses. And I'd played at one outside Vilnius in May...*Europos Centro Golfo Klubas*, I think it's called. So there was a precedent. It was also the best excuse I could come up with for leaving the country on short notice."

Grinevicius cracked a grin.

"My new sport," the lawyer said. "Took it up about a year ago. In fact I joined *Europos Centro* in April. Something endorsed by my fiancé. Call it a substitute for rock-climbing."

"Well it is safer."

"No arguments there. Are you actually going to play this weekend?"

"I'd thought about it. Obviously finding a lawyer was my first priority."

Grinevicius scribbled a line on his notepad and drew a star next to it. Morris guessed what he had in mind. Ten minutes later they were done, by which time the lawyer already seemed to be developing a plan.

"I propose to delve into Amoud al-Tikriti this afternoon on the Internet," he said, "Also research recent cases in Belarus involving foreigners, if there are any. By five-thirty or so, I should have some specific ideas about how to move forward, which I'll forward to you by e-mail. When do you plan to return to Minsk?"

"Late afternoon tomorrow...my train departs around five o'clock."

"Good, that gives us some leeway. Can we perhaps meet for dinner?"

Morris hesitated. Grinevicius sensed the reason.

"Off the clock," he said. "And dinner's on me."

For Morris this was a first, and hard to turn down. They agreed that Grinevicius would swing by his hotel on foot at seven.

"Then for tomorrow, how about a round of golf?" he said. "We can set out early. Allow plenty of time to make it back for your train. Moreover it supports your alibi, if the KGB should ever look into it."

"True."

"And you'll be my guest. No greens fees."

Morris formed a smile of his own.

"Do you have clubs with you?" Grinevicius asked.

"I'd planned on renting."

"No need. I keep a spare set for visitors. Save you some money there also."

Morris couldn't object to that either. Especially from a lawyer.

CHAPTER 29

Refrigerator shelves were emptier now, thanks to the shortened weekday shopping list Piper had given the housekeeper. Excepting three neat rows of half-liter bottles lining the door---*Alivariya White Gold,* his favorite Belarussian beer. He grabbed one, reached for the opener, and pried the cap off. His first gulp went down with languid coolness, seeping through his stomach.

His post-workout flush only accentuated the pleasure. So did a productive afternoon.

From *Bagira* he'd returned to his office tranquil and clear-headed, then with relaxed efficiency proceeded to edit and refine his briefing paper into a concise bureaucratic masterwork. He'd also quelled unruly impulses, such as inviting Svetlana out for a drink after work, an easy gesture of appreciation for her long hours on a Saturday, given that he was alone anyway...

However it was too soon for self-congratulation. He knew that Svetlana presented a more challenging proposition than Katya---separated by her safe geographic distance in Vitebsk---or the anonymous university students in the gym. She was close. She was present. And unlike the others, her age, acculturation and maturity placed her in the same general league as Caroline. Not just a one-night fling, or weekend tryst.

In short, she was *plausible.*

He pulled a deep breath, and wondered if the images he'd employed on the Stairmaster were too combustible. If he should adopt more abstracted subjects.

On the stove he ignited a burner under a large pot of water, then pulled a jar of peanuts from the pantry. He filled one fist, emptied some peanuts into his mouth, and chased them down with another swallow of beer. His solution, for now, lay in extra intensity. Several articles from *Men's Extreme Fitness* magazine supported this. The more punishing the workout, the more pronounced the effect. Adverse energies got obviated---supplanted by natural, hormone-induced euphoria.

He drew down his bottle of *Alivariya* and uncapped a second, supplemented by another fistful of peanuts. He also opened a bag of *penne rigate* and prepared some grated cheese. His approach required not just judicious application, but also adequate protein and carbohydrates.

Endorphins and beer continued to co-mingle in his bloodstream while the water reached a boil.

*   *   *

Morris donned his blazer and glanced at his watch. Before heading downstairs he sat down and re-read Grinevicius' e-mail:

Evan,
On the basis of my initial research, I can report the following:

1) *Amoud al-Tikriti vanished from public view just before the U.S. invasion of Iraq in March 2003, and resurfaced in Switzerland three weeks later along with his family. Despite his prominence in the Hussein regime he lived undisturbed in a villa outside Geneva*

*until the summer of 2006. He allegedly continued to engage in
financial activities, including interactions with several Swiss
banks. U.S. authorities never disclosed why al-Tikriti was never
placed on the "55 Most Wanted" List, and was thereafter permitted
to live openly in a Western country.*

2) *In July 2006 al-Tikriti apparently fled Switzerland. Reasons for
this have never been entirely clear, but there is widespread speculation that he suddenly ran afoul of U.S. authorities, and sought
to evade arrest. Since then his exact whereabouts have remained
unknown.*

3) *To my knowledge you are the only individual from a Western country to make random sighting of al-Tikriti from July 2006 to the
present.*

4) *Before the 55 Most Wanted List was deactivated in November
2005, the Department of Defense (DOD) distributed 27 rewards,
for a total of $113 million.*

5) *Though the U.S. has never offered a reward in connection with
al-Tikriti, there is reason to believe---based on the peculiar history of
this case--that the DOD may now be willing to pay for information
concerning his whereabouts.*

*Against this backdrop I have conceived an initiative that didn't arise dur-
ing our meeting this morning.*

*In addition to representing you if you are arrested and/or imprisoned in
Belarus, I propose to visit Washington and discreetly explore the possibility of
a reward with the DOD. Even if the DOD is uninterested, we are likely to learn
more about al-Tikriti's current international status---a possible benefit to your
future defense.*

*I also propose to undertake this initiative on a contingency basis, to allay
possible concerns about cost. I will cover all travel and other expenses, which I
will recoup only if a reward is issued, in the form of a 30-percent fee. You may
recall from my Web site I am a member of the Massachusetts and New York bars.*

This entitles me to practice law in the U.S.; when in the U.S. I am not bound by Lithuanian prohibition on contingency-based representation.

Naturally the initiative with the DOD is optional. I will continue to represent you whether you decide to proceed with it or not.

Sincerely,

John Grinevicius

P.S. – See you in your hotel lobby at seven o'clock.

Morris leaned back from his screen and crossed his arms, feeling the same involuntary rush that seized him in his apartment a week earlier. Grinevicius hadn't alluded to specific sums, but the numbers were irrepressible. Five million? $10 million? Even more, given al-Tikriti's importance as a financial figure? Certainly the contingency framework appealed to him. Also that such inquiries could be anonymous and discreet, with no repercussions in Belarus. Downsides appeared limited…Along with a way to redress recent setbacks…

He stopped himself. He'd been down this path before. And made a vow.

He was through with financial adventures. There would be no more.

After a deep breath, he re-checked his watch, closed the window of his e-mail program for safe measure, and exited his room. As he descended in the glass-enclosed lift he spotted Grinevicius waiting in the lobby. The lawyer greeted him with a relaxed handshake.

"Receive my e-mail?" he asked.

"Yes."

"We can discuss other issues over dinner. All the same…any preliminary reaction?

"I'll think about it," Morris answered.

CHAPTER 30

Bistro 18 was situated near the university district, not far from Grinevicius' office. He was obviously a regular, and Morris could understand why.

Complimentary hors d'oeuvres formed the preamble: thinly sliced local sausages on warmed slivers of fresh bread and aromatic cheese. Next, for the appetizer: *Parmentier* potato cream soup and poached quail eggs. Then unhurried procession to the main course: roast breast of duck, glazed with spinach, pine nuts and Asian plum sauce. Morris was even persuaded to share a bottle of delectable Spanish *Rioja*---his first alcohol since the *shashlik*---backstopped by a liter of *Perrier*. By way of finale: warm chocolate coolant with saffron mousse, perfectly accented by decaffeinated gourmet coffee.

Plus the staff was uniformly English-speaking: among the friendliest and most attentive Morris had ever encountered in Eastern Europe. In Minsk only one or two restaurants came close, but even they didn't quite measure up.

Throughout, Grinevicius kept business to a minimum, addressing a limited number of odds and ends just after they'd ordered---most notably their method of e-mail communication once Morris returned to Minsk. Otherwise they enjoyed the meal. At the door they said goodbye to their main waiter and maitre d' and stepped back out onto Stikliu Street, a bending, single lane of cobblestones that stood mostly un-trafficked at this hour.

The lawyer's apartment lay in the opposite direction from *Hotel Klaipeda.*

"We covered everything I wanted to tonight," he said. "I hope you found it worthwhile."

"By all means. Especially the dinner. First time I've ever been treated by a lawyer."

"Does happen, occasionally."

"Thanks."

"It was my pleasure. Tomorrow I suggest we set your case aside and focus on golf. Enjoy the full 18 holes. The initiative I outlined in my e-mail can wait awhile, now that we have our communication issues sorted out."

"I don't object. After this past week I could use the distraction."

When they'd parted ways Morris wound toward his hotel along Dominikonts Street, and encountered numerous student-age pedestrians, mostly in groupings of two or three: girls or guys-only. However he also noticed a few young couples. His positive mood made him look on the brighter side.

That maybe there was hope after all for stable, harmonious relations between the sexes. For him, too.

Minutes later the Cathedral bell tower came into view, indicating his approach to *Hotel Klaipeda.* Given that there was still plenty of daylight left, even at nine-fifteen, he considered an extended walk. A pleasant riverfront park lay just beyond the tower, he recalled, and while he stopped to check his map, he registered another pedestrian approaching along the sidewalk, from the direction of the hotel. It was a girl, walking alone. Several seconds passed before he discerned her particulars, including her short skirt. She was tall and slender-limbed, with fair skin and shoulder-length dark hair, probably in her mid-20s. An oversized handbag draped her shoulder, accenting her lissome stride. As she drew closer her attention shifted to the map in his hands then back up, together with a slight smile.

After the relaxing dinner Morris managed to reciprocate. He hadn't experienced this kind of encounter since his divorce---not even in Minsk, where girls were reputed to take reflexive interest in foreigners...Indeed a girl this beautiful had never smiled at him on the street before.

Anywhere.

About ten paces away her gaze encompassed the rest of him. He fought his usual shyness and kept his head up. She was almost upon him.

At once her attitude became clearer. Her faint smile didn't signal interest. Rather: amusement, tinged with slight condescension. She'd simply noticed that he was a foreigner with a map. To ward off a potential overture she pulled out her cell phone, staring at the screen and accelerating her pace as she overtook him on the sidewalk.

In an instant she was past. He watched her recede for a moment, knowing quite well that she wouldn't look back, and stared back down at his map, his good mood deflated. A fine meal and half-bottle of wine didn't alter reality. He'd never gotten girls like that before Nora. And now that he was no longer rich, his chances of doing so again were minimal.

Girls of that category---girls like Lena, for example---were off-bounds. In order to aspire to them again, he would have to resurrect his finances first.

He folded his map, put it back in his pocket and continued down the street. The extended walk had now lost its appeal. Near the main square he turned left and climbed the front steps of his hotel. On the way up the elevator he made up his mind. When he entered his room he immediately seated himself in front of his laptop, opened his e-mail browser, and composed a message:

John,

 On the way home after dinner this evening I reflected further on your proposal concerning Washington. Given the negligible risks involved, and the fact that you are prepared to cover all up-front expenses, I have decided to proceed. If you wish I can sign a contingency contract before I leave.

 See you in front of my hotel tomorrow morning at 6:30.

 Best regards,

 Evan

He hit the send button. Now that the question was resolved, he could better enjoy golf.

CHAPTER 31

Piper stowed the plates in the dishwasher, retrieved his remaining half-glass of red wine from the table, and then made his way through the apartment to the room that served as home office. His watch read 9:19: just after two o'clock in the afternoon in Rhode Island. Unless Caroline and the kids had gone sailing he estimated that they would just be finishing lunch back at her parents' house, after a full morning on the beach. He settled in front of the computer, connected to the Internet, and pulled up his *Skype* contact list.

Seconds later Caroline's icon turned green. When he clicked it *Skype's* futuristic ring sounded just once before she picked up, her voice as clear as if she was sitting in the same room. Moreover the connection was free.

"Perfect timing," he said. "Shall we turn on Webcams?"

"My hair's a mess from the beach...but okay."

Her digitized image appeared in the video window. Piper expanded it to full-screen. As he expected, her objection was misplaced. Sea air and sunshine had given her a radiance he associated with earlier summers, when their beachfront vacations had been longer and more numerous, together with their interludes behind closed doors.

Skype was mostly impervious to hacking. Still, work-related subjects were off-limits over this connection---except for the oblique shorthand that the two of them had developed through years of practice. She asked if he'd finished dinner.

"Just a few minutes ago."

"Good, then you must have gotten home at a decent hour."

"I suppose. Don't forget, though---it's Saturday."

Over the link, Piper could almost taste the salt air. Melanie entered the screen, already tanned and blonder, and from over Caroline's shoulder offered a cheerful greeting. Piper could see a book cradled in her hand.

"Summer reading?" he asked.

"For my AP English class."

James Joyce's *Dubliners*, she said, to which he gave a smile and thumbs-up. After a brief exchange about the book she departed, and he asked about Nick.

"Just a minute." Caroline moved out of camera---toward what Piper knew to be a window with an ocean view. She sat down again. *"...Seems he's gone back down to the Cove."*

"You mentioned in your e-mail he's swimming a lot."

"The swimming is mostly in the morning. Back and forth between the beach and the point. Every day for an hour or more."

Nick had always been strong in the water. But such dedication was new.

"He's being safe, I hope."

"Yes, thankfully. Not far from shore. And the water's been calm...perfect for it."

"Has he given any explanation?"

"Not really. He's been a little quiet since we left Minsk. When he's not on the beach, or in the water, he's often behind the computer, writing e-mails or sending instant messages back to Belarus. In Russian, as far as I know."

Piper remembered the girls Nick had brought home from his gymnasium. Also his sullenness on the way to the airport.

"Aren't there any girls there?"

"Not many…that's the problem with a private beach. Still, there are a few around his age, the same ones as last summer. I think that's why he heads back down in the afternoon."

"Give him some time."

"I don't know. He seems pretty fixated. Like he's gotten on a Russian track."

"Maybe your visit to Exeter will help change his mind."

Over the feed Caroline looked skeptical. Piper endeavored to reassure her.

"For now we should probably be glad he's swimming. There are worse things he could be doing."

This elicited a slight smile.

"Speaking of exercise…what about you? Not overdoing it? Don't forget, you're 45 now. You're not a 21-year-old university oarsman anymore."

"Well, I have gotten a little more intensive. As I said, my way of coping."

In other words: an antidote to solitude and pressures from Washington. Which was partially true.

Caroline examined him over the video connection.

"You and Nick," she said. *"Maybe you're more alike than we realize."*

Piper didn't disagree with her.

*　　*　　*

Lena's volume of Sartre lay closed on the side table by the couch, along with her notebook. During intervals like this, when she was alone, there was really only one activity that could distract her from reading.

That was thinking.

Today her midday visit to *Bagira* had triggered a chain of rumination and analysis that had lasted right through the evening. First it was the foreigner on the stair-climber, with his brutal, otherworldly exertions and inscrutable motives. Then a related conversation among several of her classmates from aerobics, her age or perhaps a little younger, whom she'd overheard in the women's locker room.

"There are simply no men here," complained one.

"That's obvious," said a second.

"What about that guy doing cardio…the foreigner?" said a third. "He's pretty good-looking, and as far as I've gathered, he speaks excellent Russian."

"Him?" responded the first. "I can't figure him out. Anyway, I'm talking about *our* guys. Belarussian, here in Minsk. They're hopeless."

Even the third woman conceded that point.

"So what's the solution?" asked the second.

"Travel. Problem is…visas are so difficult to get these days, where can we go? Turkey, Egypt, Cyprus…that's about it."

"In fact I'm going to Cyprus in a few weeks," said the third.

"Alone?"

"No, with my boyfriend."

She shrugged as she said this, as if to imply the partner in question was of no lasting consequence.

Next the two others revealed their own travel plans: one to Yalta in late August and the other to Turkey in September, both with female travelling companions. Each alluded to vague chances of meeting wealthy Muscovites----a category which had lately overtaken Westerners in desirability---but evinced little faith in the prospect.

Some minutes later the same trio had preceded Lena up the stairwell to street level. Like most young women in Minsk, they had dressed to provocative effect, with stylish clothes and makeup. One climbed into a parked Volkswagen; Lena was still behind the two others as they rounded onto the broad sidewalk of the Prospekt. As the pair separated, one donned sunglasses and iPod earpieces, while the other stared at her cell-phone.

Atomized and aloof, with moving, unbreachable barriers between themselves and the opposite sex. Earlier, the behavior had encompassed just a sub-set. Now it was the predominant motif among young *Minchane*, from mid-thirties on down. Among males, too.

Lena re-settled on the couch and glanced around her living room, with its Soviet-era bookshelves, piano, and various latter-day accoutrements. She'd not yet entered her teens when the USSR collapsed. But she possessed live memories from the era, whose hallmarks had lingered well into the 90s in Belarus. Soviet couples had generally married early---ages of 20 and 22 were rather common---and produced at least one child soon thereafter. The main impediments and disruptions to love and family life had tended to come later, in the form of alcoholism.

Divorce rates were high. Relations between the sexes were far from idyllic.

Nonetheless, men and women during Soviet times had gotten together, even if tenuously. Nowadays they seemed increasingly incapable of any kind of enduring union.

By her reckoning change had started in the late 90s. For all Belarus' isolation, Western values and behaviors had steadily supplanted the old ones, and now predominated. Natasha was a perfect example, with her mercenary attitude toward Fabrizio and pregnancy. Another was Evan Morris, a transplant straight from the source. He'd been so traumatized he'd simply hit emotional shutdown.

She celebrated most individual freedoms of the West, but doubted that this particular transformation was for the better. Disillusion, alienation, cynicism. Were those really improvements? Even worse: Belarus seemed to have absorbed the most dubious components of Western individualism, without adopting the broader, more compelling liberties that came with them.

As a Russian she was acutely acquainted with the perils of revolution. And the sexual revolution seemed to have come with its own ravages and dislocations. She was starting to suspect that Belarus was better off without it.

She reached over for her Sartre. He didn't have the answers, but at least he could distract her for a while before she went to bed.

CHAPTER 32

Grinevicius drove a 1989 Mercedes-Benz 260: in fine condition despite its age. Almost big enough to be a limousine. Streets were empty as they crossed the river and spun in regal, air-conditioned splendor out of central Vilnius.

"Nice ride," Morris commented.

The lawyer smiled behind his sunglasses. "Thanks. One of my few indulgences."

High-end computer equipment and fine dining seemed to count among the others. However given the lawyer's restraint with expenses, these were all fine by Morris.

Outside the city Grinevicius settled at cruising speed onto the northbound lane of A14 thoroughfare. The next 30 kilometers, at this early hour on Sunday, passed smooth and unimpeded. Twenty minutes later they reached the gate to *Europos Centro Golfas Klubas* and turned into the curving drive. On a hilltop to their left a semi-circle of European flags and stone column came into view.

"Did you visit the monument in May?" the lawyer asked.

"Made a quick stop. Took a few photographs."

"You know there's some dispute that this is really the center of Europe. The Poles make a different claim. They say it's on their side of the border."

"I hadn't heard that. Who's right?"

They slowed down around a bend. A golf cart pulled off to the side to let them pass. Grinevicius waved at the players and shrugged.

"Who cares? To me, the course is the main draw."

The eighth and ninth holes emerged as they wound their way further, and Morris' recollections became more distinct. The course at *Europos Centro* was challenging. Fairways were generally narrow and undulating, bounded by dense forest. Several greens abutted a small lake. Water traps abounded. Championship level.

He also remembered his previous score: two strokes behind Jeff, whom he'd usually beaten back in the States. Today he yearned for a more satisfying round---particularly after the stresses of the previous week. The rustic, log-themed clubhouse emerged ahead, with about a dozen expensive cars parked out front.

"By the way," he said, "Shall I sign your contingency contract before we start?"

"It's not urgent. We can do it afterward."

"I'd rather get it out of the way. Focus on golf."

Grinevicius, with his easy-going manner, was happy to accommodate..

"All right. First I'll confirm our tee time. Then we can review it over coffee in the clubhouse."

*   *   *

Agent 550 was a senior KGB officer who lived near the park; Agent 1300 was an army staff colonel based at the Ministry of Defense. Under Piper's variable training schedule, they kept apprised of his running days through a sliding algorithm devised in Langley, a formula which both men---possessed of characteristic Russian aptitude for mathematics---had digested and committed to memory at once. Their appellations reflected their approximate meter distances from the start of his nine-kilometer route.

Thus far he'd encountered them only on weekdays. This Sunday morning that suited him fine.

After skirting the Circus and crossing the river dam, he blew several hard exhalations, hit his stop watch, and entered the park. Once at full stride, he jacked his pace and shot down a flat, tree-lined walkway extending away from the river.

This first segment was where he moved into visualization mode, let imagination take over. Svetlana had pressed to the forefront, but Katya remained live, not yet out his system. Also further away, which made her safer...In his hotel room in Vitebsk and he was embracing her from behind, undoing the front button and zipper of her low-slung jeans, savoring her glow and fecundity...

At the park's main interior artery he swung left, back toward the Svisloch, passing a municipal cleaning crew, which he ignored. Her jeans, upon removal, left only a translucent, lime-green under-thong... she was leaning forward, arched, with eyes half-closed...his fingertips hooking her side-straps...

His breathing deepened and he ratcheted faster.

Bright yellows from *Zhar Pititsa* café came up in vague form on his right. As he approached the plaza he scanned ahead for Agent 550, then rounding the curve, stayed alert long enough to verify that there were no telltale beeps from his sports watch. The Prospekt underpass loomed fast ahead, where he experienced the first potent kick, the thrill of full penetration...

Katya's stringlet dropped to the floor. She reached back with one hand to urge him on, then shifted her weight onto her forearms, flaring her hip-joints outward and increasing the spread of her buttocks... Her wetness and engorgement became tactile as he found the necessary angle and opening, paying no heed to birth control...Consummation provoked a guttural moan and a paroxysm of raw energy. Upon confirming the absence of Agent 1300 and blasted a power-thirty, then established an unrelenting, rhythmic pace, matching the hang-swing of her breasts and light slapping of skin-on-skin: sounds and images which meshed with familiar sensations, inimitable and innate.

Slickness. Warmth. Implantation.

Over the next 250 meters, his breathing became more integrated and rhythmic, his stride more fluid. By both design and instinct, he ceded himself over to natural forces.

Once this was over he'd regain his repose. Recover his intellectual and emotional bearings, and re-fix on Caroline.

Only later. He still had seven kilometers to go.

CHAPTER 33

After they'd signed the contract, Grinevicius suggested a warm-up session before tee-off. Also that they walk the course. Morris readily agreed to the first suggestion. He also didn't mind the second, despite his habit to the contrary. However he did request a hand-cart.

The lawyer eschewed one for himself, and hoisted his bag to his shoulder as they set out, each carrying a bucket of practice balls. From the pro shop they descended a path toward a pond shaped like a lopsided eight, and at the cinch between the two sections crossed a footbridge which led to the covered tees. Just one other golfer was practicing. Golfers on surrounding holes were spaced out. In May the scene had been similar.

Morris had inferred from *Europos Centro's* Web site that the club was rather exclusive.

"Their plan is to limit the membership to one thousand," Grinevicius explained. "Next year they hope to become completely private."

"Do you mind if I ask the cost?"

"Thirty-four thousand-five hundred *Litvas* initiation...or about ten thousand Euros. But after that the yearly dues drop to about nine hundred Euros."

Morris made a quick conversion to dollars. Not as much as his own initiation fee at the Palo Alto Hills Golf and Country Club, but not too far off.

As they reached the hitting stable he pulled out his scorecard and map. Like most high-level courses, *Europos Centro* put a premium on consistent drives, prudent avoidance of hazards, and accurate pitching and chipping around the greens. Even more than most, therefore, it called for a conscientious warm-up routine.

"What scoring system do you prefer?" Grinevicius asked, before they started.

"Traditional. Why?"

"Are you opposed to some modifications?"

"What do you have in mind?"

"Sort of my own version…Call it a variation of Stableford. That is, the score for each hole is capped at par plus four."

"That's rather unorthodox. What's the point?"

"If you blow out two or three holes, it doesn't wreck your overall result."

The proposal reminded Morris of liberties he and his cousin had taken when they'd started playing in high school. Remedial. For hackers.

"Sorry. I'd prefer to stick to the book."

"Fair enough. What about a mulligan?"

"Okay. But just off the first tee."

"Agreed. Championship tees okay?"

Morris scanned distances on his scorecard. In May, he and Jeff had hit off the standard men's tees.

"I'm not really a big hitter," he said. "But I suppose that's okay."

They set up in nearby tee boxes, with one empty slot between them. Morris pulled out his wedge, planning to work up from there, and plopped a first ball on the turf. Before taking a practice swing he noticed Grinevicius already bending over his respective tee, and looked over with some curiosity.

The lawyer straightened, wielding a driver, and set up for a shot.

His backswing was relaxed and his lankiness permitted an out-sized arc. After a slight jerk at the top he brought the club-head down fast, keeping his face down and eyes well-trained. The club-face struck the ball straight and full despite minimal hip rotation before impact.

Smack.

Right on the sweet spot. The ball sailed out on a long, rising trajectory with just a faint hook. After touching ground, its core velocity propelled it another 60 meters along the grass. Morris waited for it to come to a stop and estimated the distance using nearby markers. Two-hundred-and-fifty meters. Somewhat ungainly form: mostly arms. Still, not bad for a recent initiate to the game.

"Looks like you're hardly in need of special scoring," he joked.

"It's just one shot," the lawyer responded, with a self-dismissive grin.

During Morris' first three wedge shots, he registered four additional *smacks* from the lawyer's box; as he paused to draw out his nine-iron, he then glanced out at the distances. All four surpassed the first drive, in lengths ranging from 260 to 275 meters.

Grinevicius also paused, admiring his result with a detached expression.

"You're smoking 'em," Morris said.

This time the lawyer's pleasure was less restrained.

"Who knows?" he joked. "Maybe I'll play my breakthrough round."

Morris smiled. He'd heard that line on golf courses before. Many times. More relevant to him was Grinevicius' general approach to the game. A lawyer who tried to bend the rules? And who went straight for his driver during warm-up?

He re-assumed his stance and tried not to read too much into it. They hadn't even teed off.

*   *   *

The Ambassador's official residence at Raubichi had closed in March: since occupied only by a Belarussian husband and wife who maintained the property. However today the lawn and guest annex provided the venue for a brunch picnic, for the small number of remaining Embassy personnel and their families. When Piper turned down the access road, his KGB minders split off and headed back toward Minsk. He parked his Mercedes in the driveway and rounded the house toward the back.

En route he ran into Michael Carpenter, the Embassy's Charge d'Affaires, wearing shorts and sunglasses and holding a Bloody Mary. As they walked on together, voices became audible, along with clomps of ball on mallet. Piper nodded ahead.

"Sounds like croquet," he said.

"What else? Have to keep some traditions alive."

"Can we still field enough players?"

"Perfect game for us," Carpenter laughed. "Very scalable."

Indeed when they rounded onto the lawn, Piper saw that the match in progress consisted of just three participants, two of them the teen-age children of Carpenter.

"They miss Nick and Melanie," a female voice said near his shoulder.

The speaker was Rebecca, Carpenter's wife. About the same age as Caroline, though considerably shorter, and like many Embassy wives of late, tending towards plumpness. Piper gave her dual kisses and a light hug. After his transfer she'd made Caroline and the kids feel immediately welcome.

"And we miss Caroline," she added. "Are they enjoying their vacation? Getting nice beach weather?"

"Couldn't be better. They're having a great time. Spoke to them on Skype yesterday evening."

"They wish you were there, I'm sure."

"Caroline, yes," Piper answered. "For the kids maybe my electronic presence is enough…"

When her husband laughed she poked him lightly in the ribs in mock exasperation. "Well our kids will have no choice in the matter when we leave on Wednesday. You know, Russell, I still feel some qualms about leaving you alone like this."

"Don't worry, Rebecca. I'll be fine."

"I'm glad. Anyway, we'll be back in a few weeks...What will you drink?"

"A Bloody Mary wouldn't hurt."

She signaled to a girl from the catering service. "The brunch should be out in ten minutes or so," she added, before retreating to the guest annex.

The lawn swept down to the lakefront. Apart from the croquet game, there was just one other cluster of conversation thus far: three couples closer to the water. At similar gatherings the previous summer, ninety to one hundred people had spread across the grass. Beyond, the lake looked similarly becalmed. The only ripples emanated from a lone fishing dinghy, out toward the middle.

"May I..."

The girl's English was Russian-accented, already close. Piper thanked her and took his glass. With a jovial grin Carpenter placed his empty on her tray and ordered another Bloody Mary. The girl pivoted slightly and brought her other, larger tray forward. Piper now recognized her from a previous party.

"Hors d'oeuvres?"

They plucked off cheese-and-sausage appetizers and napkins. The girl made polite eye contact with each of them in turn, though a little longer with Piper. As if she remembered him, too.

And noted he was unaccompanied.

Early 20s. Expansive gray eyes and full lips. Straight blond hair which fell to her shoulders. Somewhat more voluptuous than the norm at *Bagira*.

He caught her rear view as she retreated.

The interaction which was not lost on Carpenter, who examined Piper for an instant under amused eyebrows, and slight traces of concern. Piper gave him an offhand smile before observing the croquet game again. Thanks to his nine-kilometer expurgation along the Svisloch that morning he felt very much in control.

Then he spotted Svetlana, walking toward him with a targeted gaze. She wasn't letting up.

CHAPTER 34

The 16th hole was a 180-meter par-three and ranked second easiest on the course. Still, leftward pin placement made for a challenging shot. Morris winced as Grinevicius addressed his ball, again fearing the worst. Instead the lawyer's shot sailed in a high arc off the tee, carried the water trap and bounced picture-perfect off the front edge of the green, rolling dead just short of the flag.

Grinevicius cupped his visor against the sun to verify the result. A grin spread over his face.

"Your aggressive angle paid off," Morris commented from the side of the tee box.

"How close is it?"

"Looks like you have a chance for birdie."

The lawyer's face tinted with irony. "About time," he said, walking off the tee.

They set off toward the hole, tracking the well-worn grass that separated the tee from the teardrop-shaped fairway. A stream gurgled lightly on their left. This was their first uninterrupted walk in a while---free of unpredictable detours and hunts in the rough. Morris had played it safer, angling away from the stream and small pond; his ball now lay about five meters from the tight diagonal neck onto the green.

While the lawyer rested his bag on the turf and hung a polite distance back,

Morris parked his hand-cart and walked forward several paces to study the green. He remembered it vaguely from May, and made quick estimates of speed, distance and gravity. Together they suggested a gentle chip across the lower half of the green toward the flag. In golf he took nothing for granted.

After careful address with his wedge, he executed an abbreviated swing with clean contact. The ball popped up low onto the green, rolled along the desired path, and dribbled to a stop just a meter-and-a-half short of the pin.

"Great chip, from that distance," Grinevicius observed.

"Thanks. I'll take it. You can putt first, if you like."

"Please...You go first.."

"Okay."

After another careful set-up, Morris putt went left on a promising trajectory and found the right lip of the cup, trickling in. He also allowed a slight smile. It was his fifth up-and-down. He'd been putting well all day.

"Nice par," Grinevicius said.

"Thanks."

"Now let's see if I can also execute."

The lawyer took more time assessing angles and inclines than on previous greens, squatting at several locations around the hole. However after final address he struck the putt with far too much pace, so that it threatened to carry well past the hole and leave a longer retracement from the opposite direction. Sorry to behold.

Instead the ball caught the back of the back of the cup. *Click.* Straight up. And straight down into the hole. *Plop.*

Morris watched with surprise. But a birdie was a birdie.

"My compliments," he said.

"At that speed, I was lucky to catch the lip," the lawyer acknowledged. "What matters is the result."

Grinevicius smiled again at the remark, contemplating it a moment before he walked over and extracted his ball.

After they retreated off the green, Morris stood under the shade of a tree, marked the scorecard, and examined at the course map. The seventeenth hole was a 433-meter par-four double-dogleg that fronted a lake and crisscrossed a stream. Ranked most difficult hole on the course.

He glanced at Grinevicius again. Luck aside, the lawyer appeared more emboldened than ever.

*   *   *

Lena entered Jakuba Kolas Square and cut toward the monument: a Soviet-gigantesque rendition of a scene from one of Kolas' poems, showing young Simon playing a violin while his beloved reclines on a grassy slope. Though she had beheld it countless times, she pondered it for a moment. Lately the motif had seemed fictional in more ways than one...

She dismissed the thought, checked her watch and looked around through her sunglasses.

In keeping with Sunday pattern the small plaza was relatively empty. People filtered intermittently in and out of the two entrances to the underground *Jakuba Kolas* metro station, while five or six others milled around an adjacent bus stop. As usual many---especially the girls---had cell-phones clasped to their ears or held the screens at reading distance...

Today she evaluated Westernization from some alternative angles.

On the Prospekt three quarters of the cars zooming by were European: Peugeots, Renaults, Audis, BMWs, Mercedes---some after-market imports, but an increasing number of new, high-end models. Opposite, a bus pulled up in front of the Philharmonic

Hall, painted over with the green-and-white motif of *Tic Tac* breath
fresheners. Next to the bus-stop was an advertisement for *Christian
Dior* perfume. Alongside Stolichny supermarket: two outdoor cafes
set up under umbrellas emblazoned with brand logos: *Tuborg* beer
and *Coca-Cola*. Then there was the massive SAMSUNG atop her
building...

"Lena! You didn't even notice me. Deep in thought, as usual."

Lena checked her watch again before turning her head. Natasha
had adopted the Italian attitude toward punctuality.

"Maybe because you're 10 minutes late."

"Sorry. I was on the Internet late last night."

Lena could guess why. More preliminaries with Fabrizio, which
they were sure to discuss ad infinitum over coffee, along with Natasha's
pregnancy stratagem. For the moment, though, she preferred different lines of conversation. Rather than take the metro, they bent down
the boulevard. Pedestrians thinned as they exited the square.

"Natasha, you're on the Internet incessantly...you've traveled...you
speak several foreign languages. By those standards you're more cos-
mopolitan and informed than the majority of Belarussians."

"That's putting it politely."

"All the same I was standing in the square just now and watching
people go by. Most of them have cell-phones, text capability, and so on.
There are more cars than ever, Western products..."

"Western products?" Natasha scoffed. "A pair of jeans costs $90
here. I do all my shopping in Moscow. Or in Italy, if I can. Look at your
pupil Evan Morris. He's a Westerner. Plenty of money. Even he fled for
the weekend..."

"I'm making a theoretical case here, so bear with me. Lifestyles
have improved, or at least gotten more diverse. Shouldn't other
changes develop *eventually*? In politics, for example?"

"And my answer is no."

"Why?"

"You know our people." Natasha made an expansive gesture, as if to envelop the whole city. "They're passive. Lukashenko will be in power *forever.*"

"Forever? That can't be."

"Okay, at least for a very long time. Like Castro. *Nothing* will happen. You yourself said as much back in March, at the time of that protest…"

Lena abandoned her argument. Truth was, she agreed with Natasha, and had presented the contrary viewpoint for pure recreation.

They walked in silence to the intersection with Masherova Street and waited for the pedestrian signal. After it changed they crossed over, and Natasha became more animated, ready to talk again. "By the way," she said. "I still haven't told you what happened on Skype last night with Fabrizio…"

Through her sunglasses Lena gazed ahead toward Victory Square. They were back on main themes.

The only real novelty lay in Natasha's pregnancy gambit.

CHAPTER 35

The championship tee for the 17th hole was notched well back into the perimeter tree-line and fronted by dense rough. As they approached Morris gazed out toward the intermediate tee-box, containing standard yellow and white markers for men, situated about 80 meters closer to the fairway. In May, with Jeff, he'd played off the yellows and salvaged double bogey only by sinking a long putt.

He parked his pull-cart alongside the box and re-extracted the scorecard. Just to attain the front edge of the fairway a golfer had to hit 175 meters on a straight line. The prescribed shot was about 225 meters straight out, stopping just short of the lake and militating against long balls. The 17th was intimidating. It was ranked most difficult on the course for good reason.

Their original decision to play off the championship tees seemed more dubious than ever.

He looked up and re-examined the area near the tee. Apart from the menacing rough, forest loomed tightly on the left. Slight hooks could be deadly.

"Not much margin for error. Ever nailed this one?"

"Not yet."

"Well...your honors."

The lawyer slid out his driver with slight panache. "This is the first time all day I've had honors. Therefore I'm going to try something new."

As Grinevicius took position on the turf, teed up, and addressed his ball, his alignment---aimed about 40 degrees right---his strategy became clear. In a daring attempt to eliminate the double dog-leg, he was shooting straight for the green. Distance to the targeted fairway was about 260 meters, much of it out-of-bounds, over protracted rough and the edge of a pond. It was a shot worthy of Tiger Woods.

Daring was too tame a description. The birdie had gone to Grinevicius' head.

Morris watched his wind-up. The lawyer's height and long arms generated huge backswing, and made him at least theoretically capable of covering the distance...

Crack.

Contact was decent and launched the ball on a plausible trajectory; however it quickly veered off into a slice and hung up short, twisting down to a splash in the middle of the pond, about 230 meters out. Superior to Grinevicius' norm today but far from sufficient.

In any event the lawyer walked off the tee with an unperturbed grin, grasping his driver around the neck like a scepter.

"The concept was sound," he said. "The problem was execution."

Next Morris stepped into the box and concentrated on his own shot---with no temptation to follow suit. He teed up and aligned his stance in accordance with the prescribed trajectory: over the intermediate tee and toward the leading edge of fairway. Prior to swinging he breathed deeply and relaxed. There was no need to clobber it.

Crack.

Prevailing breezes pushed the ball a few degrees right but it descended onto smooth turf. Favorable bounces and roll carried it to about 200 meters. Most important: in bounds, clear of rough, and well-positioned for a second strike.

"Well done," Grinevicius said.

"I'll take it."

Walking back toward his bag, Morris watched with slight surprise as the lawyer returned to the box.

"Instead of dropping one up there I'm going to try another tee shot," he said.

He made another adjustment to his clubface. Morris winced on the upswing.

Snap.

Contact was sub-standard. The ball left on a low trajectory with a vicious leftward curve, and arced to the ground after about 195 meters, straight into a low-lying cluster of vines and bushes.

All the same Grinevicius gave a cheerful shrug. "At least both are in-bounds," he said. "Think I can find the second one?"

"Maybe. Could be tough, though."

They'd already hunted for plenty of others. As they set out across the rough toward the fairway, Grinevicius scanned ahead to his landing area in the brush, and seemed to sense Morris' thoughts.

"I don't regret going for it," he offered, as calm as when he'd started the round.

"Even if the second is also lost?"

"No, not really. Why should I? It's just a game. Not like climbing, for example. In climbing if you make a mistake, you put yourself in real danger. Maybe fall to your death. In golf, what happens? Some lost balls. A bad score. For me, taking risks in golf is more acceptable. There aren't any mortal consequences."

To Morris this raised analogous questions about their Washington initiative. As before, he chose to put these aside.

They were here to golf.

*   *   *

The job of station chief, to large extent, required 24-7 activation. Nevertheless Piper had long endeavored to exclude Sundays, and held to the habit today even though he was alone. His plan, now that the brunch was winding down, was to segue to a shaded café at the nearby ski complex, with a novel and undefined horizon. Moreover Svetlana had engaged him on and off during the gathering, seldom venturing from his sightline, presenting unbroken views of her shorts and stretch-fabric tank-top. So an exit also seemed prudent.

After the Carpenters bid farewell to several Russian staffers and their spouses, he seized his chance, approaching the hosts across a short expanse of grass and placing his hand on the Charge d'Affaires' shoulder. "Getting a little hot for me, Michael. I'm going to make an exit."

"I'm a little sun-burned myself, Russell. Good thing we made this a brunch."

"You orchestrated it...Thanks."

When he turned to extend the compliment to Rebecca, he found that Svetlana had also closed in, making farewells of her own. When the pleasantries were complete it was natural that he accompany her to back to her car. A slight rush ran him through him as they rounded the house. The dynamic was familiar.

He was more grateful than ever for his morning release. He hoped it would be enough.

"Back to Minsk?" he asked in Russian.

"No...It's simply too hot. I brought some drinks and snacks, something to read...My plan is to drive over to the ski complex. Take a walk, find a cool place in the woods..."

They'd attained the parking area and were approaching their cars. Piper's senses remained acute, blended with mild euphoria and agreeable fatigue in his legs. He told himself he could handle this.

"Seems we happened on the same idea, Svetlana. In fact I brought a book of my own...to read on that café terrace, outside the main hotel..."

She beeped the alarm on her car, a compact Renault. A flash crossed her eyes, visible even through her sunglasses.

"…Maybe we can combine the two," he said.

"Why not?"

Piper closed her car door behind her after she climbed in, and agreed to follow her over. As he turned the ignition in his Mercedes he glanced at the book on his passenger seat: the latest thriller by John Grisham. Already he wondered how many pages he'd get through.

Or if he'd open it at all.

CHAPTER 36

Out the window the historic architecture of central Vilnius gave way to the modern and functional apartment blocks of the suburbs, then to green meadows and forest. Morris, again with the compartment to himself, reclined against the backrest and recalled the round at *Centro Europas*. How many balls had Grinevicius driven into water traps or shanked into woods? Eight? Nine? He remembered he'd stashed the scorecard in a pocket on his laptop case, bent down and pulled it out.

In between were flashes of impressive play, including three pars and several bogeys, thanks to the lawyer's occasional ability to launch long drives or towering iron-shots off the fairway. But even with these he'd finished with a 113.

Morris didn't begrudge the score; when he'd started golfing in high school he'd produced similar totals. Of somewhat more concern was Grinevicius' tendency to go for broke, to attempt shots that befitted a tour professional rather than an intermediate hacker.

Some players were cautious on the course and off. Others hewed the odds in golf but not in their work, and vice versa...

He decided not to draw unfair conclusions. And he'd already made his call on Washington.

To his credit, the lawyer had established a sensible means of ongoing communication. On a terminal at the clubhouse, he'd set up a single account at a Lithuanian Webmail provider, under the address sundaygolfers@mail.lt. Each of them knew the password and could log in at will. According to their plan, Grinevicius would compose his outgoing messages in a "Draft A" folder. Morris would answer by creating files in another file called "Draft B." By accessing both files they could effectively correspond.

Fences appeared outside along both sides of the tracks, with parallel dirt strips creating separation from the forest. An announcement came over the speaker system, in both Russian and English. Soon additional five-meter dirt swaths cut through the forest at right angles----plowed up so as to leave footprints or tire marks. Buildings materialized and the train grated to a stop with loud expulsions of steam. Green-uniformed Lithuanian border guards boarded, and one soon appeared at Morris' door.

The guard smiled when he saw Morris' American passport, and gave a cursory glance around the cabin. He recorded the passport data with a hand-held scanner, handed the document back and said in English. "Hope you enjoyed your visit."

"I did. Thanks."

The train then left the Lithuanian side and crawled toward the Belarussian checkpoint. When it stopped again he peered forward and saw several customs officers approach the right side of the train, followed by four or five border guards---more platform activity than he remembered from Friday evening. Bodies thumped aboard, followed by heavy footfalls in the corridor. In less than 10 seconds a guard appeared outside the cabin and stared inside at him. Glints of recognition took hold, and he called down the corridor. Two others materialized in the open doorway, and the most senior-looking stepped forward into the cabin.

"Passporrt." Russian pronunciation. No please attached.

Lithuania suddenly seemed like another universe. Morris felt his stomach tighten.

The guard retreated to the corridor, and compared the passport data with what looked like a fax page. Next he scanned his bar code into a hand-held computer and studied the small screen. *"Da, eto on,"* he said, before disappearing down the aisle. Two other guards remained outside the cabin in silence. A minute later one got a signal over his walkie-talkie, raised it to his ear, listened, then turned to face Morris again in the doorway.

"Your passport will be in a minute," he said in fractured English.

"No problems, I hope?"

"No. Everything in order."

Morris felt his tension ease somewhat.

There was no real basis for concern. Much like Grinevicius and his propensity for risky golf shots.

* * *

Piper latched the bolt and leaned his back against the door. The entry-way projected its usual constancy: an assortment of umbrellas and raincoats, a floor-plant Caroline had selected at Kamarovski Market, a painting Melanie had created in art class. Hallmarks of family life, poignant in their ordinariness.

He closed his eyes and drew a deep breath. At numerable junc-tures through the afternoon---right up until about thirty minutes earlier---he could have thrown the whole rubric in play.

Strolling with Svetlana along forested cross-country trails, feeling her elbow brush his own...Pausing to sit in a clearing, setting books aside in favor of conversation, her long legs bent against her cleavage... Next, the open-ended retreat to the terrace café, chairs positioned at 90 degrees, beers and white wine that progressed to pizza...all while the windows of Hotel Raubichi hovered in the background...

Through she was too mannered and discreet for explicit ploys, she also didn't feign concealment. She'd been open to whatever he might propose. All of which led to their ostensible parting in the parking lot. As he'd done before he'd accompanied her again to her driver's-side door. Time was only 7:15. The evening, potentially, was far from over.

"Straight home?" he asked.

"That's my plan...Yours also?"

"The same. Back home." He paused.

"...I enjoyed this, though."

"I did too."

Several downbeats ensued. Their minds seemed to run on identical track. Nevertheless he'd maintained equilibrium, never truly wavered.

"I can follow you as far as the ring road, if you like, before you turn off."

"Thanks, Russell. I'd appreciate that."

After another deep breath he straightened himself and walked into his living room. He also remembered he was holding his book. And that his suspicion had been correct.

He hadn't read a single page. Still, in the crucible, his method had worked.

He'd passed his second test.

CHAPTER 37

For long journeys Lena was invariably well-prepared. Folded and packed the evening before. Ready to zip and lock.

Somehow this departure was more spontaneous....Was her luggage already in the trunk of the taxi? Or was it a private car? Her view of the vehicle was slightly out of focus...Other essentials eluded her. Was she going abroad? Just in case she checked her purse for her passport...About all she knew was that this trip was important, even urgent...She stirred, and tried to concentrate. Instead her thoughts jumbled further. Next she felt light pressing on her wrist, and a moist protuberance against her cheek.

Meow...

With reluctance she opened her eyes. Her room was dark except for moonlight filtering through the curtains, presenting dark silhouettes of furniture and other objects. Her cat was sitting by her pillow. Wide awake and demanding attention.

"Shto ti hochesh?" *What do you want?*

Meow...

Lena gently pushed her away. The feline jumped down the floor but nonetheless stayed close, unwilling to relent. Back arched and tail up. This occurred every five to six weeks during spring and summer. Unavoidable subservience to the forces of nature....

MEOW...

Vexed, Lena sat up. She found most of her nighttime visions trivial. In addition she didn't place much stock in what psychology had to say on the subject----though she'd once been curious enough to dabble through some relevant articles by Jung and Freud. Dreams were just dreams. However...she had to admit that she'd experienced occasional, somewhat bizarre exceptions, including a few scenarios that had foretold the future, after a fashion. Like the one of a tall building being constructed across the street, behind the printing factory...

MEOW...

She glanced at her bedside clock: 3:25. Too early to get up. During Marta's first year-and-a-half of adulthood she and her mother had employed anti-sex tablets, but Lena had soon determined through research on the Internet that these could be dangerous to the cat's hormonal balance. And neither one of them had thus far overcome their hesitation about sterilization, which left limited remaining options. The only solution was to contain Marta in the corridor and kitchen until morning. With a sigh she rose from bed, walked with the cat to the kitchen, and turned on the light. In almost the same instant she spotted the box of chocolates on the table, where she'd left it after devouring three pieces before going to sleep...

Sweets. Her most notable weakness.

She opened the refrigerator and found a piece of raw fish, which she hoped could distract Marta at least temporarily. She placed it on the cat's floor-plate, then sat down at the table for a moment, near the open window.

Again her eyes gravitated to the box of chocolates. She could detect their aroma from a half-meter away. *Sweet Dance* from the Minsk chocolate factory *Kommunarka*. Her favorite. Why was she even dieting this summer? To look good in a bathing suit? Persist in her vain battle to overcome her somewhat plump Ukrainian hips, which she'd inherited from her mother? She wasn't going to the Black Sea this August---probably just her grandmother's village. For what, then? Some improbable meeting with an appealing man? An adjunct to aerobics? Just in case?

It was absurd. She opened the box and extracted a piece of chocolate.

Once over the threshold, she proceeded with exquisite slowness.

First she raised the confection to her nostrils to take deeper inhalation of the distinctive scents, to allow her cravings to take full hold. Her eyelids lowered, almost in reverence, and she moved the item slightly away from her face again for intimate visual appreciation, relishing color, form and texture from several angles, then back under her nose for additional olfactory uptake. If to indulge at all, why not prolong and savor the full range of delectable sensations? Maximize the climax? At last she brought the chocolate to her mouth: allowing it to dawdle and melt on her tongue before sliding it down her digestive tract.

Sugar and cacao traveled quickly to her brain. Half in trance, she crossed her legs, took a second, unhurried nibble and glanced down at Marta. The fish had created just a momentary diversion, and the feline rubbed her shin with near-desperation, looking up with pleading, uncomprehending eyes.

Meow...

Were humans all that different, she wondered? Weren't all creatures driven, at intervals, by one innate compulsion or another? Through her spreading haze of pleasure she entertained the questions. She liked to think she was less subject to sexual craving than Marta. Or even Natasha, for that matter, with all her auxiliary fixations. Governed by intellect. Possessed of judiciousness and self-regulation. Able to balance objective and moral criteria against raw attraction.

With men she was different. With men she could choose.

Outside it was still dark. Down on the floor Marta remained agitated. Perhaps cats had certain advantage. They didn't attempt to analyze these inexplicable urges. They just surrendered to them.

Her own cravings also persisted. Within ten seconds she reached for the box and extracted another chocolate.

One more piece wouldn't hurt, after which she'd return to bed.

With luck she'd resume where she'd left off in her dream.

CHAPTER 38

After breakfast, Morris found a message from Shinkevich in his Inbox. Despite his ease the evening before he felt a jolt through his thorax.

> *Mr. Morris,*
>
> *Our border services have confirmed your re-entry to Belarus.*
>
> *Because you failed to inform me sufficiently in advance of your departure for Lithuania on Friday, I am afraid we must implement a new requirement in connection to your continued residency in Belarus. Henceforth you will be expected to notify me or my office at least five days prior to any travel outside the country.*
>
> *To ensure that you understand this, another visit to my office will be necessary. I will be in contact shortly by phone.*
>
> *Regards,*
>
> *Dimitri Shinkevich*

The message had originated at 6:45, about 20 minutes earlier. Shinkevich was up early, right back on his case.

Morris gripped his coffee mug, rose from his desk, and looked out the window into the interior courtyard. At once he spotted a black

Volga sedan, one he'd never seen before. Two men sat inside, with a view toward his entry-way. Smoke drifted out the open driver's-side window.

A chilling realization hit him. The KGB officer had waited first for his re-entry to Belarus before sending the message. Then re-closed the exits.

His sojourn in Vilnius suddenly seemed remote and long-past. Like a vanishing idyll.

*   *   *

As he climbed out from his taxi, Morris glanced back across Surganova Street through the kaleidoscope of two-way traffic; his security minders pulled up and parked along the opposite curb, observing him with bland stares. Up on the fifth floor, he found the lab locked-up and quiet. He activated the coffee machine, booted his computer, and checked his e-mail. Just one message---from his mother, asking about his golf weekend in Lithuania.

From the window, he looked back down at the Volga, and considered his position.

If all Shinkevich had in mind was another round of questioning, followed by a stern lecture, he figured he could cope. All the same it was still early. The door to the lab swung open.

"Good morning Evan."

The greeting came from Sergei, the other early bird. A small, welcome sign of normality.

*   *   *

Under normal circumstances Yuri could be counted on for regimented schedules and early starts---more so than the programmers, who'd started their working lives after the disintegration of the USSR. At twenty-past-nine Morris poured his second mug of coffee and walked down the corridor to the scientist's office, intending to discuss several issues in advance of the 10 o'clock meeting. He knocked. No answer. With his ear to the door he detected only silence. Fearing a replay of the previous week, he re-traced to the lab and encountered two more programmers, as well as Anna. He asked her if she'd heard from Yuri.

"No..." She noticed his frown. "Not yet."

At once and went back out to the corridor, stopped by the window, and hit the speed-dial.

Nummer vee zvonili ceshas ne aktirovano.

The number you have called is not activated.

Several more programmers exited the elevator, and like Anna, sensed something was askew. When Morris re-entered the lab all heads turned in his direction.

Minutes later everyone in the group was on their cell-phones, calling their wives. Their Russian was incomprehensible to him, as always. But their faces spoke volumes. As if they'd known this wasn't over.

CHAPTER 39

S artre's *Being and Nothingness* was a heavy text, especially in French. For that reason Lena had set the book aside for a several weeks, in favor of a couple of Sartre's plays and two novels by Camus. Now she was back to it, and with assistance from caffeine had plowed into Chapter Two: *The Body*. Finally Sartre was grappling directly with sex and reproduction:

> *The fundamental problem of sexuality can therefore be formulated thus: is sexuality a contingent accident bound to our physiological nature, or is it a necessary structure of being-for-itself-for-others? (page 499)...*

Over the next thirty pages, she paused intermittently to record brief observations in her notebook. The philosopher's abstractions were dexterous, as usual, but on this subject, once again, she again found him unsatisfactory. She drained the last of her coffee and put down the book with frustration.

Marta---whose frenzy had now waned----stirred on the couch nearby. Lena also affirmed her conclusion from the previous night.

Cats could be inscrutable. But they probably offered more insights in this particular domain.

She realized that Evan Morris had still not called to confirm their evening lesson, or even his return from Vilnius. She was typically wary of intrusion into his workday, but under the circumstances picked up her phone and punched his number. He answered after one ring. As if he was waiting for an urgent call.

Though not hers, it seemed.

"Evan, excuse me for phoning you at work...I hadn't heard from you. Trip go smoothly?"

"Yes, thanks. Actually Lena, I've been meaning to call you..."

She caught more uncharacteristic twangs of stress in his voice.

"...Today's proving rather demanding, and I may finish late...Could we postpone our lesson until tomorrow? Please excuse the change..."

"No need to apologize. I realize it's your first day back."

"Six-thirty, as usual?"

"Agreed. I'll expect you"

After she closed her phone, she wondered if he'd experienced some unpleasantness at the border, due to his lack of facility in Russian. But she also knew a management job like his could present unforeseen demands.

Morris could also be inscrutable, in his own way. And this was just a postponement, after all, not a cancellation.

Thus far he'd been reliable. She'd been able to count on that.

* * *

When Morris ended the call he had an immediate impulse to call straight back and cancel outright. Who knew what tomorrow held? The lesson was a diversion he didn't need. His cell-phone rang again while it was still close to his face.

"Yuri? Thank God...where are you?"

Nearby programmers focused at once on the conversation. Morris glanced out the window and saw a second dark Volga parked at the curb. Yuri's basso-profondo betrayed a quiver.

"I'm down in the lobby. I'm about to come up."

"I'll meet you by the elevator."

When the scientist emerged into the fifth-floor lobby he looked more haggard and shell-shocked than ever, and didn't utter a word as they proceeded down the long corridor, then fumbled with the key as he inserted into the lock. Once they were inside, the Russian started the coffee maker, still without a word, then seated himself on the opposite couch and lit a cigarette, with match trembling in his fingers. Finally he spoke.

"Remember when I told you about my uncle? The one who disappeared under Stalin?"

Morris nodded.

"This morning I felt I might face the same fate." He took a long drag on his cigarette, and added, "It's as if nothing's changed. As if the USSR hasn't disappeared."

"Can you tell me what happened, Yuri?"

The scientist paused for a moment and moved the ashtray closer before looking up. "Why didn't you tell me you were going to Vilnius, Evan?"

There was no animosity in his eyes. Just fear.

"It was just a golf weekend. I wasn't going to miss any workdays. And on Friday, somehow, I never got a chance to mention it."

Yuri took another drag, mulling this explanation. "I wish you'd told me. Well...it's done now. And they're holding me responsible."

"You? Why? You had nothing to do with my trip."

Yuri hesitated and glanced around his office, obviously worried about listening devices. "It's not that simple."

"What do you mean?"

He hesitated again. "After that episode near my dacha and my visit to the KGB last week, I agreed to do something for them."

"Do something? What?"

"Keep tabs on you. Let them know if you went anywhere...did anything unusual."

Morris didn't know if he should be appalled or angered by this. Somehow neither reaction seemed appropriate.

"I didn't see any harm in it," the Russian continued. "I know what happened in the berry patch…whatever it was…was just coincidence, and that what you're doing here is normal business. It's legal. Besides…I could hardly say no."

Gaps filled out and Morris retroacted a better picture. "Let's stick to the facts for now," he said, staying even. "What exactly happened to you there? At least what I should know."

The scientist appeared to organize and edit events in his head. "Well…first of all they showed up at my apartment at 6:15 this morning, when I was still eating breakfast…" Morris checked his watch, incredulous. Yuri's ordeal had lasted nearly four hours. "…This meeting wasn't in Shinkevich's office. It was down in the KGB basement, in a kind of interrogation room…I remembered that there are jail cells there in the basement as well. They're infamous. For some reason the jail has a nickname. It's called the *Amerikanka.*"

"*Amerikanka?* As in, the American?"

"Yes. I don't know exactly why. Anyway that's not important."

Morris shuddered at the coincidence, and hoped it didn't foretell his own fate. "Okay, back on what happened. Were you physically mistreated?"

"No, not really…I'll get to that in a minute. The first time Shinkevich had been hard, but I would say civilized. Today he was more impatient. His manners were gone. Like he was angry…under pressure."

"It was just Shinkevich questioning you?"

"Shinkevich was in charge. But a second official came into the room at several points. He wore a uniform. He looked cruel…" Yuri glanced nervously around his office. "I never learned his name. Let's just say I was more frightened of him than Shinkevich."

While Yuri took another drag Morris leaned forward on the couch.

"...Shinkevich kept saying that he had depended on me. That it was a serious matter. And that I had failed to keep him informed."

Yuri paused and ground out his cigarette, then rose and poured two black coffees. After re-seating himself on the couch the Russian lit another cigarette and took a pull from his cup. "At first they asked what you had told me about the berry patch. Again and again, in different ways. And I constantly repeated the truth...That you told me practically nothing. Then came more questions about you. Everything I know...About your work, your personal life. Also the trip we took together to headquarters in California in early June."

Morris took this in with a sip of coffee. "You were going to mention mistreatment."

"Shinkevich never struck me, or anything like that. Same for the other official. But I had been having breakfast earlier, with juice and coffee. They refused to let me go to the toilet. For almost three hours. It was painful, at my age...I could hardly sit in the chair."

Morris imagined the sensation and clenched his teeth. "I'm sorry Yuri. This is my fault. I should call Shinkevich now and set the record straight. Go straight down there. Get you out of trouble."

Yuri held out his palm as Morris reached for his cell-phone. "I wouldn't do that. Better just wait until he calls you."

Morris leaned back, feeling his stomach roil. The strong coffee didn't help.

"...When he does, Evan, I urge you. Tell them everything they want to know. For your sake and mine." Extra intensity came over the Russian, colored with self-preservation. He paused to exhale another column of smoke.

"...And please. Follow his instructions from now on."

CHAPTER 40

Upon payment of several utility bills, Lena emerged from the Post Office and consulted her list of remaining errands. At once her mobile rang in her purse. Finding a blocked number, she hesitated to answer, but proceeded in case it was her mother calling from Ukraine.

"Elena Grigorovna?"

Formal address. Male. Older. Lena didn't recognize the voice and frowned.

"Yes?"

"My name is Dimitri Shinkevich. I'm with the Committee of State Security."

The appellation made her stiffen. *Komitet Gosudarstvenni Bezopasnasti.* KGB. She'd had only one previous contact with the infamous state organ---when they'd attempted to recruit her as a student, an overture she'd rebuffed with certain disquiet. All her other associations were unpleasant. To her, a sinister legacy of the USSR.

"...I am calling about a matter of vital security interest. And to ask for your assistance."

"I'm listening."

"To explain further, I wish to meet you."

"When?"

"I suggest a rendezvous in fifteen minutes, in Gorky Park"

"Fifteen minutes? That's not much warning. Moreover I've done nothing wrong. As far as I'm concerned I'm under no obligations to meet you."

"As I said, this is a matter of considerable importance. Your cooperation would be appreciated."

Lena assessed this chilling phrase and raced through a gamut of possibilities. Morris came first to mind. It also occurred to her that the call might be a hoax, or some sort of con. "Wait…" she said. "How can I be sure you're who you say you are? You're just a voice on the phone. You could have obtained my number through a variety of means."

"We have a file on you here, Lena Grigorovna. Among other information, I read here that you're a professor in the Literature Department of the English faculty at the Language Institute. Naturally, your mobile number is included."

Lena shuddered slightly.

"…Moreover I can see from our tracking systems that you're now standing on Independence Prospekt…It looks like you're standing outside Post Office Number 220005."

She whirled around and checked the sign. The identification was correct. She eyed her phone for a moment, feeling a rise of anger. Then stayed contained as she replaced the device to her ear.

"Okay I'll hear you out. What do you suggest?"

"Continue straight down the Prospekt to the main entrance to Gorky Park. Go through the gate. About 20 meters ahead on your right is a birch tree. Pass by it, to a willow tree about 20 meters further. There are four benches around the willow tree. Sit on one of them and wait. As I said, I'll be there in 15 minutes."

"How will I recognize you?"

"No need. I'll recognize you."

"Can you provide at least some indication what this is about?"

"Again, I'd prefer not to discuss details over the phone. Let's just say it concerns Evan Morris."

*   *   *

When the call concluded Lena stared at her phone again. Morris had been distracted earlier for good reason. This was serious trouble. But what kind? An instant later she veered onto the sidewalk and headed toward Victory Square, collecting her thoughts and steeling herself.

She'd always eschewed politics. Opposition parties...Speaking against the regime in her classes at the Institute...What for? There was little to gain, and a lot to lose. She'd preferred to observe from safe distance. Her academic career was more important.

And now this, just because of her association with a foreigner? She'd had one foreign pupil before---a Coca Cola manager from the U.S.---and done some free-lance interpreting work for visiting businesspeople, with no adverse consequences. Morris was a computer programming manager, after all, not a newspaper reporter or human rights worker---the type who invited animosity from the government. Unless he was some kind of secret intelligence operative...

She dismissed the notion as paranoid and absurd.

Inside the park gate the main plaza was mostly empty: still early for lunchtime strollers. She spotted the birch tree that Shinkevich mentioned, then the willow tree further on, with drooping branches and deep, concealing shade. All four benches around the tree were empty. She chose one facing the gate and sat down. Her experience with such people was limited but she had an idea. She had to listen closely. Weigh her words. Not over-react. Most important was to determine what Morris had himself gotten into. And her own position in this...

"Elena Grigorovna?"

Whirling around, she saw that Shinkevich had approached from behind, out of a blind of spruce-pines abutting the Prospekt. Unexceptional face. Tightly-combed hair. Late 40s. Bland gray suit. Typical *chekist*. The breed that had never left the scene in Minsk and re-ascended in Moscow. She felt immediate aversion.

"May I sit down?"

Knowing the question was a formality, she gestured toward open space on the bench. As he seated himself she observed his features more closely. Stresses were evident, which surprised her a little. These *chekisti* were used to being in control.

However his voice held the same authority as on the phone.

"First, let me state that you are under no suspicion of wrongdoing," he said. "This matter concerns Evan Morris, an American citizen living in Minsk. We understand you know him. Is that true?"

"Yes."

"Can you describe your association?"

She reminded herself to stay cool. Nothing would be gained by confrontation.

"I'm his Russian language tutor. He pays me for private lessons. His company reimburses him for the cost."

"How did he come to employ your services?"

Lena gave a brief summary. She kept her name on a list at the U.S. Embassy. Accepted some jobs. Turned down others. In late January she'd received a call from the *Cognition Software* office manager in Minsk, a woman named Anna, and agreed. When Shinkevich asked her how much was paid, she resented the question but told him.

"Does your relationship extend beyond language lessons?"

Lena bristled but contained herself. With whom did he think he was dealing?

"If by that you mean romance…the answer is no."

"Friendship?"

"In a general sense, yes. But always in the context of lessons."

"Always in your apartment?"

"Not always. Sometimes we make the sessions more practical. I help him with certain administrative tasks in Minsk. We go on outings. I use these to introduce him to new vocabulary."

"Administrative tasks? Outings? What kind?"

"Travel arrangements, for example."

Shinkevich inclined forward and placed elbows on thighs. His eyes narrowed.

"Like his travel to Vilnius this past weekend?"

She hesitated. Evasion did not appear an option.

"Yes…I helped him buy his train ticket."

At this Shinkevich leaned back on the park bench. Through his stress he showed some satisfaction.

"I'll need to know all the details," he said.

"Did I do something wrong?" Lena answered. "Did he?"

"Again, Elena Grigorovna, leave the questions to me. Let me just say this. The assistance you gave Evan Morris was more consequential that you realize. And now it's your duty, in turn, to help us."

CHAPTER 41

After the door clanked shut Morris looked around. This room differed markedly from Shinkevich's office upstairs. Basement-level, with no windows. Concrete floor and walls: the latter painted stark white. Steel door with a small sliding hatch at eye level. Minimal furniture: just the metal chair on which he was sitting and a wooden desk, two meters opposite. Phone and intercom resting on top. Florescent lights bright enough to make him squint. Video camera mounted high in one corner, with a green light blinking at the base.

Yuri hadn't mentioned the camera. Maybe he'd been too nervous to notice.

For reassurance Morris reminded himself of positives. For example that Grinevicius now knew the facts, was safely abroad. That counted for something.

Fifteen minutes later the steel door opened and Shinkevich walked in, cell-phone in hand. Bags were visible under his eyes, along with damp spots in the armpits of his gray suit. Yuri was right. Under duress. And exuding hostility which had been absent the first time. Instead of sitting behind the desk he came round and sat on top of it, glowering down at him. His accented English came out in a scowl.

"Are you aware of the problems you've caused with your little weekend trip?"

Morris opened his mouth to speak but didn't get a chance.

"...Me especially."

Again Morris tried to open his mouth and was cut off.

"Do you know where I came from just now?"

Morris wasn't sure if the question was actual or rhetorical. At last he sputtered an interjection.

"First, let me correct any misunderstandings about Yuri…"

"Forget about him for now," Shinkevich snapped. He swept his hand backward and snarled. "We'll get to him later. Morris became conscious again of the camera, which he assumed possessed audio as well as video. "…I'll tell you where I was. I was meeting your friend Lena. And I can tell you. She was not glad to hear from me."

Acidity cut through Morris' stomach. He managed to keep his voice even.

"Lena? She had nothing to do with it."

"No? She helped you buy your train ticket…true?"

Morris hesitated. This incited slightly higher volume.

"I repeat…true?"

"Yes."

"Then whether you like or not, Mr. Morris, you got her involved."

"I just left for the weekend. I didn't…"

"Against my instructions. You tried to be clever, not contacting me until the last moment."

"I did try."

Shinkevich's glower intensified. Further defense seemed ill-advised.

"What did you do in Vilnius, Mr. Morris?"

"Golf."

"Both days?"

Morris had actually mulled this on the way down the Prospekt, sitting in the back of the BMW next to blond buzz-cut. He'd settled on amended truths.

"Just on Sunday. On Saturday I decided to do some sightseeing."

Shinkevich scrutinized him. Long seconds ticked off. "And what did you do on Saturday?" Morris recounted his walk, where he lunched, and dinner at Bistro 18. Everything as it was. Just minus Grinevicius. Shinkevich looked skeptical but kept coming. The name of the course? Transport to the course from Vilnius?

"Club Centros Europas. I went there by taxi."

The official's eyes narrowed.

"And did you golf alone?"

"No...I was paired with someone."

"Who?"

"A member of the club. I'd never met him before."

"Name?"

Morris hesitated. The delay was not lost on Shinkevich. Morris hoped the Russian would simply ascribe it to slow memory.

"John."

"No last name?"

"He mentioned it. I forgot."

Shinkevich turned sideways to scribble on a notepad on the desktop. Afterward he cast a quick glance at the camera. Worry re-creased his eyebrows. "We have a big embassy in Vilnius," he said. "Plenty of people. We'll be able to dig around. Your story better check out."

Morris struggled for a quick inventory. Most of his answers seemed astute. But he'd started to lose track. It was all going very fast. Shinkevich resumed the pace.

"Communicate with anyone while you were there? Telephone? Internet?"

"Some e-mails."

"On your laptop?"

"Yes."

Morris' acidity spiked. He felt a hollowing sensation.

"Any we should know about?"

"No...I don't think so."

"What about sites? Any worth mentioning?"

"Probably not. News. Weather. That sort of thing. Also the site of the golf club."

This last item was a lame attempt at diversion, and Shinkevich knew it. He leaned over, pressed the button on the intercom, and spoke clipped phrases in Russian. Morris thought he heard the word "computer"---same in Russian as English. When the KGB official turned back, he wore a smile that was more threatening than reassuring. He glanced again at the camera lens, apparently aware of his audience.

"I'm sending someone back to your lab for your laptop," he said, gauging Morris' reaction.

Which Morris did his best not to provide. Inside, he also grappled for confidence. On the train back to Minsk he'd scrubbed his hard disk. It was difficult, though, to be completely thorough, even for someone with a computer science degree from Cornell and years of professional experience.

"...We'll examine the memory," the official added. "Determine if you've told me the truth."

"I need my laptop for work. Will I get it back?"

Shinkevich's predatory gaze took on slight bemusement.

"Let's take this one step at a time, Mr. Morris."

CHAPTER 42

From *Bagira* Piper drove straight back to the Embassy and ran into Svetlana as she exited for lunch. Her enthusiasm hadn't waned since their parting the previous evening; if anything, the opposite. After a brief, electric interaction with her in the courtyard, he picked up his pre-ordered lunch in the cafeteria, proceeded upstairs and settled behind his desk.

Raubichi had not been a singular occurrence. That was clear.

He took a bite of turkey-and-cheese sandwich, perplexed as ever by the female mind-set. At the time of his marriage to Caroline at age 26---young by contemporary standards---he'd been struck by his immediate upgrade among members of the opposite sex. The majority of unattached females with whom he'd had contact at the time, in both near and outlying circles---particularly those that were most attractive and sought-after, somewhat paradoxically---had suddenly viewed him in a more appealing light. As if his new status conferred automatic superiority over his single male counterparts. Incidental opportunities began presenting themselves, unsought from his side. First in the States, later in Europe and Russia; the phenomenon had persisted, transcended borders, and only grown more pronounced as he'd aged.

Now, nineteen years later, it was as acute as ever. And begged the same questions.

Because he was off-limits? Desirable precisely because he was unattainable?

He took another bite, put down his sandwich, and twisted the cap off his bottle of sparkling water. His memories traced across various examples, in multiple locations, including the most consequential one in Kiev---still, thankfully, the only instance in which he'd ever succumbed.

Nineteen years on, he still had no explanations. Some female motives resisted his grasp.

All he could do was find inventive solutions, and apply them. Just as he was doing now.

*   *   *

Forty minutes later Piper seated himself in the secure communications room. Video of Stapleton blinked on over the link. It was 6:50 a.m. in Langley.

"Excellent piece, Russell. I submitted it to the White House last night."

"Hope it helps."

"It's the best we've got. In fact I think it's already had some effect. Gallstone has asked to move the NSC discussion from Tuesday to Wednesday, which is probably a good sign. Maybe he realizes that empirical indicators and logic are on our side. He wants more time to plan."

"That would be a first."

The Deputy Director allowed a smile. It was a rich theme. "By the way," he said. "Any transmissions lately from agents One and 1300?"

"None. I take that to mean the KGB and the Defense Ministry are pretty dormant this month. Vacations and so on."

"Maybe that's for the better. We have enough on our docket just now." It was an obvious understatement. Stapleton adopted a lighter tone. "…Still, it gives you a good excuse to stay in shape."

"Worse fates, I guess."

"Ah…the hazards of life in the field. No injuries, I hope? All body parts in working order?"

Piper recalled that Stapleton suffered from occasional tennis elbow.

"Yes, thank God. During the last couple of years, as you may have gathered, I've become a believer in cross-training. No more than three runs per week, seldom on consecutive days. In the gym, I keep my weightlifting regime well-rounded, and alternate my cardio training between bike and Stairmaster. The variety helps me avoid repetitive motion injuries. And this is critical…post-workout, I've become devout about stretching."

"A worthy example, Russell. Especially to us more sedentary types back in Washington."

Once they'd signed off and the screen went blank, Piper leaned back in the upholstered chair and contemplated the exchange, enfolded by the silence. Postponement of the NSC discussion until Wednesday freed up extra time in the interim. The exchange also prompted an idea. He rose to his feet and exited the room. The corridor was empty, and he made straight back for his office.

He had a call to make. This one was local.

*   *   *

Shinkevich's authoritative attitude dissolved when he answered the phone. During the ensuing call he mostly listened, glancing once at the video camera. After slowly replacing the receiver, he contemplated Morris with an oblique gaze. "I'll be back," he said, getting up to leave.

Morris' first reflex was to check his watch, but the guards had taken it along with other personal items. His best guess was two p.m.

The video camera stayed trained on him from the corner, green light blinking. By his reckoning another full hour passed. Clanking doors, footfalls or muffled voices sounded occasionally from the corridor. Otherwise just deadening silence. At last the door swung open and Shinkevich returned. The official's preoccupation remained but he got right back on pace.

"Your laptop shows signs of erasure on the hard disk," he said. "Any explanation?"

"I regularly clean off files from the Internet," he answered. "Just routine system maintenance."

Shinkevich came around and leaned again on the front of the desk, staring down at him again. "Our programmers said it was done with unusual thoroughness. As if you're hiding something."

Morris cleared his throat. "I'm a programmer by profession. I try to be thorough in these matters."

He snorted and eyed Morris through narrowed lids. "Don't rest too easy. We still have to check out your story about Vilnius." He paused for effect. "...But that may take a few days. What are we going to do with you in the meantime?"

Morris imagined sleeping on a cot in a concrete cell.

"I won't leave Belarus," he said. "Will that help?"

"Not an option in any case. We'd stop you at border control if you tried. In fact you wouldn't even get past city limits. After what's happened, you can count on tighter surveillance. And that's this week. What are your travel plans for August? And September for that matter?"

"I've scheduled a week's vacation in Cyprus during the last week of August...just some time on the beach...."

"Cancel it," Shinkevich interrupted. "What next?"

Morris cleared this throat. "...I'm scheduled to visit corporate headquarters in California on September 20th. A conference...all the development managers are required to be there."

"Cancel it as well."

"Wait…That's my work. I'm willing to cooperate. But that kind of restriction can create real problems for me."

Shinkevich folded his arms, stroked his chin and beheld Morris with a look of exasperation. "I don't think you realize the severity of your predicament, Mr. Morris."

Acid re-hollowed Morris' stomach.

"Let me be specific," the official continued. "If you try anything unwise…seeking refuge in your embassy, hiding, escaping the country…that is, anything resembling what you pulled this past weekend, I can guarantee you. Yuri and Lena will suffer consequences. Arrest. Detention. Destruction of their careers. We have that power."

Morris swallowed hard. "That would be unjust. They…"

Shinkevich flipped his hand back, cutting him off. "Justice has nothing to do with it. And your programmers? We'd shut down the lab. They'd all lose their jobs. Of course it also goes without saying that your company would lose their entire investment here."

He paused and let his threats saturate the room. In the silence Morris groped for normality. Some way forward. "I've gotten your message," he said finally. "As I stated, I'm prepared to cooperate, to meet your stipulations. I have just one question…"

This time the official did not interrupt.

"…When will these conditions be lifted? I can't go on like this indefinitely."

Shinkevich brought his hand to his chin again, looked down at the floor. Flickers of pragmatism in his expression, even decency, provided some basis for hope.

"I don't have an easy answer for that, Mr. Morris. But I will say I can play a stabilizing role here. I don't want this to escalate any more that you do. For now, let's just get through the next three or four weeks."

CHAPTER 43

S tanding barefoot and bare-torsoed before the mirror, Piper moist-
ened his stubble with hot water, applied a layer of shaving gel, and
began from right to left, employing mostly down-strokes. First his
face; next the area below his jaw-line. Then his neck, along with final
retouches beneath his nose and lower-lip. On running days shaving
constituted an exquisite postlude. Replete with fresh discharges, he
felt at once spent and invigorated, calmed and empowered, as if he'd
unshackled himself, even just briefly, from his own mortality.

Much as he did after superlative sex.

Self-satisfaction by hand, that eternal male standby, still had its
place before bed-time during solitary periods like this, and no doubt
constituted a physiological safety valve. But in his estimation the relief
it brought was glandular, temporary, and often gratuitous, particularly
if the starting point was a photograph or video.

Effects from his workouts, he'd concluded, were more systemic
and lasting.

When he was done he rinsed the razor under the tap and dabbed
his face with a hand-towel. Confident for the moment in his powers of
self-regulation, he allowed an alternate line of thinking.

In practical terms Svetlana seemed to expect nothing permanent. She was aware Caroline was returning in early September. Parameters were clear; she was not the type to precipitate a blowup. Beautiful and cultured. Discreet. No obvious strings attached. A philanderer's dream.

He half-closed his eyes and summoned exhilarating scenarios back to the fore---an easy progression, so soon after his run, then stripped off his athletic trunks and hung them on the drying rack in the hall-way, before retracing to the shower and opening the tap.

While he waited for the water temperature to stabilize, the jets and streams reverberated off the tiled walls. Another scenario came back to him, all the more exhilarating because it was real.

He let the memories cascade.

CHAPTER 44

The swish of running water from the bathroom had already acquired a reassuring, even domestic quality to Piper, one that offset the rush and tumult of events outside and assuaged the longer-term ramifications of the plunge he and Oksana had taken. Politics and regime change had thrown them together, at least according to own his self-serving rationalizations. Cleanliness, routine and normalcy, he imagined, were at least in some measure what allowed them to shed their limitations and merge into each other behind closed doors during yet another night. To flow with the ardors of the moment without disconnecting completely from previous fixtures and habits, before re-descending into the fast-moving, orange-themed groundswell down on the square.

Movement of the nozzle and the squeak of Oksana's bare feet on the shower floor emanated along the short hallway. By now he knew her rituals required about ten minutes, which coincided perfectly with his last round of quick phone calls and text messages, including one final text to Caroline. He reclined in his armchair in the living room and relished warming sensations in his extremities and the quiet of the fifth-floor safe apartment. For some inchoate and entirely baseless reason her cleanliness imparted a gauze of safety and propriety to their couplings, just as the sweeping changes outside justified their cession to these impulses in the first place.

What he and Oksana were doing, he knew in intermittent bouts of clarity, was hardly safe.

Even if it did spring from the rhythm of the demonstrations.

Numbers on the *Maydan* invariably surged between seven and ten in the evening for speeches by opposition figures, including Yushenko's habitual galvanizing address at eight or nine. That was also when the media dove into the whirl, relaying the drama and jubilation around the world. Denizens of tent-city remained overnight, braving the cold in their sleeping bags and blankets, but everyone knew that that was when the revolution was at its most vulnerable---that if Kuchma's militia acted to re-take control of the square it was likely to do so in the early hours of the morning or crack of dawn, which compelled Piper to stay close-by in case bedlam intervened.

In mid-morning he re-emerged from his safe house and participated in another planning session with the organizers, primarily observing, providing counsel when called upon. His only real chance to break free and foray home came around mid-day.

It was only then---during these half-hour treks through kicked-up snow and un-shoveled sidewalks to join Caroline for lunch at their apartment near Mariinsky Park, and see the kids at least briefly upon their return from school---that he sometimes thought of ducking into a pharmacy or any other store that was still operating and more or less normally stocked. Though truth was, he didn't really desire the items in question. Even if he could find them he'd long fallen out of the habit. He and Oksana were past that anyway.

On their first night there together they'd dispensed with condoms for the straightforward reason that they didn't have them. From there, through momentum and sheer sensate voracity, birth control---or absence of it---had remained a deferred and mostly unconsidered question, which neither one of them was inclined to advance. Their caution, such as it was, rested on initial, on-the-go assurances from

Oksana that she was at a more-or-less safe point in her cycle. This coupled with his retention of enough self-command---just enough---to withdraw before climax.

This was already night four.

Perhaps most astonishing to him was that he had little real desire to back up and reverse their tumbling, impetuous progression. His exhilaration was just too intense, imbued with raw power he hadn't experienced since his early years with Caroline, and augmented, he believed---in another of his self-serving rationalizations---by surrounding political currents...At ten-thirty, while still on *Maydan*, he'd called Caroline for the third and final time that day, shortly before she'd gone to bed, assuring her he was all right and soon en route to the Agency-financed apartment, all while Oksana, with calm discretion, had stood close-by and listened...Now the rest of the night was clear of responsibilities, straight through to morning. From the bathroom, he heard the taps close, which meant that she was almost ready.

On cue, Piper rose and walked into the bedroom, and had undressed down to his boxer briefs when Oksana emerged into the hallway. Intercepting her at the door, he found her hair tied up and her body wrapped in a short-hemmed night-robe. She smiled as he pulled her into a tight embrace, and felt the outlines of her panties under the silk---her lingering gesture toward modesty and restraint.

"This is never far from my mind all evening, despite everything else that's going on."

"For me too, Russell."

He smiled, blocking out the earlier part of the day. The skin around her neck and was still damp, and she emitted fragrances of a soap she'd somehow garnered by their second night. Energy swelled out from his center as he pulled her tighter and gave her a kiss.

"I'll be right out," he said, before entering the bathroom himself.

At the sink he washed his face and hands with warm water, and after he'd toweled off, examined his reflection in the mirror. What also astonished him, from the beginning of this liaison right through the present, was Oksana's utter *availability* to him. Prior to the election, his contacts with her had been intermittent, occurring by virtue of her role as an organizer for the Yushenko campaign, where she was one of the few females in a cohort of graduate students on the youth committee. In that early context he'd seen her display nothing but rectitude and focus, as well as disinterest in the overtures from other men in their circles. Then, as the balloting turned fraudulent, the election led to protest and became tent cities on *Maydan* and gripped the whole world's attention, the two of them had found themselves in frequent proximity, operating almost in tandem, Oksana serving as a vital conduit on the intentions of the students while Piper fulfilled his role as advisor and observer with more senior leaders. Several quick meals slipped toward an impromptu invitation back to the apartment, and unpremeditated advancement to bed, where to his amazement---for all her acculturation, discrimination and refined attractiveness---she'd given herself over to him completely, with no filters or impediments, despite the fact that he was married and offered no long-term assurances apart from his own decency and good will.

Yet it was precisely this completeness---her total abandonment of reserve, for all the risks and profound implications---that thrilled him the most and made it impossible to pull back.

In the mirror he saw that his chest was heaving and that his eyes bore a gloss of urgency. From his reserves of alertness he registered that she was now four days further into her cycle, and remembered a flash in her eyes as they'd neared climax the night before, aware what it portended.

Instead of dwelling on the question he quickly brushed his teeth and walked back toward the bedroom.

He was still wearing his briefs when he slid in next to her under the thick comforter, finding as usual that she'd taken off her robe, leaving her body bare except for the delicate undergarment around her middle. All the same there were still two layers of fabric between them; she did not attempt his overt seduction; nothing was definite or foreordained. Savoring their shared warmth, he propped himself on his elbows, draped half his body over hers, and kissed her again. His next words were spontaneous and didn't linger long in the slight space between them.

"We never talk about where this is going," he said.

She looked into his eyes for lingering instants. The observation didn't seem to discomfit her.

"We shouldn't have to," she answered.

With that she turned on her side, brushing her fingers across his protruding appendage to confirm what she knew already, and jutted her posterior into the crook at his hips. The flesh-contact shot stimuli through his core and overran his brain, inciting several deeper breaths. He gently swept her hair back with his free hand, and still panting, planted his open lips on the nape of her neck.

The thin barriers between them had become less meaningful now and no longer acceptable. With the same hand Piper reached down and pulled off his undergarment by the waist-band, freeing himself so that he sprang back into the crevice between her buttocks as he nestled forward again. Seconds later he hooked his thumb under her side-string and pulled down hers as well. She offered no resistance.

Instead she took a few deep breaths of her own, then twisted her head back with open lips and placed her palm on his thigh.

In his recesses of reason and self-control Piper remembered Caroline, and knew that his next act, and the ensuing seven or ten minutes, could be among the most decisive and consequential in his life. He didn't pause.

By now he was past pausing.

CHAPTER 45

With the 10-hour time difference between Minsk and Santa Clara, news didn't filter back to headquarters right away. However some of the programmers had obviously gone on-line from home, communicating with their U.S. counterparts by text or voice conference. From there, exaggeration and distortion had taken over, and compounded overnight. This was clear from the slew of sensational, alarmist e-mails that awaited Morris when he logged on after breakfast. Rumors and mad speculations were already running rampant, including:

* He had been tortured by either electric shock or water-boarding at KGB headquarters
* His passport had been confiscated and he was awaiting trial
* Yuri had been sent to a prison camp

Given the extremity of these reactions, from top management on down, perhaps the most remarkable aspect was that events from the previous weekend had remained under wraps until now---something Morris attributed to Russian reserve. However everyone was past that stage now. A new dynamic was in effect.

When he arrived at 7:45 hoping to contain the damage, the entry door was already unlocked. Inside he found Anna already at her desk, eyes riveted, shaken and on edge. "Malcolm called me during breakfast," she said when Morris stopped in front of her desk. "He asked me to get to the lab as soon as possible."

Malcolm Crowder was the company's President and CEO. He had visited the lab once in April, but had never telephoned the Russian employees directly, least of all at home. Still, Morris was not surprised. When Crowder leapt into crisis mode, standard parameters got discarded.

"Why?"

Anna's expression remained tense.

"First, he wanted to be alerted if you didn't show up at your usual time...He also wanted to speak to you as soon as possible."

"Okay, I'll boot up my laptop..."

As he turned toward his desk she interrupted him.

"He's worried that typical channels aren't secure...He wants to talk to you on my cell-phone."

Crowder could be over-the-top, but Morris knew this particular idea had some merit.

"Give me ten or fifteen minutes to review my e-mails and organize my thoughts," he said. "Then we'll make the call."

*   *   *

Lena was not intimidated. She seldom was.

Her principal reaction to Shinkevich, she supposed, was loathing. She detested men like him, and even more the power structures they represented.

Historical record was clear. State security organs had oppressed and diminished people of her parents' and grandparents' generations across numerous decades during the USSR---and even worse, imprisoned and killed them by the millions under Stalin. In Belarus, by her reckoning, the latter-day versions of these same organs still smothered society like a respiratory illness, stifling basic freedoms, and keeping the population confined, isolated and chronically short of full potential. This was why she'd steered clear of them. She had her political views, which she sometimes shared with close friends, in the kitchen over tea or coffee. Even if that was where her opposition stopped, her opinions were firm.

All the same she now found herself entangled with a soulless, despicable KGB functionary, and at odds with the state structure behind him, through no fault of her own. Which brought her back to Morris.

After rinsing out the coffee pot she placed it in the drying rack by the kitchen sink, then brought her full mug into the living room and settled onto the couch, revisiting the questions that had bedeviled her the previous afternoon.

She remained convinced he wasn't a spy. He simply wasn't the type. Too polite. Too technical. Too straightforward.

Still, that left a lot of questions unanswered.

She examined the walls and bookcases around her, and wondered again if the KGB had bugged her apartment during her meeting in the park with Shinkevich. Her guess was that they had. Moreover the space was already heating to excess in the morning sun.

Neither condition helped her concentration.

Normally she did her best thinking here. But these were not normal circumstances.

This morning she needed a change in venue. Someplace that could stimulate fresh insights, and enable her to develop an intellectual map with which to go forward, along with an action plan. One location was not long in coming; it suited her needs perfectly.

Her lesson with Morris was scheduled for 6:30 p.m. And she wanted to be ready.

CHAPTER 46

Morris reviewed the emails he'd opened at home, and read several new ones which had arrived during his commute to the lab. In the process further outlines emerged from the reaction at headquarters.

First: Crowder perceived this as a grave crisis, shot with mortal danger, requiring utmost priority. Second: he had mobilized most of top management to shape a response.

Three or four vice presidents, with Crowder at their nexus, were now bivouacked in a conference room, awaiting his call. Morris steeled himself and checked his watch. It was approaching 10:15 p.m. in Santa Clara. When he looked up Anna remained alert and upright, phone in hand.

"I'm ready," he said.

He watched while she punched in the number. As it rang through she handed him the phone. Crowder answered up after two rings, tautness in his voice.

"We're all waiting, Evan. I'm putting you on conference."

A slight increase in ambient noise came over the line, including the squeaks of a chair.

"Where are you now?"

"In the lab. With Anna."

"We would ask that you go outside into to the corridor."

Morris held the phone down and gestured correspondingly to Anna, who acknowledged with a nod. He then proceeded outside the entryway and took up position by the large window nearby.

"Okay, I'm outside now," he said. "Just across from the elevator."

"Good. We're concerned about listening devices. Is that a possibility?"

Morris hesitated.

"Yes, I suppose it is."

During the ensuing pause Morris could sense the tension ratchet up on the other end. He visualized Crowder at the head of the table: mid-forties, expanding midriff, eyes blazing with animal intensity behind wire-rimmed glasses. He waited while further consultations transpired.

"...It's probably best if you take the stairs down, then exit the building. We've opened an aerial view of the Institute on Google Earth. We'll tell you where to go when you're out the door. And keep the line open, in case something happens to you on the way down."

This was classic Crowder: on one hand, astute and aware, alert to all angles; on the other, paranoid and obsessive, subject to over-the-top delusions. Indeed there was a fine line between the two, which blurred under certain circumstances---altogether common among high-tech entrepreneurs, in Morris' experience. He had some direct acquaintance with Crowder's wacko side, but company folklore was even richer. Most notable episodes seemed to occur on the road at trade shows or investment conferences. Precipitants varied; dangers to physical safety were a recurring motif. Often results were abrupt and sweeping for those concerned---firings, trans-global re-assignments or even promotion. Not to mention mesmerizing drama for the company at large.

For his own sake, and the sake of the lab, Morris hoped this would not be one of those episodes. He re-raised the phone as he walked through the lobby, and passed just one in-comer. The guard at the booth at the door paid him little attention.

"Okay, I'm out the front door," he said. "What next?"

"Take the steps down to your left. There's a large open area past the end of the building. The one that fronts the swimming pool complex which is set back off the street...called the Palace of Water Sports. Correct?"

"Yes."

"Head straight there. Keep the connection open and don't talk again until you've passed the corner of the Institute."

Following instructions, Morris turned left off the front steps and proceeded along the tree-lined walkway that fronted the building. Simultaneously he made discreet survey of the front parking lot, and scanned Surganova Street. When he passed the corner he got back on-line.

"Anyone in the area?" Crowder asked.

The closest pedestrians were three athletic-looking teenage boys, almost 100 meters ahead, probably en route to the pool complex.

"No."

"Good. Cross the driveway to the back lot, and turn left toward the pool complex. Tell us when you approach the adjoining parking area."

"I'm approaching it now."

"Any cars parked there?"

"Seven or eight, as far as I can see. All empty."

"Okay...cut across. Keep heading toward the pool...See the cluster of trees just ahead to your right?"

"Yes."

"Head into it. Find a place where you're mostly out of view....preferably next too a tree trunk."

Even under the circumstances, the precautions were beginning to border on bizarre. Morris finally took up position.

"There are five of us here," Crowder said. "Bob, Neil, Ed, Manny and myself." Morris visualized the individuals in the group, all of them vice-presidents. Crowder pressed on. "Let's first get the facts. We understand this originated with something you saw at Yuri's dacha a week ago Saturday. True?

"Yes."

"Can you tell us what it was?"

"For my own sake the sake of the lab, I think it's better if I don't. That's why I didn't inform anyone at headquarters in the first place."

There was a pause on the other end as everyone digested this.

"We appreciate your self-reliance, Evan. But from what we heard yesterday, the situation has gotten serious. We gathered you were called into the KGB for questioning not just once but twice. True?"

"Yes."

Crowder sounded as if he caught his breath.

"Were you mistreated?...Let me be more precise...Were you tortured?"

The last verb hung for an instant before Morris redacted it.

"No, nothing so extreme."

This seemed to bring slight relief, though Crowder didn't relent.

"What can you tell us about your trip to Vilnius this past weekend? Was that connected to this?"

Morris hesitated. Telling them about Grinevicius just opened up a whole additional set of complications. "Not really. I just felt the need to get away for some golf...Unfortunately the KGB didn't take kindly to that."

A short conference ensued at the other end. After about 45 seconds Crowder came back on.

"Even though you haven't told us what you saw, Evan, the picture's coming into clearer focus. However we're going to need some time to formulate a response. It's now 8:20 in Minsk? Correct?"

"Yes."

"We suggest the following. Go back to the lab. At precisely ten o'clock, return to the same location by the pool complex, using Anna's phone. We'll call you again. By then we should have a plan."

Morris agreed and signed off. As he started back toward the Institute he re-glanced at his watch. Crowder and his crew would be working through midnight in Santa Clara.

And Morris knew Crowder. From this point forward, anything could happen.

CHAPTER 47

On her way down the Prospekt Lena determined she might find practical application for Sartre after all. Also for his dialectical forebears, for that matter, whom she'd read as a student.

Hypothesis, antithesis, synthesis. Force, counter-force, resolution.

Intellect was her best weapon. And she would bring it to bear.

After rounding onto Saharova Street, she mounted the terrace of the Language Institute and proceeded through the main entrance, where her unexpected presentation---she hadn't stopped by several weeks---prompted the duty-guard to stand from his desk, even though he quickly recognized her and offered a polite nod. This had been her main habitat, apart from home, since her first year as an undergraduate eleven years earlier.

Otherwise the lobby was empty. The only artifacts of recent activity were several boards standing in the corner, on which the results of entrance exams were still posted from early July. In another week or so the Institute would close down entirely for three weeks prior to reopening in late August. She walked up stairs and down a deserted corridor to the Department of English Literature and found the door unlocked. One of her more senior colleagues---late middle-aged and perpetually cheerful, also the department chair---was inside, and looked up from a computer screen as she entered.

"Lena! This is an unexpected surprise."

"For me also, Olga Petrovna. I was sure the department would be empty."

"What brings you here?"

Lena had to improvise.

"I was in the vicinity." She spied an open text next to her older colleague's computer. "...Some questions occurred to me for my syllabus, so I decided to stop by and look through some materials."

Olga Petrovna eyed her, curious. "Well, I can't fault that."

Lena managed a half smile, as she sat down. Abruptly Olga Petrovna checked her watch. "Listen," she said. "The main reason I'm here is that I'm meeting Alexandra Evgenovna for coffee and pastries. Right here close-by...at the Beriozka Café. Why don't you join us?"

This overture was just what Lena needed. She made a show of opening a file drawer and extracting an academic journal.

"Thanks very much, Olga" she said. "But I just had breakfast. Plus I want to re-read some articles, while these questions are fresh in mind."

Olga Petrovna reacted good-naturedly. "Well, if you're still here when I get back, I wouldn't mind having a chat. I've hardly seen you since the semester ended."

A minute later Olga's footsteps faded down the corridor and Lena leaned back in her chair. Her desk was situated with four others in one room of a three-room suite; she now had the entire department to herself. The only illumined computer screen was Olga's. Shelves lined two nearby walls, crammed with books and mish-mashed academic journals, both English and Russian. A dormant coffee maker and unplugged electric kettle rested on a side table. Potted tropical plants rooted spare surfaces throughout the room, including the window sills. Her second home. Her workday sanctuary. A lone car passed by outside on Voiskovoi, a side street. As the noise subsided she leaned forward onto her desk and interlaced her fingers.

Even though she doubted Morris was a spy, she would nonetheless ask him straightaway, that evening before their lesson. It couldn't hurt. At least gauge his response. Assuming she was correct, that still left numerous vexing questions. Most central: what on earth had he done to arouse the ire of the KGB? Hacked into a government computer? Impinged upon secret, state-owned technology at the Institute?

Second: why had his trip to Vilnius provoked such harsh reaction? By the same token, why had he risked such an excursion, under the circumstances?

At this stage it was all guesswork.

She opened a drawer and pulled out a blank piece of paper. To organize her thoughts she settled on outline form, the same method she employed for her lectures and articles.

The page filled up quickly.

*   *   *

When Lena straightened and placed her pen aside, she looked over the result. This was just a first-pass analysis, but it was a start:

Reasons for KGB interest in Morris:
Intelligence work?	**Unlikely**
Illicit business activity?	**Less plausible**
Accidental knowledge of sensitive issue	**More plausible**

Explanations for Morris' travel to Vilnius:
To buy something not available in Minsk?	**Possible**
To visit a woman?	**Less plausible**
To play golf?	**Probable**

Dangers from KGB:
Cell-phone tracked?   **Established**
Phone conversations monitored?   **Almost certain**
Apartment bugged?   **Probable**

General risks:
Loss of position at the Institute
Revocation of passport
Complications/unpleasantness for mother
Imprisonment

Principal dialectics:
Cooperation with KGB vs. outright refusal
Actual cooperation vs. symbolic cooperation
Reaction vs. pro-action
Joint effort with Morris vs. autonomous response

Immediate measures:
Re-configure lesson with Morris around outdoor location
Turn off cell-phones
Simulate teacher/student interaction
Level direct questions

She mulled the outline for about 10 minutes, and considered re-classifying several components. Before she did, footfalls sounded down the corridor.

CHAPTER 48

The sun had risen higher by the time Morris returned to his designated location among the trees, casting deeper shadows and offering welcome refuge from the heat. At precisely 10 o'clock, Anna's phone rang. First Crowder confirmed his position, then asked if he was out of earshot of passersby and unobserved by the KGB. However the CEO wasn't reassured; his tone was even graver than before.

"…We can't forget who we're up against here," he said. "Therefore we'll have to speak in general terms. First, let me say that we have a provisional plan. But before we get to that, let's revisit the basics. Do you believe yourself to be in immediate physical danger?"

"I don't think so, no."

"Same hold true for Yuri and everyone else in the lab?"

Morris noted that they seemed in even less danger.

"Good. However we've also proceeded on the premise that the current situation is volatile and unsustainable, and requires a coordinated response by the company. Around this table, we're in full agreement on that."

Brief affirmations issued from Bob Lamont, Neil Nordquist and the other two vice presidents. Crowder resumed.

"We'll need several days to work out the specifics of our plan. At that time we'll make further contact by alternative channel, and communicate them to you directly. Meanwhile we urge you to carry on as usual with the business of the lab. Will you do that?"

"We'll certainly try."

"That's all we can ask. And Evan?"

"Yes?"

"We can assure you of one thing. You're not in this alone. The company is behind you one hundred percent."

After the call concluded Morris remained standing under the shade for a moment. Paranoia could serve useful purpose. But within limits.

With headquarters, from this point forward, his main hope was to avoid extremes.

*   *   *

Four programmers had arrived over the previous 20 minutes, and stood huddled around the coffee maker with acute expressions when Morris re-entered the lab. They quietly disaggregated to offer morning greetings. During the ensuing handshakes the office phone rang, and Anna answered after one ring.

"Yes, he's here," she said, placing the call on hold. She looked across the room to catch his attention. "It's Keith Brockton. This is already his second call since you left."

Keith was another team leader in the programming group, based back in Santa Clara. Another post-midnight probe from the Pacific time zone.

"I'll take it at my desk."

"Jeff Esposito also called, from Warsaw Airport. He's heard about your problems through the grapevine and wants to know what's going on. He said he'll be in Tallinn later today."

Morris nodded and continued on to his desk. His extension chortled and blinked as he lowered himself into his chair.

The day had started with an onslaught. And the deluge wouldn't stop.

CHAPTER 49

In an instant Lena folded the page and stuck it in her purse, then immobilized herself and listened. As the footsteps grew closer she soon discerned that they were Olga Petrovna's, and with slight relief moved the academic journal back to the center of her desk, opening it to a previous bookmark. Upon entering the department Olga glanced at the materials and smiled.

"Still at it?" she said.

"You know me Olga. Once I get absorbed, I have trouble tearing myself away."

Olga approached a file cabinet against the adjacent wall, appearing to be in transition. "It turns out Alexandra Evgenovna and I decided to head up to the National Library for a few hours. Both of us have some things to do there. We'll probably tack on a late lunch at the library cafe. Can we interest you in joining us? Don't forget...the building is air-conditioned. And it's getting pretty hot today."

Lena made a show of checking her watch. "Tempting. But I've really got to be on my way in an hour or so...I'll tell you what though, Olga. I need to run out quickly to purchase a few items. Can I walk you out?"

"With pleasure."

While Olga collected some folders, Lena rose and took hold of her purse; the two of them then traversed empty corridors down to the lobby, where Alexandra Evgenovna was waiting, then on to Rumjanksaya Street, at which point Lena bid farewell. She felt somewhat remiss about her artifice, but reckoned these were exceptional circumstances.

Most relevant among them: the KGB was tracking her cell-phone signal. And that was just fine. Nothing would vary from the ordinary.

Her first stop was the *Okean* grocery store, just around the corner, where she purchased a *bulochka* bread roll, a *sirok* dairy sweet, and a bottle of mineral water. Across from the grocery store she stopped at a curbside kiosk.

"A copy of *Belarusskya Gazeta*, please," she said.

The attendant laid the newspaper across the sill. Lena was a regular here, though she'd never purchased her next item.

"Also a box of matches."

Without blinking, the attendant placed the second article on top.

Five minutes later Lena was back at her desk in the department. To ensure that she was alone, she double-checked to make sure the corridor was quiet before extracting her sheet of notes. Then she took out her *bulochka* and mineral water, mulling her outline as she chewed and swallowed. Her eyes gravitated at once to the second and third lines under <u>*Principal dialectics*</u>: *Actual cooperation vs. symbolic cooperation* and *Reaction vs. pro-action.*

With quick strokes of her pen she crossed out **Preferred** in both instances, and substituted **Decided.**

Of all the components she'd identified, these two stood out. The core dialectics. Her antitheses to Shinkevich's theses. These would constitute the main battlefield. One where she would prevail.

Another quotation from Sartre came back to her. She added it to the bottom of her page:

Freedom is what you do with what's been done to you.

She picked up the phone and punched Morris' speed dial.

*   *   *

When Morris came over the connection his voice sounded even more distracted and preoccupied than the previous day. Silence fell on his end when she mentioned a new lesson plan. As if he'd already been pounded by disruption that morning.

"As you know, my apartment is hot and unpleasant after days like this," she explained. An addendum occurred to her, for the benefit of KGB listeners. "Do you remember the Russian word for 'stuffy'?"

"No, I'm afraid I don't."

Lena was not surprised.

"Dushno," she said.

"Dushno," Morris repeated in a robotic tone.

She presumed he forgot the word the instant it rolled off his tongue. Vocabulary building was not her current intent anyway. "Remember the lesson we conducted on a similar evening earlier this month?"

"Yes."

"I have in mind something similar."

"That's fine. However I'm really swamped today. Could we make it a little later, at seven?"

Lena agreed and specified their meeting place, leaving out their ultimate destination. Over the next 15 minutes she reviewed the outline, committing the essentials to memory. She then stood, re-folded the page, and snatched the box of matches off her desk. Outside the department the corridor remained clear. She headed straight to the women's restroom, halfway down, keeping her footsteps as discreet as possible, and glanced both ways before entering. The odor inside was strong and familiar: a fusion of cigarette smoke and liquid cleaning solutions. Though smoking had been officially prohibited throughout the building since 2006, students tended to congregate in the restrooms and indulge anyway, so much so that the odor still lingered, even a month after the end of the semester.

Just now these violations suited her purposes. She walked straight to the sink, then scanned her notes one last time before igniting the lighter.

Conflagration was quick. She held onto the corner of the sheet until the last possible instant, and dropped the smoldering remnants into the basin. Without further delay she opened the tap and washed the black ashes down the drain.

She wouldn't try to defy the KGB. That would be foolish.

Just stymie them. Use her brain.

Above all take the initiative.

*   *   *

Stopped at a traffic light on Kiselova Street, Piper drifted back to his morning recollections, and experienced another powerful upsurge from his loins before the signal turned green and he continued toward the Lithuanian Embassy.

With some effort, he refocused on traffic as he descended to Victory Square and navigated the encircling roadway. When he was past it, climbing up Saharova, he glanced back again at the obelisk in his rear-view mirror.

His excitement soon subsided. Such spontaneous arousals had become somewhat more frequent of late, a development he chalked up to his recent cardio-vascular improvements. However he saw no particular cause for alarm and got his mind back on his upcoming appointment with his Lithuanian counterpart.

Moreover, his recollections of Oksana had been too selective.

For the sake of balance, he needed to retain a more complete perspective. Play his recollections further forward.

There'd been a postlude in Kiev. One he'd also never forget.

CHAPTER 50

What stunned Piper most of all when the passions of revolution had subsided---after the tents were taken down, the trampled, kicked-up snow cleared away, the defiant banners and general detritus of civil disorder sequestered and removed---was not that Oksana worried she was pregnant. It was that she appeared unfazed and even eager to proceed.

First inklings came over the phone. For him the two weeks after the Revolution had been more intense than the event itself: a never-ending cycle of unpublicized conferences and consultations in government ministries and parliamentary offices, just as critical to the democratic movement as his earlier interventions were to the popular groundswell. Which by necessity relegated Oksana to the margins: quick calls on his mobile and two chaste, outdoor meetings near her graduate faculty in the frosty environs of Schevshenko Park. On the day in question he'd barely been able to step off the carousel for a 20-minute rendezvous in a café near the Embassy, where they'd unbundled scarves and overcoats before sitting down.

"My period is a little late," she said. "I just thought I should let you know."

Terrain seemed to shift under his chair. Ambient sounds—conversations, clinking saucers, the swinging door into the kitchen---faded to periphery. Across the table, in person, she appeared even more untroubled and serene than she'd sounded by telephone. He took a sip of coffee and swallowed hard.

"I know we took some risks, Oksana, but this is serious..."

She observed him with unblinking eyes.

"Shouldn't you take a test?" he added. "I mean...as soon as possible?"

"All the pharmacies seem to be out of the instant kits. And the clinics are backed up. The earliest I've been able to make an appointment is in two days."

He took another sip and hard swallow.

"If you are pregnant, what will you do?" He caught himself and instinctively reached for her hand. "...Let me rephrase that. What will *we* do?"

She squeezed his fingers lightly and beheld him in turn, letting the question hang.

"Let's not get ahead of ourselves. We don't even know yet, one way or the other."

While he stopped to consider his next words, her composure didn't waver, or allow a frown. Instead she sealed the void.

"...Although I've already made up my mind. If I am pregnant, I would go ahead and have the baby."

Her declaration took a moment to gather force. Shifting escalated to tremor, then to seismic quake. To ward off the instability Piper reached out his other hand for hers, so that they formed interlocking pairs.

"I want to face this with you, Oksana. This concerns both of us... Whatever the outcome of this test."

She formed a smile, projecting even more confidence and placidity than before. "I was hoping you'd say that, Russell. And to be honest, I thought you would."

"We're in this together. Right?"
"Right."

*   *   *

Rattled by the words they'd exchanged that December morning, Piper kept one arm braced on the railing as he stood back and raised his beer. Almost four years later, the scene hadn't lost its force and imprint. That was no less true of the two days that followed, when the multiple currents and cross-struts he'd discerned only vaguely in the café had acquired clearer, jarring focus. Family, work, his life writ large.

With Caroline at the vortex.

He took another pull from the bottle and gazed out from his balcony across the green of Kupala Park, catching glimpses over the treetops of evening recreators on the river basin.

Over his shoulder he heard the pot boiling in the kitchen, and realized he'd been standing outdoors, engrossed in his recollections, for nearly 10 minutes. As he returned inside, he resolved to extend the narrative while the pasta cooked, and complete it during dinner.

That would help him avoid repeat cataclysms.

CHAPTER 51

Phone calls and e-mails from corporate kept Morris tethered to his desk for most of the afternoon, and he finally escaped the lab at 6:40. A vacant taxi materialized immediately on Surganova Street, which struck him as about the only favorable occurrence all day. Several programmers were visible again in the fifth-floor windows as he climbed in, as if expecting another intervention by the KGB.

No black *Volgas* showed themselves, at least for now.

En route to his rendezvous with Lena, he disencumbered himself of his laptop at his apartment, and got dropped off at the southern edge of Kupala Park with a few minutes to spare. Kupala, situated across the Prospekt from the National Circus, was the smaller sibling of Gorky Park; entering its diagonal walkway, he proceeded to a recessed, cobble-stoned plaza, dotted with park benches and set off from the din of traffic. Straight ahead was a Soviet-gigantesque statue which he had seen before: a man wearing a cape, of late middle age, one foot thrust forward in a confident stance. His right hand clasped a cane; he held his left over his heart and gazed ahead, appearing to contemplate the future with comprehending eyes. Morris guessed that the statue represented Kupala, whoever he was.

The area was quieter than Gorky. No children's amusement rides. Just paddleboats down at the riverfront. More adult and sedate. Appropriate not just for a language lesson, but for more sensitive exchanges. Such as a private, one-on-one discussion about the KGB, with direct questions and answers.

The kind for which he wasn't prepared. He hadn't even contemplated what to divulge or what to withhold. There'd been no time to think. At the base of the statue he took a deep breath, taking in the scent of cut grass, and checked his watch. Lena tended to arrive neither early nor late. Right on time. Three teenagers sat on the opposite corner of the plaza, drinking beer and smoking. Closer by, an elderly women tossed bread crumbs to several pigeons.

The incongruity hit him again. He had gone to Vilnius to contain risks.

His position was unraveling anyway.

"I'm here."

Lena's voice came from over his shoulder. She'd approached the statue from a back angle, carrying a plastic bag. He was too worn out to startle. She propped her sunglasses on her forehead and made a subtle scan of the plaza, including the teenagers and old woman. Then she examined his face.

"You made it."

"It's been a hard day."

"So I gathered."

Morris had a chance to examine her demeanor in turn. More or less composed, though with an edge. "First, Lena...let me apologize for getting you involved in this...I mean the Vilnius trip. I should have known better."

She continued looking at him. Long seconds passed. Instead of responding she gestured up toward the statue.

"Do you remember the Russian word for monument?"

Morris drew a blank. This was not the opening he expected.

"*Pamyatnik,*" she answered.

"*Pamyatnik*," he repeated.

"And do you know who this one represents?"

"Kupala, the same name as the park?"

"*Yanka* Kupala. Do you know what he did?"

Morris noticed she didn't repeat this last question in Russian. This evening she seemed to lack the patience. Her edge sharpened as she answered her own question.

"He was a writer, born in Belarus, who wrote in the Belarussian language. Poetry mostly, though a few plays as well. Before the war he actually lived in a wooden house in this area, where the park is now, then moved to Moscow as the Germans advanced in 1941. In 1942 he died in a so-called 'accident.' Fell from a window. More likely he was pushed, on orders from Stalin. 'Defenestrated' as I think you say in English."

Morris shuddered. It seemed a horrible way to die.

"Over what?"

"His dedication to Belarussian language and culture, one would guess. Some would even say his Belarussian patriotism. But who knows, exactly? For one reason or another he displeased Stalin. That was enough."

After the day's events, this account was jarring. Morris wondered what she was getting at. Lena didn't pause.

"Are you a spy, Evan?"

Her blunt delivery surprised him. He cleared his throat.

"No, Lena. I'm not."

She searched his face again. "Are you engaged in illegal activity? Criminal, maybe?"

"No. Absolutely not."

"Nothing at all irregular?"

"No."

"Then how did you antagonize the KGB?"

"It was an accident. I stumbled into something. I'm not supposed to tell you what, exactly, for your sake as well as my own."

Lena weighed his words. Gradually a frown crossed her face. After a moment she gestured up again at the statue.

"Do you know why I mention Yanka Kupala?"

Morris could guess. But he stayed silent.

"…I mention him because here in Belarus, things haven't really changed much since that time. State authorities can still squash a person. Do you realize that?"

Morris cleared his throat again. "Yes."

"Do you understand you've placed both of us in a serious situation?"

"I do, Lena. I don't minimize it."

"…For now, I'm assuming you're being honest with me." She studied him again. "Even if you can't tell me what got you into trouble, you've got to at least tell me what's necessary for my own well-being. Will you do that?"

He stared down at the cobblestones for a moment. But not too long. He didn't want to convey doubt.

"Yes, I will."

"We've got to cooperate, Evan. We have no choice."

*   *   *

Lena knew spies were trained liars. But indicators and instinct still told her Morris was telling the truth. Particularly his eyes---decent, guilt-ridden, almost pleading. The dark circles underneath suggested he'd been through a ringer. But he was still composed, despite everything. She had to give him that. Anyway she had little choice.

"We'll get to those matters in a moment," she said. "…I've conceived a plan."

Morris showed no reluctance as she paused. It was a favorable sign. She continued by gesturing again at the statue:

"I'll tell you another reason I mention Yanka Kupala. Because this is supposed to be a language lesson. And we can presume we're being watched. Therefore we've got to go through suitable motions." She paused to open her plastic bag, to show him the loose-leaf materials she'd prepared, and closed it again. "Our first step? Turning off our cell-phones. Just as we always do when we start."

Morris hesitated.

"I'm not sure that's a good idea, Lena," he said. "I've been told to do otherwise."

"By Shinkevich?"

He nodded.

"So have I."

"Did he also tell you to follow usual patterns?" she asked.

"Yes."

"Then let's follow that instruction instead. We can justify it later."

His eyes narrowed for a moment. Then he reached into his back pocket, pulled out his phone, and switched it off, while she did likewise. He scanned the plaza and nearby trees, narrowing his eyes again.

"Lena, we've already said plenty of incriminating things."

"Not really. Moreover we're standing next to this statue. If they're using directional microphones in parallel, I think we're safe."

It didn't take him long to comprehend. Lena expected as much, given his scientific background.

"Of course. Steel and cast iron. Radio-magnetic interference."

She nodded.

"So far your plan seems well-thought through," he said. "What do you have in mind next?"

"This part varies from past patterns," she said. "But I've already formulated an explanation for Shinkevich. A *legend*, someone in his profession would probably say. "

* * *

The sunken plaza gave way to a promenade lined with nineteenth-century-style streetlamps. Traffic noise from the Prospekt receded further, and Lena kept their pace slow, determined to preserve appearances as they headed toward a circular fountain. Dozens of pressurized spouts formed an umbrella of water at its center; these swished into the pool in sheets and released a mist of droplets into the still evening air. Another jet of water shot from a pair of female statues on the periphery, with hyper-slenderized figures. Each held a wreath. She gestured toward them.

"Do you have any idea what they represent?" She repeated the question in Russian.

Morris smiled slightly at the play-acting. Lena shot him a gentle glare.

"Something to do with Belarussian mythology?"

His answer was in English. Lena didn't wait for his vain attempt at the Russian equivalent. This evening there were limits.

"Not exactly. It's more tradition. The statues represent an ancient Slavic holiday, with pagan origins, called *Kupalya,* or bathing, which was celebrated around the summer solstice. See how one of the girls holds her wreath aloft?"

This area of the park was somewhat busier; most park benches on the periphery were occupied. A nearby cluster of three young women chatted around parked strollers. Lena veered around the assemblage. Morris examined the female figure in question and nodded.

"...And see how the other is holding hers toward the water?" Morris nodded again. "According to the tradition, young maidens would float their wreaths on a lake or stream, bearing lit candles. The drift-paths of these wreaths---and who would ultimately retrieve them---would determine whether or not the maidens would marry, and with whom. The holiday formed the basis for a poem by Kupala, which began: ....." They pulled up and stopped, two meters from statues. Lena allowed him to follow script and gaze at the figures. She also assessed ambient noise. Voices of other people in the vicinity were muted and unintelligible. Just what she wanted.

"Okay, enough of the lyricism. Stay angled toward the fountain. The water will hush our voices."

Morris took only a second to realize why, and followed her instruction. She positioned her body likewise.

"We can probably linger for about five minutes here…at the most," she continued. "We have to stick to our lesson template."

Morris opened his mouth to speak. Lena interrupted him.

"I'd like to ask some more questions, if you don't mind. We have to be efficient. First of all…Can you at least tell me when this began, and where?"

For several beats Morris stared down at the rim of the fountain, appearing to reach a decision, then raised his head.

"It began the weekend before last. While I was staying at Yuri's dacha. I saw someone during a walk. During berry-picking, to be exact. By accident. Someone I wasn't supposed to see."

He fixed his eyes on hers. His posture remained immobile as a wave of mist grazed his shoulder and forehead. He continued.

"For now, as I said …I think it's best not to tell you who he was. But I'll summarize everything else that happened that day."

"Okay. That's a start."

CHAPTER 52

Lena reminded him to glance at intervals toward the fountain, to "adhere to the lesson motif." Otherwise she just listened. Her only question came at the end, after Morris alluded in vague terms to his *Google* investigation.

"You're pretty sure you know who this man is?"

"Ninety-five percent sure."

"You call him an 'international fugitive'...Is he a terrorist, or more of a criminal figure?"

"Please, Lena. Can we leave it at that?"

Her eyes focused hard on him through her sunglasses. After an obvious effort at self-containment, she checked her watch.

"Okay. We've been here long enough," she said. "Let's walk toward the river."

Along the circumference of the fountain two young children ran shrieking across their path, then stopped at the edge and splashed their hands in the water, while their mothers observed from a nearby park bench. Lena and Morris veered unobtrusively around them, and ten steps later left the small disturbance behind. She gestured straight ahead.

"Ever tried one of those?"

Morris extrapolated the line and saw a gray kiosk and short queue of people. Beyond was a floating dock. On it, two attendants helped people into small paddleboats.

"Not here in Minsk. But I see them all the time from my apartment."

"My plan is to rent one and paddle around. Is that okay with you?"

He gazed through two tall pine trees and over the basin, noting his building in the background. "It's out in the open, which…" He stopped himself. "Of course. Audio interference from the paddles. I have to admit, Lena, you seem to have thought this through."

For the first time that evening she smiled slightly.

At the ticket window she examined the price board and informed him of the cost, which he paid. They descended the aluminum gangplank leading to the floating dock, and he held her plastic bag with lesson materials while she clambered onto her seat. An instant later an attendant shoved them off. Pedal coordination took a moment, but they were soon underway. Rudder control was on Morris' side of the craft: a simple lever. He pointed toward the middle, not too close to other recreators. Sounds were those they'd anticipated: rhythmic splashes that almost obviated their voices at normal volume:

Flop-flop-flop flop flop flop…

"Straight chronology seems easiest, Evan. Any objections?"

"Makes sense to me." They were now near the middle of the basin. "I suggest we keep moving at this speed," he added. "…in a gentle circle."

As he adjusted the rudder, early-evening sunshine struck low across the water. She adjusted her sunglasses and checked her watch.

"Next I'd like to cover the rest," she said. "Right through Vilnius and what happened to both us with the KGB today. We have almost an hour. You'd gotten up to your *Google* search. You can pick up from there."

*   *   *

While Morris talked he occasionally neglected his steering, drawing warnings from Lena. In each instance he suspended his monologue until he'd corrected course, then hewed again to his narrative: his motives for enlisting a lawyer, his criteria for selecting Grinevicius, and the basic outlines of his weekend in Vilnius. And lastly: the day's turmoil with Yuri and his own visit to the KGB. To his relief she didn't fault his decision-making---his golf alibi or even his employment of her help for his travel arrangements. After about 40 minutes he was done. She followed with a summary of her encounter with Shinkevich. Finally they took stock.

"Have you told Yuri about your lawyer?" she asked.

"No. Just that I went golfing."

"Anything about my involvement?"

"Not yet."

"Good. Let's keep it that way. I feel sorry for Yuri. He's gotten caught up in this just like I have. But let's not forget...he agreed to inform for the KGB almost a week ago. I wouldn't rush to tell him about your lawyer."

"My thinking exactly."

"Okay, let's take a rest."

They drifted in silence toward the stone citadel on the embankment, just left of the yellow façade of Morris' apartment building. Lena also affected a display for the benefit of would-be surveillance: extracting some pages from her bag and pretending to consult them. Before they got too close to shore she put the materials away and they started paddling again.

"The facts are becoming clearer," she resumed. "Are you sure you've told me everything?"

"I think so."

She eyed him through her sunglasses.

"Are you sure? I...we...need to come up with a strategy. Based, I hope, on common purpose. That requires a complete picture."

Thus far he hadn't mentioned Grinevicius' trip to Washington. He didn't respond right away.

"We still have a little time left," she persisted. "Please...take a moment to be certain."

Morris stared down at his knees, moving in rhythm against the pedals. It didn't take long to make a determination. The reward was hypothetical. An add-on. There were no parallels with his previous bust-up.

Money, in this case, was a side-show.

He adjusted the rudder and steered out of their arc, so that the bow angled back toward the dock on the opposite bank. He looked at her again sideways.

"Yes," he said. "I'm sure."

CHAPTER 53

Forty-eight hours probably broached his limit, Piper reckoned. Much longer, and the constituent strands might have unraveled.

Over this period---to his later astonishment---he'd somehow managed to stave off the oppositional forces that asserted themselves in the café. To conceal the development from Caroline. To maintain positive interaction with Oksana. To nevertheless overcome tugging, relentless guilt and sustain one of the most unforgiving workloads of his career, all on negligible sleep.

He'd held the fabric together, and kept his life intact. Just barely.

And that was when Oksana's pregnancy test came back negative.

He rose from the table and carried his empty plate and utensils to the sink, where the pot was already soaking. After a quick brush under the tap, he placed the items in the dishwasher, then refilled his wine glass and retraced to the balcony, taking in the first hues of dusk.

At first he'd assumed Oksana's attitude stemmed from the unique political passions of those weeks, mingled perhaps with Soviet cultural legacies, particularly the uneven and often careless use of birth control. That was: until he'd opened up to his cousin four months later, a Manhattan corporate lawyer in his early forties who'd recently divorced after an eleven-year marriage. They'd met for drinks at a downtown watering hole, during one of Piper's rare passages through New York.

The cousin had shaken his head with wry sympathy, and taken a swill of draft microbrew.

"Unfortunately, your experience is hardly unique, Russell. I've been just as shocked myself."

Piper had looked back at him with surprise.

"You're saying this is also common here in the States?"

"Absolutely. It's not only common…It's almost the norm. I've now been divorced for almost two years. Every woman I've been with during that time…four or five of them, late twenties, early thirties, for the most part…has depended entirely on me. Condoms, if I have them. That's it."

"Are you serious? Even with all the methods at their disposal?"

"Oh yes. What's more…after the relationship develops to some extent…Say, after the third or fourth time…if they see you as a serious prospect they're quite willing to dispense with them altogether. In fact, they're often eager to do so."

Unsettled by this, Piper took a swill of beer himself.

"What happened to women taking responsibility for their own reproduction?" he asked. "…The rules…unspoken, granted…that prevailed back in the eighties and earlier?"

"Forget it. Sometime in the mid 90s…around the time I got married…those rules apparently went out the window."

"Wow. I had little idea. How do you account for it?"

"One could argue that AIDS was one precipitant. Public mantras took hold by the late 80s, more or less saying that unmarried couples were supposed to use condoms at all times. That implicitly de-emphasized other methods. But we both know that's not realistic. Anyway, women who were sexually active in the 80s seemed to utilize female contraception nevertheless---that is, condoms in combination with something else."

"Hence my remark about rules."

"Precisely. Therefore I've developed some explanations, some hypotheses, if you will. First and most important---since around the mid-90s---DNA testing has taken all the ambiguity away...That is, paternity is no longer disputable. On that basis, a new body of child support laws has been created. These place the man on the hook for child support regardless of the circumstances of conception. Under this new rubric, it doesn't matter if a man never agreed to conceive a child, or was tricked. In any event he has to pay primary support, right to age eighteen. All men are subject to these laws, whether they realize it or not. But celebrities...professional athletes, music stars and so on...have it worst of all. From what I gather they often have entourages of unattached women following them around to games, concert venues, hotels and the like, with the express objective of getting pregnant. These women know that if they succeed, they'll basically be able to claim eighteen years of financial support, not just for their child, but for themselves as well. Rappers seem particularly vulnerable, and sing about this problem constantly."

Further disturbed, Piper stared for a moment into the unfiltered hues of his microbrew.

"I'd picked up on some of that in the media, but only in passing," he commented. "It strikes me as fundamentally unjust."

"Tell me about it. What it means is that a man has to have the discipline to use condoms at all times, or refrain from sex altogether. If by chance he lets his guard down...even for a minute or two...a woman is legally empowered to place him under de facto material bondage...essentially, eighteen years of indentured servitude. Evidence is everywhere. Courts are now choked with child support cases. Men should beware...Women---many of them, at least---have evolved into mercenary predators." His cousin paused for effect. "...The Sexual Revolution didn't begin this way. But for men, it's become a path to slavery. It's over."

"Over?"

"Over."

It was a stark picture. Piper resisted some of the implications.

"I must say…" he shook his head. "Whatever the ramifications for the Sexual Revolution, I hesitate to place Oksana in that category. She's responsible, well-intentioned…She was just overcome by the atmosphere…the spell of liberation. I guess we both were."

For all his bluntness, his cousin was sensitive to the trauma. "Of course I've stated the case in rather extreme terms," he added. "There are all sorts of gradations. Maybe she just fell under the sway of this new ethos. Or more benignly…she simply wanted to have a child with you."

In open pronunciation, the words hit Piper like Oksana's in the café, four months earlier. He and his cousin paused again and re-contemplated their beers.

"What's happened with her since then, by the way?"

"Oksana?"

His cousin nodded.

"I was so shaken by that episode, I immediately downshifted. We still saw each other, but on a platonic basis. We never had sex again."

"That's probably for the best. You'd be a fool to lose Caroline."

"I know."

"One-time occurrence then?"

"That's my intention."

His cousin appraised him. Seeing this, Piper elaborated.

"The political situation in Ukraine has quieted down. That's helped. I admit though…What I really need is some kind of permanent solution. Some method of pre-empting these impulses, so that in the future I avoid such situations altogether."

"Hmmm…Any luck finding one?"

"I'm still experimenting. But I think I may have identified something."

"You mean a solution? …This I've got to hear."

His cousin drained the rest of his mug. Piper did likewise.

"Another round?"

"All right."

His cousin signaled across the bar to the waiter.

*   *   *

Over the Prospekt and across the two adjoining parks, illumination went active on the Ferris wheel. Piper leaned back from the railing and glanced at his empty wine glass. Since that conversation in New York—and particularly over the past two weeks---he'd put his method into full execution.

Because Svetlana was entwined in his daily reality, he figured he would have little choice but to incorporate her in his workouts, at least until Caroline returned. In parallel he also decided to employ occasional, anonymous girls at *Bagira*, as he'd done earlier, to bolster his general defenses. Perhaps even ratchet up the intensity another degree or two.

In addition he had a mid-morning appointment the next day, made a month earlier. One which was turning out to be quite well-timed.

It would confirm that his plan remained viable.

CHAPTER 54

The dog was a mongrel; he lifted his head and gave Lena a baleful, beseeching look as she exited her apartment building. By now she recognized him. He was medium-sized, with multi-colored fur that was ragged and blotched with dirt. He'd inhabited the semi-enclosed yard off and on since late spring, and now sheltered under the shade of a tree, in tenuous repose. She stopped and looked back at him, wrenched by pity.

In his eyes she glimpsed more gentleness and goodwill than she found in most humans. Yet the poor creature had apparently been abandoned by his masters---that is, if he'd ever had any in the first place---and had no constant companions, canine or otherwise. Thus far he'd subsisted on handouts of food scraps from a coalition of kind souls from surrounding apartments, Lena's mother among them. But how long would that last? Three weeks earlier she'd seen him hobbling and bloodied---the victim of attack by hostile dogs, fighting over territory. If he wasn't picked up by animal control officials in the coming weeks, he would soon face the onset of cold weather. He was alone. Every day was precarious---a struggle just to exist.

The dog's fate was random. Senseless. Unjust. Entirely undeserved.

Somewhat like her current predicament with Morris and the KGB.

To fill the void left by her mother, she resolved to pick up some extra meat on her trip to Kamarovski market---even the cheaper variety---and feed it to the dog on her way home. She took out her grocery list and added "meat for dog," then re-read the phrase and found odd reassurance.

The action would be real and constructive. What the existentialists might counsel.

And her predicament with Morris was not life or death. Serious, yes, but not as dire as the one faced by the dog.

That was something.

*   *   *

The yawning, arena-sized interior of Kamarovski was bustling as usual. Before proceeding to the meat section, Lena swung by her favorite fruit vendor, and while the woman looked on encouragingly, inspected a rack of pears, picking one up to measure its freshness. Several shoppers milled the aisle behind her; she sensed one person over her shoulder but took no notice.

"Meet your standards, Lena?"

The voice was male: both familiar and disquieting. She whirled around.

The speaker was indeed Shinkevich. Same combed hair and gray suit, with a different tie. Her distaste came back.

While she stared back at him he glanced down at her hand.

"I was talking about the pear."

She replaced the item on the rack, then turned back to face him.

"Seems fresh," she answered. "In general, I avoid products that have been preserved for too long."

He squinted at her insinuation, though didn't lash back. "I wish to talk to you, Elena Grigorovna."

"We've already spoken once. I have nothing more to add."

He inhaled hard through his nostrils. She detected a new edge. "I thought you'd say that. So after your meeting with Evan Morris yesterday evening, I obtained a warrant, requiring your further cooperation." He handed the document over. Lena gave it quick examination, and saw that it was signed and stamped by a prosecutor---another lackey of the state structures.

"It was just a language lesson," she said. "There's not much to discuss."

"Don't play coy, Lena. Anyway you have little choice."

She took a deep breath of her own, glancing again at the warrant. Then down at her bag, which already contained vegetables.

"...I'll give you 10 minutes," he added. "I'll be waiting near the exit."

The KGB official turned heel and headed away down the aisle. Lena watched him go, her distaste compounding.

She'd half-expected another ambush. And she was ready.

CHAPTER 55

One receptionist was standing when Piper walked in; two others sat behind computers. All three glanced his way as he approached the counter.

"Russell Piper," he said. "I have a 10:30 appointment with Dr. Ivanov."

Upon hearing his name and accent, they proffered full attention. The one who was standing consulted her schedule pad, and established an especially forthright gaze, informing him of the cost: 75,000 rubles. Her light tunic, unfastened low, entered his sightline as he opened his wallet. She allowed an extended view while writing out the appointment slip and receipt.

"Room 302. Down the hall on your left."

"Thanks."

The corridor was long and narrow, empty except for another female staff member who passed him along the way. The door to Room 302 was closed. Piper listened for a moment, heard only silence, and knocked. Beckoned inside, he saw a lone figure sat at a desk, examining a folder. He was pale, with thick brown hair, around 40, wearing a white lab coat. Following brief introduction Piper handed over his slip and took a seat.

"Your Russian sounds excellent," the doctor said. "No need for English?"

"No."

"Good. I'd inferred that from your file." Dr. Ivanov gestured with one hand at the folder on his desk. "Your physician in Kiev...Dr. Pavlichenko...forwarded it to me when you were transferred, so I've had a chance to review your history. Seems you've come to Minsk with an immaculate bill of health. Since your last examination, have you developed any problems or concerns?"

"None, really. But I do have some issues I'd like to discuss." Ivanov raised his eyebrows and gave him closer inspection. "...They concern exercise," Piper added.

The doctor seemed to relax somewhat, and flicked his eyes back at the folder. "Yes, Dr. Pavlichenko noted that you're quite the sportsman, with a rather serious training regime."

"Yes. You could say that. Ever since university, I've always stayed in decent condition. But I re-started in earnest about three years ago."

"Are you referring to injuries, then?"

"No. Until now I've avoided injuries through cross-training and stretching. My concern is more general. Over the past two or three weeks I've ratcheted the intensity higher, particularly during my runs and cardio sessions, consisting of either stationary bike or stair-climber. Six or even seven days per week, right to my limit. I haven't trained this hard since I rowed in college."

"Is it your heart you're concerned about?"

"Well, perhaps somewhat..."

At once the doctor swiveled in his chair and shuffled through some pages in the folder. He pulled out two sheets and took a moment to study them, then swiveled back again. "I see here you underwent an electro-cardiogram and an electro-sonogram in Kiev. Results were excellent for a man of forty-five. Also: quick recovery during your stress test. Resting pulse of fifty-three...As far as I can see here you have no reason for concern. Let me ask you this…Are you training for some sort of competition?"

"Well, in my recent training runs I've broken four-and-a-half-minute kilometer splits for probably the first time since…" here Piper refrained from mentioning his baptismal regime at the 'Farm', before his commissioning into the Directorate of Operations "…my mid-to-late twenties, around the time I got married. And that's even without any sprint training or interval work. In light of these improvements, I am now considering getting back into sports on a more serious level, perhaps with a couple of 10K races in autumn, and even some half-triathlons back in the States next summer. But that's not my main motivation."

Ivanov nodded upon hearing the pace, obviously impressed. Then waited, curious again.

"…To be open, it's become a way to release excess energy. Stress from work, in part…" Piper hesitated for a moment. "…But more importantly…my family is away from Minsk for about five weeks, including my wife…those kinds of energies."

The doctor brought a thumb and crooked index finger to his lips. "I see…at least I think I do. Is it working?"

"Yes, for the most part. Almost too well."

Now the doctor's interest was truly piqued.

"…I do succeed in expending these forces on a day-to-day basis," Piper elaborated. "That's to say, after each workout I feel purged and relaxed. However it's also yielding a kind of paradoxical result. The more my body adapts, and my condition improves, the baseline only seems to increase…To the point where I've regained the sort underlying physical desire I experienced in my 20s. And this, in turn, is forcing me to make my workouts ever-more intensive, just to keep the formula in place."

"Most men your age would envy you, I suppose. But I see your dilemma."

"Do you have any suggestions?"

The doctor contemplated this for a moment.

"When is your wife returning?"

"Not for another three-and-a-half weeks."

"From a physiological standpoint I cannot not find fault with your solution. My main suggestion for now is that you take care not to injure yourself, by continuing what you've been doing: cross-training, stretching, and so on, simply persevering until your wife returns...." He paused. "I do admit, though, this is the first time I've encountered this particular question from a patient. And I'm intrigued. Consequently I will also undertake some research, to see if I come up with additional answers."

"I appreciate that. I realize my case may be somewhat unusual."

"To a degree, yes. Though perhaps not so unique as one might think..." He paused and adopted a more philosophical cast. "To large extent, testosterone is what makes the male of our species, on average, faster and stronger than the female in youth and middle age. But it also, in the end, is what leads to our earlier demise."

"Our fate, for better or worse."

For the first time since the appointment began, Ivanov offered a slight smile, which Piper reciprocated.

"Shall we proceed with your examination?"

"Yes. That's the main reason I'm here, after all."

As Piper stood and unbuttoned his shirt, he knew he'd omitted the particulars. There were some aspects he preferred not to reveal, even to a doctor.

*　　*　　*

When Lena climbed the stairs toward the main entry/exit Shinkevich was standing at a nearby snack bar, finishing an espresso. At his request she followed him out the door, down the short flight of steps, and onto the broad sidewalk toward Janka Kupala Square. He made no offer to help with one of her two grocery bags, which didn't surprise her. From his breed, superiority was assumed: one of many foul legacies from the

Bolsheviks. Traffic from the Prospekt howled close-by. She raised her voice to be heard.

"Where are we going?"

"To the underground passage straight ahead. Then the *Philharmonia*."

To Lena's knowledge the concert hall was closed at his hour; even the ticket office didn't open until eleven. Once they'd traversed the tunnel and re-emerged above ground she sighted the building ahead, and noted a young man in suit and sunglasses, standing on the entry terrace; thirty seconds later he opened the front door, let them in, and locked up afterward. No employees were visible in the lobby. The two ticket windows were dark. Lena's heels resonated off the marble floor.

"Straight ahead," Shinkevich said, pointing forward with extended fingers.

One of the doors into the auditorium was open; the same young functionary closed this behind them as well. Lena followed Shinkevich, descending along the right aisle, noting that the stage curtain was open; about halfway down the KGB man stopped and gestured into a row of center seats. She carried her grocery bags several places in and sat down, placing her items beside her. Instead of assuming position beside her Shinkevich leaned against the backrest of a seat in the next row, one space over. He crossed his arms and gazed over her toward the back balcony, in no rush to fill the silence.

Then the real point struck home. This was a show of mastery. In addition to the warrant, if Shinkevich could commandeer the *Philharmonia* at moments' notice, limits on his power were few. Certainly none that would prevent him from rolling over someone like herself, a junior professor at the Language Institute. Lena took a deep breath, as determined as before not to be intimidated. Shinkevich re-established hard eye contact.

"Unusual lesson plan yesterday, Lena. Care to explain?"

"It was hot...too hot for my apartment."

"And the paddleboat?"

"A last-minute improvisation."

Shinkevich squinted down at her.

"Same go for turning off your cell-phones?"

"We always do that, so as not to be disturbed. Your instruction was to stick to usual patterns."

The KGB official reacted with an angry snort. "Beware Elena Grigorovna..." he said, wielding her patronymic with disdain. "You're not as clever as you think." He paused, using silence to re-emphasis the vast indoor space. "...Next I suppose you'll tell me you didn't talk about your contacts with me."

"No. We did. And Morris' first gesture was to apologize."

Shinkevich unfolded his arms and straightened them over the backrest. "Now we're getting somewhere. Tell me more."

Academia had given Lena plenty of experience with redaction. So she was ready. Before continuing, she also remembered the dog. The canine faced peril much worse than hers.

Somehow his example helped.

CHAPTER 56

By now Piper had distilled his requirements. Even developed a checklist of sorts. What he needed for maximum release. These included the following:

1) Late teens to early 30s, tilted toward the lower half of the range
2) Ample hips and thighs, well-adapted to vigorous sex
3) Radiant health
4) Lengths and circumferences in suitable proportions
5) Clean complexion
6) Absence of wedding band
7) Outward marks of intelligence
8) Inklings of good humor
9) Hints, however slight, of underlying tenderness and empathy
10) Workout gear that complemented all of the above

And then: connection, however fleeting. A curious glance. A glimmer of interest. Lingering appreciation.

First he had to complete his reverse curls. He half-closed his eyes, summoned one last gauzy projection of Svetlana, and muscled through ten repetitions each over his last two sets. Just as he finished, early arrivals for the noontime aerobics class materialized across the training hall. Pleased about the timing, he removed the collars and plates from the bar, stowed all items on the storage rack, and made his way to the cardio area. Finding his favorite bike unoccupied, he leaned over and checked the stirrup settings, raised the adjustable seat to his customary height, and released the spring-loaded pin.

"Russell, I need your advice..."

Even before looking up Piper recognized the speaker. Vika, the owner of the club. Divorced. Broaching forty though looking rather younger. Well-known in Minsk, thanks to the prominence of her establishment. Toned and attractive enough to appear on her own billboard advertisements. Somehow, in the course of casual conversation the week before, she'd tuned into the fact that his wife was in the States. Piper liked her well enough, but also divined her angle. She stood tight by the handlebars.

"Sure Vika. How can I help?"

"I've decided to study English. I'd like to find a tutor."

"Great. Just beginning?"

"I took a couple of years in school. But it was so long ago I've mostly forgotten. Now I'd like to get serious about it. I want to speak with foreigners. Maybe travel to the U.S.A."

"That's no problem. I know some tutors who are associated with the Embassy."

"Russian tutors? That wasn't what I had in mind."

"There are lots of talented local linguists in Minsk. They're more than capable of getting you started with English."

She considered this for an instant. Then smiled and edged nearer, just centimeters from his elbow.

"Can you give me a few contacts, in the coming week or so?"

"No problem. I'll bring some along on my next workout."

"I appreciate that." She paused and smiled. "And if I want to practice with a native speaker?"

Piper imagined incidental exchanges at the club---coinciding with
breaks in his workouts, or ideally, during stretching sessions at the
end. She obviously had something else in mind. He smiled back at her,
affected all the same by her closeness.

"I'll always be happy to help, Vika."

"I'll let you get on with your workout, then."

As she walked off, Piper mounted the bike and renewed his assessment from his first days at the club. Vika was an entrepreneur. Not
afraid of going after what she wanted, which he appreciated to certain
extent. Even though she fell outside his usual parameters she was an
explicit, magnetic presence and he considered inserting her into his
cardio phase, if only for one day.

Svetlana, a more potent hazard, was in any case likely to dominate
his training sessions for the rest of the week.

Before inputting his workout settings, he nonetheless made discreet survey of the latest arrivals for aerobics, and fastened onto one
lush and chestnut-haired exemplar, in her early 20s, sporting a bared
midriff. The girl began loosening up with toe touches, her hips com-
pressing and releasing against the taut spandex of her workout briefs.
Detecting his gaze, she looked up and made eye contact for several
seconds; not going so far as to smile, but obviously pleased she'd been
noticed...After she looked away Piper allowed the 10 seconds for her
image to embed his memory. Then, while increasing his RPMs, he
punched in his program, session time and difficulty level, and pressed
"Enter."

As his vision blurred, he caught one last sight of the girl before
he closed his eyes. That was sufficient. In his interior visualizations
he imagined himself standing behind her, unclothed except for final
items. There were no pretenses, or artificial barriers; she bent forward,
arched and receptive, briefs already off...He pulled her elasticized
thong off her rounded haunches and let it fall to her feet, while he

spaced his feet and drew closer, readying himself....At infiltration she gasped, triggering the same reaction from him...As his RPMs steadied he pictured the jiggle of soft flesh around her flanks, her warm slickness overran his other senses, and his oxygen flow became integrated and primal...

Breathing was vital during the beginning and middle portions of his programs---particularly his exhalations, to prevent CO_2 buildup. So was relaxation, for efficient distribution of energy. He kept his palms on the spread of her hips, guiding rather than gripping, losing himself, surrendering to the moment. As long as he stayed wholly focused on the act, all the other optimizations took care of themselves.

Sometimes he felt guilty about these tableaus. But not for long.

He just had to remember the purpose behind them.

And to keep them abstract.

*   *   *

To Lena the soaring ceilings and grand décor of the concert hall amplified short silences---much like the hush between symphony movements. Same held for opening bars that followed, of whatever variety. Here, words acquired wider reverberation. Probably another reason Shinkevich had chosen the location.

Therefore she paused for several cadences before continuing.

"I followed your instructions in that regard," she said, re-fixing her gaze upward onto the KGB official. Shinkevich's arms remained uncrossed. He leaned further forward. "...That is, I waited for him to mention your meeting with me."

"And he apologized?"

"The very first moment we met at the monument."

"What were his exact words?"

Lena wasn't sure if the KGB had been able to eavesdrop on this first portion, due to the statue. She and Morris had not yet turned off their cell-phones. So she told the truth. Shinkevich eased his eyebrows by a miniscule degree. Test passed. "We heard most of your little lecture on Kupala," he said. "What was the point?"

"Twofold. First, it was a lesson. So I held to subject. Second, I wanted to make sure he understood the seriousness of his situation."

"Does he?"

"Seems so. You heard his response."

Kuabashin eyes re-narrowed. He didn't like such directness.

"I'm not saying that to be flip, Dimitri Nikaelovich. I really sought to clarify the picture. For myself also as much as anyone. That Morris is not a spy. And that he wants to put this matter to rest as much as I do."

Shinkevich assessed her for a moment and scoffed. "That doesn't square with his trip to Vilnius. We still don't know what he did there."

Lena had thought this through.

"I believe he's told me the full story. He's talked frequently about golf since I've known him. It really seems he just needed to get away for the weekend, playing a game he enjoys."

Shinkevich's eyes narrowed even further.

"Again, Lena don't think you're able to mislead me. It won't work."

She waited another downbeat.

"Why would I do that? I've concluded that cooperation with you is the best means of ensuring Morris' safety and my own."

"Well-worded phrase, Elena Grigorovna. For your sake I hope it's true."

Shinkevich hung silent for a cadence or two of his own, using the setting for more menacing effect. His last words reverberated against her backrest.

"...Otherwise, for all your cleverness, you may be getting in over your head."

CHAPTER 57

Well before Morris showed up on the main plaza at the Academy of Sciences, Lena spotted the KGB surveillance vehicle: a black Volga parked in the small lot next to the children's hospital across the street. Two men were inside; the one in the passenger seat giving her a blunt stare. Obviously anticipating this rendezvous. She wondered if other agents were already situated in surrounding offices or apartment, equipped with electronic eavesdropping gear. This time, in any event, she'd resolved to play along. Make it easier for them.

When Morris finally emerged along the Prospekt, one minute late, she stepped out from the towering columns of the Presidium building and waved. He crossed the square and ascended the steps, carrying his laptop case.

"Thanks for meeting me on such short notice, Evan."

He glanced among the columns. She could tell what he was thinking.

"These are concrete," she said.

Morris intuited her meaning. He appeared unsure whether to keep his guard up. "You said this wasn't a lesson."

"No. And I chose this location for a reason. It's away from your Institute---and the curiosity of your programmers. I wanted this to be discreet and open at the same time."

He gave her a quizzical look.

"...Partly to reassure the KGB." She nodded over toward the Volga. He followed her glance and didn't take long to recognize the vehicle, then re-examined her.

"Problems?"

"Well, let me put it this way," she answered. "I met Dimitri Shinkevich again this morning. Another unexpected encounter." She waited for a bus to pass by the Volga. When she resumed she was careful to enunciate her words. "He wasn't exactly pleased about our outdoor lesson yesterday. He's obviously tired of surprises. After Vilnius, I mean."

Morris winced and cast his eyes upward along the columns, while an older man with a briefcase passed by them and descended the steps---perhaps a senior scientist from the Academy. Rush-hour foot traffic crisscrossed the square below.

"He re-iterated his expectations," she continued. "I said I understood. I tried to convince him that I could be an asset to him."

"You? How? I wish I'd never gotten you involved."

"It's too late for that, Evan. We're in this together. We have the same interests. I told him that."

She paused, making sure their faces were unobstructed to surveillance.

"...He wants you to be open. Again, no more surprises."

Morris looked down over at the Volga again, increasingly catching on. "You know Lena..." he said. "I've thought more about this since last night. Shinkevich's taken a hard line so far. But he hasn't really mistreated us. He seems like an intelligent guy. My guess is that we can reason with him."

Lena had to refrain from grimacing. There were limits to her play-acting. A cluster of traffic roared by on the Prospekt.

"Our next lesson isn't until tomorrow," she concluded. "I said this would be brief. Call it an exercise in confidence-building. By the way I'm taking the metro home. Are you headed home also?"

"That's my plan."

"Care to join me? I'm just going one stop,"

He intuited her purpose at once.

*   *   *

Both of them stayed silent as they descended into the station. At Lena's prompting they walked halfway down the platform and stood close to one of the square pillars. She scanned nearby faces, seeing no one who appeared suspicious, and waited until a train pulled into the opposite track, drowning out most voices. She drew close to Morris and spoke into his ear. "Okay, let's turn off our phones," she said, extracting hers from her purse. "That will let us speak freely, at least for a minute or two."

When both their phones were off, Morris didn't waste any seconds. "You realize my last remark up there was for KGB consumption, Lena."

"Thank goodness. I was worried."

A southbound train pulled into the platform. Several people boarded with them into the same car. Lena assessed them quickly and stood close to Morris; the two of them faced the doors as they closed. "I want to ask you about one element in particular," she said. "It's essential that you not withhold anything from me."

"Go ahead."

"Your lawyer. Have you been in contact with him?"

"Not yet. But we have a system set up. Secure e-mail. I should check it soon. If not tonight, then tomorrow."

"Why? What's he up to?"

Morris glanced down at the floor of the train car. Lena sensed an instant of hesitation.

"He's an insurance policy, as I said."

"He's not going to produce any surprises of his own?"

"Not if I can help it."

Their train was already slowing.

"This is my stop. For both our sakes, I would suggest you keep a close handle on whatever he's doing."

"I'll stay on it, Lena. Don't worry."

The platform showed through the windows. After she exited she turned back to remind him to turn his phone back on, before the doors closed, and found him already doing just that. He really was catching on to their new exigencies.

That presented at least one cause for reassurance.

CHAPTER 58

Instead of exiting at *Victory Square* station, Morris stood back from the door and gripped the support rail. Lena's exhortations were on the mark; there was no sense in postponement.. After the bustle and interchanges of the *Oktyabraska* nexus, the usual canned voice came over the subway speakers. Unintelligible to him, but he knew the sequence and got off at the next stop. On the platform he turned right toward the west-side exit and mounted the stairs. At the top, rather than splitting right or left, he stopped at the outsized bust of Lenin and pretended to check his cell-phone screen. Other passengers streamed by him until the passage emptied out. There were no lingerers or KGB trackers.

Tonight he didn't mind if Shinkevich knew his location. However he preferred to be unobserved, at least for the remainder of the evening.

Outside the station he crossed the sidewalk fronting Independence Square, and descended an escalator into the underground mall. Along its main concourse he paused to examine a few shop windows, checking again to make sure he wasn't followed. Several minutes later, he boarded the express elevator to the top floor of *Hotel Minsk*, and pressed number seven for the *Seven Skies* restaurant. There were only a few people in the bar area as he passed through, and as he anticipated he found the restaurant empty.

The female maitre d' seemed to recognize him. He hoped nothing had changed since his last visit.

"By the window, please," he said in English.

The girl led him to a table alongside an expanse of plate glass, where he'd positioned himself several times before, and handed him a menu. Minutes later a young blond waitress walked over, polite and attentive, who'd waited on him before. Once she took his order and left, he shifted his place setting, reached down, unzipped his case, and set up his laptop on the table, trying to appear unhurried. While the computer booted he looked over at the red-brick spire of the city's main Roman Catholic church, then onto the public gardens below. Several fountains were interspersed among the greenery. About ten people were sitting on benches. No one was looking up.

His next glance was diagonal, to a four-story, rose-colored office building, between the gardens and Independence Square. Home of the Belarussian State Architecture Committee---a fact he'd discovered during a lone dinner in May, when he'd turned on his computer to review that day's coding from the lab...He returned his gaze to his screen...

The wireless icon appeared on his task bar. Active. He clicked on it.

Just as he'd hoped. The network identifier for the Architecture Committee. Still configured for open access. Signal strength, from his position two stories higher and about 50 meters away was "Very Good." In seconds he was on-line.

In his planning with Grinevicius, he'd counted on this surreptitious resource. Still, in the unlikely event that the KGB detected his connection, he opened multiple browsers. First his company e-mail. Then the *Wall Street Journal* and *Investors' Daily*, followed by his Charles Schwab account. At last he opened the @mail.lt site. He entered the username *sundaygolfers*. Then the password: *centroklubas*.

The Inbox was empty. But there was a message in the Drafts folder:

Evan,

I booked an earlier flight than planned; I'm already in Washington.

I called in to the DOD this afternoon seeking an appointment. I had trouble navigating the bureaucracy---until I mentioned the "55 Most Wanted List" and a possible Iraqi fugitive. That got their attention.

I have an appointment tomorrow morning at 10 a.m. with William McCosker, department head for the DOD's special counter-terrorism task force.

Don't worry---in keeping with your instructions I will reveal little at this stage. My objective will be exploration. No more.

Regards,

John

The phrase "special counter-terrorism task force" stood out and unsettled Morris a little. While he mulled it, the waitress returned with his bread tray and Coke; he switched screens to his *Wall Street Journal* browser until she'd gone again. In short order he reached a decision, which he punctuated by sitting up straight in his chair. Given all the unknowns, he determined the lawyer needed some latitude. Rather than a cautionary note, he opted for a factual summary, covering events in Minsk since his return.

Grinevicius was primarily his defense attorney, after all. Monetary reward, if there was any, was tangential to his case.

The main complication was what to tell Lena. Though he had the whole next day to figure that out. He took a bite of bread roll, washed it down, and started typing. He wished to finish the message and store it in the Drafts folder before dinner arrived.

CHAPTER 59

Piper rounded the corner on the lookout, and spotted Agent 550 descending steps onto the promenade: brief case in hand, bound for work, bang on schedule. Maintaining pace, Piper melded to his standard course along the embankment, and seconds later, near the Gorky statue, converged to within four meters of the KGB officer, who gave him a cursory glance. Underneath his sport-watch, a buzz vibrated his skin. Without breaking stride, he blew into the pedestrian tunnel and launched a power-thirty out the other end.

Along the curve toward the Ministry of Defense, no youthful female pedestrians came into view, with or without their short-skirts and satin-stretch trousers. Today, in any case, he didn't need them. Agent 1300 was still on vacation. Moreover he had a subject at the ready and could skip preliminaries.

…Svetlana's tank top and shorts already lay on the floor of the hotel room at *Raubichi*, and she didn't protest as he removed her fine under-layers and dropped them beside the king-sized bed. An animalistic rumble rose from his thorax as she kneeled on the mattress, raising her backside….

Rear-entry always supplied the strongest energy blast, especially under forward momentum. He preferred to finish that way as well.

Which still allowed a gamut of other positions in between, each transition delivering a fresh jack and spurt of locomotion. Spine angled up or down...Knees bent or straight, splayed or together... Face-to-face or chest-to back...Standing or sitting...Calves raised or wrapped...

Always driving forward, up and inside. *Always forward...*

Based on 550's previous productivity, he suspected his watch carried some worthwhile intelligence. But he had to hold to pattern.

There were still seven kilometers to go.

*   *   *

Around halfway Piper hit his rhythmic zone. His strides lengthened, his breathing became pervasive, his movements automatic. Unforced but intense. Concentrated but natural. He felt transported, uplifted, in concord with nature.

The same way he did during exceptional sex.

Before re-attaining the Prospekt he leaned into a hard-right corner, passed a stone staircase on his left, and aimed down a long, shaded alley, smooth and unobstructed, which constituted his finish. An elderly man on a park bench scarcely registered as he flew by, increasing tempo and opening up speed. Thirty meters further he quick-timed his breathing to match his stride pace and maximize oxygen intake, and at a designated lamppost began counting his final power-fifty. All considerations of form---squared-loose shoulders, forearms in parallel motion, gentle tilt, fluid back-kick---came together. Instinct overrode conscious decision.

His body ascended toward simulated climax, propelling him into a trance. Svetlana's words came out half in a moan, together with inklings of immortality.

Zakonchi vnuytri menya.
Finish inside me.

At the twenty-count his lamppost-finish approached in a blur on the right. He exploded faster...penetrating to the fullest extent...all energy directed toward one purpose as he glided over the finish line. At the line he hit his stop-watch and slowed to a walk, turning his face skyward and gasping for air.

When he refocused his vision he noted with satisfaction that he'd shaved another 14 seconds off his time---another peak performance. As recovery took hold and his breathing slowed, he cut into the park's main plaza, turning his eyes half-closed again toward the sky, overrun with exquisite, countervailing sensations.

Expenditure and renewal. Obliteration and fulfillment. Conclusion and perpetuation.

The closest he came to post-coital rapture, minus actual consummation.

At his customary location he placed one foot on the marble ledge, leaned over, and elongated a hamstring. Clarity returned by gradations, together with fresh insights. First, this energy---this incomparable strength, speed and endurance that he'd identified and exploited in his effort toward self-regulation---was not available from any other source. Not from competition. Not from frustration or anger or narcissism. Least of all from aspirations for longevity.

Second, these tableaus weren't just about energy expenditure. They were also about energy *optimization*, particularly during his runs. Only through simulated sex did he achieve his most graceful and efficient form, with integrated oxygen intake, absence of superfluous vertical motion, and unnecessary joint impact. The key was focus: not to let his mind wander beyond the two or three square meters that encompassed the act, and to center in particular on the point of genital contact---the most basic and powerful energy source of all. As long as he adhered to this construct, critical juices flowed to affected tissues, and his movements became unitary and forward-directed, which in turn made him less prone to injuries: the sort of nascent twinges and aches in his hamstrings, knees and ligaments that often nagged runners his age. He was more attuned to self-preservation, less susceptible to harm.

He grasped the ledge with both hands, and pushed one leg straight backward, distending an Achilles tendon and continuing the line of thought.

Always it was the endpoint that kept him going, driving though kilometers, ever-closer to blissful culmination. In broad sense, he supposed it represented one facet of the survival instinct---the same one that kept pre-civilized males running for their lives through forests or across savannas, at least long enough to propagate, before perishing to the desolations of nature or the predations of enemy savages.

Delivery. Deliverance. *The importance of finishing.*

After stretching his other Achilles he pulled back from the ledge and paced a dozen steps back into the plaza, shaking out his arms and legs to transmit extra oxygen to his extremities. In the process another association flushed up, from closer timeline. He wondered if Pheidippides, the original marathoner, had visualized a woman to propel himself back to Athens to warn of the approaching Persians---employing a similar method in service to his state.

The Greek had perhaps directed testosterone to noble ends. And persevered to completion, even if his particular form of immortal glory was different than the one he had in mind.

On this more detached and historical note Piper glanced at his sport-watch and remembered 550's intelligence report. At once he pivoted back to the corner of the park, toward his apartment building. Ruminations were fine. And his tableaus served a constructive purpose, as long as he didn't get sidetracked.

He didn't face the lethal threats of pre-civilized man, or the military exigencies of Pheidippides. But he couldn't forget he still had work to do.

CHAPTER 60

Lena spotted Morris while waiting near the kiosk; he was the only person in the area carrying a laptop case. Upon noticing her in turn, he walked over, displaying the same concern he'd evinced on the phone.

"Didn't we decide this was asking for trouble? I mean outdoor lessons."

"I tried to alert Shinkevich by phone several times. I couldn't get through. His secretary kept saying he was 'indisposed.' "

He frowned and set down his case. "All the same I have some qualms about it. "I'm going to trying calling his mobile," he said. Lena didn't object as he punched the number. Ten seconds later he clicked off the connection. "Turned off," he confirmed. "Couldn't even leave a message." After a moment of reflection he glanced around the small plaza. Most other people in the area were parents, with young children. He now appeared a little puzzled.

"Okay, now that we're here, what do you have in mind?"

She gestured upward with her left hand, to the gently moving assembly that towered overhead.

"I thought we'd take a ride on the Ferris Wheel."

Morris stiffened a little, showing obvious discomfort. Lena hadn't expected this reaction.

"That's my plan, anyway. Ever ridden it before?"

"No."

He did retain enough focus to turn off his phone. She did likewise.

"…It suits our purposes for two reasons. First, the metal struts and rotating movement should thwart any directional listening devices. Second, it provides quite a panorama of the city, and therefore a pretext for our lesson."

Morris looked up, contemplating the prospect. "The cabins seem to offer more protection than the open-air seats."

"That's what I thought also."

As they purchased tickets at the kiosk he relaxed somewhat but still evinced little enthusiasm. After a short wait in a queue, they boarded one of the red-and-gold plastic-and-plexiglass cabins, sitting opposite each other across the small table affixed to the side. Once the attendant had bolted the door and their enclosure had left the boarding area, Lena swept her hand out toward the city. The gesture was for show, in case they were subject to visual surveillance from below.

"I want to talk about your lawyer," she said. "My apartment obviously isn't safe for that." Morris held eye contact with her across the plastic table in the middle of the cabin, looking neither right nor left out the windows. "Did you manage to receive his e-mail communication last night?".

"Yes." He took a long inhalation. "…He's in Washington now. It's part of the plan I outlined with him in Vilnius. Doing some research on the man I encountered in the berry patch."

"Washington? Does that mean the man you saw is American?"

"I'd rather not say, at this point."

Lena took this in. Morris hesitated, weighing his words

"I'm starting to have doubts about this policy of keeping me in the dark," she said. "Are you sure that these investigations by your lawyer won't cause additional problems for us?"

"I don't see why they should."

"Okay, for now I'll have to take your word for it."

Lena looked around. They'd risen above the treetops and were approaching the quarter-point in the rotation, so that the city spread about below them in full quadrants. For the sake of their lesson ruse, she scooted to one side of her bench and pointed eastward across the park. "See Victory Square down there? The monument is plainly visible. It's a great perspective."

When she repeated the phrase in Russian, instead of sliding closer to the window himself, he remained seated in the center of the bench and shot only a passing glance in the indicated direction. Then looked straight forward again.

Lena had never seen a fissure in his composure, and this wasn't one either. Nonetheless she wondered if he suffered from vertigo. Though every individual had quirks of one kind or another, she supposed, even someone as inscrutable as Morris.

"Sure you don't want to take a longer look?" she said. "It's really a great view."

"I'll also take your word for it," he said.

CHAPTER 61

Piper re-read the hard copy of 550's transmission, shook his head, and released a hard exhalation through his nostrils. American citizens in Belarus were so few in number that they'd never presented problems during his tenure. Seconds later Stapleton's image materialized on the flat-screen. A digital readout in the lower-right corner displayed Washington time: 13:20.

"Sorry for my unavailability this morning, Russell. I've delayed your dinner."

"Summer. I eat late anyway."

The bags under the Deputy Director's eyes had acquired a grayish tinge. Gallstone tended to have that effect.

550's report didn't hedge. There'd been a spasm of internal recrimination and turmoil within the Belarussian KGB. A high-ranking department head named Shinkevich had been re-assigned. The American citizen in question---thus far unknown to One K---had become an obsession. According to 550 that often presaged some kind of aggressive operation. Even liquidation, or so-called "wet job." Bottom line: this was serious.

"When do you expect your next report from 550?" Stapleton asked.

"My next run on Saturday, perhaps. No earlier."

"Our late schedule today may work to our advantage, then."

Piper straightened a little with surprise. Belarus was such a centralized and isolated regime that worthwhile intelligence seldom emanated from outside the country.

"Remember 'Iraq's 55 Most Wanted,'" Stapleton continued. "...Put out by Defense in 2003?"

"Of course. A little cartoonish, for my taste. But the media latched onto it."

Stapleton conveyed a sardonic nod.

"...Wasn't that shut down in 2005, or thereabouts?"

"That's right. Most were apprehended, as you know."

Mention of the program made Piper recollect reports from early 2003---rumors, really---that certain Iraqi fugitives had taken refuge in Belarus. The Agency had never confirmed any leads. Stapleton resumed.

"...Turns out an American lawyer---one who practices in Vilnius, named John Grinevicius---has just contacted the Defense Department. Claims he has information on the whereabouts of Amoud al-Tikriti..."

"Hussein's main financial guy?"

"Right. Not on the list. Evaded the dragnet. Lived for a while in Switzerland, then ran afoul of...certain powerful patrons, let's say... and disappeared, for reasons I'll describe later. This lawyer Grinevicius says al-Tikriti has been sighted by his client---as yet unnamed---an American citizen. In Belarus."

"And you think there's a connection between this and 550's report?"

"Pretty striking coincidence, I'd say."

"Indeed." Piper paused to digest the implications. "...I'm surprised Defense volunteered the information so readily."

"One would wish. The fact is we found out through back channels. Defense isn't aware yet that we know."

Piper nodded. "Are we able to run it further?"

"I already have, thanks to help from the Lithuanian STT…"During Piper's regular visits to Vilnius he often interacted with the Lithuanian intelligence organization. Small but professional. "…They provided me the identities of all American citizens who entered Lithuania during the past two weeks. Two hundred forty-two in all. Big number. But they broke it down. Only five crossed the border from Belarus. One by train and four by car."

"I can handle that."

"You won't have to. The four in the car were the Wellingtons, from our Embassy in Riga. Parents and two kids. En route home from a vacation in Ukraine. That leaves just one possibility, the one on the train. His name is Evan Morris."

"Doesn't ring a bell."

"It probably wouldn't. He's a manager for Cognition Software, a U.S. high-tech firm based in Silicon Valley. Supervises an offshore software lab in Minsk. I'll send over what we've got."

"Thanks."

Piper at once suspected some kind of set-up by Gallstone. Precedents were abundant. He asked if Stapleton would bring it up in his meeting with the President the next day.

"I've been thinking about that. Strictly speaking it doesn't fall within my briefing parameters. However I'm not sure it will make a difference. You know how tight Gallstone is with Defense. I'm sure he's fully informed." Stapleton's on-screen expression said the rest. "My biggest worry is that Gallstone, in his quest to turn up the heat…to move to 'elevated status,' will latch onto this. That he may finally have the pretext he's been looking for."

"Namely, Evan Morris."

The Deputy Director nodded.

"Start girding yourself, Russell."

*　　*　　*

Lena stood in the bathtub and squeezed some of the water from her hair. Her cell-phone chortled from the hallway the instant she reached for her towel. She let it ring through to messaging.

Baths and showers fell on her inviolable list. Particularly after the stresses of the past few days.

With deliberate movements, she ran the towel down her all sides of her hair, then rubbed it lightly over her body with two hands: first over her breasts and shoulders, then her back and abdomen, and in turn down her legs, soothed by the terrycloth on her skin.

Next she re-addressed her hair, mussing it slightly to dry her scalp, then pushing upward and wrapping it in the towel. She looked down and beheld her own nakedness for a moment, more or less liking what she saw, though never fully satisfied, before finally reached for a second towel, which she circled over her breasts and under her arms, cinching it on one side.

To her, some of life's best therapies occurred in solitude.

Her phone rang again. In case the caller was Morris, she stepped out of the tub and walked to the hallway. Seeing the number, she flipped open the mouthpiece with a trace of resignation.

"Hi Natasha…just got out of the shower. I see you called twice."

"For a moment I thought you'd extended your lesson with Evan Morris," Natasha said with a chiding tone.

Once again, Lena didn't indulge the joke. She asked if it was something important.

"Sort of…Remember that U.S. Embassy party I mentioned a couple of weeks ago? Well, it's on Friday evening. And I have to respond tomorrow, for the guest list. Still planning on attending?"

There was enough else going on without the distraction of a social event. Until she identified another angle.

"What time?"

"Six o'clock. It's a pre-dinner cocktail party…in honor of a couple of writers, as far as I understand. You should be in your element."

"Okay. I'll be there."

After Lena closed her phone she proceeded to her room, sat down in front of her mirror, and removed the damp towel from her head. She contemplated her image for a moment, then re-smoothed her hair with two hands and reached for her brush. Her hair was tangled, so her first brush strokes were gentle.

She was in no rush. She needed time to think through her idea. She wanted to be sure before she ran it by Morris.

CHAPTER 62

Straight from an obliterating, late-morning blowout at *Bagira*, Piper rendezvoused with Anthony Fletcher and Leonid Kravchuk, his British and Ukrainian counterparts, also posted to their embassies under diplomatic cover. Today's venue: an outdoor terrace at *Ristorante Ostia Antica* at Troistkoe Predmetsva, table under the canopy overlooking his running route, well-exposed to cooling breezes off the Svisloch. Piper ordered salad and risotto. Fletcher chose cold celery soup and rigatoni, Kravchuk, the more substantial *Vitello Milanese* with spaghetti.

The Ukrainian station chief was sturdy and about Piper's age. His inclusion in these conclaves since the spring clearly galled the Russians, not least because the operative language was English. The three men scanned the other tables for signs of surveillance, and checked their directional-listening sensors. Only then did Piper open the week's business, alerting them to the pending National Security Council meeting.

Fletcher---in his mid-thirties, normally amiable and detached--- gloomed whenever they discussed initiatives from the White House. The Briton swallowed some sparkling water and took a long, slow breath; it was clear he was also counting days until the presidential election in November.

"I'm aware what that status entails in a general sense, Russell," he said. "Bigger spotlight, more pressure…Question is: what's it likely to mean here in Minsk, on the ground?"

Piper outlined basics: face-to-face briefings with Gallstone every three weeks, either in Europe or Washington; more aggressive benchmarks and stricter timetables; insistence on new agents; intensified rhetoric from the White House. "Also more funding," he added. "Gallstone has few qualms about that. I myself would prefer to see taxpayer monies used toward saner ends."

Fletcher shook his head. Kravchuk, with his beefy joviality and suffering the opposite problem, endeavored to lighten the tone.

"Send some my way, if you like," he said with a laugh.

The three of them paused with the arrival of the salad and celery soup. As Fletcher and Kravchuk took first spoonfuls, Piper shifted to Morris, recounting the intelligence he had received the previous day from 550, without, as usual, disclosing the source. A light gust blew off the river. Fletcher looked up from his soup, while Kravchuk straightened, dabbing his chin with his napkin.

The discussion turned serious again.

*   *   *

An hour later Piper was back at his desk. Two folders lay before him. One contained a printout of additional information on Morris, just forwarded from Langley:

Birthplace: *New York, NY, 1974*
Parents: *Eugene b. 1948, dentist; Laura, born 1949, housewife and substitute mathematics teacher*
Siblings: *Caitlin (Kate) sister, b. 1973; Blake, sister b. 1976*

Education: *Millburn High School, Short Hills, NJ; graduated 1992 Cornell University, B.S. Computer Science/Applied Mathematics, graduated 1996*

Career: Computer programmer, Cognition Software Corporation, 1996-2000
Head of IP sub-structure development department 1997-2000
Unsalaried activity 2000-2004 (independent investor) active in equity and options markets
Programming manager, Cognition Software Corporation 2006-present

Residency: Palo Alto, CA 1996-2006
Minsk, Belarus January 2007 - present
Spouse: Nora, married 2001, divorced 2006
Children: none
Foreign Travel: Hannover Germany (business), 1997, 1998, 1999
Italy, Spain 2001 (honeymoon)
Australia, French Polynesia 2002; Bali, Indonesia 2003

Special note on income: IRS filings from 1996-2000 indicate annual salary and bonus totaling from $65,000 and $90,000. In the year 2000 Morris realized approximately $5.5 million in long and short-term capital gains through exercise of Cognition Software stock options. In 2001-2002, he realized another $4.2 million in short and long-term capital gains through self-initiated options transactions. For tax years 2004 and 2005 he reported zero income. Since returning to work for Cognition Software his salary and bonus have averaged between $110,000 and $135,000 per year.

Additional background investigation currently in progress. More details to follow.

Piper contemplated the portrait. What most caught his eye was the data on income, notable for someone in his late 20s. Followed, perhaps, by some sort of financial plunge, and/or material setback from his divorce. Then re-employment by Cognition and posting to Minsk, of all places...

Morris' passport photo was attached. Dark hair---neatly parted and combed. Slender, judging by rather bony neck and shoulders. Careful, non-descript smile. Fastidious. Not a face one normally associated with high-stakes options trading. Or with misbegotten marriages, for that matter.

Even less---the type to rummage in politics and fun afoul of foreign intelligence services.

He turned to his computer and typed a quick message to the domestic research department at Langley, requesting additional financial information about Morris for the 2003-2006 tax years. He then opened the other folder, containing a report from the Quentin Hill, Acting Consul in Minsk:

Through further search of our database I discovered that that Evan Morris has has had two contacts with the Embassy during his current period of residency----not one as I initially reported. The first occurred on 9 January 2008, one week after his arrival in Minsk, when he filled out the on-line U.S. citizen registration form on the Embassy web site. He listed his coordinates as follows:

Residence: Communisticheskaya Street 5
            Apartment 37
            Tel. 172-84-71-29

Office: Institute of Engineering Cybernetics
          Surganova Street 6, Suite 501
          Tel. 172-89-32-73
          Mobile Tel. 8-029-3543116

The second occurred six days later, when he sent a query to Consular Services, requesting the name of a local Russian language tutor. One of our staffers suggested three options, with whom the Embassy has

extensive previous experience, all previously vetted. From these Morris
selected Lena Antonova, aged 28.

    Ms. Antonova has tutored eight spouses and teenage children of
Embassy personnel during the previous five years, for periods of three
to eight months, and received consistent and glowing reviews. She also
worked on a temporary basis for the Embassy in the summer of 2001
as a telephone receptionist, while still a graduate student. Due to her
previous employment and continuing association we have kept Ms.
Antonova's profile on file. Here is what we have:

When Piper flipped to the next page his eyes went straight to the color,
passport-sized photograph in the upper right corner. Blond hair, clear
gray eyes, smooth complexion. Even in mug-shot, a composed allure
he associated with a certain category of well-educated Russian women.
Feminine. Unpretentious about her beauty. Never intimidated.

    A little like Svetlana. He read further:

Name: *Elena Grigorovna Antonova*
Birthplace: *Minsk, Belarus; 23 October 1979*
Parents: *Grigori Alexeivich Antonov b. 1947, architect, deceased*
2003; Olesya Ivanovna Antonova, born 1951, economist
Siblings: *None*

Education: *Minsk English Language Gymnasia No. 2, graduated*
1995; five gold medals; victor 1995 nationwide all-schools English
language competition
Minsk State Linguistic University, Master's Degree in English, with
minor in French, graduated 2000, Highest Honors
Minsk State Linguistic University, PhD. Comparative English
Literature, conferred June 2005
Career: *Associate Professor, Department of English and American*
Literature, Minsk State Linguistic University 2005- present

Residency: *Minsk, Belarus*
Marital status: *Unmarried in 2001; current status unknown*
Children: *Unknown*
Foreign Travel: *Russia (1999, 2003); Ukraine (numerous occasions through summer 2007; Lithuania (2004 and 2005); France and Italy (2006); Great Britain (2002 and 2007)*

Piper re-examined the photograph, which incited an extra frisson upon second glance. His contemplation was interrupted by a knock at his door. His first guess was Svetlana; however the knocker was Hill.

"Timely entry, Quentin. Just reading your brief on Lena Antonova."

"Speaking of timely entries," he asked "Still going to the cocktail party tomorrow evening, at Zhuravinka?"

"Why? Will she be there?"

"You guessed it."

CHAPTER 63

What Lena noticed first were the expensive cars: late-model Mercedes, Jaguars, Volvos and Citroens, gleaming clean, most bearing the *CD* prefix on their plates for *Corps Diplomatique*. A subset bore flags, forward-mounted on their hoods---ambassadors' limousines, attended by drivers. Dual Stars and Stripes jutted from a black SUV parked front-and-center near the entrance, now used by the acting U.S. Charge d'Affaires. Also in evidence: the Union Jack and French and Italian tricolors. As she and Natasha approached the entrance the Polish Ambassador pulled up and disembarked, identified by his red-and-white standard.

The West was out in force. Albeit for a social event.

Two solemn but courteous security personnel in dark suits checked their invitations and directed them through a metal detector. Inside the lower lobby a young Belarussian employee of the Embassy greeted them more decorously, supplying nametags and a pamphlet on the two Belarussian novelists: the honored guests. In short order they joined a procession up the curving staircase. Natasha glanced at the pamphlet.

"I've never read any books by either of these writers. What about you?"

"One of them. In the original Russian."

"Worthwhile?"

"Mediocre, to be frank."

Natasha observed her.

"You look so concentrated, Lena. "Don't tell me it's because you're keen on meeting foreigners…" She smiled. "You're usually so nonchalant."

Lena gave her friend a forbearing glance.

"…Well, for my part I'm not out to get acquainted with our writers," Natasha added. "Let's put it that way."

Upstairs, the restaurant was sequestered off by the buffet and open bar, pushing activity to the terrace. Natasha's eyes went into scan-mode as they proceeded outside. Lena hardly paid attention. She was performing a scan of her own.

Her preferred nationality was different. So were her motives.

Of the two sections on the terrace, the first was semi-enclosed, with all-weather roof and large, retractable windows which were now open onto the river. The second was full-outdoors except for an overhead canopy. They ambled through both, and positioned themselves next to the railing, where a waiter served them wine. From fixed vantage Americans didn't prove difficult to spot, despite their small number. In their role as hosts they wore nametags, along with small American-flag pins. And Lena was seeking just one---the only one with whom she had a pretext for direct contact---despite the fact that she didn't know what he looked like.

"Who are you looking for again?" Natasha asked taking a sip.

Lena pulled in her gaze. "The official who organized the function. Quentin Hill. So happens he referred Evan Morris to me in January, based on my past record with the Embassy…Seems like a good place to start."

Natasha's attention was already elsewhere. She nudged Lena with her elbow.

"See that guy standing near the window over there? Just walked in? Dark hair?"

Lena reluctantly followed Natasha's sightline and nodded.

"I met him once. Works here for a charitable organization... Italian. Let's go over. "That guy he's talking to doesn't look bad either. English, maybe. And young."

Lena didn't bother with a second look. "I would, Natasha, but I'd prefer to thank this Quentin Hill before I start mingling. You're probably better off starting on your own anyway." Natasha shrugged, glanced down and smoothed her dress. "Well, let's reconnect a little later," she said. In an instant she was off, clasping her wine glass by the stem. At once Lena reached into her purse to turn off her cell-phone, then wrapped it in a handkerchief and zipped it inside her cosmetics case.

After a small sip of wine and deep breath, she began a circumnavigation of the outer terrace, and soon spotted a diplomat whom she guessed to be Hill. Drawing closer and reading his name tag, she confirmed it. He was conversing with two Belarussians in their 30s; whom she presumed to be the novelists. To her surprise, she quickly garnered Hill's attention, then mustered a smile, walked up, an introduced herself.

"I thought you were Lena Antonova," he said. "Also of the Language Institute, are you not?" Hill said.

"That's right. Thank you for inviting me. I also wished to meet you in person, after you referred me to Evan Morris last January."

"Our pleasure. He's in capable hands, I'm sure."

He switched to Russian and introduced her to the two Belarussians, who turned out to be the novelists. She greeted each in turn, exchanging the customary "priatno". *Pleased.* She noted to one that she had read his work. Both writers were polite but reserved. Hill re-addressed Lena, noting she seemed to be the only representative from academia present. "And we're delighted you've come...." He swept his hand across the gathering. "You help balance out the diplomats and businesspeople..." He checked his watch. "Now if you'll excuse me, it's time for me to fulfill one of my duties as acting head of mission."

Hill retreated with the two writers to a central position near the railing, where they were joined by a stout man in his early 60s wearing and expensive suit and gold cufflinks, and another man, slenderer, somewhat younger, with no tie. Hill took a moment to gain wider attention. "I'd like to present our honored guests," he said. "Whose splendid work we are celebrating this evening." Each writer made brief remarks in halting English. Hill then performed similar introductions for the other two men, who turned out to be the American publisher and Russian translator. The publisher made a brief speech of his own, before Hill concluded. "Before the evening is over...I urge all of you to stop over and say hello. I also urge you to read these fine books!"

After light applause, conversational clusters reformed and the party resumed. Accepting a wedge of brie-on-bread from a passing waiter, Lena took a bite and contemplated her options. Hill remained near the railing with the writers and translator. Discreet contact with an Embassy official was proving more difficult than she'd envisioned...Another face and figure caught her attention to Hill's right, taller than the others. Male, athletic shoulders, somehow familiar...

She needed an instant to place him. But not longer. The foreigner from *Bagira*.

He stood in quarter-profile, engaged in conversation with two other men about his own age, probably European diplomats. She shifted position slightly to gain a better view. This evening he wore a well-tailored light-gray summer suit and aquamarine silk tie. His nametag and flag-pin marked him as American, just as she'd guessed when he'd worn workout gear. If she got closer she'd be able to read his tag. But what then? Contrive an overture based on their shared membership at the health club? Try to maneuver him into one-on-one conversation? It was a stretch. Respectable Russian girls were never that forward with men---not even Natasha, for all her brazenness...

She took a small sip of wine and mulled her predicament. As she did, the American's interlocutors paused to deposit empty glasses on a passing tray, and the American performed a relaxed half-turn. His gaze found her at once; his face didn't change expression but she saw an unmistakable glimmer of identification in his eyes.

Maybe he'd noticed her at *Bagira* after all.

CHAPTER 64

Piper beheld Lena for a long instant, then turned back and swallowed the rest of his sparkling water. His first head-to-toe impression overrode the evening's other exigencies, numerous as they were. In live ensemble she was even more compelling than her file photograph. And she'd noticed him. Question was: why? As he deposited his empty glass on the waiter's tray he rifled through venues where they might have intersected.

Fletcher and Klaus Roeder now had free hands, not the latter's standard pose at events like this. Roeder, a German, quickly rectified the void and ordered another scotch.

"Don't tell my I'm the only one," he said.

"Sympathy, Klaus," Fletcher responded. "Some of us are on the front lines."

Roeder shrugged, corralled a waitress and plucked a spear of sausage and olive. His posting as Minsk liaison for the European Bank for Reconstruction and Development was largely figurehead. Albeit one with tax-free salary, abundant holidays and a six-week vacation, coupled with plans for August that centered on a rented, beach-front villa in Turkey. Here for the sole purpose of enjoying himself, which set him apart from Piper and Fletcher this evening, agreeable as he was. From across the terrace, Kravchuk assessed their threesome and came over, gripping what appeared to be gin-and-tonic. Apart from his other merits, the Ukrainian station chief was adept at orchestrating tame exits, thanks in part to his experience in soothing the truculent Russian bear.

Roeder broke into a smile as he saw him. "Timely approach, Leonid...We were speaking of front lines."

"Less so than usual tonight," Kravchuk joked.

"What? No one from Moscow to keep an eye on you?"

"Most of them are back in Moscow for consultations now, I'm happy to say. Only the Ambassador is here this evening, and he's leaving this weekend."

As if on cue, Russian Ambassador Grilov, who had just filtered onto the outdoor area, noticed their assemblage and shot them a distrustful glance. He appeared to be unaccompanied. The Russian FSB station chief Mironov, Piper knew, had just been re-assigned.

True to form, Kravchuk extended Grilov a polite nod before engaging Roeder on his vacation plans, allowing Piper and Fletcher to excuse themselves and split off in separate directions. Piper angled across the terrace, slid another glance over at Lena while he sidestepped two groups of conversationalists. The delay created an opening for Terrence Graybill, the publisher, to approach her from the side. Lena appeared too polite to brush him off. As Piper drew closer Graybill's gravelly intonation became audible.

"Are you here because of the books?"

"You could say that."

"I hoped so!"

Piper had heard worse lines. Especially from Western businessmen in Minsk, unattended by wives and on the prowl. Lena, appearing unimpressed by either the line or the cufflinks, mustered a passable smile and refracted her view-line back toward him. He nodded toward the buffet, which she seemed to understand, then heard her speak again as he passed by.

Her accent in English was slight and more pleasant to the ear than that of most Russians---precise diction without any forfeiture of femininity. At closer distance he also became more aware of her dimensions: average height, not towering, like some Russian girls. Gray eyes. Flawless pale skin. Slender without being underfed, with a little extra around the hips. His gaze then swept downward, taking in calves and tapered ankles, all of which only enhanced the composition.

As he continued toward the buffet, he re-combed memories outside her case file, and finally recognized where he might have seen her. At *Bagira*, an instantaneous glimpse, a flash in the mirror...

In any event she'd exited the realm of abstraction.

CHAPTER 65

At *Bagira,* Lena recalled, the American's eyes had appeared closed or half-closed. This evening, by contrast, his visual contact was unambiguous, even prolonged. Not lewd or propositional, exactly, but still...What aims did he have in mind? She hoped they weren't the same as those of Charles Graybill.

"Charlie," the publisher insisted.

"I'm Lena."

Lena returned a polite smile and took another small sip of wine. Graybill was overbearing, with his ostentatious cufflinks and superfluous suspenders, but engaging enough. Under different circumstances she might have even welcomed his company---for five or ten minutes. Just now she felt compelled to fill the pause before brushing him off.

While Graybill sipped his martini she flicked a glance onto the retreating back-and-shoulders of the American diplomat. Vectors and timing had been unfavorable as he'd passed; she'd been unable to read the name or position on his Embassy tag. However she now had an opening with someone other than Quentin Hill. That was, if she could shake off Graybill.

"American literature..." he asked. "Twentieth-century?"

"For the most part. Dreiser, London, Fitzgerald, Steinbeck, Hemingway, among others. You know. Standard canon."

The publisher's grin widened. "Ah…London, a longtime favorite in the Soviet Union. Fine writer. Nothing against him. But Hemingway. Well…Category all his own."

"I can't really disagree."

With no additional prompting Graybill launched into an encomium to the famous author. Lena listened enough to grasp the essence, which was that Hemingway's capacity to distill foreign cultures and political dislocations into powerful, accessible stories might have attracted him to the contemporary ex-USSR. The American diplomat was still within her sightline when he pulled up short and turned sideways. Concerned, she altered her stance slightly. Waylaid by a woman: younger…about her own age, a little taller, standing close and speaking into his ear. His wife, maneuvering him into a new cluster? Exhorting him to leave early? Lena squinted through the thicket of partygoers. The woman's coloring and manner of dress were immediate giveaways. Russian: a certain type of strawberry blond that was common in Minsk. She also noted a nametag on the woman's blouse. Part of the local staff at the Embassy. She exhaled slightly and refocused on Graybill.

"…If Hemingway were alive today and in his prime," the publisher continued. "I doubt he'd gravitate toward Italy and Spain. Too stable. Too settled."

"You might be right."

"…Though Cuba might still interest him."

"True. The climate and the fishing are still good."

Graybill smiled at the jibe and swilled his martini. "Bear with me," he said. "I'm talking about the younger Hemingway."

Lena flicked another glance at the diplomat, still standing on the enclosed terrace and talking to the young Embassy staffer. "How about Afghanistan?" she suggested. "Mountainous terrain. Guerilla warfare in the rocks and snow. All the right ingredients."

"As good a guess as any. But I admit I was trying to bait you in a certain direction. You didn't oblige me."

She gave him a skeptical look. "You mean Belarus?"

"Well…"

For the first time in the conversation the publisher, paused, gave off a chastened look, and tacked off his intended course. "You're right," he said. "I read about those protests last spring, and last year as well. But now that I'm here…" He swept his arm vaguely around the cocktail party, encompassing the tailored suits and civilized chatter, then over the scene below the terrace, where teenagers milled on the promenade and a young couple dawdled by with a baby stroller. A veritable picture of calm. Graybill lowered his arm and resumed. "…Now that I'm here, it's obvious that Belarus is quiet. Perhaps not suited to an action-based narrative."

"That's probably accurate. We're known for being a quiet country."

"Okay, Lena…The idea was a stretch." Graybill recovered his grin. "As for Hemingway…you're more on the mark. Today, Central Asia probably offers much richer material. Not to mention Iraq, Lebanon… the list is long."

"Yes. Hemingway would be bored here."

A sly look fell over Graybill. "Bored?" he said. "I don't know if I'd go that far…"

Lena shot another glance over the publisher's shoulder. The American diplomat took several steps away from the female staffer, making an affable gesture. He resumed his path, zigzagging around a cluster of guests, toward the bar and buffet. She also guessed what was coming next from Graybill.

"…If you're in any way representative…" he said. "He might change his mind."

She nodded at the compliment. "You're too kind, Mr. Graybill."

"Please…Charlie."

"Charlie."

Lena waited a beat.

"On similar note…representation, I mean…I'm afraid I'll have to excuse myself. I still wish to thank one of the hosts from the U.S. Embassy."

Disappointment flickered over the publisher. But he held his grin.

"Perhaps we'll run into each later, before the party finishes?"

"Perhaps….If not, my compliments on your publication of our writers, and your interest in Belarus."

She extracted herself and moved away as fast as decorum allowed. When she reached the door to the inner terrace she saw the diplomat's tailored shoulders disappear into the restaurant area. She hoped he really was heading to the bar or buffet.

She put down her unfinished wine on a vacant table. If he was leaving the party her options were diminishing.

CHAPTER 66

Svetlana was unapprised of Piper's main objective this evening, so she didn't fault her when she intercepted him. Once they separated he resumed course toward the bar and ordered a mineral water. When it came he picked up his glass and turned back for another appraisal of Lena's entanglement with Graybill, and found her right behind him. With deliberation and small traces of tension she signaled the bartender, then turned her gaze upward.

"I believe I recognize you," he said in English.

"Probably from *Bagira*. I think I've seen you there."

"I thought so."

She paused to order white wine, in Russian. Piper waited a polite downbeat before introducing himself.

"I saw your name on the guest list beforehand, Lena," he said. "With a note that you teach English at the Language Institute. Also that you're on our list of recommended tutors."

"All true. Though I obtained this invitation through a friend." When the bartender re-appeared with an open bottle of Chardonnay, Lena eyed him as he filled an empty glass. Afterward the young man stayed rooted in place, contriving to neaten the countertop. "...So happens Quentin Hill is the only person with whom I have a connection here," she resumed, with distinct diction. "I did manage to thank him briefly. But I also wanted to express my appreciation to at least one other representative from your Embassy...that is, before the evening was out."

"The pleasure is ours."

Piper re-examined the bartender, who diverted his eyes but showed no discomfiture.

"Why don't we move over here, Lena...You can tell me more about your teaching duties, and maybe share your assessments of these two writers." With extended palm he guided her along a line of empty banquet booths that marked the edge of the restaurant, then stopped next to potted ferns overlooking of the curved staircase, which presented a pocket of seclusion from both guests and serving staff "...This is better," he resumed. "More out of the way."

"In other words," she said with a sidelong glance, "The bartender is KGB. Or at least an informant."

He hadn't expected such directness.

"...I said those things in front of him for a reason," she continued. "I have to have some defensible basis for speaking to you, if I'm ever questioned about it."

At once Piper made two assessments. First, Lena Antonova was on guard. Second, she had not come to this party to socialize. He also realized she had gotten rid of her first glass of wine. She had not yet sipped the Chardonnay.

"Did you seek me out for another reason this evening, Lena?"

"Not exactly, Mr. Piper." She hesitated a moment---as if pausing on a threshold of wider consequence. Then she re-appraised his nametag. "Political officer...What are your responsibilities, if I may ask?"

"They're varied. Generally speaking I analyze the policies of the government here, and also promote links between the Embassy and various civic organizations and political parties in Belarus."

The phrase "civic organizations" made her squint for an instant. She absorbed this and eyed him. Indicators were obvious. CIA, though this time she refrained from stark statements. Instead she adjusted her position slightly, so that her back was to the rest of the party as well as the bartender. "What if told you I was here on behalf of an American citizen? One who's in trouble here with the authorities…on a national security matter, let's say. And that he's gotten me in trouble as well?"

"I'd help you both."

"*Both* of us?"

"Yes."

"How?"

"Anyway I could. Diplomatic efforts by our team here, temporary refuge in the Embassy…even political asylum, in your case."

Lena appeared at once gratified and unsettled by the latter terms.

"Of course that's an extreme scenario," he added. "…We'd only resort to that if necessary."

During ensuing seconds, conversation buzz rose more audibly from the terrace. Piper used this as a pretext to glance around, and verify their detachment from potential listeners. Her attention stayed on him. At last she pressed ahead.

"Then I'd like to ask your help, Mr. Piper. The situation I describe is not hypothetical."

"Go on."

"I'm the language tutor of Evan Morris, an American citizen here in Minsk. We've run afoul of the KGB. Our trouble is real."

CHAPTER 67

Now that her plan was in motion, Lena didn't second-guess herself; she'd reviewed her rationale too many times for that. Prior to the party she'd even found corroboration in Sartre, despite his other shortcomings. She was facing adversity. Following the philosopher's prescriptions for concrete action.

Still, certain markers made her uncomfortable.

For example: she'd long heard rumors that catering staff at these diplomatic functions were often KGB informants, and the bartender's behavior seemed to substantiate them. Still---KGB or not---he was Belarussian. One of her own. While Russell Piper was likely CIA, a foreign spy in her own country. She was already entangled with Morris. And now she'd enmeshed herself with another American, an intelligence operative, with his varied and obscure motives. He'd supplied the words she wanted to hear, but they also carried a traitorous ring.... For all its retrograde politics and other faults Belarus was hers. Where she'd been born...Where she remained rooted in countless ways...

She felt a new spike of resentment toward Shinkevich. He'd forced her into this. Pushing these thoughts aside, she re-focused. Piper spoke in low tones, quickly and efficiently, aware that their time was limited.

"So you've remained in continuous contact with Evan Morris through this period?" he asked.

"Lessons twice per week. Also phone calls, mainly to organize our lessons."

He asked where they took place.

"They used to be in my apartment. Now they're often outside. Parks, historical locations, and so on. For additional lesson topics. And because of the warm weather."

"Monitored?"

Lena nodded and summarized their last several sessions, including the KGB trackers and ensuing reactions from Shinkevich. Piper asked little about the KGB officer. As if he already knew who he was.

"Why has Evan Morris not come to us directly?"

"First, he hasn't been arrested, so he's hoping these problems will subside. Second, he doesn't want the lab to close, and the employees to suffer repercussions."

For the first time the Piper paused to drink from his sparkling water. Lena raised her wine glass as well, taking an infinitesimal sip. In small quantity, somehow, the chardonnay lingered longer on her tongue.

"...There's no way he'd risk an event like this," she added, gesturing out toward the terrace. "Out of apprehension of antagonizing the organs...I mean Shinkevich and the KGB. Otherwise I might have brought him. After all I'd been invited. I had an excuse."

Piper appraised her again.

"The cars from the KGB seemed to have disappeared over the last couple of days," she continued. "But it's hard to tell. I would guess they're keeping closer tabs on Morris than on me. And tracking both of us through our cell-phones...which by the way Shinkevich has insisted we leave on most of the time, though of course I turned it off here."

"That can also be an advantage."

"An advantage? How?"

"If you give me your number, we can track you just like the KGB does." The remark made Lena shudder slightly as he pulled out his cell-phone; this facet of information age had always alarmed her, and no less now. He observed her reaction. "...Brave new world, for better or worse." Without hesitating further she relayed the digits, which he entered immediately on his keypad while pretending to check messages. "Let me also give you a special number, to be used only in emergencies," he continued. He pronounced it; she repeated it once and committed it to memory. "...Registered to a Ukrainian trucking company. It's safe, and can't be tracked to the Embassy. If you need immediate assistance, call it. Let the phone ring phone five times and hang up. We'll identify your location and make every effort to come and extract you. Please give it to Morris as well."

Piper glanced over her shoulder and drained the rest of his mineral water. Lena sensed their conclave was nearing its end.

"...Otherwise we should probably avoid contact."

"What if I see you at *Bagira*?"

"We're formally acquainted now. So we should behave accordingly. Polite chats and the like."

"Even if I need to speak to you for some reason?"

He looked down at the floor, but appeared to have already thought this through.

"The only place at *Bagira* where we can have a private conversation is the sauna. Let me know...discreetly, somehow...that you'll be taking one. I'll join you there."

"Understood."

"All right...We've been talking over here long enough. Let's make a short show of ending our conversation. Wander back onto the terrace. I'll stay here for a moment and pretend to re-check my cell-phone messages." Lena nodded and followed script. They exchanged courteous goodbyes, raising their voices somewhat for effect before she strolled back toward the terrace, taking her time and refraining from glancing back.

She also sensed Piper's gaze scorching her posterior, though she couldn't be sure.

In all other respects, he'd been an exemplar of professionalism and probity. And she'd noticed his wedding ring, an item he hadn't worn in the gym. So those questions were closed and irrelevant.

Which was for the better.

She and Morris would have to depend on him. There was no room for unnecessary complication.

CHAPTER 68

Undulations of green swelled out across Gorky and Kupala parks, replete with accrued energy and sliding into the lush rhythms of nighttime. Fertile expulsions, mingled with other live scents and sounds, issued through Piper's open window: human voices, spurting fountains, oscillations of traffic. To his right the Ferris wheel, newly illumined, moved in indefatigable revolution. Further along the Prospekt the black obelisk at Victory Square stabbed the dusk.

Almost three hours had passed since the end of the party. He swiveled his desk chair and resettled his fingers on the keyboard.

Even around social occasions, he was often compelled to draw lines. Though in this case he wasn't sure his reticence issued from defensible motives. He paused for an instant before he began typing:

Dearest Caroline,

   When I called your parents' house after the Embassy cocktail party, your mother said that your father convinced you and the kids to take the boat out for a sail, toward Martha's Vineyard and back. Glad to hear about your excursion, not least because you managed to pull Nick away from his swimming obsession for a day. Plus he's available to take the helm if your father needs a break (we can't forget

he's almost 75), or if any equipment problems arise, given that you're
out of cell-phone range for most of the day.

Send me some photos, if you took some!

How to encapsulate my workday, over a non-secure connection?
Manageable load, but requirements from Washington have only inten-
sified lately. Notions of breaking away next week for a quick visit are
looking less and less plausible. But I think you already gathered that
from our brief chat by cell-phone yesterday.

The Embassy party this evening took place at Zhuravinka and aimed
for a highbrow tone. Writers always seem to be suitable for that, almost
like props...Still, I think you would have enjoyed meeting the American
editor and various other cultural and academic types who turned out.
We both know that one can tire of the diplomatic breed week after week.

Piper paused and cleared his throat, decided to say no more about the
party and resumed writing:

Meanwhile Quentin Hill is also leaving on vacation in a few days,
leaving behind just me and our Russian personnel. That means I'll
be the ranking representative and saddled with general management
responsibilities along with my other duties.

All the same I'm holding my balance. My workouts really do help.
I also hope my physical examination with Dr. Ivanov on Tuesday has
helped reassure you.

As much as I miss you, I'm gratified that you're now in one of your
favorite places in the world---with your parents, Melanie and Nick.
Relish your time on the water and don't fret about me!

Love always,
Russell

Piper re-read the message, corrected a few typographical errors, and
hit the *send* button. Upon confirming transmission he rose from his
chair and walked onto the balcony; at almost the same instant, in

response to impinging darkness, street lamps went on up and down the Prospekt. He took a deep breath through his nostrils, throwing open his senses. The two parks and the surrounding city smelled and sounded as alive as ever.

He traced his vision along the early portion of his nine-kilometer course, now partially obscured. His next run couldn't come soon enough.

The crisis involving Evan Morris was unpredictable, and could develop along any number of dangerous lines. But he was able to discern one feature.

Lena could be his third test.

CHAPTER 69

Friday, August 1ˢᵗ

Morris jolted awake, his bedroom suffused with natural light, quiet except for chirping birds. The digital clock on his nightstand showed 4:32---another reminder that Minsk lay at northern latitude. He scrunched his eyes and stared at the ceiling. Whatever had transpired from Lena's initiative at the Embassy party, he and Lena had opted for greater pro-action. Last time he'd done that he'd only inflamed his predicament and entangled her in the first place.

Even if her foray had succeeded, the U.S. Embassy now constituted yet another factor in an increasingly complex equation, with him at the center. Others included: the KGB, Yuri and the programmers, Grinevicius, Crowder and corporate headquarters, and now even the Pentagon, based on Grinevicius' first report from Washington.

From his study of mathematics he knew that each new random variable magnified the possibility of unforeseeable outcomes. Same was true of software programs. And options trading, or for that matter, anything involving money. Probably even more with international politics.

In these matters, the fewer random variables the better.

He sat up on the edge of the bed with a sigh, and massaged his brows with the thumb and middle finger of one hand. After a moment he stood and moved to the window, stretching his arms and back. There was no point in getting back in bed; it made more sense to get to the lab early. He walked to the kitchen and made the day's first pot of coffee.

*   *   *

Outside the entry to his building Morris paused and surveyed the courtyard. No parked Volgas wafting with cigarette smoke, or crew-cut goons idling under trees. There was just one lone male figure at the far end of the long courtyard: wearing sunglasses and a baseball cap, sitting on a bench and talking on a bulky portable phone. The man's physiognomy was solid and suggested relative youth; he flicked a glance toward Morris through then inclined forward onto his knees. Apparently absorbed in conversation.

The KGB never wore shorts, to his knowledge. Moreover the man looked somewhat familiar, and the portable phone---probably linked to a nearby apartment---suggested he was a resident.

Drawing a cue, Morris pulled out his cell-phone phone and checked the log---just in case Lena had called or sent a message. Finding none, he rounded onto Communisticheskaya Street and passed the city mar-riage bureau, which was still closed...And somehow presenting a fit-ting motif. Instead of stabilizing and consolidating his life after his last bust-up, which had been his intention, he seemed to spiraling into even greater precariousness. Remarriage seemed even more implausible than before...He pushed the thought aside, and two minutes later descended into Victory Square station, where the platform was mostly empty---the norm at this early hour. He walked two-thirds of the way down to his preferred location, then stood next to a column and waited for the next train.

He sensed a presence behind him. He pivoted slightly, hampered by the laptop case on his shoulder.

"Keep cool, Evan. It's me."

The intonation was American. Recognizable at once. Morris completed his turn. It was Jeff Esposito, now minus his sunglasses and cap. Also wearing a backpack.

"Jeff? Good God..."

Esposito glanced up and down the platform before completing his movement around the column. He kept his voice low. "I'm here to help," he said.

"...You scared the daylights out of me."

Morris took in the floral silk shirt, as well as the sunglasses hanging around Esposito's neck on a sports strap. "That was you in my courtyard?" He re-checked his watch. "...At 6:30 in the morning?"

Esposito nodded. His face showed strain and fatigue---far from his usual state.

"I was on a direct connection to Crowder," he explained. "Or I should say with Crowder and the emergency action committee he's set up back in Santa Clara. When I told him you'd come out of your building, he instructed me to hang back and make 'covert' contact. That was the word he used."

Morris did a quick calculation. It was 8:40 the previous evening in California. Not yet the middle of the night. Still, the phrase "emergency action committee" jarred him.

"They're standing by," Esposito continued. "We're to find a suitable location and call him back as soon as we can manage."

The tracks rumbled with the next train.

"I suggest we get on the train," Esposito said. "But I'll take your cue about where we should go."

Morris made a quick assessment and decided a minor detour was the most they should risk. "Our best bet is probably to go one station beyond the Academy of Sciences," he said. "To Park Chel...I can't really pronounce it. Anyway, we can get out there. But we can't take long."

"Sounds okay to me."

Esposito's response was almost drowned out as the train lead car barreled down the platform and the train came to a stop. The closest car contained only about a half-dozen passengers.

"We probably shouldn't speak English on the train," Morris said as the doors jangled open. "We'll just attract attention to ourselves."

Esposito nodded.

"...We'll go through two stations and get off at the third. Just get up and follow me out."

They filed in and took seats near the door. Doors slammed shut behind them and the train started moving. Morris registered stares from a few other passengers. He looked down at his laptop case, now resting on his knees, and over at Esposito's colorful shirt and shorts. Not terribly unusual in Minsk in mid-summer.

They were attracting attention all the same.

CHAPTER 70

Just two other passengers disembarked at Park Chelunskinstev station: male pensioners, up early for their morning constitutionals. Still early for the commuter crowd, which suited Morris just fine. He watched the men turn left toward the south end of the platform and pointed Esposito toward the north exit. Out on the broad sidewalk of the Prospekt, they passed through an arched gate into the park, then turned onto a diagonal walkway, largely shaded from the rising sun--- and from binoculars and directional listening devices. Morris was now habituated to thinking in those terms. He checked his watch.

"This is a back way to the Institute," he said. "It gives us a little extra time. But only fifteen or twenty minutes."

"It's not even seven o'clock...Do you usually get in so early?"

"No...But I've seen surveillance vehicles in front of the Institute, off and on."

Esposito's back stiffened while he shot a glance over his shoulder, then ahead along the curving walkway: empty except for an elderly woman sitting on a bench, about 50 meters ahead. "I'm here alone," he explained, keeping his voice down and talking fast. "Malcolm wanted to send two or three of us, but everyone who applied for visas back in the States had their applications rejected or delayed. And he doesn't trust the Europeans in our Paris office with this kind of thing…which I'm sure doesn't surprise you. Why me? I happened to be in Estonia on a business trip, which you knew. I was able to slip in on a tourist visa. You could say my job is reconnaissance. To orchestrate contact with you and report back directly."

"Besides Malcolm, who else is involved in this?"

"This emergency committee has six or seven people on it. Along with Malcolm, Neil Lamont, Dyson, and MacPherson are the main players. They're on call around the clock. Malcolm's consumed by this situation, Evan. Especially since…."

As they drew closer to the elderly woman on the park bench, Morris flicked his eyes ahead, and Esposito paused. The woman wore a scarf over her gray hair, her face tanned from the outdoors, and sat straight, with two hands propped on an upright cane. Her blue eyes followed them with intent curiosity as they passed. Esposito soon picked up where he'd left off.

"…Something happened in Santa Clara yesterday, which raised the urgency level for him."

"In Santa Clara?" Morris was at a loss.

"I think Malcolm wants to tell you himself."

Esposito unzipped his backpack and pulled out a bulky satellite phone---the same one Morris had earlier mistaken for a home-based portable. It wasn't standard company gear.

"Scrambled signal," Esposito explained.

As they resumed progress Esposito punched the number and waited about 10 seconds for the through-link. He exchanged a few words with Crowder, mentioned that time was short, and handed the device over.

*   *   *

In Crowder's rich history of paranoia and off-key management behavior Morris could not think of another incident that paralleled the current one. Numerous crises had erupted over the years, most associated with real or contrived physical dangers---unpredictable reactions from fired employees, suspected sabotage of physical plant and system infrastructure by competitors or other shadowy adversaries, traffic accidents of indeterminate origin, and the like. Overseas locations figured prominently, including, most memorably, a major trade show in Singapore 15 months earlier. Typical outgrowths were a day or two of electric tension at headquarters, furious rumor-mongering by corporate e-mail, and bolstered security at affected facilities.

However none of these previous instances had involved a hostile foreign government.

Along with Crowder other members of the action committee were on hand, arrayed around a conference room. They signaled their presence in perfunctory fashion and let Crowder begin. True to form, he focused first on safety-related questions. Was Morris still physically unharmed, and Yuri, too? Had they been further harassed by the KGB during the past three days? Was their situation time critical? To all three queries Morris answered in the negative. Meanwhile he and Esposito approached an intersection with the park's main, tree-lined alley, interspersed with refreshment kiosks and food tents, all still closed. Then Crowder got to his kicker.

"Evan, we didn't realize just how serious this was, until today. Just after lunch two officials from the federal government stopped by my office, completely unannounced. One was from Vice President Gallstone's office. The other was from the Defense Intelligence Agency. They asked questions about you and about our lab in Minsk."

Morris first reaction was disbelief. It didn't last long; he drew immediate connection to Grinevicius.

"....I asked them to explain their purpose. They said it was 'a matter of national security.' Otherwise, nothing. And they were insistent. Your employment history with the company. Lines of reporting. Personal characteristics...they had a whole list of questions."

After a pause Crowder resumed, his voice larded with consequence.

"...I told them as little as I could, and got them the hell out of here. But of course it raised all sorts of serious concerns. But don't answer those over this connection, Evan, even if it's scrambled. We're dealing with the Defense Department here. If you can shed some light on this, fill in Jeff. He'll communicate the information to us through separate channels."

"Agreed, Malcolm. All the same, I hope this will eventually settle down on its own."

Crowder took this in. Several murmured voices, audible though indistinct, issued around the conference room.

"We appreciate your optimism, Evan," he said. "We wish we could share it. For that reason, we're already entertaining various options, even including a private rescue operation."

"A rescue operation? I would advise strongly against that, Malcolm..." Morris transmitted a dismayed glance to Esposito. Before he had a chance to object further Crowder continued.

"...Again, that's just one option among many on the table. At this point we just want to make one thing is clear. We're committed to you and the entire team there. This will remain high priority for the company until it's resolved."

*   *   *

After Morris signed off and handed back the satellite phone, he stayed silent for a moment, guiding Esposito onto another diagonal which cut to the park's southwest corner and main gate. Thanks to the visit by the DIA, Crowder had gone into crazy mode. Morris had little doubt about the origin of Washington's interest. He also realized he and Grinevicius had been a little naïve.

"I take it you already knew about this episode with the government yesterday?" he said.

"Just heard this morning, as you came out of your apartment building." Esposito then raised his eyebrows and formed a simulated whistle.

"Vice President's office...DIA? This seems pretty high stakes, whatever you've gotten yourself into. Also a company first. You've made history, that's for sure."

Morris had trouble sharing the humor. Esposito, under stress himself, cut short his smile before resuming.

"...Malcolm's always suspected the government is out to screw him. Now he's convinced of it. It feeds into his whole Ayn Rand obsession. You know what I'm talking about..."

"Oh God."

Shaking his head, Morris remembered that he'd once read "Atlas Shrugged" at Crowder's prompting, and subsequently discussed it with the CEO en route to an industry conference in San Diego. The novel's heroes and heroines were entrepreneurs struggling against insidious opponents and a confiscatory, oppressive government. The protagonist, in the end, responds by taking matters into his own hands. Which in the current context gave rise to all sorts of new and unsettling implications.

"...Will you at least try to dissuade him from this rescue idea?"

"I'll try my best, Evan."

A small plaza came into view ahead, with the main gate behind it. Morris did a quick calculation.

"We can only talk for four or five more minutes," he said. "You can walk with me out the other side of the park, to a back-street and another gate that leads onto some athletic fields. But the path there is visible from Yuri's office, so we'll have to separate at that point."

Esposito nodded. "Then we should address Malcolm's main question, Evan. That is...what provoked this interest by the Vice President and the Pentagon?"

"It probably concerns my lawyer, Jeff. I'll tell you what I can."

CHAPTER 71

Piper's passport was routinely red-flagged by Belarussian border security, which meant his checked baggage was subjected to tampering. Therefore he preferred carry-on. Who wanted KGB electronic devices sewn into one's suitcase lining, or embedded in one's deodorant stick?

For today's flight, in any event, his bag contained just one change of clothes. The secure communication from Stapleton had awaited him when he'd arrived at the Embassy at nine o'clock: that morning:

Russell,

We've gained an unexpected respite from today's NSC meeting. Gallstone postponed consideration of his proposal for Belarus, to permit "further assessment and preparation" by his staff. He even cited your analysis from last week, among other factors.

We can both presume that other influences are at work. Among them: Evan Morris.

Indeed Morris' case now appears more multi-faceted than either of us supposed---enough to warrant an immediate face-to-face conference in Europe, and onward travel to Moscow on my part. I depart from Dulles at 01:30, EDT, on an Agency jet. Scheduled arrival in Frankfurt is 14:05 local time. You're already booked in business class on today's Lufthansa flight from Minsk II International Airport, departing at 14:40; scheduled arrival in Frankfurt at 16:00. I'll expect you at 17:00, at our usual rendezvous location...

When Piper's aircraft, a Boeing 737-500, climbed over green fields and clusters of dachas west of the airport it was soon engulfed by cumulus clouds, then a brief period of turbulence. When the plane ascended higher, to clearer skies, he leaned back and closed his eyes.

His thoughts soon gravitated to Lena. She was his only conduit to Morris, and would likely retain than role for a while.

The tableau which he'd generated at *Bagira* that morning sprung back for a moment.

Along with Morris, she was front and center.

*   *   *

Throngs of mid-summer vacation travelers swarmed the concourses of Frankfurt International Airport, though most were transferring to and from long-haul flights, which allowed Piper to clear passport control without delay. From the second-floor departure level, he ascended an escalator and traversed several skywalks to the Frankfurt Airport Sheraton, and less than fifteen minutes after disembarking was in his room. There he unpacked his few personal items, washed his face and headed straight back out, to Frankfurt Airport Center, a complex of offices and conference facilities connected to both the airport and hotel by another series of climate-controlled walkways. Numerous high-profile organizations such as ABC News and American Express leased space there, while other tenants were more obscure: Swiss private banks, oil-rich principalities in the Middle East, and trading companies of unspecified provenance. The CIA fell in this latter category, operating under the rubric *Transcontinental Arbitrage, AG.*

Otherwise known, within Agency circles, as Frankfurt station.

Piper showed his U.S. government identification to the German security guard in the lobby and rode the elevator to the fifth floor, where he underwent another security check, this one by a youthful and plain-clothed American. As always he found the Agency's suite of offices spare but pleasingly appointed. A secretary ushered him to a small conference room, with windows overlooking the A3 Autobahn. Long stretches of green forest stretched out beyond, rush-hour traffic barely audible through the triple-paned glass.

Stapleton stood over the hardwood table, reading contents of a classified folder. Notwithstanding his time-zone change and slightly rumpled summer-weight suit, he appeared somewhat less weary than Piper had observed him during their last video conference, even if the bags remained under his eyes. As if he was relieved to escape Washington for the field. The impression was reinforced as they shook hands and seated themselves.

"In one sense, Russell, Evan Morris has been a godsend. Gallstone has backed away from this initiative of his, which promised to vex both of us for who knows how long.

"But brought new problems."

"I'm afraid so." The Deputy Director paused. Some of his lightness faded. "Turns out Morris didn't see just any Iraqi. Remember Amoud al-Tikriti?"

"Of course..." Outlines emerged to Piper and became more distinct. "Now it makes sense. The connection to oil...Gallstone's own contacts with al-Tikriti back in the eighties. Am I right?"

Stapleton nodded and let him fill out the picture.

"...In other words, Gallstone was trying to distract attention away from those legacies. To pin some of the blame for our failures in Iraq on unfriendly regimes like Belarus."

"Naturally we can't yet verify that Morris made correct identification," Stapleton noted. "What I did learn yesterday is that Morris' lawyer..." He glanced down at a sheet from his folder. "...One John Grinevicius, an American based in Vilnius....revealed al-Tikriti's identity to his contacts at the Pentagon. Apparently on the assumption that there might be some chance of a reward."

Piper raised his eyebrows and blew out his cheeks.

"You recall all the nasty details, then?"

"Most of them. A little refresher wouldn't hurt."

Stapleton reached for another folder, opened it, and perused the contents. "Al-Tikriti's prominence under Saddam Hussein goes all the way back to the mid-70s. Not the usual Baathist: he was from a well-to-do merchant family, educated in Europe, multilingual. Supposedly a distant cousin of Hussein, which certainly helped. His main expertise was money. At the end of the last oil boom, he made astute investments on behalf of the Iraqi State Treasury and Hussein's immediate clan. Operated mostly through Swiss banks and offshore tax havens, stayed highly liquid, and was skilled at covering trails. Kept a low profile, gained Hussein's trust. When the Iran-Iraq war began in 1981, he extended his responsibilities to arms purchases. Not weapons themselves, just the payments for them. That brought him into contact with Western defense contractors, not to mention high-ranking government officials. British, French, Russian...and of course, American."

"Like Gallstone."

"Exactly. Gallstone was an undersecretary at Defense during early 80s, as you know, and later Deputy Chief of Staff at the White House. In both jobs, he maintained regular contacts with al-Tikriti. And signed off on some murky deals, including purchases of binary chemicals from Germany necessary for the manufacture of mustard gas. But when Hussein also used gas against the Kurds in 1988, we lost our stomach. Cooperation got ratcheted down. Including contacts between Gallstone and al-Tikriti. That's when Hussein fell into stronger embrace with the Russians."

Piper needed no briefing on that. And al-Tikriti's activities during the first Gulf War, he asked?

"Stayed out of harm's way in Europe. Shifted assets around, prevented them from getting frozen. For al-Tikriti, the biggest challenges came after the conflict. Oil prices continued their downward trend. Restrictions on Iraqi exports, the U.N. oil-for-food program....but you know all that. Through the 90s, he had to juggle resources and orchestrate a lot of back-channel transactions to keep the regime afloat."

"Oil-for-food," Piper observed. "Not the most admirable chapter in UN diplomacy."

Stapleton expelled a slight snort and shook his head. "And al-Tikriti was right in the thick of it, cutting deals in Zurich and Geneva, lining pockets in numerous Western capitals, not to mention the UN. Everybody elbowed back up to the trough. French and Russian companies were the greediest offenders. However no one was completely clean. British and American oil interests became riled not because the program was corrupt, but because they were largely boxed out of the action."

"Though not entirely."

"Sadly, no. And that's where the connection between Gallstone and al-Tikriti comes back into play. When Gallstone became CEO of Carleton Energy in 1993, he also become a private citizen again, which meant we faced fewer obstacles in keeping tabs on him---especially his overseas activities. So of course we did. It was during this period, starting in 1995, that he renewed his contacts with al-Tikriti. In Europe, for the most part, though occasionally in one of the Gulf states. Dinners in private dining rooms, breakfasts in hotel suites, always very discreet. We managed to plant listening devices on a few occasions, and learned Gallstone was nibbling around the edges of the free-for-all."

"You mean Carleton itself actually evaded oil-for-food strictures?"

"No. At least not in such a way that he could be definitively incriminated. Instead Gallstone used his meetings with al-Tikriti to steer illicit deals to commodities dealers...agile, transnational types....who did parallel business with Carleton. In so doing, he spread corporate quid pro quos and generated extra revenue for Carleton by indirect means. Disgusting, given what came later."

"Still downsides were significant. Especially for a political figure like Gallstone. So why bother? Why take such risks?"

"That's where these interactions became most hazardous for Gallstone. He used these meetings not just to orchestrate side deals like the ones I just described, but also to receive briefings from al-Tikriti on the Iraqi oil industry. Productivity at specific oil fields, state of repair at refining and storage facilities, locations of computer databases, and the like. In short, steady, updated intelligence on the Iraqi economy---precisely the sort we craved at the Agency during that period. Unfortunately, as I said, our eavesdropping was limited."

"Incredible."

"Not really, knowing Gallstone as we do."

Piper nodded to acknowledge the point. "And let me guess," he said. "Weapons programs, real or fictitious, never came up in those meetings."

The Deputy Director snorted again, and shook his head with distaste. "Certainly not our knowledge."

"Did Gallstone ever pass anything along to the Agency, or to the last Administration?"

"Just bits and pieces. Enough to keep the last Administration placated. They hoped, after all, that economic pressures would bring Hussein to heel, or force an internal collapse of his regime, so they were keen on that sort of data. Unfortunately Gallstone never gave them the choicest information. That, he kept for Carleton and himself. For later use."

The Deputy Director's phrase reverberated in the room for a moment, and required no elaboration. Piper asked what was in it for al-Tikriti.

"Al-Tikriti was a shrewd player, and covered himself in two ways. First, he was conducting illicit business through Gallstone, outside the oil-for-for-food framework. He therefore possessed a pretext for these meetings. I would presume he also informed Hussein about them. And why would Hussein object? The U.S. had been playing a duplicitous game with him for decades; such cynicism from the American side fit his pre-existing schema. Second, I'd guess Hussein hoped this back-channel with Gallstone would prove useful down the road. And it did. In early 2003, when U.S. and international financial sanctions were tightened, many Iraqi assets were left unscathed, because they were buried deep in the Swiss banking system, and simply couldn't be pried out by U.S. and British banking regulators. However they were nonetheless impeded from ready access: difficult to draw upon quickly in those crisis weeks of March and April, when the regime crumbled and the various individuals in the Iraqi hierarchy scrambled to save themselves. With an exception. A subset of Iraqi assets, including al-Tikriti's own, as it turned out, were given free passage in the international banking system. And I don't mean just marginal offshore conduits. I mean through Luxembourg, Paris, Frankfurt, even New York. In other words, when action was fast and hot, and when the U.S. and the rest of the world were focused on the military invasion and its immediate aftermath, al-Tikriti managed to re-allocate his own holdings, stay clear of restrictions, and thereby preserve a flexible financial profile that he could carry into the post-war period."

"With connivance by U.S. banks? You're kidding."

"I wish I were."

"How much are we talking about?"

"The majority of al-Tikriti's personal holdings---at least two-and-a-half billion dollars, by our reckoning---remains embedded in Switzerland. However through these maneuvers in spring 2003, he also dispersed $400-$500 million into new assets in Western Europe and the U.S. Liquid, for the most part. Heavy on government bonds. But also real estate. Four or five villas on Lac Leman and the Cote d'Azur, as well as a ski chalet in Zermatt. Now used by his daughters and grandchildren, as far as we know."

"Thanks to intercession by Gallstone?"

Stapleton nodded. He took in Piper's expression before elaborating.

"And there's the nub. According to our assessments, the information al-Tikriti supplied to Gallstone from 1995-2001 gave Carleton detailed blueprints for the seizure and exploitation of Iraqi oil installations, once the invasion happened. It also explains why Carleton was in prime position to bid on billions of dollars in U.S. government contracts."

"Because al-Tikriti and Gallstone had cut a deal well in advance," Piper observed. "In fact before the Administration even took office."

"That's the gist, Russell. One you won't hear on the nightly news."

Piper leaned back in his chair and issued a snort of his own. The narrative could hardly be more repulsive.

In that regard he was mistaken.

CHAPTER 72

News reports on al-Tikriti during the period were few, Piper recalled, and mostly emanated from an iconoclastic reporter from the *Boston World Tribune* who posed unscripted, insubordinate questions at press conferences in Baghdad and Washington. The Pentagon had responded with curt dismissals, preferring to focus on Hussein and his sons, as well as other Iraqi figures who played roles in internal repressions. Roundups, they assured, were hewing to plan.

Hussein's sons were killed that June. Hussein himself was captured in November. Media reports on al-Tikriti dissipated and finally stopped. Even the reporter from Boston lost interest. Stapleton resumed the narrative there.

"He stayed tranquilly sequestered in one of his new villas on Lac Leman," he said. "Popped down to Geneva by limousine for occasional visits to banks, accompanied by one escort vehicle and a couple of bodyguards. Obviously felt reasonably secure. We knew his whereabouts at all times, but the word from the White House was hands-off."

"From Gallstone."

"That was fairly clear."

"Did al-Tikriti try to help any of his former Baathist comrades, or even Hussein himself?"

"He did help orchestrate and finance the relocation of Hussein's wife and family to Syria, as well as the families and associates of other Baathist officials. When we reported this back to the White House, Gallstone didn't object. Part of the deal, maybe."

"He had his oil," Piper observed. "And Carleton had their contracts."

"Quite so. First things first."

Piper issued another long exhalation. "Sounds like al-Tikriti made a smooth transition," he said. "One of the few leading Baathists to land on his feet. No one else was inclined to interfere with him?"

"On the contrary...why would they? He held incriminating information on dozens of prominent political and economic figures, from the halls of the UN to corporate boardrooms and ministries all over Europe. As we've noted, the French and Russians were the most grievous offenders. Everyone preferred him content...and most of all, quiet. Along with Gallstone, in other words, he had some powerful protectors."

"How long did this go on?"

"Quite a long stretch. Up until late 2006."

And why, Piper asked, didn't he just stay serenely ensconced in Geneva?

"That's where the dynamic with Gallstone took a bizarre turn. By this time, of course, Iraq was sliding into civil chaos. Casualties mounting week to week. After the 2006 Congressional elections, Gallstone himself was seething and increasingly isolated in Washington. Starting to reach out for diversions like Belarus. Meanwhile al-Tikriti was thriving. Began moving about more freely. Despite his earlier accommodations he continued to fulfill his role as primary, remaining pillar of the former Iraqi regime, managing portfolios of Hussein's family and others. And rather effectively, too. From 2004 onward, he tilted more toward equities, especially energy companies. From 2003 to autumn 2006, according to certain secondary indicators we obtained, he approximately doubled his own wealth, as well as other assets under his supervision. When we reported this back to Gallstone, it obviously rankled him. While he wallowed in frustration and failure, his old co-conspirator was living a lordly life on Lac Leman and the Cote d'Azur----indeed, about the only figure in the entire Iraqi equation to come out ahead. Round about mid-December 2006, Gallstone apparently decided he'd had enough. The deal was off."

"Just like that? Out of spite?"

"That may have been the primary impetus. But not the only one. Hussein was sentenced to death in early November. Most other Baathist leaders were already rotting in prison. And a certain impression had taken hold, especially with the American public. That was that trying and convicting former Baathists was one domain---there were really no others---in which the Iraqi Coalition Government produced demonstrable results. Problem was, the Coalition had run out of individuals to put on trial. Therefore various Iraqi politicians---Shiite of course---began lobbying Gallstone to feed al-Tikriti into the machine."

"And Gallstone was receptive? I would think he wouldn't want him on the stand, re-dredging their deals from the 90s."

"Evidently Gallstone presumed he could deny al-Tikriti's claims, based on Carleton's employment of middle-men. Or better yet, suppress the information altogether. Manipulate the proceedings and shift the spotlight onto the Russians and French."

"Usual culprits."

"Of course. True to form."

Piper felt another wave of disgust. Stapleton observed him and resumed.

"Still, there were obstacles. Gallstone couldn't ask the Agency to perform a rendition of al-Tikriti into Iraq. First, he was a long-established, legal resident of Switzerland. He couldn't credibly be labeled a terrorist. Second, controversy in Europe over earlier Agency renditions was by now too intense for us to consider any more. So the Coalition's request gave Gallstone the opening he needed. He determined he would use the Iraqis as proxy for an extraction operation."

"Abroad? I didn't even know the Coalition Government had a foreign secret service."

"They don't, really. But that didn't stop the plan from going ahead. The Coalition cobbled together a seven-man team. Former Republican Guard-types with no previous experience in such operations. More likely to be against the Coalition than loyal to it."

"Sounds like disaster in the making."

"In other circumstances I might have called it a circus. But the stakes were too serious for that."

Piper managed to smile at the dark humor. "And how was the Agency supposed to react?" he asked.

"Somehow Gallstone believed he could keep us half-unaware. Relegate us to the sidelines....Asked us to suspend our surveillance, on some contrived pretext. Of course that was absurd. We remained privy to his enterprise from the get-go. And the more we learned, the more we worried. We had little choice but to stay on top of it. On November 29th, the Coalition team arrived from Baghdad and set up at a hotel in Geneva. Our communication intercepts indicated that they intended to identify al-Tikriti's daily schedule and patterns of movement, and abduct him about 10 days later. From there they planned an improbable and hazardous itinerary, including overland transfer to Genoa, smuggling by fishing boat to Egypt, and chartered flight to Baghdad."

Piper shook his head, half-incredulous. Stapleton continued.

"Two days later on November 25th, when al-Tikriti emerged from his villa with his limousine and escort vehicle, they trailed him down the lakeside at close range. So close that we worried they would rear-end his limousine. It was clumsy in the extreme. Fortunately al-Tikriti's security kept their cool. The morning ended on a benign note when the Coalition's SUVs ran a red light in Geneva and were pulled over by traffic police."

"All the same al-Tikriti must have gotten spooked."

"Naturally. The episode broke four years of relative calm. Throughout that day and the next, al-Tikriti tried to make direct contact with Gallstone, seeking explanation. With no success. Concluding that Gallstone had turned on him, he made quick contact with the Russians. Within three days he was gone. That's where our trail went cold."

"And what was the word from the White House? Was the Agency supposed to seek him out, and identify his new location?"

"No. Gallstone deduced---with good reason---that al-Tikriti was now out of reach. And that this botched abduction constituted yet another Iraq-related fiasco...another potential blot on his record. So he re-retreated to his bunker, still angry but somewhat chastened."

"Until Evan Morris sighted him in Belarus. Or I should say...until his lawyer Grinevicius materialized in Washington this week."

"Correct..."

Before continuing, Stapleton rose from his chair, clasped his hands behind his waist, and moved by deliberate steps over to the window. Piper swiveled his chair and watched him until he stopped, silhouetted in natural light against the plate glass, appearing to contemplate rush-hour traffic, then the forest beyond. After a long instant he turned back.

"Thereby reviving Gallstone's old obsession," he said. "And adding to our troubles."

*   *   *

Prompted by an urge to stretch his legs, Piper rose and joined Stapleton along the window, where he shared the view over the autobahn. A truck horn infiltrated the plate glass; he waited several seconds for the hush to resettle.

"So you're assuming Grinevicius' claim is valid?" he said.

"For now, yes."

"Why would the Russians stick al-Tikriti in Belarus? Why not Russia proper?"

"Belarus is more closed off to foreigners than many Western regions of Russia….Small as the country is, it's easy to hide someone there. Especially outside major cities. And it's convenient to Europe."

Piper couldn't fault the logic, particularly since Belarus was in no position to object. Moreover the country offered reasonable flying times for Swiss bankers, which he noted.

"Quite right," Stapleton responded. "Something we're now investigating, through international flight logs and passenger manifests. But there's more. Appeared just yesterday. Once we re-focused energies on al-Tikriti, we learned that in this case Belarus...or Lukashenko, I should say...didn't just take orders from Moscow. Let's say he got a little sweetener...According to preliminary intelligence, $27 million in transfers, so far."

"Not a bad sum, over 18 months."

"Not at all."

"Where did it go, exactly?"

"As far as we can tell, directly into a special "presidential" account controlled by Lukashenko himself. Not into the state treasury, let's put it that way."

"Hardly suprising. Guess the one or two billion dollars he's accumulated so far isn't enough."

"You know these dictators, Russell. There can never be enough."

Stapleton found some murky humor in the observation, but his amusement quickly dissipated. They had come back round to Morris.

"…In many ways that highlights our core worry, Russell. Gallstone has retreated for now. But Defense can't bottle Grinevicius up forever. After that, Gallstone's position will become exposed, which he's not apt to take well. You've observed him over the past seven years, sometimes up close. He has trouble handling reversals. In every instance I've witnessed, his response is to become even more secretive, commandeering, and worst of all...unpredictable. Meanwhile Lukashenko---and by extension his lieutenants in the KGB and other security organs---will be on a hair-trigger, fearful of losing this asylum fee. It's an unstable equation."

"One in which Morris is caught in the middle."

"Precisely"

At once Piper comprehended the urgency of their meeting. Disturbing scenarios barreled into view. Rash action by Gallstone... Retaliation by the KGB against Morris....Arrest...Sudden disappearance...Or worse. Moreover, whatever befell Morris was likely to encompass Lena as well. He drew away from the plate-glass view of the Autobahn. There was only one solution.

"Looks like we should involve the Russians," he said.

Stapleton drew a long inhalation and stood back as well. "I agree. That's why my onward flight is to Moscow."

CHAPTER 73

Once they'd straightened out Lena felt freer of constraints, and pumped her thighs with additional vigor, while Morris, also exerting himself in the dormant air, broke an uncharacteristic gloss of perspiration. This evening there'd been little pretense of a lesson. More urgent priorities had taken over. For the next 30-40 seconds they remained wordless, losing themselves in thuds and splashes, focusing on concerted movement.

Lena wanted to get clear of other paddleboats. Then get down to business. When they reached a secluded corner of the river basin, near the Kupala Street Bridge. Morris steered into a perpendicular drift and waited to catch his breath.

"I hope this doesn't antagonize Shinkevich again," he said.

"We haven't heard from him all week."

"I prefer to keep it that way."

She considered him, appreciating his coolness despite events the last 48 hours. The discomfort he'd shown on the Ferris wheel was absent. To this point she'd still not briefed him on the Embassy party. At the bridge railing above, several student-age males leaned over within easy ear-shot, observing them. Noting their attentions, Morris promptly re-directed the craft up-river. They resumed pedaling at

slower pace, ducked their heads under the concrete spans, and steered
a gradual arc past Zhuravinka. Near the glass-sided exhibition center
they at last found a modicum of solitude, and slowed their rotations.
Morris had also implied he had important news of his own, but suggested she begin.

Without further delay Lena launched into succinct summary of
the previous evening at Zhuravinka: her arrival with Natasha, her
search for Quentin Hill, and the unsolicited overture from Russell
Piper. She left out preliminaries and stuck to the facts. The telephone
from Piper, she stressed, was the most concrete outcome.

When she was done Morris took all this in. He locked the rudder.

"Sounds positive," he observed. "Under the circumstances, we
could hardly have hoped for better."

"It's a step."

"Do you trust him?"

"Yes."

"What about the telephone he number he gave you? The sooner I
memorize it, the better."

She gave it to him.

By now they'd drifted past the exhibition center, and were
approaching the Bogdanovich Street overpass; through the arches the
basin along Pobedetelei appeared empty. As Lena sat up straighter on
the seat and firmed her feet on the pedals, they re-acquired momentum and proceeded under the bridge at controlled pace, then passed
the out-jutting island of the Afghan war memorial into open water.
Morris glanced around, and finding no other boats close, next scrutinized the high-rise apartment building which stretched along the
northern riverbank. With succinctness of his own, he recounted his
unexpected encounter that morning with Jeff Esposito. Also the prospect of a private rescue operation by Cognition Software, under the
direction of Malcolm Crowder.

For all her foresight, Lena had never even considered such a
development.

"Incredible," she said. "Do you think he'll attempt it?"

"Ever heard of the operation mounted by Ross Perot in Iran in 1980, to extract some of his employees from the Ayatollah?"

She shook her head.

"Well anyway, Crowder resembles Perot in many ways. A successful high-tech entrepreneur, with deep pockets. Smart, but also a little crazy. In other words, he just might do it."

"If it does go forward, where would it leave me?"

"I did raise the subject with Jeff, but he didn't have an answer. The planning hasn't gotten that far."

Lena stopped pedaling, making her dissatisfaction evident. For the moment she forgot her caution.

"Great," she said.

"I'm doing my best, Lena."

The platitude seemed sincere. Still, not sufficient for her to let up. "Meanwhile, what about your lawyer? Is he going to help us if we need him? Or just complicate our situation, like this Crowder of yours?"

Showing slight hesitation, Morris checked their drift-heading, adjusting the rudder. He angled his face inward, toward the hull, and lowered his voice. "His last e-mail didn't have any concrete news. I hope to check our link again later this evening."

"And you'll fill me in tomorrow?"

"Of course."

Lena looked over the bow of the boat at a grouping of ducks 20 meters ahead. The birds appeared wary: already altering course and ready to take flight. She still sensed Morris wasn't telling her everything about his lawyer. This excursion to Washington remained puzzling and vague.

Another reason she might have to count on Piper, for better or worse.

* * *

Wearing a fresh shirt and repossessed of his laptop, Morris ascended the elevator to Seven Skies, and upon entering the lounge area heard festive voices from the restaurant, more numerous than usual. Several staff congregated along the bar: one, a waitress whom he recognized, stepped forward holding a menu. She smiled, but made no move to lead him onward, instead gesturing backward with a half turn.

"There's a party," she said in English.

"Does that mean there are no tables?"

She offered another polite smile. "Maybe you'd like to have dinner in the bar instead?" With another gesture she indicated several small tables nearby, arrayed along the windows.

"I'd really prefer the restaurant."

The girl received the request evenly and disappeared through the door into the clamor. A moment later she returned, beckoned him to follow, and conducted him to his usual location: just off the forward edge of the dance-floor, overlooking the courtyard, with a clear view to the Architecture Commission. He glanced over his shoulder; two tables behind him were empty; beyond that was an extended banquette with 25 to 30 settings, occupied by a talkative ensemble, mixed male and female, of varying ages. One couple in their late 40s or early 50s sat at the head of the grouping, perhaps celebrating their anniversary. Another man stood and took hold of a microphone, preparing a toast.

Morris at once unpacked his laptop, and relaxed somewhat when he saw the wireless icon materialize in the lower-right corner of his screen; the network of the Architecture Commission remained on and available. Within 20 seconds he was logged onto sundaygolfers@mail. lt. A message from Grinevicius waited in the draft folder:

Evan,

Over the past two days I've provoked reactions here that I hadn't anticipated. In short: overt hostility from the Defense Department and other elements in the U.S. government, perhaps even including the

White House. Suffice it to say that your own position is more exposed and complex than either of us presumed in Vilnius.

I now worry that this communication link is compromised. For this and other reasons, I will depart Washington shortly and make contact by alternative means.

Best regards,

John

Tightness took hold in Morris' throat, together with another fit of self-rebuke. The short text carried portents of impending crackup... Here was more proof---as if any was needed---of the perils of financial overreaching...

"Are you ready to order?"

Startled, he looked up to find the waitress standing at his shoulder, holding her pad. As she retreated with his order, the band---three instrumentalists and a female vocalist---emerged across the dance-floor. The quartet took positions around their equipment, already in place from their first set. After a remark to the partygoers, completely incomprehensible to him, the singer launched into a Russian popular tune, one he'd heard before. Banquettes behind him quickly emptied as couples took to the floor.

Lyrics went up-tempo and the conjoined dancers became more energetic. And highlighted a larger reality. They belonged to a context in which he had no part. More than ever he felt on alien footing.

Which underscored a more unsettling fact. Lena was his only real cohort here. And he hadn't told her the whole truth.

CHAPTER 74

Monday, *August 4th*

Piper turned the lever hard-right and angled his face to the nozzle, letting the ice-cold jets smack his face and cascade down his torso. Twenty seconds later he rotated, exposed the nape of his neck, and replicated the pattern backside. Afterward a brisk towel-off, he hung his towel on the rack, and exited the bathroom, forgoing his occasional, vain impulse to pause before the full-length hall mirror, even for a few seconds. Instead he strode straight back to his study, where 550's latest report remained illumined on his laptop.

550 had come into view as soon as he rounded onto the park's main alley, having already closed half the distance from the river embankment.

Their shared glance had been quick---though long enough to discern 550's consequential demeanor and beep from his sport-watch. For the remainder of his run he'd maintained ripping, adrenaline-saturated pace, powered by a new dualism: sexual imagery of Lena fused with something else.

Visceral fear for her well-being. Whatever affected Morris was bound to affect her, too.

He refocused on the text, which he'd already transcribed from encoded Russian:

The special committee dealing with the Morris case has been meeting daily over these past several days---each meeting lasting an hour. Yesterday I learned that Yevgeny Bezrukov was called before the committee to give a briefing. Bezrukov is the head of the section for "Special Assignments." His role in KGB has always been vaguely defined, but he is reputed to have master-minded the abductions and "disappearances" of opposition figures Zakharenko, Gonchar and Krasovsky in 1999.

Bezrukov's presentation before the committee does not necessarily mean that a similar operation against Evan Morris has been activated. However the possibility exists, and should be taken seriously. If Morris is not in mortal danger already, he may well be in the immediate future.

I will try to alert you to further developments.

Nineteen-ninety-nine had been a particularly gruesome year in Belarus, Piper recalled. In May former Interior Minister and opposition figure Yuri Zakharenko vanished while walking home from a political meeting. In September, opposition leader Victor Gonchar and his deputy, Anatoli Krasovksy, disappeared on a Sunday sauna excursion. In the interim, in July, a Russian cameraman from the television station ORT also vanished, supposedly for his unfavorable reporting on the regime. None of the men were heard from again; Western intelligence agencies believed, without exception, that the four men had been murdered.

Nine years on, the regime was still in place, more rooted and paranoid than ever.

Aware now of the precise location of Morris' fifth-floor apartment on Kommunisticheskaya, Piper looked out the window over the treetops and re-sighted the three of Morris' windows that overlooked the Svisloch. He'd inferred from the Agency's profile that Morris was probably an early riser; was he already in his office? And Lena's apartment was just several blocks further north. Where was she at this early hour? Still naked, he stood up, strode to the bedroom and dressed.

There would be no more 1999s. For either Morris or Lena. Not if he could help it.

With his laptop slung over one shoulder, he exited his building onto the courtyard and at once noticed a lone and unfamiliar man standing near his parked Mercedes, smoking. By bearing the man appeared Russian; he gave Piper a forthright stare, ground out his cigarette, and initiated an approach.

Piper stopped and stared back. Was this an overture? Or first salvo in a full confrontation? 550's report was just two hours fresh, and he hadn't even conceived any counter-measures.

*   *   *

At closer distance, the first attribute of the man that caught Piper's attention was the striking light blue color of his irises. Otherwise his appearance was unexceptional: brown hair; medium height and build; conventional, moderately handsome features; early-to-mid-thirties. Piper had vague inkling he'd seen him before, incidentally---perhaps in a file photo rather than in person. The man stopped one meter away and spoke with courteous directness, in slightly accented English.

"Mr. Piper, my name is Oleg Mikhailov. I'm from the Russian FSB."

Piper took him in further, acknowledging nothing. Then scanned the parking lot to confirm that the man was alone. He was.

"I know about you from your file, including your address," he continued. "This manner of meeting is not to my taste, but I had little choice."

If this sudden materialization of the FSB on his doorstep was an outgrowth of Stapleton's trip to Moscow, Piper speculated, it could be just what he needed. He ratcheted down his hard expression.

"Would you prefer Russian or English?" Mikhailov asked.

"Russian would be less conspicuous."

The FSB man made a quick switch. "Can we talk? I only need about 30 minutes."

"Yes, we can."

"I propose walking across the street into the park."

"I have no objections," Piper answered.

CHAPTER 75

Piper and Mikhailov exited the courtyard in silence, and cut right toward the Prospekt. At the intersection, Piper considered where he might have encountered the Russian, even just on paper. Earlier in his career, in the waning days of the USSR, when he'd served a three-year stint in Moscow? Mikhailov looked too young to have worked for the KGB during that period. He continued rummaging his memories as the signal turned green and they traversed the crosswalk. On the opposite corner the name clicked. He bided confirmation until they were 20 meters into the park, and traffic noise had receded.

"Were you the plant who posed as interpreter and accompanied that American journalist to Tajikistan last year?" he asked. "His name was Conley, as I recall, a reporter from the *Boston World Tribune*. The story was all over the newspapers and television."

Mikhailov traced an ironic smile. "The FSB has never publicly commented on my role in that episode."

"I know."

The Russian kept his eyes forward. "If nothing else, my involvement with Conley spoiled my capacity for undercover work. For the record, I was recruited afterward."

Piper responded on similar pitch. "Okay, let's leave that aside. What's your role now?"

"Call me an all-purpose troubleshooter. I'm assigned to high-priority situations, developing crises, you could say. Sent out from Moscow with superseding authorizations."

Looking ahead, Piper saw that they were closing in on the statue of Janka Kupala. He drew to a stop, preferring the initiative. Mikhailov did likewise and turned to face him. "Are you here because of Evan Morris?"

The Russian paused to choose his phrasing. "Your Deputy Director, James Stapleton, made a persuasive case yesterday in Moscow. Let's put it that way."

Piper evaluated him and waited for more.

"…My assignment is to prevent my Belarussian counterparts from doing anything rash," he continued. "…Toward Morris or anyone else connected with this matter. The last thing Moscow wants in Belarus just now is an international crisis, or another story that makes headlines."

"Then I'm glad you're here, Mr. Mikhailov."

"Call me Oleg."

CHAPTER 76

To Piper Putin's first term had generated real progress: tax and legal reform, anti-corruption initiatives, better management of the sclerotic Russian bureaucracy, more-or-less honest parliamentary elections. Not to mention deepening cooperation between Russia and Western countries, particularly against terrorism and the narcotics trade. Then he'd been assigned to Ukraine, and witnessed, first-hand, resurgence of the other, more traditional side of Russian political conduct: cynical, brutish and domineering, particularly toward countries in its periphery. During the Orange Revolution his main adversaries had been the FSB and their Ukrainian proxies. Evidence suggested Russian intelligence had even been involved, on some level, in the poisoning of Victor Yushenko, the Western-oriented opposition candidate.

Stung by perceptions of defeat afterward, Putin and his second-term government had become more belligerent and mistrusting. They'd tightened control over Russian media and walled the country off from outside influences, while also exporting the same retrograde attitudes to Belarus, propping up the regime, making Belarus a de facto vassal state. And thus far, despite some improved rhetoric, the new Medvedev-Putin tandem had just offered more of the same.

On the future of Russian democracy, therefore, Piper considered himself agnostic, but still hopeful. It was from this vantage point that he now assessed Oleg.

They remained standing in front of the monument. For now the square was void of other people.

"Likewise. You can call me Russell."

Mikhailov acknowledged the invitation with a nod. Piper continued.

"Were you were aware of the situation with Morris before Stapleton's visit?"

"Almost from the beginning. Not much happens here without our knowledge."

"I'd grown concerned. Your embassy seems mostly empty this month."

The Russian frowned for an instant, not appreciating the remark. His brows shifted to inquisitive. "Does that imply you've also been aware of this from the beginning?"

"Hardly. I've had no direct contact with Morris. Our information came to us piecemeal, just in the past few days. And oddly, mostly through Washington."

Mikhailov knew better than to inquire about Piper's local sources. Belarus remained contentious terrain, whatever the outgrowths of Stapleton's trip.

"I assume you're aware of the origin of Morris' trouble?"

"We have an idea."

"Then perhaps we've come to the core."

Piper waited for Mikhailov to make first broach.

"I'm referring to Amoud al-Tikriti," the Russian said.

"That's a good place to start," Piper answered.

*   *   *

Piper was not yet briefed on Stapleton's dialogues in Moscow. In any event Mikhailov confirmed what the Agency had already presumed:

that Russian special services had organized al-Tikriti's flight from Switzerland and secret relocation to Belarus. Due to information from the Russians, and from al-Tikriti himself, Lukashenko now also possessed full knowledge of al-Tikriti's sensitive role in the early days of the Iraq war, as well as the Iraqi's continuing connection to Gallstone. And thus far been paid abundantly for his trouble. Mikhailov didn't cite figures, or refer to a special "presidential" account, as Stapleton had, but admitted that the transfers were a meaningful source of hard currency for the Belarussian government, given its weakening economy.

This last fact, more than any other, explained the vigilance by the Belarussian KGB.

Thus far Piper could only speculate how Morris had seen al-Tikriti. Random encounter in the countryside? Freak sighting in Minsk? Second-hand information from an opposition sympathizer, or from one of his Belarussian employees? He declared his ignorance on this point.

"He's been moved anyway," Mikhailov said.

"I would expect that."

"And for obvious reasons, we prefer not to disclose his current whereabouts."

Piper sought to reassure the Russian. "To us al-Tikriti's exact location in Belarus is immaterial. An extraction operation has never been considered."

"Your Deputy Director said the same in Moscow. We would hope you're not that reckless."

"We're not."

Mikhailov clamped his lips with traces of sarcasm, a trait Piper had encountered before among Russians of his approximate age. Residual reflex from the USSR, he supposed. There was also the more recent matter of Iraq.

Again Mikhailov put the reaction aside, seeming intent on cooperation.

"I should note Al-Tikriti has not just been moved," he said. "He's also been placed under much stricter concealment. In other words, Morris may be the only foreigner who ever sees him here."

"That's part of what worries me," Piper noted. "For the Belarussians, this crisis boils down to one individual. Or two, I should say."

"The second being Lena Antonova?"

"Yes."

CHAPTER 77

The subject of Lena engendered a pause, and Piper and Mikhailov shifted a few paces further around the monument. Mikhailov was no doubt informed of the coercions the KGB had employed against her---whatever these were---and that she'd sought him out at the Embassy Party. So there was little sense in dissembling.

"My knowledge of Lena's role arose just days ago. My assessment is that she's an innocent bystander, involved only by virtue of Morris."

"That may be," Mikhailov answered. "Unfortunately my Belarussian colleagues don't see it quite the same way."

"Can that be rectified?"

"I'm already taking steps to alleviate her exposure, just as I'm doing with Morris." The Russian turned his head for more direct appraisal. "What's your interest in Lena exactly? Unlike Morris, she's not a U.S. citizen."

"Call it a moral consideration."

"Not everyday words from an intelligence operative."

Piper didn't react to the comment.

"Anyway I intend to meet her," Mikhailov added. "Maybe on Wednesday. She needs to be reassured."

Piper imagined a phone call and/or impromptu rendezvous in a public area, in keeping with templates handed down from the Soviets.

"At some point soon I should do the same with Morris," he said.

Mikhailov frowned slightly. "I would respectfully ask that you hold off on such contact, at least another week. I'm still trying to tamp down excess among my Belarussian counterparts. A direct meeting between Morris and the CIA station chief in Minsk at this juncture will only complicate my efforts."

"I'll think about it."

Another short pause ensued, and Piper took stock. In most respects Mikhailov's appearance in Minsk was fortuitous: the sort of responsible, elder-brother intervention with the Belarussian KGB that he and Stapleton had wanted. Still, he looked up at the massive figure of Kupala, who'd hovered over them for the previous few minutes. Mikhailov followed his gaze, before Piper turned back to address him.

"As I suggested earlier, Oleg, I welcome your appearance here. However I'm sure you can understand my caution."

Mikhailov's light blues were curious but unwavering.

"I'm referring to the mixed trends in Moscow. Backsliding toward old habits. Hopeful signs nonetheless from Medvedev. Where you fall in that rubric."

Deducing the connection to Kupala, Mikhailov glanced up at the statue and formed a restrained smile, revealing traces of the sarcasm that Piper had detected earlier. Yet with seeming absence of artifice.

"Don't worry, Russell. Those dark days are past."

"I hope so. If so, we're all better off."

Piper let the theme conclude on this concordant note. But he was thankful that Lena had her emergency phone number.

And that he had a backstop.

CHAPTER 78

From a small terrace outside the terminal, Piper scanned the softening hues in the East and spotted the Learjet in slow descent, about three kilometers behind a commercial airliner from Baltic Airways. The larger craft came in with a roar and smoky expulsions of burnt rubber, trailed by the Lear, with higher pitch and elegant, near-frictionless touchdown. He then turned to find Scott Ewald, Vilnius station chief, a recent initiate in his mid-30s, dressed in a beige summer suit. He smiled and shook Ewald's hand.

"Hello, Scott. What's this about?"

"Stapleton didn't fill you in?"

"No."

Ewald glanced toward the end of the runway, one of two principal landing strips at Vilnius International Airport. The Lear turned, still whirring its fan-jets, and began taxiing toward the terminal.

"Well, he's arrived. I suppose you'll hear soon enough."

In keeping with Agency norms, the Lear was white and bore no fuselage markings except for the numerical identifier. It parked on open tarmac, about 40 meters from the terminal, and an attendant lowered the side-hatch. First to appear was a fit-looking bodyguard, succeeded by Stapleton, carrying a slim briefcase. After brief greetings on the terrace, their quartet proceeded into the terminal, where Ewald's Lithuanian assistant was waiting. She ushered Stapleton, Piper and Ewald down a narrow hallway to a door labeled *Foreign Ministry/ NATO*. Inside was a small, spare conference room capable of accommodating five-six people, which Piper had visited once before, to meet a traveling contingent of European intelligence officials.

Stapleton got settled, pulled out a folder, and inquired about Piper's drive.

"No bottlenecks at the border, thank God. Two-and-a-half hours, door to door."

"Good. I wouldn't have called you up here so soon after our meeting in Frankfurt if it wasn't urgent. I also wanted Scott on hand." The Deputy Director nodded at Ewald. "He has news on another unexpected development with the Morris case, I'm afraid."

Ewald nodded once but said nothing.

"...But we'll get to that in a moment. First, I'd like to hear about your contact with Oleg Mikhailov this morning."

Piper obliged, opening a folder holding several pages of handwritten notes and copies of his typed brief, which he passed over. Stapleton skimmed down the report. "Even in the FSB there are tints and shades, as we all know. Mikhailov has been a cipher to us, ever since Tajikistan. Now that you've met him, Russell, where do you think he falls?"

"First impression? He seems well-disposed toward the West in general, which may help on the margins. Nonetheless, it goes without saying that he'll follow his orders to the letter, whatever those are."

"Of course. I assume you received my brief on Moscow before you left?"

Piper nodded.

"Good. As I described, my counterparts in the FSB are wary of this situation with Morris, just as we supposed. But we're talking about Belarus here. Cooperation doesn't come naturally. Best case? We consider this a one-off." The Deputy Director paused and shook his head.

"...That is, if we can keep all the other pieces aligned, on our side. With that, I'll cede to Scott."

Ewald passed over a four-page brief.

"This is probably the last distraction you need, Russell, but here's the latest. On the first page you'll see a photograph of Malcolm Crowder. CEO and largest single shareholder of Cognition Software."

Piper glanced down at the image, showing a stocky man of about 50 with wire-rimmed glances and a half-wild glint in his eye, perceptible even in the photograph. Ewald continued.

"Crowder arrived in Lithuania two days ago with a couple of vice presidents and a contingent of technicians. They've already rented a house on the outskirts of Vilnius, where they've proceeding to set up an operational base."

This last phrase alarmed Piper.

"Don't tell me they're about to attempt something rash."

"I'm afraid so. Their undertaking first came to our attention through our intelligence contacts in the Lithuanian VSD. We've since been able to assemble a decent picture ourselves. Crowder apparently intends to mount a rescue operation, for Morris and other company employees in Minsk. Toward this end he and his team are making contacts among ex-military and intelligence operatives. You know the type...ones who've gravitated toward private security firms since the collapse of the Soviet Union. There's still quite a number of them floating around the Baltics, just as there in the rest of the ex-Soviet space. Through these contacts, he's attempting to secure two or three fast-bore military helicopters, still in relative abundance thanks to hardware the Soviets left behind."

"Good God. And fly them into Belarus? Doesn't Crowder...or his Lithuanian associates, for that matter...appreciate that the western Belarus border is one of the most heavily defended in Europe?"

"If so, the obstacle doesn't seem to faze him. And the people he's cooperating with will probably undertake just about any operation for the right price."

Stapleton interjected from the head of the table.

"Just before I left Moscow," he said. "I received a report from Langley, gleaned from other agencies in Washington. On his way to Europe from the States, Crowder met privately in Bermuda with Ross Perot."

"Don't tell me he's modeling this on Perot's 1980 Iran operation."

"Perhaps Crowder figures he can learn from Perot's mistakes," Ewald noted. "Bottom line? He's here. And he appears to be serious."

"Can't you have a talk with him, Scott?" Piper asked. "Convince him that this is a reckless fantasy?"

"I considered that, Russell. Easier said than done."

Stapleton elaborated.

"Based on past indicators Crowder is very wary toward the U.S. government," he said. "Or any government for that matter. Suasion will likely get us nowhere."

Cradling his chin between thumb and forefinger, Piper shook his head, still half-incredulous.

"What about just shutting him down? Enlisting help from the VSD?"

"We'll stymie him, of course," Ewald answered. "But the Lithuanian economy isn't exactly booming just now. Cash goes a long way here. A private citizen with two billion dollars in personal wealth and thousands of employees at his disposal can be awfully hard to keep in a box."

"I've already warned my counterparts in Moscow," Stapleton added. "But I would suggest, Russell, that you also broach the subject with Mikhailov at the earliest opportunity. Also keep him apprised of continuing developments. The last thing we need, given our new and tenuous cooperation with the Russians in Belarus, is to withhold information from them. Otherwise they'll think we're behind this."

Piper brought his hand down and inflated his cheeks with a long exhalation, while Stapleton collected his papers to his brief-case, preparing to re-board.

"You're right, Jim," he answered. "I'll attend to that tomorrow."

CHAPTER 79

Views from Piper's ninth-floor room at Novotel-Vilnius encompassed the Lithuanian Parliament and National Opera building, and the gentle curves of the Neris River just beyond. On the tributary's northern bank, dusk-light refracted off glass-sheeted skyscrapers in the new business district, icons to the recent, ill-fated boom in commercial real estate.

The lightweight blazer Piper had donned for dinner still hung comfortably on his shoulders, along with the meal's after-effects. He and Ewald had selected a tranquil, courtyard restaurant in the Old Town, and thanks to satisfying cuisine, a bottle of Bordeaux, and their free-ranging discussion on current East European politics, he felt more relaxed than he had in Minsk, despite the new intelligence he'd gleaned at the airport.

Until his thoughts gravitated back to Lena. To counteract them he crossed at once to his desk, made a quick check of his e-mail, plugged in his web-cam and opened Skype. To his relief he found Caroline's Skype icon active.

Despite her relaxed glow when she came on-screen she seemed vaguely preoccupied. She took in his image across the connection.

"Thank goodness for Skype, Russell. The distance is less noticeable than the phone."

"Everything okay?" he asked.

"Well...our ideal beach weather continues. And we just finished a delicious lunch---cold cuts, cheeses and French bread from that new bakery in town, capped off by fresh blueberries. You know how my mother loves to prepare for guests."

"I can imagine what awaits you for dinner. Is she still fixing desserts every night?"

"Key lime pies, rhubarb crisp, peach cobbler...The best I can do is moderate my portions."

"Well, your indulgence doesn't show. I wouldn't worry about it."

His remark prompted a quick smile, before the clouds returned. She glanced around, to make sure she was alone. "Actually my figure is the least of my concerns," she said. "I'm still concerned about Nick."

"Uh oh."

"...Nothing extreme. Just restlessness. He's kept up this habit of long swims. Another one this morning...more than an hour long. He disappears way up the beach, before he turns around and comes back."

"Better than drinking or smoking."

"You're right on that score. He does look fit."

"That's evident in the photos. Quite the young Adonis."

The remark did not hearten her, as Piper expected.

"He opened up as we were walking down to the beach this morning. Which is rare. Apparently he has trouble meeting girls his own age here, or even in town. Most girls are younger or older, he says. Maybe because he was on the tail end of the baby bust. My mother attempted one introduction. Somehow it didn't work out."

Caroline deliberated for an instant, weighing the follow-on. "I hesitate to spring this on you, Russell. But he also asked this morning if he could forego our college tour next week and fly back to Minsk early."

Piper leaned back, unprepared. "And miss out on exploring all those campuses with you and Melanie? Should be a fun trip. Once he got there I thought he'd get more excited about it."

"I hoped the same."

Both of them fell silent for a moment. Piper recollected Nick's comments on the drive to the airport.

"What was your response?"

"That I'd wait and talk it over with you."

As Piper considered the prospect, Caroline observed him over the connection.

"I'm not in favor of the idea, Russell. And I know you're wrapped up with work. Still, do you think we should consider it?

"Well...the timing *is* inopportune. Let's mull this over for a day or two."

CHAPTER 80

Wednesday, 5 August 2008

Under-ventilated air tended to afflict *Okean* later in the day, especially in summer, so Lena preferred to visit the store in mid-morning. Also to meet the day's first fresh bread. Just as she started on her list Natasha called her mobile. She got right to the point.

"I've decided to go."

Lena stepped into an alcove near the beer coolers. "Go where?"

"To Italy, of course. To take that vacation with Fabrizio."

"Natasha, I'm in the food store now, shopping. Can I call you back when I get home?"

Reluctantly, Natasha agreed. Lena sighed and replaced her phone in her purse. Natasha remained completely unaware of her travails with the KGB. She still didn't approve of her friend's plan, but felt engulfed now by more pressing priorities. She glanced at her list again and resumed progress.

After a stop in the produce section she made her way to the bakery rack in the rear. Prominent among this morning's selections was a full bin of wheat loaves, which she prodded with metal tongs and found soft to the touch. She selected a half-loaf and bagged it, pleased to find it still warm. Next she proceeded to the dairy section, where the woman behind the cheese counter, to her surprise, had not yet succumbed to adverse moods and even offered a polite smile. Lena reciprocated, ordered a half-kilogram of Russian-made *Edam*, and continued to the yogurt cooler while her basket was still light.

Most yogurts these days---even the Western brand names---were also manufactured in Russia. The trend had been underway for three or four years and cut across most food-products, with the exception of baked goods, fresh meat and produce. Russian food companies, bit by bit, appeared to be taking over.

Which didn't really matter that much to her. Quality was more important than provenance. She selected a container of peach yogurt, the Russian brand *Emigurt*, and checked the calorie-content and expiration date. While her hands were still full her cell-phone rang in her purse. Assuming it was Natasha again, calling with some additional announcement or angle that couldn't wait, she answered without glancing at the display number.

"Hello, Elena Grigorovna?"

Not Natasha at all. The voice was male, about her age, maybe a little older; standard Russian accent. Educated. She answered cautiously.

"Yes?"

"My name is Oleg Mikhailov. I'm with the Russian FSB. The SVR branch, to be precise."

Lena straightened and dropped the yogurt in her basket.

"...I'm now in Minsk," he continued, *"and aware of your current predicament with the Belarussian KGB, in connection with Evan Morris."*

Mention of Morris' name gave her a little chill. The man's courteous tone didn't correspond to his content.

"I'm listening," she said.

"I wish to be of assistance. Toward that end I wish to meet you."

Remembering her earlier encounter with Shinkevich, her first instinct was to scan surrounding aisles for a man on a cell-phone. None came to her attention. She chose directness, to signal she was not intimidated.

"Are you nearby?"

"No. I admit I know where you are, Lena Grigorovna. But I'm elsewhere in the city. That sort of approach is not to my liking."

"What do you propose, then?"

"Time is rather critical, so I'd prefer to meet you today. However I'll let you designate the exact time and place."

By now Lena felt steeled to this. She weighed her options before responding.

*   *   *

At his office window Piper stopped pacing and re-checked his watch. Three-fifty: Lena's rendezvous with Oleg would occur in ten minutes. Oleg's alert had occurred by telephone: *"...Due to the mutual interest this matter entails."* However, with no venue specified.

Still, the Russian's omission was deliberate. Therefore a basis for worry.

Oleg had already out-maneuvered the U.S. once; the FSB might well have instructed him to repeat the feat here, on what they viewed as home turf. Piper gazed down on the Embassy courtyard, partly shaded from the late-afternoon sun, a de facto refuge from such hazards, worried he had ceded too may prerogatives to the Russian.

He exited his office and hastened downstairs to the operations center: a sizeable, basement-level chamber packed with electronics gear. Tommy Worthen, the chief of security systems, was already seated along a bank of screens along the far wall: what he called the tracking console. Worthen was the youngest American staffer in the Embassy, possessed of a recent master's degree in computer science; he probably also received the least exposure to sunlight. Piper sat down in the empty chair beside him, and laid his secure cell-phone on the console's protruding counter.

"Already established coverage, Tommy?"

"Five minutes ago for her phone signal. All of greater Minsk. However our satellite won't pass overhead for another twenty-three minutes. Until then, we won't have any live shots. Just images from the last fly-over."

Piper glanced up at the central display, an LCD flat-screen. Longitude and latitude were superimposed over a static image of the city, taken about fifty minutes earlier. It showed the familiar arteries emanating from the center, out to the two ring roads.

"And you'll know if her phone is switched on, and where?"

"Instant it happens, as long as she's above ground. Location down to the meter."

They fixed their eyes on the screen. Still free of flashing indicators. A digital clock just above read 3:55. Through previous experiences with Piper, Worthen was acquainted with boundaries. What he could ask and what he couldn't.

"Are you expecting the subject to make a call, Russell?"

"Only if she perceives herself to be in danger. And only to one number."

Piper gestured toward the cell-phone on the counter.

"In other words," Worthen said," You'd prefer just to observe the signal location, for starters."

"You could say that."

"Wait, here she is," Worthen interjected, pointing toward the screen. "Looks like she's coming out of the metro."

CHAPTER 81

From *Vostok* station Lena curved in along the northeast approach. When it came to Russians, this venue was one she associated with official delegations. For that reason she half-expected Oleg Mikahailov to materialize by chauffeured car, asserting implicit domain over the plaza. And over her, by extension.

Instead she spotted a solitary figure waiting near the entrance, dwarfed by the backdrops of stone mural and glass. Rather than an apparatchik's suit---like Shinkevich's---he wore a silk shirt and cream-colored slacks, and fixed on her through modish sunglasses as she drew closer. His age was also younger, corresponding to the voice on the phone.

She returned his gaze without breaking stride. When distance closed to a few meters he removed his frames and revealed light blue eyes----a hue she associated more with remote regions of northern Russia than Moscow. She drew to a stop.

"Elena Grigorovna?"

"Yes."

"I'm Oleg Mikhailov. Thank you for coming."

"You're welcome."

Her voice carried a biting overtone, which she intended.

It didn't seem to irritate him. Compared to Shinkevich, the more polished variety of *chekist*. Maybe Russian provenance, in this case, did denote higher quality. By instinct and experience, she at once ranked him her peer.

Maintaining his relaxed posture, Mikhailov smiled slightly and nodded over his shoulder at the massive form of the National Library, triangular panes glistening in the sunlight. "Seems suitable for an academic. Is that why you chose it?"

"I chose it because it's quiet this time of year. And it's close to the metro."

"I approve."

"I wouldn't imagine you took the metro."

"As a matter of fact, I did."

Lena smiled to the polite minimum. She wouldn't be disarmed that easily.

Mikhailov swept a hand over the sun-baked paving stones of the plaza. "It's still rather warm out here…Would you care to meet inside, and take advantage of the air conditioning?"

"You have to be a member of the library to gain access."

"I've already made arrangements."

"Including a room in which to talk?"

"Yes. In the conference center."

The new Belarussian National Library was designed to resemble a hexagonally-cut diamond, with angular glass facets and a narrow base--- Belarus' jewel of knowledge, according to official declarations. A pretension discredited, to Lena's slight perturbation, by numerous awkward foreign-language translations of the library's official slogan, carved over the main entrance. Particularly the English variant: "To knowledge are furnished all good works." Probably effected by a hack in-good-standing in the Foreign Ministry…Why hadn't they called her for a proper rendition?

Otherwise she had to admit the Library was probably the best-appointed public building in Belarus. She visualized the conference room accordingly: polished wood table, and chairs cushioned with the Library's signature light-green upholstery. Not to mention state-of-the art climate control. The picture was tempting, except for the prospect of hidden microphones and one-way mirror, preconfigured with video camera and technicians. She thought the better of it.

"I prefer the outdoors," she answered. "I hope you're not opposed to a walk by the canal?"

Mikhailov re-donned his sunglasses.

"Not at all, Elena Grigorovna."

* * *

Few people were present on the southern half the plaza; Lena observed one scholarly-looking young woman crossing toward the Library entrance, and several idlers sitting on a bench, exploiting shade from a recently-planted tree. Almost two hours remained before Library employees and visitors would disgorge onto the space on truncated summer schedule.

They strolled across the blank expanse, then bent down a walkway toward the canal. Along the way Mikhailov complimented the landscaping and layout of the Library grounds, which allowed her to take more nuanced stock of the FSB man.

Although her mother was Ukrainian and her father had been born in Russia, she'd always identified most of all with Russia. What was Belarus, after all? Even to Belarussians themselves, the country was a latter-day historical anomaly, arising from the chaotic breakup of the USSR. Most Belarussians didn't even speak their own language. Russia, by contrast, was a formidable, centuries-old world power, boasting 150 million souls and cutting across nine time zones. Possessed of deep, abundant culture and commensurate national identity.

Still, Belarus was where she lived. Not Russia. *Minsk*. Not Moscow. Regardless of Oleg's Mikhailov's smoothness and modernity.

They reached the canal and turned north, away from the Prospect. Mikailhov's eyes settled on an upcoming park bench. Pre-chosen? Another setup?

Rather than follow his cue she gestured toward the opposite bank.

"I suggest we walk over there," she said.

"As you wish."

They proceeded toward a footbridge which connected the two sides. The Russian seemed to take stock of his own.

"I remind you, Elena Grigorovna. I'm here to help."

"We'll see," she answered.

CHAPTER 82

"Can you zoom down, Tommy?"

Worthen outlined a sub-quadrant with his cursor and expanded the static image. Topography became more distinct. "They're right alongside the canal, there," he said, tracing the cursor across. "Near the end of that new pedestrian bridge. Again, these images are about an hour old. But our satellite is approaching. In another nineteen minutes we'll have live overhead shots."

"Do you have any lateral views on file, apart from the satellite images?"

With several quick movements of his mouse, Worthen opened a window on an adjacent screen and displayed two recent photographs of the bridge, with its gentle arc and modernistic design: one taken from the south bank of the canal, with the library in the background, the other from the north bank. After a glance back at the phone-signal tracking screen he activated a second cursor on the south-facing view and indicated three park benches, set up along the promenade.

"The subjects appear to be stationary," he said. "Probably seated on one of those benches."

Piper recalled not just the bridge but the park's general environs. Due to the newness of the plantings, the area remained wide open,

visible from both the Library and the tall, 70s-era apartment blocks on
the other side of the Prospekt. Not conducive to abductions or other
malefaction, especially in broad daylight.

Lena had chosen well. Everything he'd postulated about her thus
far was bearing out.

While he waited he imagined her sitting next to Mikhailov on the
bench, legs crossed under a summer dress like the one she'd worn to
Zhuravinka, knees exposed to the afternoon sun. He rolled back his
chair from the console and stood up, taking a deep breath.

"Thinking about driving out there?" Worthen asked.

"No. I'm staying put. Just need to stretch."

*   *   *

Expanding upon her initial assessment, Lena gained the impression
that Mikhailov accorded women special respect: the sort that issued
from a current of Russian culture that pre-dated the Bolsheviks and
had persisted to the present, despite countless setbacks. She also
noticed he wore a wedding ring, and for all her caution supposed on
that general basis that his wife was content with him---something she
doubted held true of his erstwhile confederates in the Belarussian
KGB.

Another contrast with Shinkevich registered on her: Mikhailov
did not hurry. Once they'd seated themselves he contemplated the
Library, whose southerly facets glinted with the quartering sunlight.
She did likewise, letting the dialogue play out slowly.

"A positive symbol for Belarus, it seems to me," he commented.

"Built with Russian oil subsidies, essentially."

Mikhailov considered the premise. He did not contest it.

"And you object to that?"

"In one sense, yes. Those subsidies have made us dependent on
you. Cut-price oil...massive state credits, natural gas at half the market
cost. We have no economic self-determination, which in turn extends

to other domains, not least of which is our internal politics and foreign policy."

"Most subsidies involve some degree of dependence, Elena Grigorovna. There are bound to be quid pro quos."

"To a point. But where does it stop?"

Mikhailov said nothing and observed her through his sunglasses.

"...Every year you squeeze a little harder, extract more and more concessions. Lately Russian companies have been taking over the Belarussian economy piece by piece, gradually assuming control of both consumer markets and Belarussian state enterprises."

"Does that really matter?"

"It matters if you live here."

"Even if one has Russian roots?" Mikhailov paused, his implication obvious.

"I assume you're referring to my father?" When he didn't answer she leveled another shot. "...Is that in my Belarussian file? Or the Russian one?"

"Belarussian, if that matters. Reading it is part of my job."

Lena pursed her lips for an instant and exhaled through her nostrils. Staying even, he let her reaction pass before he continued.

"If Russian owners invest their capital here, and introduce better management, doesn't that benefit you?"

"Not necessarily. The problem is lack of other options."

With this pronouncement Lena became suddenly emboldened. These ideas had been kicking around her head since his earlier phone call. Now they discharged. She gestured toward the library.

"While you were waiting for me, did you read the slogan over the main entrance? The one translated into multiple languages?"

"Only in passing."

"I assume you speak English?"

Mikhailov nodded.

"The English translation is horrendous, almost incomprehensible. The French isn't much better."

"They obviously should have consulted you, Elena Grigorovna."

In matters of intellect, Lena was not susceptible to compliments---in part because she was used to them. "Seriously, look at it before you leave," she said. "It exemplifies how isolated we are. We have so little interaction with foreigners that our own linguists can't create proper renderings."

Mikhailov held his courteous, inquisitive look. This only increased her edge.

"...Let me provide immediate frame of reference." She swept her hand toward the Prospekt. "...See many foreigners on the streets today? There are almost none, even in the capital city. The government's driven most of them out of the country."

"And that's the fault of Russia?"

"To large extent, yes. You've supported a crude, dictatorial regime which is hostile to the West. And the result is clear. Politically and economically, we're a virtual island, totally beholden to Moscow."

"This dynamic is nothing new, as you know. It goes back to Peter the Great."

"A dynamic which you perpetuate."

When Mikhailov offered neither acquiescence nor rebuttal, Lena re-fixed on the Library with a hard stare, suppressing the impulse to cross her arms. At last the Russian answered.

"Dependence isn't always bad, Elena Grigorovna. Sometimes it can work in your favor. In this instance I would suggest that's true."

First Morris and Piper. Now possibly Mikhailov as well. Any one of whom could let her down.

Lena didn't like to depend on anyone. Yet the list was only growing.

CHAPTER 83

At intervals Piper paced behind Worthen along the console, rarely diverting his gaze from the screen. He could tell he was making Worthen somewhat tense.

"Is the subject in danger?" Worthen asked.

"At this stage, probably not," Piper responded.

"Anyway, here comes our satellite. In thirty seconds we'll have live coverage, and know with more certainty."

Piper forced himself to sit down. He'd endorsed this rendezvous beforehand. Risks were low. Still, Lena and Mikhailov had been anchored to their park bench for nearly twenty minutes. Was the Russian going beyond reassurance? Proposing something more? The thought occurred to him that the FSB man had now stepped forward as her protector, supplanting himself from the same role. Which yielded mixed reactions, he had to admit.

At last the live image flickered onto the screen, overriding the old one. Worthen zoomed down at once onto the bench from a quartering angle, the two figures unmistakable.

"No signs of trouble," Worthen observed. "In fact they appear in no hurry to leave."

"Looks that way," Piper answered. "Could you zoom down a little more?"

"Sure."

The image enlarged by several more orders of magnitude, rendering it almost intimate. Hand gestures became discernible, postures, the color and cut of clothing.

Piper's gaze settled straight onto Lena's knees.

*   *   *

Lena knew that by stating her views so openly she risked antagonizing the Russian. On the other hand she saw benefit in defining her ground---in refusing to accept the enduring Russia/Belarus template of master and subordinate, even if it did constitute current reality for both herself and the country at large.

Mikhailov did not appear antagonized in any case. Willing to engage her in her own lexis. To meld abstraction with fact.

"My current assignment in Minsk corroborates my assertion," he said. "Allow me to explain."

"I'm listening."

"What has transpired recently between the Belarussian KGB and Evan Morris---and you by extension, Elena Grigorovna---quickly came to our attention in Moscow. We investigated and determined that this matter was developing along unstable, even dangerous course. For all concerned: for Russia, for Belarus, and most of all for you and Evan Morris. The information that Morris uncovered...by accident, it seems...has international political ramifications."

"Because Morris is American?"

"In part. But there's a much wider context than that. Russia's national interests are involved, as well as those of other countries such as the United States. On that note, may I ask you one question before I proceed?"

"If you must."

"Has Evan Morris ever revealed to you how he provoked the KGB in the first place?"

"No. He said it would be better if I didn't know."

"Good. It makes my assignment easier."

Lena wondered again who Morris had seen at Yuri's dacha. And what would happen to her if she did know.

"Now to specifics," Mikhailov continued. "In short, I'm here to forestall further damage, and to ensure a benign outcome. Toward that end, I have already outlined concrete measures with my Belarussian colleagues."

Lena rankled at the last word. Colleagues? What was the Belarussian KGB, in the end, except a tool of Moscow---a means of keeping a benighted, provincial population under the Kremlin's thumb? Though in this particular context Mikhailov was right; Belarussian subordination could also bring advantages.

What measures, she asked him?

"I have stipulated that the KGB is to refrain from all further action in this case. That includes direct contact with you and Evan Morris."

Lena weighed this. "Is that why neither one of us has heard from Dimitri Shinkevich for several days?"

"Not precisely. But that's irrelevant, now."

"Easy for you to say. As far as we could tell we remained under surveillance."

"That will also cease, as of today."

"Does that mean our case is closed?"

"No. That would be premature. But I can tell you that I have taken de facto control. From this point forward, nothing will happen without my knowledge or consent, to either you or Evan Morris."

"And what do you expect of us in return?"

"That's a natural question, Elena Grigorovna. "And I'll give a straightforward answer."

Lena braced herself. In Belarus, Russian largesse seldom came free.

CHAPTER 84

Mikhailov took care to emphasize that his next remarks were "guidelines, nothing more." Still, his gentle phrasing and inflection meant little to Lena. Here in Belarus, Russian intelligence officers---however smooth or cosmopolitan---did not issue guidelines. They issued instructions. Or to borrow a well-worn Soviet term: "firm requests."

Therefore she waited for him to finally reveal the sort of domineering core she'd glimpsed in Shinkevich. To her continued surprise, it did not appear.

"Both you and Evan Morris are to continue as you're doing now," he said. "Discussing the matter with no one. Carrying on with your lives."

"Can we leave the country?"

"You are under no prohibitions. But I would ask that both of you remain for the next two weeks. By then the matter should be closed."

Lena considered the timeline. Two weeks was manageable, for her or Morris and both. In her case she would just delay her vacation to Ukraine, which had been tentative anyway.

"I take it I should communicate this to Evan Morris?" she asked.

"Yes. In fact I encourage you to do so as soon as possible. Later, in four or five days, Morris will also be contacted by a member of the U.S. Embassy, with whom I have undertaken limited cooperation on this matter. His name is Russell Piper."

Lena checked any outward reaction. She kept her tone as bland as she could.

"I see."

Mikhailov scrutinized her with equal blandness. She presumed that he knew about their contact at the Embassy party, but had chosen not to broach it. Most surprising to her was ostensible cooperation between the FSB and CIA. In Belarus? In other parts of the world, maybe. Not here. Though standard geo-political equations seemed less and less relevant of late. Mikhailov was well-positioned to help her, like it or not. And Morris as well. Probably more than any CIA operative.

All the same she found herself wishing this initiative had originated from Piper. And that Piper's next contact would occur with her, rather than Morris. She couldn't specify exactly why.

*   *   *

After work Morris consumed a simple dinner in his apartment: ham and cheese cold-cuts, bread, and a medium-sized bag of potato chips, washed down with Coke. He also digested Lena's phone call, which he'd received before leaving the office. According to her report, Mikhailov had been sent from Moscow to ensure that their case didn't deteriorate further. "Russia wishes to avoid any international crisis here," she'd explained. "It's not in their interest." And, by way of clarification, that "organs in Moscow exercise dominant influence over the Belarussian KGB," and that "Russia is ultimately in charge." Despite several cautionary notes, she'd suggested their situation was now less precarious. Also that they proceed with their upcoming lesson plan, at which time she would provide more details.

He wanted to draw a modicum of optimism from the development. However Crowder's intentions remained open-ended, and she still didn't know the full scope of Grinevicius' initiative in Washington.

Upon finishing dinner he washed his dishes, wiped down the kitchen table, and moved to his living room to settle into his armchair. He resolved, at minimum, to warn her again about Crowder during their meeting.

The matter of Grinevicius was more complicated. On that, he resolved to wait a little longer.

CHAPTER 85

Across from the biathlon stadium Piper curved up the short incline and parked between the ski jumps and the base lodge. Most other spaces were empty, like Raubiche in general on a weekday. Warm air engulfed him as he emerged from his air-conditioning and stood on the asphalt, mixed with recollections of Svetlana. He pulled his mind off them and re-focused on his upcoming dialogue with Oleg Mikhailov.

By all indications: new, de-facto pro-consul from Moscow. About whom he'd formed another impression over the past few days. Unlike many other FSB men, and even in contravention of the general collectivist bent of Slavic culture, the Russian seemed to be a loner---one who preferred operating outside conventional guard-rails. This rendezvous only corroborated the notion.

"Our interactions are, how shall I put it...unorthodox," Mikhailov had said the previous evening by phone, "We'll invite less scrutiny outside the capital." His subtext: Russian-American cooperation in Belarus had no precedent, even on matters as tightly delineated as this, and the Belarussians were nervous.

Piper exited the parking lot and climbed steps toward the ski jumps, ten minutes early. Though Mikhailov had suggested Raubiche, he'd left the exact choice of locale within the complex to him---a gesture to which he wasn't accustomed after his chess games in Kiev. Stapleton's overture to Moscow had obviously laid the groundwork. Still, a Russian intelligence officer showing accommodation to the CIA? Rare, in the first place. And in Belarus?

Concerned about being lulled, he remained on guard.

He sidled between two mid-level bleachers and sat down in the approximate center of the spectator area. Two ski jumps towered up to his right: one 60 meters and the other 40 meters, supported by metal scaffolding. Their snow-free surfaces were now green, covered with material that looked like artificial turf. Narrow stairs lined the left edge of each jump. Piper had earlier surmised that the ski-jumpers faced long climbs before waiting their turns at the starter's box. He squinted against the sunlight and imagined the perspective on top.

Less than a minute later Mikhailov materialized at the end of the bleachers, also early. The Russian removed his sunglasses and greeted Piper with a handshake. "Ever watch a competition?" he asked in English, flicking a glancing at the jumps.

"Just on television."

"These are mid-size jumps, by Olympic standards."

"I know."

"Even at that scale, the sport is supposedly not as dangerous as it looks." He paused. "….Though naturally, that depends very much on your competence."

"Perhaps like intelligence work."

Both men smiled slightly. Mikhailov sat down and they switched to Russian.

With no obvious redaction, the Russian provided a comprehensive account of his meeting with Lena, including his phone call. She'd been wary in early stages, but had nonetheless seen fit to level some forceful criticisms of Moscow. When their discussion progressed to particulars, he said, Lena had parried him with questions. Despite misgivings she'd agreed to describe the altered schema to Morris, and knew that Morris would soon be contacted by Piper.

Thus far, Piper realized, he'd been much less forthcoming with Mikhailov than vice versa. He figured it was now time to give, in order to keep on getting. Meanwhile the sun was climbing higher. The aluminum seats were absorbing heat.

"Shall we get up and walk?" he asked the Russian.

"Fine with me."

Donning sunglasses, they navigated down from the bleachers onto the level grass of the landing zone, and began an unhurried stroll, skirting perimeter embankments as they talked. Piper's first subject was Malcolm Crowder and Cognition Software's would-be, private rescue operation from Lithuania. He covered all essentials, including base locations, financial resources, and evacuation objectives. The FSB, he figured, would soon uncover the scheme anyway, not least because many of the operatives were former Soviet military personnel.

Mikhailov clasped his hands behind his waist and listened stoically, in the manner of an older man. Piper didn't need to characterize the plan as reckless and ill-conceived; that was obvious.

"I appreciate your forthrightness, Russell," Mikhailov said when he'd finished. "It's not often the CIA informs us about undertakings abroad by U.S. citizens."

"Same goes for your openness with regard to al-Tikriti."

The Russian nodded once in acknowledgement.

"....In Eastern Europe," Piper added. "This may even be a first."

Tinges of concern flashed under Mikhailov's dark lenses. Since Tajikistan, the Agency had not identified his exact position in the FSB/SVR organizational chart, but presumed him to be mid-grade---until now. This assignment to Minsk confirmed his status as a rising star. Also his increased exposure to back-currents in Moscow.

"Novel initiatives are risky for field agents," he observed. "If things go wrong, we're the most vulnerable. Both of us know that."

Piper recalled Gallstone and experienced some twinges of his own. "Yes, I do. Particularly in arenas like Belarus."

"*Particularly* in arenas like Belarus."

The Russian glanced up at the ski jumps again.

"…Small arenas sometimes present breathtaking events, Russell. That's our problem."

*   *   *

While addressing remaining details they completed a semi-circle and drew under the base of the 60-meter jump. Mikhailov performed some unspoken calculations and suggested they angle out toward the center, underneath the trajectory line. Piper obliged him. About fifty paces out the Russian drew to a stop and examined the matted grass.

"This is about where they land."

Piper assumed the area had witnessed some spectacular crashes over the years.

"Preferably under full control."

The Russian formed a sardonic half-smile behind his sunglasses, and when they turned upward again, the ramp seemed to loom higher than from the bleachers. Piper tried to visualize the jumper's perspective.

"I've wondered about the sensation," he said, adding an ironic inflection of his own. "Must resemble flying."

"In jumping parlance, they call it 'gliding.'"

"Appealing term, if you know what you're doing…Here in Belarus, we're making jumps we can handle, right Oleg?"

"I hope so, Russell. Because it will hurt if we take a tumble."

CHAPTER 86

They'd abandoned any pretense of language instruction. They hadn't spoken a single word of Russian all evening. They'd also eschewed monuments, paddleboats and the Ferris wheel, opting instead for the second-floor terrace at the Firebird Café. Still, despite their now-more-conventional environs, Lena added some final, cautious notes to her summary, stressing that she and Morris were bit players in what appeared to be a much larger international dynamic, involving the governments and intelligence services of three countries. Meaning---despite the current de-escalation---that they had little ultimate control over their fates.

Russian power could be stabilizing, she explained. But it could also turn arbitrary and brutal if its interests were impinged. The key was Oleg Mikhailov.

Morris gulped the remainder of his Coke and placed the empty glass on the plastic table. He glanced around the terrace---occupied mostly by teenagers and young families with children----then down onto passersby, co-mingling at the intersection of the park's two main promenades. Children's music emanated from the speakers on ground level, casting a cheery, innocent vibe.

He did agree their ordeal was not over. Starting with the loose end of John Grinevicius. A subject he'd avoided thus far.

He put it off a little longer.

"So…I'm to expect Piper to contact me shortly?"

"In five days or so. That's what's Mikhailov told me."

"Toward what end?"

"First and foremost, reassurance, as far as I gathered."

Morris mulled this. He suspected Grinevicius would also be on the agenda, but kept the thought to himself.

Instead he re-addressed the issue of Malcolm Crowder, and whether he should raise this subject with Piper.

CHAPTER 87

Friday, 7 August 2008

Engaging all major muscle groups, Lena pivoted left and pumped her right knee high across her waist, splaying her elbows back and bosom forward. Her eye caught peripheral movement at the corner entrance as Piper materialized, clad in workout gear. He paused on the threshold of the training area and made quick eye contact.

At once she flicked her eyes back toward the mirror.

Re-glimpsing him from refracted angle, she watched him progress to the cardio area, where he mounted a Stairmaster, draped his towel around the upright handlebars and punched in a program. From earlier observation she remembered that his session lasted about 30 minutes. Timing was favorable, if they were to make contact...

While the routine wound down she began thinking ahead.

For the next number, at behest of the instructor, the class adopted wide stances, knees partially bent, and pushed their hands overhead in alternation. Feeling anchored again, Lena couldn't resist another quick check, and saw that Piper remained at slow tempo, still in his warm-up phase.

And that his eyes were not only open, but fixed unmistakably on her jutting hind-quarters. She turned quickly away. Lyrics from Madonna interposed themselves.

I know you want me.

So set yourself free…

Maybe she was mistaken, or overreacting? Several refrains later she re-twisted her view-line, and exhaled with reprieve when she saw his eyes had closed in the way she remembered. His program was gathering intensity; sweat dripped down his bare legs, and parts of his t-shirt were already plastering to his chest and abdominal muscles…

She hoped he stayed that way for the rest of his session. They could do without hindrances or diversions.

Though she had to admit his attention had transmitted a thrill.

*   *   *

The programmers were unapprised of Mikhailov's intervention and had remained skittish all morning, staring at their screens and tapping on their keyboards only occasionally. Yuri, for his part, had sequestered himself in his office; during a conference on technical issues Morris had found him brooding and taciturn.

In response Morris had tried to project general confidence, and re-emphasize software development. The approach wasn't working. Moreover Grinevicius had been incommunicado over the previous thirty-six hours; their shared e-mail account had gone cold. Frustrated, he finally rose from his desk. Several glances flicked over.

"I'm going to lunch at McDonald's," he told Anna.

She scrutinized his face for an instant, then checked the wall clock. Time was 11:40.

"…I want to beat the midday rush."

Everyone kept an eye on him as he got up and left.

Out in front of the building, he didn't look back and kept his cell-phone in his pocket until he approached the Prospekt. Before crossing to the Academy station entrance he ducked around the corner and speed-dialed Grinevicius' cell-phone number. To his slight surprise the call rang through. But with no answer. Deciding he'd had enough of delays and protocols, he called the lawyer's office. His secretary answered, in English, and became immediately careful when Morris identified himself.

"I'm afraid John is not in the office," she said.

"I've been trying to reach him since he left the U.S. Is he back in Vilnius?"

She hesitated. "Yes"

"In the office?"

"Off and on. I suggest you leave a message."

His frustration rising, Morris requested a call-back in ten to fifteen minutes and headed into the station. Nine minutes later, after a straight shot down the north-south metro axis, he emerged onto Oktryabraska Square. Halfway across his phone rang, with Grinevicius' office number on the display. The lawyer came on the line himself this time, harried and apologetic.

"It's about time, John. Until today I wasn't even sure you were back from Washington."

"I got back on Monday, actually."

"That was three days ago. What's going on?"

"Our situation is heating up, Evan. Let's put it that way."

"Can you give me the short version?"

"I'd like to. But not over the phone."

At the crosswalk on Engels Street Morris stopped and exhaled. The pedestrian signal turned green. "One way or another, John, I've got to talk to you. Even if that means you coming to Minsk."

"I can probably obtain a visa tomorrow, and get there by Saturday. How's that?"

"The sooner the better."

"Understood. I'll call again tomorrow and confirm my travel plans."

Still dissatisfied, Morris snapped his phone shut. The situation in Minsk seemed to be stabilizing. But events in Washington remained a disquieting blank.

Which also meant keeping Lena in the dark a while longer.

His mood elevated somewhat when he climbed the steps into McDonald's and was greeted by familiar aromas of hamburgers and French fries. The ambience was clean and bright, as always, with just a few people standing in line at the counter. He walked straight to a free register and ordered---the polite young female attendant more than happy to speak English. While he was withdrawing the necessary Belarussian rubles he sensed a tall figure draw up beside him. A familiar American accent issued his way, both cheery and nervous.

"I thought you might be heading to McDonald's."

Morris glanced up from his wallet. The speaker was Grinevicius.

CHAPTER 88

The instructor was ecumenical in her approach, often blending Pilates and other latter-day techniques with classical aerobics. Lena therefore anticipated some stretching and centering moves to close out the routine---particularly when a ballad from Beyonce commenced over the sound system. To her partial relief, the class adopted the bland "roll-up", followed by the "spine stretch," rather than the more demonstrative "bicycle" or "rocker with open legs".

Simultaneously, from the cardio zone, Piper unleashed a torrent of extreme breathing, overwhelming the ambiance. Sensing that he'd reached culmination---Lena couldn't resist another sidelong look.

Even after her earlier observations, she wasn't quite prepared for what she saw.

Sheens of saliva had formed on his lips and chin, and his eyes rolled wild under his eyelids. During the furious final seconds, he boosted his air intake even higher, then half-bared his teeth and emitted a visceral, half-audible groan.

The blatant, raw animalism of the display was a little frightening to her.

Almost on cue, the music subsided and the class engaged in mutual applause. Everyone rose from the floor to put away their mats, and Lena

ventured another glance via mirror, catching him wiping face and forearms with his hand towel. Impediments to direct contact had diminished
since the Embassy Party, thanks to Mikhailov. Aware of what came next
in his routine, she attached herself to a wall-railing and lingered over
some additional stretching exercises. She didn't have to wait long; two
minutes later Piper climbed off the machine, draped the towel around
his neck and sauntered over toward her position, limbering his legs.

His movements, lithe and dominant, resembled those of a satiated
safari animal. Lena averted her eyes. Then re-established contact as
he drew up.

"Hello," he said, in English.

"Hello."

Their interaction drew instant attention from the instructor, who
was crouching in the corner near the audio system. In Lena's view the
instructor was well-meaning but also a little over-proprietary toward
her students. She didn't know if she spoke English.

"Good work out?"

"All right. Though not as intense as yours, it seems."

Piper grabbed the railing, straightened one leg behind him, and
stretched his Achilles tendons. At the same time he angled his face
inward, away from the instructor, and spoke half into his towel, so his
voice was muffled. "We shouldn't talk here for too long."

She nodded, while he observed her reaction.

"...Can you meet me in the sauna in about ten minutes?"

Lena exhaled and nodded again, glad the initiative had issued
from him.

"Let's exchange a few more pleasantries," he continued. "And finish our stretching. Then I suggest you head for the locker rooms first."
He switched legs, elongating the other set of tendons, then, after a
pause, wiped his face and examined her again.

Her thoughts zipped ahead. The sauna was less utilized in summer
than in other months, but they couldn't be sure they would have it to
themselves.

And either way, she'd be clad in only a towel.

"Agreed."

* * *

Morris emptied warm fries onto his tray, sprinkled on extra salt, and poked several into his mouth. Meanwhile Grinevicius uncapped his bottle of *BonAqua* and surveyed other lunch-goers from their second-floor table, partially shielded by a granite planter topped with artificial ferns. A foursome of teenage girls was camped immediately behind them: giggling and glancing at their mobile phones. Two places over, a mother watched her young son devour his "Happy Meal", intent on his manners. None looked like KGB. Most other customers had gravitated to the umbrella-shaded seating outside.

Grinevicius relaxed a little, though much of his laid-back affability from Vilnius was gone.

"Unconventional, John," Morris said. "But well done. Where did you pick me up?"

"Outside your office. From there I tracked you onto the metro, and onto the square. I tried to be careful."

"You'd make a good intelligence agent yourself."

Grinevicius conveyed a sheepish smile and un-wrapped his *MacFish* sandwich.

"No problems getting a visa?"

"Not really. I came on my Lithuanian passport. Got here by train at mid-morning. I'm already checked into *Hotel Minsk*."

The lawyer paused and swilled down his first bite of fish sandwich with mineral water. Morris did likewise, sipping his chocolate shake. "Thankfully things have calmed down here in Minsk over the past few days," he said. "But I'll get to that later. Let's start with Washington. Your last message sounded downright ominous. What's going on?"

Grinevicius shifted his lanky frame, unable to manufacture another smile. "We knew Amoud al-Tikriti was an enigmatic figure.

Turns out that wasn't the half of it. This guy, even after all this time, remains a figure of major importance to the U.S. Government...to the point where they don't have the patience for rewards."

"I was afraid of that. Better give it to me straight. Don't leave anything out."

Without referring to notes, the lawyer proceeded chronologically, starting with his meeting with the Pentagon's Public Affairs Bureau. At the appointed time, he'd met a junior civilian official, who'd first shown puzzlement, together with suspicion that their interaction was a waste time. Until Grinevicius mentioned Amoud al-Tikriti by name. At once the official had excused himself to make a phone call. Ten minutes later he conducted Grinevicius up to the office of a senior Army officer on the fifth floor. One Colonel Harold Hodges, Army Intelligence. Two junior-looking officers, who remained unidentified, had listened to the dialogue from the back of the office. Grinevicius had stayed cool and matter-of-fact, emphasizing that he was a licensed attorney representing a U.S. citizen "currently residing overseas." And that this was just an exploratory contact. The colonel had bored back with queries. In what country? Grinevicius deferred. Was the sighting visual? Yes. In full daylight and from less than 10 feet away. Definitive? Again yes: based on multiple photographs of the Iraqi. The colonel had exchanged consequential glances with the two officers over Grinevicius' shoulders, and suggested another meeting the next morning. He'd also asked where Grinevicius was staying, and how long he'd be in Washington.

"And you told them?" Morris asked, clasping the last of his fries and transferring them to his mouth.

"Of course not. I already sensed I'd touched a nerve. I didn't want to get my sister mixed up in this."

"Makes sense."

"Right afterward I left my sister's apartment, and checked into the Crystal City *Marriott*."

More to calm himself now than satisfy his appetite, Morris reached for his double cheeseburger. The lawyer chewed and swallowed a bite of fish sandwich before resuming.

His appointment the next day was at nine a.m.; he materialized at Entrance D ten minutes in advance. Before he could approach reception/security, he was pre-empted by a uniformed Intelligence officer, who diverted him to a side office and processed him separately from other visitors, scanning and scrutinizing his passport. Instead of returning to Colonel Hodges' office on the fourth floor, as he expected, he was ushered into a small amphitheatre---accessed from the second floor---and up to the stage. Already in the audience were about fifteen men and two women, scattered among the first few rows of seats. About half appeared to be civilians, expressions intent and solemn. Colonel Hodges stepped forward. He didn't identify the observers, except to say that several "worked for the White House and National Security Council" and that other civilian agencies were also participating, "due to "the serious and wide-ranging ramifications of this matter for national security." When Grinevicius asked to be informed of everyone's identities, Colonel Hodges bristled. Tried to intimidate him, with no success. The colonel finally pledged to provide a list after the meeting.

"Did he carry through?" Morris asked.

"I'll get to that later."

Morris lowered his cheeseburger, pulled a deep breath, and drew again from his chocolate shake.

Next Hodges re-commenced. Queries: acute and aggressive, with occasional interjections from the audience. Much the same as the previous day, just more detailed. Grinevicius added little to what he'd already stated. Impatience buzzed up among assembled parties. With such meager information, asked a middle-aged suit from the audience, why had Grinevicius contacted the Pentagon?

To explore the possibility of a reward, the lawyer reiterated. Hodges had waited a downbeat. As if this juncture was pre-planned.

Another suit stood up in the fourth row---somewhat plumper and older than the previous questioner, his face hardly distinguishable under the offstage lighting. His diction carried twangs and clipped suffixes which Grinevicius associated with Texas or the rural Rocky Mountains. Without naming himself, he said he worked for the National Security Council, and spoke on behalf "of all the bodies represented here today." The U.S. government, he declared, was prepared to offer $10 million for information leading to killing or capture of al-Tikriti. The only stipulation was secrecy; Grinevicius' client was forbidden to disclose the transaction and the U.S. Government would deny it in any case.

And what if the information doesn't lead to killing or capture, Grinevicius inquired?

Then Grinevicius' "hitherto unnamed client" could at least draw satisfaction from fulfillment of their "patriotic duty as U.S. citizens."

And if his client was exposed, saw his life up-ended, and received no money in return? Were there intermediate variants? Was the government open to negotiation?

"I'm afraid not," said the unnamed speaker from the fourth row. "On national security matters such as this, the U.S. Government does not negotiate."

Eerie silence had fallen over the gathering, while Grinevicius sat stupefied onstage. This was the territorial United States, under rule of law. Did these political appointees and military officers really expect that they could dictate terms? After considering a moment, he inserted his notepad in his briefcase and stood up to leave.

At once Hodges stepped forward from the edge of the stage.

"I must inform you that broader issues are involved here, Mr. Grinevicius," the colonel declared. "Walking away isn't as easy as that."

Morris put down his milkshake and stared across the table, just as stunned the lawyer professed to be at the time.

"Good God."

Grinevicius allowed the ramifications to expand on their own.

"To apply rock climbing jargon," he observed. "That's when I knew we'd gotten into a heinous spot."

CHAPTER 89

Two knocks sounded through the door and made Lena's pulse bounce. Piper's smooth baritone penetrated the damp wood; is it possible to enter, he asked in Russian? She re-checked the bind in her towel, and verified that the terrycloth edge wrapped neither too high nor too low over her breasts before responding, first in Russian then again in English---recognizing too late that the redundancy signaled her nerves and over-eagerness, both of which she wished to conceal.

At the threshold Piper made courteous, direct eye contact through the dim light, then turned sideways as he closed the door. His elasticized bathing trunks amplified his lean waist, and drew attention upward to the bared muscles of his torso, still glinting with perspiration from his workout.

"Looks like we have it to ourselves," he said.

"A pair of women just left."

She straightened her posture and waited for his next move. He smiled and stayed businesslike.

"Okay if I sit up there?"

She scooted sideways and gestured toward the space next to her on the second-level bench.

"Of course."

With deliberate movements he climbed up and spread his towel out on the hot slats, settling into position no more than 30 centimeters away. Her eyes traveled involuntarily up the lines of his thighs to the close-fitting fabric over his male organs, and it occurred to her she'd probably never been in such intimate proximity to a well-built man in a closed space. Particularly one who was more-or-less unknown.

He waited a respectful interlude before looking at her again. If he'd indeed fixed on her during his workout, he'd now reasserted control of himself. "I've gathered you know about my contacts with Oleg Mikhailov. He also informed me about your meeting yesterday."

"Yes, and I'll admit, Mr. Piper…"

"Russell."

She nodded. "…Cooperation between Russia and the U.S. is not something I ever expected to see here."

"I didn't either, to be frank. However these circumstances are unique. It seems to offer the best solution."

"What does it mean for the arrangement we made at the Embassy party?"

"We're just as committed to you as before. In fact now that the heat is off, we're going to add another safety measure. After our sauna I'll give you a dedicated emergency phone, registered to the same Ukrainian trucking company. You can turn it on whenever you feel threatened, and use it to call me directly, if necessary, rather than the other number I gave you. I'll give one to Morris as well, when I see him."

She nodded her appreciation. Their first-person plurals also hung for a moment in the overheated air. Lena felt her flush rise again. This time she didn't attempt to hide it.

They'd crossed a subtle threshold.

Once again she became conscious that they were sitting mostly unclothed in a confined space. She glanced over at the metal container with its superheated rocks, then at the wall-mounted thermometer.

The dial indicated 108 degrees Celsius. Out of some inborn reflex---she arched her spine, rendering taut the fabric of her towel and protruding her buttocks backward on the bench.

After a slight pause she re-appraised him.

His attentions locked for a second or two on her flanks. Then ascended to her partially exposed cleavage, and where his eyes lingered for another long instant before disengaging.

All the same he appeared very much in control.

"We shouldn't overdo this conversation, Lena," he said. "Even with recent changes, protocols still matter."

"Okay. I'll keep my remaining questions brief."

She smiled at him, figuring she could tolerate the heat about five minutes more. Her confidence also ascended several tiers.

His attraction---if it indeed existed---didn't have to cause problems. Russell Piper appeared quite capable of self-regulation.

*   *   *

Grinevicius paused to partake further of his MacFish sandwich, before laying it back in the wrapper only two-thirds finished. He then sipped his mineral water and watched dubiously as Morris consumed the rest of his Big Mac, punctuated by sips from his chocolate shake. Sensing the lawyer's attitude, Morris looked over.

"You're not going to finish it?" he asked.

"I've lost my taste for this stuff since I moved overseas."

"Not me. I never will."

The lawyer refrained from comment.

"What happened after you left the Pentagon?"

Grinevicius resumed. During his tense exit from the auditorium, Colonel Hodges' had assured him, unconvincingly, that the list of participants would be supplied "a short time later." From there a black SUV trailed him out of Lot D all the way to the Crystal City Marriott, where two plainclothes observers, their assignment unmistakable, already awaited his arrival in the lobby.

On these bases he surmised that e-mails from his hotel room would be monitored, and that his only safe means of communication was his auxiliary cell-phone, for which he'd purchased an anonymous SIM card at Dulles Airport. That was, until Hodges called him on the phone soon afterward and requested another conference at the Pentagon the following day. The Colonel cited several clauses in the Patriot Act and "Executive Order 271." His tone implied that compliance was mandatory.

Subsequent Internet searches revealed that Executive Order 271 established staggeringly wide power for the government to survey, detain and question individuals deemed threatening to U.S. national interests. Shaken, Grinevicius hunkered in his hotel room and mulled what to do.

Later, according to prior arrangement, he left for dinner with an old college friend at a restaurant near DuPont Circle.

"Because I didn't want to mix him up in this, I was determined to shake off surveillance," he recalled. "I brought my laptop with me, and walked through the lobby toward the parking lot, holding my car keys. Once I was outside, I doubled back around the hotel and jogged to the Crystal City metro station. On the train I turned off my phones."

"Pretty serious move. Did it work?"

"Almost too well, as it turned out. My surveillance apparently got unnerved. They rifled through my room...briefcase, clothes, everything...probably trying to figure out where I'd gone. When I got back around 11 o'clock, Hodges called me immediately. He demanded to know my previous whereabouts. He also implied I'd face 'appropriate measures' if I tried to slip my surveillance again."

Morris shook his head, astonished.

"I can't believe this was happening in the United States," he said. "To a U.S. citizen, besides."

"I couldn't either. I'd tangled with the IRS before, but this reached a whole different level."

The lawyer paused to sip his mineral water, as if additional hydration would fortify him.

"The next morning I eluded them again, and took the earliest flight I could back to Europe."

CHAPTER 90

Following the five-block drive back to the Embassy Piper parked along a vacant curb near the Consular entrance---free of visa queues since March's diplomatic bust-up---and rounded through the main gate, glad to attain the cool sanctuary of his office. In the tight, over-heated confines of the sauna Lena had re-kindled his energy surfeits, partly annulling the effects of his cardio blow-out. Juices he'd just expelled were already surging back, which concerned him somewhat.

At his desk he picked up his phone and ordered a turkey and cheese sandwich, with carrot salad and mineral water, from the Embassy's cafeteria service. Next he clicked his laptop out of hibernation; no new e-mails awaited him; it was still early in Washington.

While waiting, he reclined in his chair, closed his eyes, and let his mind drift back to Lena, contours emphasized by the taut terry-cloth of her wrap, arching her spine on the hot slats. He'd been right. She was indeed his third test. Far and away the most demanding...It wasn't over, but despite this post-workout regression he'd passed through one installment...Held up under trial, which presented another validation of his method...And he wouldn't see her again before tomorrow.

During his run, convey her back within safe limits and rebalance himself...

Abstraction. That was still the key.

*　*　*

Strolling down the Lenin Street pedestrian mall through noon-hour foot traffic, Morris and Grinevicius found a vacant bench which abutted the street side, shaded by a large tree. Fountain jets splashed into a basin of polished granite, several meters to their right. Grinevicius surveyed the area through sunglasses he'd put on as they'd exited McDonald's, then continued his narrative.

There'd been immediate indications of further trouble at Vilnius Airport.

"I re-entered on my Lithuanian passport---the same way I exited," he recounted. "All the same I was flagged at passport control. Asked to step aside, with no explanation. For about 15 minutes I stood and cooled my heels, while a supervisor eyed me through a glass partition and made several phone calls. I got the impression it was serious. I also had a pretty good idea who was behind it."

"The Pentagon."

"If not the White House. Remember the speaker I described in the auditorium...the civilian?"

Morris nodded.

"Needless to say I never got the list of participants from Hodges.... As I said I left Washington as quickly as I could. But just before I checked out of the Marriott I managed to do some quick research, and confirmed the man's identity." The lawyer paused for effect. "... Richard Wolfson, the Vice President's chief of staff."

"Damn. Are you sure?"

"One-hundred percent. Even with the soft lighting."

Morris looked down at the pavement, absorbing this fact. He could make a general guess what happened next, during the lawyer's intervening days in Vilnius, though he almost hesitated to ask.

Grinevicius obliged without prompting.

Next alarms issued from Grinevicius' fiancé, who informed him that a strange car, bearing standard-issue Polish plates, had parked at long intervals outside their apartment building during the previous two days. Sometimes with one man inside, sometimes two. One took a photograph of her as she'd left for work. At his office Grinevicius also found his secretary unnerved. An American had stopped by the day before his return, asking questions about the practice, identifying himself only as a representative of a "U.S. private security firm". Declined to leave a card; said he'd call later. Upon her arrival at work the next morning, the secretary noticed Grinevicius' desk chair out of position, convincing her that someone had broken in overnight.

The lawyer's first response had been surreptitious evacuation of his fiance to her parents' house outside the city. Over the next three days he'd laid low: staying mostly at home, sometimes departing his building by fire escape, stopping by his office only twice for short interludes, keeping in touch with his secretary by phone. The strange car remained parked outside. Ominous calls started coming into his office, all in American-accented English.

Through another evasion, similar to the one he'd pulled in Washington, he nonetheless managed to slip away to the Belarussian Consulate for a tourist visa. That same night he'd driven his Mercedes to the Airport, where he'd parked and doubled back to the central city by taxi. Finally he'd vacated Vilnius by late-night train, somehow escaping scrutiny on the border.

"But I'm sure my passport fed back into U.S. databases," he noted. "Therefore I paid cash for my hotel room. And you saw the precautions I took with my cell-phone."

"I appreciate your carefulness," Morris responded. "But things have calmed down here. Maybe there's not so much to worry about."

The lawyer looked skeptical.

Morris continued: "In short, Russia has intervened. The Belarussian KGB has backed off. And here in Minsk at least, the U.S. is cooperating with the Russians to defuse the situation."

Grinevicius' skepticism transmuted to dismay. He made another careful survey of the pedestrian mall.

"The U.S.?"

"That's right. I'm expecting a call any day now from an American diplomat…apparently the CIA station chief in Minsk. His name is Russell Piper. He wants to meet me."

"Then I got here just in time," the lawyer said, sitting up straighter on the bench with sudden clarity.

Morris was a little perplexed.

"Why? You want to join the meeting?"

"Not by a long shot. Don't you get it? After what happened in Washington, we can't trust the CIA any more than we trust anyone else."

CHAPTER 91

S tapleton's message was tagged *URGENT*. Piper clicked on it at once:

Russell,

We just learned that Richard Wolfson conducted a back-channel meeting yesterday with Sergei Kirikorov, the Belarussian Ambassador to Washington.

Speaking on behalf of Gallstone, Wolfson threatened to expose al-Tikriti's presence in Belarus, and use it as a basis for new and harsher financial and trade sanctions against the Lukashenko regime. Even worse: Wolfson stated that the U.S. would consider "search and render" operations if Belarus did not expel al-Tikriti voluntarily, in the name of the "broader war on terror".

Ramifications with Russia, obviously, could be calamitous. More immediately, Evan Morris faces extreme jeopardy.

I've requested an emergency meeting of the National Security Council and will leave for the White House at 1130. Please make your-self available for a video conference in at 1230 East Coast/1930 East European time.

James Stapleton
Deputy Director

The clock on the lower-right of Piper's screen read 5:53. He grabbed his handset and punched the speed-dial.

"Thank God you're still here, Svetlana. Have you made all the contingency arrangements we discussed?"

"Yes."

"Good. Please bring all the materials to my office. And cancel your evening plans, if you have any. I'm going to need your help."

Next he reached for his mobile and entered the number Lena had given him for Morris. The call rang through, but with no answer. He clicked off, hoping Morris was simply occupied by a late-day conference.

And that Lena's situation remained just as benign.

Her name did not appear on his incoming call log. He verified the ring volume and kept the device within arm's length. Just in case.

*　　*　　*

A bright yellow taxi---a Volga---was on hand when Lena emerged from her building entrance. Drawing closer, she noticed a tall young man in front, next to the driver. Over the phone Morris had described him as "a friend, visiting from Lithuania." Knowing his probable identify, she'd accepted the invitation at once. Once she'd seated herself in the back seat with Morris, the visitor twisted around, with a sheepish smile, and extended his hand. Lena reciprocated and they made quick introduction in English, while the taxi exited the parking lot. Out on the Prospect, Morris lowered his voice.

"John is my lawyer," he said. "He just arrived here today. I hadn't expected him."

Lena glanced at the taxi driver. Plain-looking, in his fifties. Not the type to speak English. In the adjacent seat Grinevicius nodded, visible in profile. His sideways eye contact was affable enough, but also guarded.

"Things have come up," Morris continued. "Things we should tell you."

The evening wasn't unfolding as she'd envisioned. She'd wanted clarity. Not crisis.

"Our plan is to fill you in at the restaurant. *Zolotoi Vek* still okay?"

"Yes."

"Meanwhile I suggest you turn off your phone, if you haven't done so already."

She reached into her purse.

"That goes without saying," she said.

*   *   *

"In effect, the president just chuckled and told Gallstone to 'cool it for a few days.' That's the best I could do."

Over the feed the bags under Stapleton's eyes looked bigger than ever. His link originated from a secure communications room in the Old Executive Office Building, next door to the White House; he hadn't even been able to make it back to Langley. There wasn't time. Fallout was bound to be instantaneous. "Even if Gallstone's threat of extraction was mostly bluster," he continued, "This is the sort of thing that could send the Russians into high alert---even the nuclear kind. Needless to say, all bets in Minsk are off, unless we act fast."

"I'm already trying to arrange an emergency conference with Mikhailov."

"Good. We're thinking along the same lines."

Piper exhaled hard through his nostrils. Dependence on a rival intelligence service had been delicate enough. Under this new hair-trigger, he could hardly guess how the Russian would behave.

"With Morris, meanwhile, I'm now preparing emergency measures," he said. "Either refuge in the Embassy or full evacuation."

Stapleton ran his thumb and index finger over his puffed-out eyelids. There were countless other debacles of similar stripe, all across the globe. The Administration had been in charge a long time.

"Gallstone may be indifferent to Evan Morris and Lena Antonova. Despite the wider issues involved here, Russell, they're the ones on the front line. We can't leave them to their fates."

"That's not my intention, Jim."

"I know. Therefore I won't detain you any longer."

CHAPTER 92

Even under high tension Morris preferred linear progression to distillation, a habit ingrained, Lena figured, by his training in computer science and mathematics. Problems needed first to be broken down, then addressed in increments. Totality---and resolution---occurred only at the end. She therefore contained her dismay while he recounted the full genesis of his U.S. initiative, starting in Vilnius. Grinevicius, after listening with a slightly pained expression, next launched a step-by-step recapitulation of his misadventures in Washington, hewing to Morris' wish to include every painstaking detail.

Their primary motivation was evident to her throughout their account. That central, incessant shortcoming of Western culture.... The same one that had incited a ruinous and irresponsible sacking of Constantinople by Crusaders and pitted the West against Russia, off and on, for centuries ever since...

Greed.

She sliced off small forkfuls of her chicken-and-cheese cutlet and interjected more frequent questions as Grinevicius reached his pivotal conference at the Pentagon. She also sensed that Morris aimed, at least in some measure, to obfuscate his avarice---and the severity of his omissions---through retracement. Finally she put down her utensils. She'd had enough.

"Why didn't you tell me at that point, Evan?"

"I didn't really know everything myself, until today."

"But you understood something had gone wrong."

"Yes."

She glowered at him and shook her head. It was not the reaction he'd wanted.

"...All in pursuit of money."

"It was obviously a bad idea."

"Obviously. So where does this put us now?"

Guiltiness submersed his features. He cleared his throat.

"I'm trying to make amends, Lena. Please let us finish."

They were almost alone in the high-ceilinged, Soviet-style space; only one other table was occupied, on the other side of the restaurant's semi-circular wall of windows. Staff remained cloistered in the bar area. Live music, if there was any in store, would come later. For now, *Zolotoi Vek* offered near-total privacy. And air conditioning. At least Morris and Grinevicius had done something right. She re-wielded her knife and sliced hard through her cutlet---the squeak on her plate muffled by the drapes and two-tiered carpeting.

"Go on."

Grinevicius continued, just as uncomfortable as before, relating the deterioration of his conference at the Pentagon, his abrupt exit, and premature departure from Washington. With each new detail Lena became more alarmed, especially when Grinevicius identified the mysterious spokesman in the amphitheater as the Vice President's Chief of Staff.

Adversity from Washington? For her, it was the unlikeliest quarter of all. Then the lawyer conveyed his conclusion about the CIA. She was dumbstruck.

"Russell Piper?" she said. "Are you serious?"

"There's logic to it," Morris seconded.

"That simply doesn't square. I just saw him again today."

She summarized her impromptu encounter with Piper at *Bagira*. Morris looked unconvinced. Grinevicius even more.

"Has he called you yet?" she asked.

"I think he already did. Just before I left the office. I didn't answer."

Lena stared at him.

"You've gone mad…He's our only resource!"

For all his remorse Morris' expression remained immobile, which garnered obvious approval from Grinevicius. Lena reached into her purse. She held out her mobile and punched the security code. The device beeped to life. "We've already covered sensitive matters," she said. "We should turn our phones back on."

Morris had recovered his usual unflappability. Her disbelief ratcheted higher.

"You especially, Evan. Piper is probably still trying to reach you."

Across the restaurant Lena noticed a musical duo, man and woman, take the stage and begin set-up. Given the preponderance of empty tables, they only amplified the unreality of the moment.

Morris remained stationary.

"Please," she reiterated. "You're making a huge mistake."

"Maybe our assumptions were faulty, Lena," he said. "We should be prepared to accept that."

*   *   *

From basement level Piper bounded stairs two-at-a-time to the second floor. Svetlana was still standing near his desk, brandishing two cell-phones. Prior to this evening her swells and contours and translucent dress might have distracted him; now they only amplified his focus.

"Any luck reaching Morris?" he asked.

"I'm afraid not."

"What about Mikhailov?"

"His calls ring through. No answer."

He exhaled through his nostrils, unsurprised. In the Embassy's operations center Tommy Worthen had just tracked Mikhailov's signal; it emanated from KGB Headquarters on the Prospekt.

Where the FSB operative might well be in the process of determining Lena and Morris' fates.

The passports and tickets which Svetlana had organized were laid out on the end of his desk. Piper glanced at them, already confident that they were in order, then paced away with folded arms. When he'd reached the opposite wall, his inter-office phone rang. He nodded and Svetlana picked it up in mid-ring.

"It's Tommy," she said, holding out the handset.

Piper strode straight back over and took it from her. Worthen's voice bore new urgency.

"Unwelcome news, Russell."

"On Mikhailov?"

"Worse. Stavrolenskaya and Communisticheskaya Streets have been sealed off. Two dark sedans are parked near your Mercedes. Looks like KGB."

"Hang on."

Piper put down the handset and stepped to the nearest window. Indeed, there was no sound of traffic from either street. Over the top of the wall he caught sight of two militiamen and a couple of barriers, at the intersection in front of the Ukrainian Embassy. He returned quickly to the phone.

"I see what you mean."

"By the looks of it, they don't want you to leave in a hurry. And they've impeded your way to the Ukrainian Embassy for good measure."

"What about back walls?"

"Also manned. Several KGB goons on foot--the young, athletic variety. Along the basketball courts of the Military Academy."

Piper drew a deep breath. He'd envisioned this scenario, well before Lena and Morris. Routes pre-considered; contingencies in place.

"Thanks, Tommy. And don't be surprised when you see me on your feeds in a few minutes, checking out the situation first-hand."

"Not so fast, Russell…"

Piper withdrew his hand from the speaker button.

"Subject F29 just appeared on-screen."

Lena's designation. First activation of her emergency phone. Piper clasped the handset more tightly and leaned closer to the console. "Where is she?"

"Southern end of Jakuba Kolis Square. In the courtyard."

"Coming or going?"

"Stationary, for now."

Piper glanced at Svetlana. He could already feel his adrenaline pumping.

"Then we've got to get ready for action," he said.

CHAPTER 93

Through graying dusk Lena watched the Prospekt flow past her side-window, and her building appear just ahead. By her reckoning, omission, at least in this context, was tantamount to deception. Why trust Morris now? Or least of all Grinevicius, the overreaching lawyer who'd arrived late to the scene with an oversupply of strong opinions? Her security seemed more tenuous than ever.

While Morris paid the taxi driver, and Grinevicius glanced around the courtyard, temporarily distracted, she reached into her purse and turned on her emergency phone.

Time had come to cast her lot. And she was betting on Russell Piper.

The taxi performed a three-point turn and quick exit, leaving the three of them standing by her entrance. Several clusters of people, most of whom she recognized, reposed in different corners of the area, though none were within earshot.

"We'll walk back from here," Morris said. "But I wanted to make one last attempt to convince you, Lena."

"You made your case in the restaurant."

"Will you at least agree that we should avoid precipitous action?"

"I hadn't planned to call Piper tonight and flee to the U.S. Embassy," she answered. "If that's what you mean."

Morris eyed her, obviously conflicted.

"Again, I'm sorry Lena."

"So am I, Lena," Grinevicius added. "I'm partly responsible for the way this played out."

To Lena the lawyer still looked more resolute than repentant. She let her skepticism show.

"I only wish the two of you had thought of that sooner."

"The best we can probably do now is to sleep on it," Morris offered, as wan conclusion. They bid her good night and waited until she'd opened the entry door. Inside the darkening stairwell she pushed the timed lighting button by the mailboxes then paused on the first land-ing and gazed out at their retreating figures: both slender, Grinevicius a head taller than his client. The two Americans slipped through the half-open gate by the adjacent high school and headed onto the Prospekt. As they disappeared she reached into her purse and made sure her emergency phone was active.

She hoped that she'd made correct determination. That her judg-ment was not impeded by other factors.

She'd not yet put the proposition to test.

*   *   *

Neither Morris nor Grinevicius spoke until they were out on the Prospekt. The broad sidewalk stretched ahead, dotted with evening strollers. "Maybe she'll come around," the lawyer offered. "As you said, perhaps all the three of us need is one night to adjust."

"Then what?"

"Then it's time to think seriously about an exit strategy…and I say this as your lawyer…with or without her."

Morris was about to object when the lawyer reached his hand in front of his chest, cutting him off.

"Keep on walking," he said. "Don't make any sudden moves..."

Morris tensed somewhat and didn't break stride; they'd nearly passed the high school that abutted the back of Lena's building. Grinevicius paused, appearing to examine something on wide diagonal.

"See the car to your right? Try to be casual."

Heeding the instruction, Morris spotted a sedan in shadows along the wall of the high school. Two figures were inside, barely visible. The car appeared to be a BMW five-series. Dark in color. The two heads inside were close-cropped. One was blond. He looked away and took a deep breath. The BMW would be imprinted in his memory forever.

"I think I recognize it," he said. "KGB. The worst kind."

"Are you sure?"

"Ninety-nine percent."

"Could also be CIA."

"I'm telling you, I know those guys! They were the same ones who were guarding al-Tikriti, and brought me back to Minsk."

To both of them Lena's interpretation gained sudden, extra legitimacy.

For the next 30 paces both of them refrained from looking back, until the lawyer glanced over his shoulder again and related what he saw. The car had pulled out on the sidewalk parked perpendicularly. Not following. Observing their further progress. Morris' reckoned blond buzz-cut and his cohort would be unlikely to apprehend them in the public expanse of the Prospekt. More likely was that they would wait for them to return to his apartment building, for an interception in the courtyard. Passing a shoe store, he ventured the next glance back. The vehicle had turned right onto the Prospect, and inched along the right-hand lane about 50 meters back, hazard lights flashing, its slow progress provoking honks from overtaking traffic. Under the starker light---indisputably the BMW he remembered.

"It's definitely them," he said. "I don't think we should head straight back to my apartment."

"Any ideas?"

At Masherova Street the pedestrian signal turned red. They stopped short of the curb.

"See that metro entrance ahead?"

Grinevicius scanned across the intersection. Pedestrians from the tram stop were flowing into the passage. He nodded.

"...Let's try to lose ourselves in the crowd. Take a metro back to your hotel. Then we'll figure out what to do."

"Agreed."

A young man pulled up alongside them near the curb, obviously in a hurry. When the signal turned green he strode fast toward the median, attaining it while Morris and Grinevicius were barely onto asphalt. Squealing tires sounded from behind, accompanied by a gunning engine. The young man's face swiveled back in alarm.

"Look out!" Grinevicius shouted, lunging backward and yanking Morris along by his left arm.

The curb made both of them stumble and lose their footing. On his way down Morris twisted left and observed the BMW, as if in slow motion, rounding the corner at high speed. He glimpsed blond buzz-cut in the passenger seat, while his cohort gripped the wheel into the turn. The BMW tilted on its chassis, and just as he hit the pavement, quivered on its curving trajectory, losing control and missing his outstretched leg by less than a meter. Rolling back, he watched the vehicle skid sideways across two-and-a-half lanes, hit a tram rail and launch upward off its left wheels. Its roof slammed into the front corner of a parked tram, shattering glass, crunching metal, and emitting a fan of sparks.

Screams and shouts erupted at once from the tram stop. Morris turned to Grinevicius, his shock just taking hold.

"Incredible...They tried to kill us."

Grinevicius stared at the wrecked vehicle, and with dazed movements rose from the asphalt and helped Morris up to his feet. His voice was unsteady.

"That was f**king clear," he answered.

CHAPTER 94

Two KGB plainclothesmen stood across from the Embassy gate; upon seeing Piper, one lifted his arm and spoke into a cuff-transmitter. Looking left down Starovilenskaya Street, Piper also saw that a pair of squad cars, attended by four uniformed militiamen, had sealed off the southerly approach, while at the nearby intersection with Communistichkeskaya, another deployment obstructed both sides of the Ukrainian Embassy. When he approached his Mercedes near the Consular entrance, he noted two additional sedans 40 meters further, manned by plainclothes operatives. At once they turned over their engines, ready to follow.

Tommy had been accurate. The KGB was determined to control all access. In and out.

Completing his reconnaissance, he re-entered through the Consulate and strode down the connecting alley toward the Embassy. Svetlana met him in the courtyard.

"Just as we thought," he said. "Are you ready?"

"Yes." She looked alert and composed.

"You go first, as planned. Straight to your usual tram stop."

She nodded once, slung her purse over her shoulder, and strode to the gate. When she was gone Piper limbered his legs and took deep ventilating breaths. He also checked the buttons on his back pockets, making sure both his cell-phones were secure, including the one dedicated to Lena. After two minutes he re-exited the gate, turned immediately left, and walked down the middle of the empty street to the militia barrier, aware that the two KGB men trailed about 10 paces behind.

He bisected the squad cars and took off running.

*   *   *

Traffic on both sides of the tram stop remained blocked or immobile, even when lights turned green. Passengers emptied onto the street, unnerved and half-panicked, through the tram-car remained on its rails, only superficially damaged. Rising to his feet, Morris checked his limbs and flexed primary joints. Apart from a sore hip and bruises and scrapes on his elbows, he was uninjured.

"Are you okay?" he asked Grinevicius.

"I've had much worse tumbles. You were the one who nearly got hit."

"I would have been, if not for you."

In the midst of the commotion they withdrew back onto the sidewalk. Several bystanders who had observed the incident examined them with blends of concern and dismay, including one middle-aged woman who asked Grinevicius if they were uninjured.

Most attention still swirled around the point of collision, where the BMW remained on its side, its undercarriage exposed. Morris didn't detect any injured pedestrians, and saw the young man, previously in a hurry, standing by unhurt but shaken. He presumed the two KGB operatives were alive but trapped inside the vehicle. Several men in the vicinity made tentative steps toward the wreck, ascertaining their condition. He retreated several more steps with Grinevicius, and they positioned themselves near a newly-planted tree. Uniformed militiamen were running to the scene from several directions, including a contingent from the nearby Ministry of Interior Academy. A compact squad car soon blared along Masherova, weaving through stalled traffic. When lights changed again, cars became stranded perpendicularly across the intersection and created further gridlock on the Prospekt.

"Let's get out of here while we have the chance," Grinevicius said.

"First we've got to go back for Lena."

The lawyer winced.

"I would advise against it. We made our case. She turned us down."

"This changes everything. All bets are off."

Grinevicius looked down at the pavement, hesitating further. Morris had no doubts of his own.

"...Can't you tell? She's probably next. We have to get back and warn her."

At last the lawyer relented, and they turned back up the Prospekt, moderating their stride just enough to avoid notice. Along the way Morris gained new resolve.

Time had come to make amends.

CHAPTER 95

At full stride Piper began adapting to his footwear, though for years he'd chosen dress shoes with exactly this contingency in mind: rubber-soled, durable, and with soft-leather uppers that would neither chafe nor distend under duress. Less cushioned and coiled than his running shoes, but affording closer, more intimate contact with surface details, such that they transmitted every bulge and granule into his central nervous system---a sensation that was somehow more primal and joined to the earth.

About 10 meters behind he heard clapping leather soles of the two KGB plainclothesmen. Both had appeared to be in their late 20s, with athletic builds. Apart from gear, he reckoned that he enjoyed two other advantages that offset their youth. One was his fitness level.

The other was drive.

Along the descending incline he elongated his kick and notched up his pace, bearing down on the massive, 80s-era apartment complex fronting the Svisloch. Screeching tires and gunning engines sounded back near the Embassy; however he had lead to spare and didn't flinch when the asphalt narrowed into the building's squared opening, launching him into the open space of the river basin. About 10 seconds later the same archway amplified the harried strides and labored breathing of his pursuers, after which he glanced back. As the vehicles also emerged behind them, he cut hard to his left, up a grassy embankment, leaving shouts in his wake.

His soles tracked tightly on the moistening grass, enabling him to pump his arms and power up the slope. Entering a small residential courtyard at the top, he surmised he'd gained 30 meters over the KGB runners and lost visual contact with their sedans. Intent on building the distance, he rounded an interior building, passed a gaggle of startled housewives, and burst back onto the street. The two sedans were crawling up the curve with their headlights illumined in the dusk, on the lookout. They spotted him and immediately accelerated.

Keeping his focus forward, Piper dodged evening strollers along the narrow sidewalk, honing on the pedestrian signal, sighting it when he breached the corner. It was red, flashing signal digits...*three, two, one...*

When the signal hit zero he was first over the curb.

Once across he cut a clean diagonal into the Opera grounds, and didn't glance back again until his course was wide and unobstructed. His foot pursuers thudded off several pedestrians on the crosswalk, causing shouts and commotion and falling even further back. The two sedans pulled up helplessly by the hospital on opposite lane, then took off again toward Kubesheva Street and the general direction of Morris' apartment---exactly as he'd anticipated.

They'd guessed wrong. His objective lay elsewhere.

Piper opened up his stride and re-established sensory connection with the walkway. The Opera building and its grounds remained in the late throes of renovation, still presenting unlighted detours and busted-up surfaces, and beyond he would have to make a hazardous dash across Kubasheva into the park---the sort of random adversities, he speculated in a flash, that characterized the starker, more unpredictable runs of antiquity. Demanding not just endurance but adaptation and instinct.

His next thought was of Lena, and of reaching her on time.

In the same instant he initiated the pervasive, integrated breathing that had become reflexive during his training runs. Sweat began to soak through his dress shirt and suit trousers---affirming vitality and potential rather than portending limits. Behind him, the footfalls and breathing of the two KGB men were fading; by corresponding measure they ceased to provide real impetus.

Instead he visualized Lena, haunches bared, bending over, arching to receive him.

He let imagery take over.

He sensed he'd have no trouble finishing.

*   *   *

Like most felines Marta was alert to signs of crisis, and stayed in close proximity on Lena's lap. Two wailing police sirens raced by outside, exacerbating her edge. Lena observed the cat's nervousness and wide-open eyes, and reciprocated with attentive strokes.

Her emergency phone remained close-by on the side-table.

Once her rile subsided, she reached two conclusions. First, Grinevicius had overreacted to his reception in Washington. The figure in question was a key Iraqi from the old regime; U.S. government was bound to want full information. What did Morris and Grinevicius expect? Second, the U.S. was not Belarus. It was a democracy, where individual rights and basic justice held sway, by and large. Grinevicius had just been monitored, after all, not apprehended and menaced. And even if certain elements in the U.S. government did turn up pressure on Morris and Grinevicius---through various subtle means---why did that necessarily bear on her? She was a non-U.S. national, not on U.S. territory, with limited knowledge of the affair in any case.

And then there was Piper. She'd spoken to him twice, assessed his intentions. Even though he was a U.S. intelligence officer---an agent of American state power, no matter how she demarcated his role---she could almost say she trusted him. At least more than she trusted Morris and Grinevicius after this latest travesty. Moreover, after the sauna, when she'd seen him stripped of adornment and formality, she was also fairly sure of his professionalism and detachment...She exhaled and looked down at Marta.

An instant later her intercom chortled. The cat startled with alarm and leapt from her lap. She strode to the hallway and picked up the handset. It was Morris, his voice fraught.

"Something serious has just happened, Lena."

"What?"

"The KGB tried to run us down on a crosswalk."

"Tried to kill you? Are you sure?

"Yes. You're probably also in danger. We've got to act fast."

Lena felt her heart-rate jump. The scenario was altogether plausible. Still, after Oleg's assurances it came like a bolt from blue.

More police sirens sounded through her windows.

"We suggest you leave with us immediately," Morris added.

"And go where?"

"Maybe to the U.S. Embassy. Even John's hotel. Anywhere but here."

She thought quickly. A pell-mell dash toward the Embassy seemed like a bad idea, with militia racing down adjoining streets. They first had to call Piper. "We can't afford to panic. I'll buzz you up. We'll call a new emergency phone which Piper gave me." She detected an unintelligible statement from Grinevicius, followed by a curt, muffled response from Morris. When they agreed she pressed the switch, listened for the sound of the elevator, then retraced to the living room and grabbed the phone.

Danger was now in full visitation. To her, at least, Piper was resource number one.

*   *   *

When Morris and Grinevicius stepped into her apartment she quickly double-bolted the door behind them. Both were shaken, but more or less composed. They stood in the hallway while Morris quickly recounted the episode. It took less than a minute for her to confirm they were victims of a genuine assassination attempt. She raised the phone.

"That's it," she said. "I'm calling Russell Piper."

Grinevicius started to object, with less conviction than over dinner. Morris held up his hand.

"She's right, John. We have no other choice."

Lena punched the speed-dial. There was just one number entered.

Relief swelled inside her when Piper answered at once.

"There's an emergency," she said. "We need your help."

"I know, Lena. I'm at your entrance, right outside."

She buzzed the door before he completed the sentence.

CHAPTER 96

Aware that every minute was critical, Lena took quick charge while Piper ascended the elevator. First Morris would summarize the incident with the BMW. Facts had to be rendered as efficiently as possible. Nevertheless she was in agreement with Morris and Grinevicius on one point. They probably couldn't remain in her apartment for long.

In her foyer Piper required little more than 30 seconds to glean essentials. News of the assassination attempt made his eyes harden, though with no sign of shock. Grinevicius' presence also seemed to come as no surprise to him. While he listened Lena noticed sweat coursing down his neck, and that his dress shirt was half-soaked.

His focus remained tight, as it had in the sauna. Addressing them as a group, he declared that they should leave as soon as possible.

"To take refuge in the Embassy?" Grinevicius asked.

"I'm afraid that option is no longer available."

With a start Lena registered an appalling omission. "I can't leave my cat here," she interjected. "..Not if the KGB is coming."

Grinevicius and Morris stiffened. She allowed no opportunity for objection.

"...She has a travelling case."

Piper required all of two seconds.

"Okay. Please hurry."

Knowing exactly where to look, Lena scampered to her bedroom and found Marta crouched under the headboard. Within seconds she managed to extract the apprehensive feline and enclose her in her case, overruling her protests. Upon re-attaining the foyer, her first impulse was to thank Piper for the accommodation before they set out.

She didn't have the chance. Seeing just Morris and Grinevicius by the door, she spun around and saw Piper emerging from the kitchen. New concentration showed on his face.

"We'll have to devise another plan," he said.

"What do you mean?"

"The KGB just arrived in your courtyard."

$$* \quad * \quad *$$

In Piper's original training at the Farm, completed almost 17 years earlier, he'd absorbed two core requirements for covert intelligence operations in hostile environments. The first was meticulous planning. The second was adaptability.

He'd already made one adjustment this evening. He was ready for another.

At his request Lena put down her cat carrier and he led her back into the kitchen. They refrained from turning on the lights and gazed down into the courtyard, careful not to lean too close to the window. Below were two parked sedans, parked end-to-end. The two vehicles and the four men standing around them appeared different from those that had pursued Piper from the Embassy. For the moment the men made no move to enter the building. They appeared to be waiting, for either reinforcements or instructions.

"Is this the only room in the apartment with an interior view?"

Lena nodded.

"Is there another exit off the stairwell?"

"No, just one."

Keeping his voice low due to the open *fortichka,* Piper called Morris and Grinevicius into the kitchen. While they stood in the door-way, he maintained his position near the window-sill, and glanced outside at quick intervals as he briefed them on their predicament. He didn't hedge. The KGB operatives in the courtyard were prob-ably either awaiting a lock specialist or authorization to break down Lena's door. With every passing minute, their chances of escaping were diminishing.

An alternative seized him. He turned to Lena.

"Are you friendly with anyone on your stairwell? Some who might give us refuge for half an hour...an hour?"

Lena thought for an instant.

"Unfortunately, no. One can only depend on close friends or rela-tives in this kind of situation..."

She appeared to experience an epiphany of her own.

"However I have keys to my aunt's apartment...I've been watering her plants this summer. Only problem is...it's on the next stairwell."

Piper hardly paused. Did Lena's stairwell have roof access?

Access-hatch one floor up, off the top floor. Last she'd noticed: un-padlocked.

With a corresponding hatch on the other stairwell?

"I'm pretty sure there is. However I don't know if it's locked or not. I also have no idea about how easy it is to walk across the roof. Though there is that Samsung sign...that might provide some concealment."

Before Piper could react further, Grinevicius stepped forward.

"Luckily I'm experienced in this area," he said. He turned to Lena. "Do you have any rope?"

"I think so. In the hall closet. My father used it once to hoist up a piano."

Morris and Grinevicius filed out first. For an instant by the refrig-erator Piper beheld Lena's rear contours, enunciated by her rather tight-fitting skirt, two steps more distant than during his dash by the Opera.

At once he reverted to context. Jeans were suitable for climbing across rooftops. Tonight that was what mattered most. He advised her to make a quick change, and to slip on comfortable shoes.

Adaptability was essential. The ability to move from one tableau to another.

CHAPTER 97

Whatever misgivings Grinevicius retained toward Piper, as far as Morris could tell, dissipated with the escape plan. Re-animated with the same purpose he'd displayed earlier in the day, the lawyer placed three rope coils over one shoulder and ascended the steel ladder alone. His proposal, which Piper endorsed, was to perform a quick reconnaissance of the rooftop before the four of them set out as a group.

The hatch, about twelve feet up, yielded to a quick shove and creaked open. Early nighttime sky glimmered through the aperture before he hoisted himself through and disappeared, noiselessly re-sealing the barrier. Morris stood underneath and waited while Lena crouched nearby with her carrying case, soothing her cat with gentle strokes, quieting the creature's soft meowing. Half a flight below, Piper kept watch over the courtyard from a stairwell window.

As ramifications took hold Morris felt a growing unease, bordering on dread. He was determined not to show it.

He'd deceived and disappointed Lena enough already.

About 40 seconds later the hatch re-opened and Grinevicius hung his head down, speaking just loud enough to be heard: "It's a mansard roof, with three sections. The main section, in which we're located, is about 50 meters long and 15 meters wide. We're about 20 meters from the edge that abuts the Prospekt, so it won't be easy to spot us as we climb out, which is good, and the Samsung sign gives us some decent concealment from the square. As for the roof, the surface is aluminum sheeting. It's still warm from the sun, and a little slippery now with evening condensation. Given its changing temperature it might also be prone to buckling. But the pitch is moderate. Nothing we can't manage with ropes...Other than that I have good news and bad news."

Piper turned sideways from his position on the landing, angling one ear upward. Lena rose from her crouch. Morris swallowed hard.

"Bad news: the next hatch is locked."

The lawyer waited a downbeat.

"...Good news: there's a drainpipe on the opposite corner and a sturdy overhang. With the ropes we can easily lower ourselves onto the balcony."

Grinevicius looked down at Lena.

"Is the door on your aunt's balcony locked?"

"Yes. But I leave the *fortichka* open at the top, in order to let air inside for the plants."

"I can handle that," Piper said without hesitation. "The key will be getting everyone onto the balcony."

The lawyer craned his head lower. "As I said, no problem there, as far as I'm concerned. What's your verdict, Russell?"

With heart pounding, Morris looked down the stairs. Piper's reaction wasn't long in coming.

"Seems like our only option," he said. "Let's do it." The CIA man re-glanced out the window, then turned his gaze back inward. "Are you ready, Lena?"

"Yes."

"I suggest you go first. Leave your cat behind. I'll put the case over my shoulder and bring her up myself."

Lena agreed and took at once to the ladder. When she was halfway up Piper addressed Morris.

"You next please, Evan. As soon as Lena gets onto the roof."

Morris nodded and looked up. Grinevicius already helping Lena through the hatch. Night sky yawned around them, encompassing a smattering of stars. He took hold of a shoulder-level rung.

He tightened his grip and re-swallowed. The ladder wasn't what worried him.

*   *   *

When Lena broke through her first impression was space. She was accustomed to seventh-floor panoramas from her apartment and knew her building was the tallest in the area, taller than other signature residential blocks that lined this stretch of Prospekt. But roof-level, just two stories up, was appreciably higher, and the hatch emerged near the peak, presenting views in every direction. Traffic emitted familiar, aggregated buzz from below, but individual cars on the Prospekt and Krasnaya Street appeared several scales more distant and miniaturized. If not for the Samsung sign and scattered chimneys and ventilation pipes she might have even experienced vertigo.

After determining she was sufficiently collected, Grinevicius indicated a place several meters down the roofline, behind the middle "S" that demarked her apartment, warning again that aluminum sheeting was smooth and slippery. He then watched as she part-slid, part-crab-walked down and braced her feet against and low chimney, clasping a vertical strut that backstopped the sign. Once she was stationary she signaled back to Grinevicius, who helped Morris in turn.

Visibility derived from a combination of starlight, ambient illumination from the central city, and incidental spillover from the sign; together they allowed Lena to observe Morris' movements and facial expressions as he climbed out. His transition into open air looked awkward and tense, and he fixed his gaze on the roof-surface until he was seated. He then re-concentrated on his underpinnings while Grinevicius communicated instructions, indicating a second down-slope position near Lena's, between two ventilation pipes, just behind the "U". The act of following the lawyer's outstretched finger appeared a test of will.

It also made Lena remember Morris' reaction on the Ferris wheel---the only other occasion in which she'd observed cracks in his composure.

Tonight the cracks were noticeably wider. Nonetheless he didn't hesitate. His rib cage tugged an abbreviated inhalation before he set out. Eyes half-closed, limbs stiff, sliding more than crab-walking, each increment laborious as he compelled himself down the incline toward his designated position. She considered encouragement, but determined that any statements on her part would only distract him.

An instant later she caught a plaintive meow---and relieved to shift her attention---looked back up the incline. Piper emerged from the hatch, the cat carrier slung over his shoulder. After quick visual survey he reached her position in seconds, walking rather than crawling, crouching forward only to lower his profile. As he set the case beside her Lena's nostrils caught his zing of dried perspiration through the night air. He made visual connection through the diffuse light.

"Please take the cat, Lena," he said. "Just for a moment."

She nodded and clasped the case close to her body.

"...I'm going to check the courtyard again. I'll be right back."

With another series of economical movements he transited back across the peak, pausing only long enough to exchange a few words with Grinevicius, showing no shortfalls of strength or energy, whatever distance he'd run moments earlier. While he was out of sight on the opposite incline Grinevicius re-secured the hatch. In tandem they presented a reassuring picture. Especially Piper. He'd taken charge, even if she'd never visualized this particular scenario...

Marta meowed again. Lena unfastened one corner-flap and reached inside the case. The cat was breathing fast and her pulse was palpable and elevated; still, her protestations were soft and within her enclosure she remained crouched and stationary. Given her modest size and weight, she presented no major problems.

Lena raised her head and looked back across at Morris. At his designated drainpipe he was clasping a back-strut double-handed, with protruding knuckles, his eyes half-closed and his body rigid.

They still had a lot of roofline to cover. Then there would be the challenge of descending onto the balcony.

Morris was obviously fighting fear, just like the cat. Thus far, though, he was holding himself together.

CHAPTER 98

The roof's perimeter was rimmed by safety grating about 20 centimeters high, which hindered downward sight-lines. Noting this, Piper identified a joint between two grills five meters to his right with the best possible angle, and elbowed down sideways until he reached the obstruction. Bars were spaced about 8 cm apart; he grasped two of them for stability, slid closer, and extended his forehead into an opening. Just as he did, two additional dark sedans entered the courtyard and parked behind the other KGB vehicles, disgorging a second quartet of operatives. The most senior-looking among them conferred briefly, while also glancing at their watches, as if anticipating a third vehicle. Piper recalled that KGB technical units, including locksmiths, were deployed in specialized trucks. So were *Spetznatz* detachments, which given the degree of escalation, suddenly didn't seem farfetched.

The KGB appeared certain that Lena was in her apartment. He presumed by now that they'd searched Morris' apartment along the river, found it empty, and concluded that he and Grinevicius had fled there after the botched assassination attempt…

When the implications registered, he pushed back from grill---and staying low to the roofline---scampered back across the peak to Lena on the other side. Upon reaching her he grasped the same strut she was holding and reclined in parallel; so that all that separated them was the cat carrier.

"Do you have your cell-phone with you?"

"Both of them, including the one you gave me," she answered.

"Is your main one on?"

"No, it's off. I turned it on briefly back in the apartment, then turned it off again before we left for the roof. I though it would throw them off. Maybe buy time."

Piper beheld her for an instant.

"Smart thinking...The ruse seems to be working."

He twisted and glanced down the roofline. Morris remained immobile and rigid two meters away, wedged against his drainpipe; Grinevicius was further down, stringing one rope along chimneys and back-supports of the Samsung sign as a hand-hold. Piper was about to disengage in order to move along and repeat the same query to each of them when Lena interjected.

"Evan and John still have their phones," she said. "But they're off."

Piper re-fixed on her.

"...I verified it in my apartment. While you were in the lift."

Before he moved along again to assist Grinevicius, Piper realized two things. One was that he couldn't foresee all eventualities this evening. His mastery wasn't total.

The other was that Lena was anticipating certain developments more accurately than he was.

*   *   *

Morris' older sister had first made the suggestion in the upper reaches of a towering maple tree in the family's backyard, where he'd clamped in place with raw fear and she'd sat unperturbed on an adjoining limb, legs dangling into nothingness. "One small move after another," she'd said. "Just don't look down." In subsequent years and in other high places---spraying and dislodging a hornet's nest on second-story dormer with this father; sitting atop a giant retaining wall at Cornell, during what was supposed to be a weekend lark; an unavoidable ridge-line on a hiking trail at Yosemite---he had elaborated upon these core maxims. Additions included: "block out wider vision", "focus on imme-diate surface areas" and "breathe deeply."

He'd applied all of these tenets tonight. So far they were more or less working. He sensed Piper approaching from his right, and looked at him only when he was crouched alongside.

"How are you faring, Evan?"

"Hanging on. I'll manage."

"That's the spirit. John is creating a safety line. We'll do this as a team."

Piper moved past him, on to Grinevicius. Just 30 seconds later he crossed back again, passing above overhead toward the peak, and returned to Lena. Morris caught fragments of instruction; when he turned his head again and opened his eyes for a clear view, they were crouching beside him. Piper held the cat case in his right hand, toward the sign; with his left he grasped a rope which was secured to the next chimney. Lena flanked him up the incline, grasping his upper arm with both hands.

"Ready for the next phase?" Piper asked.

Morris nodded.

"As you've observed, the aluminum can be a little slippery. As John suspected, some panels are unbuckling and resetting as they lose their accumulated heat. Therefore we've strung across a fixed line, starting from the next chimney. It's easiest to stay below the line, using it to angle your body weight into the slope of the roof. You can also steady yourself at different points against framing of the sign."

Morris blurred his vision, rotated his left and refocused. Horizontal framing elements lower down, together with the sign's large letters, provided a last-ditch safety impediment, just in case. "Got it."

"Just one caveat. Try not to stand straight up. We don't want to be spot-ted from below. Last thing we want is a crowd of onlookers in the square."

Morris nodded again. Piper didn't waste a second. "This is a mansard roof, and the next part, after the sign, toward Krasnaya Street, is wide open and a little trickier. But John and I will help you there. Can you handle this first part on your own?"

Morris cleared his throat. "Seems straightforward."

"Good. I'll begin with Lena and the cat. For now, take hold of this pivot line. That will help get you up to the start-point in the traverse. Just leave it slack for a moment until Lena and I are on our way. Further on, when we're at the end point, I'll signal back. Then you can go."

Morris took hold of the line and resisted the urge to pull it taut.

"Good luck, Evan. We'll see you at the next section."

Before they gathered themselves and moved away Morris glimpsed Lena's eyes in the ambient light. Despite fleeting contact, he thought he saw a degree of worry, joined to acute self-possession. She was soon off, hewing close to Piper. He felt tension on the line fluctuate in his hands as they progressed up along the diagonal. Within ten seconds the connection went slack.

Keeping his eyes half-closed, he pulled the line tight and shifted to his side, propping himself on one elbow and preparing for Piper's signal. While he waited he looked down at the rope within his closed fingers, and the roof-sheets underneath. Each piece stood out from the others: distinct and dull gray, though with enough luster and smoothness to refract the night sky. Details helped. He couldn't get overwhelmed by context.

He had to vanquish his doubts. And Lena's, too.

CHAPTER 99

Piper's advancement along the traverse was balanced and profi-
cient, incarnating the same animal-like command Lena had earlier observed at *Bagira*. Each step forward, which she matched in their
moving tandem without resorting to the safety line, corresponded
exactly to the exigencies of surface and space, while his bicep---too
sizeable for her to encircle with double-grip through his thin shirt-
sleeve---was rock-hard.

She tightened her hold. At last she recognized the utility of his
concentrated pumping and sweat-soaked agonies.

Marta remained slung over his opposite shoulder. Despite her
moving suspension in the case and the unaccustomed milieu of the
rooftop, the cat's meows had subsided---as if reassured by Piper's
physical wherewithal. Even she seemed ready to forego her habitual
independence.

In these matters, Lena figured, felines were usually right.

They passed between a second chimney and the letter "G". Except
for end-framing, they were clear of the Samsung sign and more exposed
out in the open. Leveraging his weight off the safety line, Piper bent
lower at the waist and asked that she do likewise. She complied without reservation. Their final steps along the traverse proceeded with

smooth equilibration. Piper helped her settle into a half-meter gap between a ventilation pipe and the outermost chimney. Once she was secure, he deposited the cat case beside her.

"Time for another pause," he said. "I'm going to survey the next section with John."

She nodded.

He raised himself slightly and gave a thumbs-up sign back to Morris, 20 meters back, now visible mostly in silhouette. "You can start across, Evan," he pronounced at low volume, cupping one hand to his mouth. After slight delay, Morris started up the initial diagonal by measured but steady increments. Piper watched for a moment turned back to her.

"Once he's underway, please keep an eye on him. Let us know if he runs into trouble."

"Okay."

Lena could tell the next section would be more hazardous---especially getting down onto the balcony. She unfastened a flap in the case in order to reach in and re-connect with Marta, feeling the cat's beating heart. For an instant she took in the night sky. Her initial daze was gone. Clarity and concord took over.

She suddenly comprehended where Sartre had fallen short. For all his insight, the philosopher had overlooked the integral link between action and capability. In his over-abstraction, in his cigarettes and coffee and endless ponderings, he'd become detached from his physiological core. Her own intellectualizations had been just as overdone. These challenges---so unforeseeable and extreme that they bordered on fantastic---provided proof. Tonight she was ceding to Piper's directives for good reason; it was the only way to survive.

She looked back at Morris across the traverse. He was a somewhat different story.

She worried he was making the same mistake as Sartre. He was thinking too much.

*   *   *

Most chimneys were coupled with ventilation pipes; after the first pair Morris established method and rhythm. His sidesteps and alternating handholds, while still measured, became more fluid. By degrees his breathing deepened and his pulse decelerated. One quick glance over his shoulder indicated that these improvements coincided with the second "S" in SAMSUNG. He was about halfway across.

Continuing forward, he kept the sign to his back, focusing on the roof rather than the twinkling cityscapes that stretched out in three directions. It helped that Grinevicius had created a well-secured, user-friendly safety line. He was also conscious that Lena was watching him, about 15 meters away. Given all his other infractions over previous weeks, he was determined to avoid further missteps. Even less to show weakness.

Without warning Grinevicius appeared from his right and sauntered across low like a panther.

"Don't mind me," he said, staying above the safety line.

Morris halted and looked up, maintaining his narrow gaze.

"Where are you going?"

"Back for the third line. Turns out we need it."

Some ten seconds later there was a screech of crumpling metal from behind, accompanied by a grunt. By reflex Morris pivoted his head and glanced back, shocked to see Grinevicius sliding down the incline on his backside, groping in vain against the sheeting to slow his descent. He came to an abrupt stop, back-first against two horizontal bars underneath the sign, emitting another guttural "Ugh". The impact looked violent, causing the lawyer to clench his jaw and screw his eyes shut. "Damn," he said, half-moaning.

Shooting a glance back up to the genesis, Morris saw one of the drainpipes half-ripped off its base, exposing a sharp edge of sheet metal. Without thinking he reversed and started back over across the traverse, glancing intermittently down at Grinevicius, who remained in place, eyes still closed, feeling his lower back with one hand. When he got closer, he angled sideways off the safety line and examined the lawyer in more detail.

"Are you hurt, John?"

Grinevicius opened his eyes, unmistakably in pain. "Nasty bruise on my lower back. Kind of like a hip pointer." With effort he looked down and dabbed his shin, then examined his fingers in the half-light. His trousers showed a short rip. "Also opened a small gash on my leg."

The panorama behind the sign came belatedly into focus. Morris reeled for an instant, then fought off the resulting vertigo.

"What happened?"

"I was coiling the rope, leaning against the pipe." He pointed back up and shook his head in disgust. "…Careless."

"Stay there," Morris said, continuing to slide over. "I'll retie the line and lower myself down to help."

At last the lawyer righted himself into vertical position, bracing his feet against the horizontal supports and flexing his lower back.

"No need, Evan," he said. "But you could re-gather the rope."

CHAPTER 100

Grinevicius' tumble shook Lena out of her reverie, not least because he'd seemed so practiced and comfortable in this milieu---the least likely candidate for such a mishap. What came next stunned her even more. Morris evinced an utter transformation.

His excess caution vanished. Inhibitions dispersed. Decisiveness and surety took their place.

Piper soon materialized beside her from the Krasnaya Street incline. He squinted down the main roofline through the half light---first alarmed, then performing worried assessment. "I heard the noise," he said. "What happened?"

Lena told him.

Across the separating distance he exchanged some quick words with Morris, which he muffled with a cupped hand. The report seemed to reassure him somewhat. Through the background din of the city she discerned an embarrassed "I'll manage" from Grinevicius. The change in Morris also appeared to catch Piper's notice.

In no time Morris and Grinevicius covered half the distance from the incident, proceeding along the safety line: Grinevicius first, Morris trailing behind in case the lawyer's injury induced another mishap. Piper went partway out to meet them, while Lena stayed anchored in place with Marta. Ten seconds later they were all clustered around her, Grinevicius sitting on one hind-quarter, flexing his leg and wincing.

Morris handed Piper the coiled rope. "Would the first line also help?" he asked. "I can go back and untie from the starting point."

Piper thought for an instant, and said, "Couldn't hurt." For endorsement he shifted gaze to Grinevicius. "You're right," the lawyer responded, regaining his focus. "Two stabilization lines, plus a descent line. Together, they're the best variant."

"I'll go back and untie the safety line then, by segment," Morris said. "I'll be quick."

Lena, Piper and Grinevicius watched him set back out for the start-point. His movements were swift, but well-considered. He appeared to employ the safety line not because he needed it, but because it was available.

"He seems to have adjusted," Grinevicius commented.

"We're all adapting as we go," Piper answered. "Most important is that we work as a team."

In that instant Lena forgave Morris for all his earlier misjudgments and concealments. Those transgressions now seemed irrelevant or overruled.

And her estimation of Piper scaled even higher.

*　　*　　*

Stiffness in Grinevicius' lower back truncated his movements slightly, but his underlying strength and agility appeared to Piper to be unaffected. When Piper had finished configuring the two stabilization lines, as well the descent line from Morris, he suggested the lawyer should go first, based on the assumption that his climbing experience made him best able to cope with unanticipated problems; he would stay in place on the balcony to assist Lena when she made second descent.

Speed, he emphasized, would also be important. Though architectural illumination on the west face of the building was less extensive than on the Square and along the Prospekt, and pedestrians on Krasnaya Street were fewer, they nonetheless risked being spotted. And once Lena was down, she and Grinevicius could wait discreetly on the balcony.

Piper and Grinevicius splayed themselves out and peered over the edge. A tram was approaching from the south. It also gave Piper an idea.

"Trams create noise," he said. "Especially at street level."

"In other words. A natural distraction."

"Right."

"Okay, I'm off."

While Piper steadied the descent line, Grinevicius climbed over, holding the conjoined safety lines. He was halfway down the balcony as the tram passed below. Within seconds he dropped the final meters, released the lines, and stood back from the railing, sticking to shadows. He flashed a thumbs-up sign.

Next Piper turned back up toward Lena, who reclined with Morris next to the last chimney on the peak. She left the cat case with Morris and slid herself down, keeping herself low. When she was beside him he explained the tram stratagem, then leaned out to scan Krasnaya Street. The nearest tram-car was just pulling into the stop at Kolis Square. They had about a minute to wait. Their reclined positions yielded an electric charge. Piper shook it off.

"Once you get onto the balcony," he said. "Pretend you're just standing there talking with John, enjoying the night air. All the same try not to attract attention to yourselves. I'll lower your cat down to John when the next tram comes along."

"Are you coming last?"

"Yes, after Evan."

"I'll be waiting. Be careful."

"I will." Piper glanced at the street and confirmed Grinevicius' preparedness below. "...Here comes the tram."

Lena rotated onto her stomach, took firmer hold of the conjoined lines, and pushed her feet into the void. While he steadied her, she bent at the waist and thrust out her haunches before going the rest of the way over. On descent her alternating handholds seemed adroit and instinctive---hardly the mark of someone habituated to libraries and classrooms. Grinevicius was waiting to receive her at the bottom. After she released the lines, Piper gave her a thumbs-up sign. She reciprocated, held his gaze for an instant.

He exhaled, inhaled...exhaled again. He had to keep moving. Tonight's challenges had just started.

CHAPTER 101

From his vantage near the chimney Morris watched Piper lower the cat over. The transfer took less than 10 seconds; afterward Piper darted back up the exposed incline, keeping low. "There are no trams in sight yet," he said.

Morris nodded.

"I'm going to use this interval to re-check the courtyard. While I'm gone, Evan, can you lower yourself closer to the edge? That way you'll be ready to go when the time comes."

"I'll start right down."

Piper gave him a pat on the shoulder and gestured down the incline. Morris took a deep breath, cleared the chimney, and began sliding down along the descent, feet first. The exposed surface and open space incited new frissons of disequilibrium, but he subdued them and kept up his momentum, intent not to lose time. When he reached the juncture with the stabilization lines, he stopped. Gaping views opened up in three directions, infused once more with the surrealism of nighttime illumination, and sensations re-asserted themselves.

For a moment he re-closed his eyes, attempting re-capture the surety he'd discovered just minutes earlier. He remembered the prelude...Grinevicius' saunter across the peak...The ensuing accident and his own impromptu reaction...Perspectives stretched...Connections formed...His misadventures in options markets two years earlier had arisen from similar origins...Proficiency had engendered carelessness and overconfidence...Together with the additives of wealth and success, imbued him with an absurd propensity for financial risk...

Just as Grinevicius would henceforth return to more methodical climbing habits, he himself would know better than to take another multi-million dollar flier with un-hedged derivatives, no matter how convinced he was of his conclusions. Now he was more attuned to realities. Better equipped for crises. He opened his eyes, tranquil and lucid again. Piper reappeared alongside him seconds later.

"The KGB utility truck just pulled up," he said. "Within minutes they'll be in Lena's apartment."

"Sounds like we're just in time."

"Yes and no. When they realize we're gone, their first reflex will be to lock down and search the building. I don't know how we're going to get out of here."

"That is a problem."

Piper glanced toward the street and spotted an approaching tram, then back up along the southbound line, from which a second tram was also approaching. He looked back at Morris.

"You go next, Evan. The second tram should pass by soon afterward from the other direction. When it does I'll come down right after you, in order to open the balcony door and get us all into the apartment without further delay. Are you ready?"

"Yes."

"Good. Here comes the first tram. Good luck."

Morris registered details of the conjoined lines as he swung his feet out over the edge, re-twined his ankles, and lowered himself into free-hang. His adrenaline surged as space engulfed him, though he did not block out his wider vision. Halfway to the balcony, he heard the tram round the bend below. He managed to glance down and take in the vehicle's ovular top-side and collapsible electrical framework.

Several sparks shot off into the night air. And he conceived an idea.

* * *

As the interval elongated Lena crouched back in the recess of the balcony doorway and reached into the cat carrier to stroke Marta. At last a pair of trams approached from opposite directions with their distinctive rumbles and clang, causing the feline to tense slightly. Then in a sudden flurry of activity, Morris' feet and legs appeared from above, followed by the rest of his body, and Grinevicius guided him to a smooth touchdown. Just half a minute later Piper trailed behind, rappelling down with the same coiled agility he had displayed on the rooftop. Without pausing he pulled a plastic card from his wallet, jimmied the door latch, and let the three of them inside.

With relief Lena sat down on the divan, and watched him through the open doorway as he coiled the three intertwined lines they had just employed, leaned out against the railing, and heaved them back onto the rooftop. After glancing around to confirm that he remained unobserved, he also entered the apartment.

"I think I managed to throw them back up near the chimney," he said. "Near where I left the other two. Hopefully they won't be noticed. If they are, the KGB won't necessarily know how we used them, or into what apartment we've escaped."

"So we're safe," Grinevicius said. "At least for now."

"Not really. All we've really done is buy ourselves additional time."

Morris got up from the armchair near Lena.

"An idea occurred to me on the way down," he said.

Lena swiveled to look at him. Grinevicius did likewise.

"Presumably they're looking for my cell-phone signal."

"Lena's too," Piper noted.

"What if we turned them on, and tossed them immediately onto a moving tram?"

"In other words...draw them out of the courtyard, after the trams."

"Right."

Piper's reaction was instantaneous. "It's viable, if we can make accurate drops from the balcony, and get the phones to adhere to the roof of the tram..."

Several beats ensued while he considered the challenge.

"...And perhaps not so hard, if we have some old towels and grease."

* * *

During the next several minutes Morris saw his idea put into execution. Lena responded first; in her aunt's kitchen she found two hand towels of appropriate size, along with a can of cooking lard and various lengths of string, and brought the items to the living room. Piper laid out the towels and opened the can. As sweet odors from lard suffused the room, Morris remembered an introductory course in mechanical engineering. Grease possessed properties of both lubricant and adhesive. It was an appropriate choice.

Piper elaborated upon the plan.

"We have to play odds," he said. "Therefore we'll drop each phone separately. That way, if one of the bundles bounces off into the street, we still have a chance with the second. We also should turn on each phone for as little time as possible before we toss it off the balcony, so the KGB can't localize us here in the apartment. No more than 30 seconds, I would say, from the time the phone goes active."

He assigned roles. Morris would wrap the phones in the towels. Lena would tie the strings. Grinevicius would smear on the lard and pass the bundles to Grinevicius. Everyone took their positions. Morris' phone would be first.

The next tram clanked along Krasnaya Street in less than a minute.

"Okay, go!" Piper said, gesturing toward Morris.

Morris turned on his phone and punched in the security code. Ten seconds later the screen went active.

He had a text message waiting. He punched it up in an instant:

Have been unable to locate you this evening. Rescue operation in progress. Staging area situated outside athletic facility where Jeff last saw you. Bus will depart at 0100 tonight. Border crossing planned at 0330. Yuri and the programming team are being alerted through secure channels. Malcolm.

"Hurry!" Piper said.

There was no time to re-read it. Morris hit the delete button, wrapped his phone in the towel and put the assembly process in motion.

CHAPTER 102

Most of the trams on the Krasnaya-Kolis line appeared to be of Soviet provenance, with rounded corners and protruding forward cabs, painted bright red and yellow. Their heavy-steel top-plates bore inch-high ridges along both sides, and undergirded collapsible conductors that made contact with the overhead lines. They also offered the biggest target and best chance of adhesion; the key was to avoid inadvertent impact with electrical elements.

Piper knew the northbound trams slowed before entering the curve. He timed his release accordingly.

To his relief the bundle dropped perfectly between the conducting apparatus and circular capacitor, emitting a barely discernible *thup* as it hit the plate. Despite a small slide backward it did not bounce off. He watched the tram pull into the stop alongside the square, disgorge about a dozen passengers and receive an equivalent number, then angle up Kolis Street. No one inside seemed to have noticed, including the tram-driver. Morris' phone was on its way. Another tram approached from the same direction, southbound. Piper let it pass, and instead waited about two minutes for the next northbound tram to appear at the end of Krasnaya Street. He leaned back into the apartment.

"Okay, go ahead Lena."

She activated her phone and re-initiated the assembly. Less than 30 seconds later Piper had the bundle in hand, and took similar aim. This time he was too early. The bundle glanced off the capacitor and tumbled backward, lodging against the conducting frame with a flurry of sparks.

He held his breath, fearing he'd caused a short circuit.

Instead the tram sputtered for two or three seconds around the bend, then regained normal power. Piper waited until it pulled into the stop with no incident, and started off again, then re-entered the apartment.

"Not quite as accurate as the first one," he announced. "But it stuck."

Lena relaxed her shoulders. Grinevicius offered token applause.

"Does this apartment have any rooms with a view onto the court-yard?" he asked Lena.

"No. They all look outward."

"In that case I'm going to venture back onto the stairwell, to check on the KGB."

At the front door she stood by while he peered through the peep-hole. Finding no one in view, he exited the apartment and surveyed the courtyard from the closest interior window, half a flight down. Instants later, six KGB men burst out of Lena's entrance and made for their vehicles. Both performed hasty three-point turns, scattering several fearful residents from their paths, and with revving engines and screeching tires shot onto Krasnaya Street and disappeared. In their wake the KGB technical truck remained behind, unattended. Though not for long. Within 90 seconds three technicians also emerged, clad in overalls and carrying toolboxes. With less haste, they also climbed into their vehicle and departed.

The ruse had worked. Lena let him back into the apartment, and accompanied him back to the living room where he conveyed the good news. Grinevicius leapt from the couch and performed a fist pump.

Morris was more restrained, but also stood up in relief. Lena was first to ask what lay next.

"The train station," he answered.

Her eyes traveled down the cat case. He recognized why and conceived an immediate solution.

"You have the keys to the apartment, don't you, Lena?"

She nodded and reached into the pocket of her jeans, holding out the bundle.

"I can leave the keys with my assistant...whom we'll see shortly," he said. "She can come back to the apartment and feed the cat after we're gone."

Upon consideration, she formed a smile and opened the case. The cat fled at once to the bedroom, and she made a quick detour to the kitchen to leave water and food. When she got back he checked his watch. "We should get going," he said. "Our best option is to shoot down to the train station by metro. I'll provide details when we get there."

Piper started toward the door, followed by Lena and Grinevicius. He noticed Morris lagging behind them.

"I should tell you something before we leave," he interjected.

Everyone stopped and turned to look at him.

"...It's horrible timing, to say the least."

*   *   *

As she exited the living room Lena contemplated the keys in her hand. Thus far Piper had overcome every challenge they'd encountered. He'd even formulated a neat, clever solution for Marta. Her earlier judgment had not proven misplaced. She felt confident taking his cues. Right through the rest of the escape.

Morris' pronouncement---and the edge in this voice---hit her just as she reached the threshold with the hallway, making her halt in her tracks. She'd thought he'd run through his bombshells. Now he looked ready to drop another.

"I'll keep this brief," he said. "Just before we tossed my phone onto the tram I received a text message." With a burdened expression he proceeded to summarize the pending corporate rescue operation by Cognition Software, also mentioning that Lena had been encompassed in the plan. Hearing this, Lena didn't know whether to be angry at Morris…again…for withholding additional information, or gratified that her welfare had been considered.

She tended toward the latter. That still didn't lessen her dismay.

Either way, Piper looked rueful rather than surprised. "I knew about their preparations," he said. "And you're right…the timing is unfortunate. I hope none of your employees go along with it."

"I can't speak for them," Morris answered. "But I know they're not stupid. And I know I want no part of it."

Piper considered the development for another instant, and appeared to register another angle. "In fact," he said, "The timing may help."

Lena couldn't conceive how, but readied her aunt's keys again as they filed out.

CHAPTER 103

Descent by elevator, Piper reckoned, exposed them to potential surprises on the ground floor. He therefore opted for the more predictable increments of the stairway and led the way down. Lena followed close behind, while Morris and Grinevicius brought up the rear. They passed no one en route, and he halted their ensemble on the last landing, in front of the mailboxes. He addressed Morris:

"There's a chance that the KGB showed your photograph to some of the residents in the courtyard. That means they may be on the lookout, and ready to call in alerts. Therefore I'll walk out first with Lena. We'll assess their reactions but also appear casual. We'll stroll to the other side of the courtyard, stop there and linger. We'll also gain full view of all the people in the area. You go next, Evan. Pass by us...and unless I raise my hand to my nose...proceed at a normal pace to the side of the building, near the gate onto the sidewalk, and wait. John, keep your eye on me from the window in the entrance door."

"What do I do if you touch your nose?" Morris asked.

"That's a signal that we've got to get out of here as quickly as possible...to you too, John. We should all run to the side of the building then on to the metro station, before the KGB respond."

All three accepted the logic behind the sequence. Morris and Grinevicius took position by the window. Lena drew next to him.

"Ready, Lena?" Piper asked her.

She nodded.

Outside the entrance several teenagers on a nearby bench brought their gazes over, checking them out. Piper refrained from staring back but didn't notice any of them reach for cell-phones. To his slight surprise Lena took his arm.

"This will seem more conventional," she said. "…Even if they haven't seen me with a man in quite some time."

In execution, Piper had to admit, the act felt natural and unfeigned.

They proceeded across to the opposite side of the courtyard, stood between two trees, and turned back and gained 180-degree view, watching Morris emerge in turn. From the teenagers, and another man who had stepped out onto a third-floor balcony to smoke, Piper detected nothing more than incidental glances.

"Looks okay to me," Lena said

"So far, so good," he agreed.

Morris continued to the side of the building. About 30 seconds later Grinevicius repeated the pattern and joined him. Once Piper was assured their collective exit had gone unremarked, he and Lena walked over as well, Lena keeping hold of his arm. As they re-formed their foursome, Grinevicius took passing note of her deportment, seeming to recognize that it was tactical.

Morris' reaction was somehow more acute.

Piper didn't know what to make of the sentiment. He hoped it didn't augur complications. Lena lingered a moment long before she relinquished his arm.

"Our luck is holding," he said. "Now, on to the metro."

*   *   *

Time and cohesion now seemed more critical than subterfuge, so Piper maintained their loose grouping as they traversed the southern edge of the square. After-dark ambience added to their inconspicuousness; most people they passed were teenagers or young adults, intent on socializing. They reached the south entrance without incident, descended into the underground passage, and entered the station. Everyone had tokens, even Grinevicius. There were no militiamen or other danger signs on the platform, just more milling teenagers. The center part was least populated; they took position between two columns.

While they waited Piper fast-forwarded over details of their escape plan. During his formulations the previous week, he'd focused on operational efficacy, and little else. Now, on the verge of implementation, certain correlations came closer to the fore.

A southbound subway train barreled onto the platform two minutes later. They boarded and stood along the closed outer door. "Just three stops to the train station," he said in English, keeping his voice in undertone.

Lena reached across him to grasp a vertical support pole, regaining her close position. Morris took notice again, this time with a more beleaguered expression.

Which made Piper wonder if there was a back-story between Morris and Lena about which he was ignorant.

"What then?" she asked.

"As I mentioned, my assistant is meeting us there. She'll have documents, tickets. If all goes well, we'll proceed straight to the departure platform."

"And our destination?"

Over Lena's shoulder Piper noticed a young man with a backpack, of approximate university age, arm hoisted on the handrail. He appeared to be listening with curiosity to their English.

"Better if I reveal that at the station," he answered.

CHAPTER 104

Although Morris supposed Lena's alignment was borne of exigencies of the moment rather than genuine inclination, he nonetheless found it difficult to behold. Even more because he had no right to object. He'd had his chances to extract her somehow before this crisis degenerated and Piper intervened. Those chances had come and gone.

As the subway train reached full speed he looked away, overrun with second thoughts.

Piper had materialized when needed, with plans already in place, and thus far his judgment seemed exemplary. Yes, the Cognition Software rescue operation was ill-advised, Morris recognized. But he was nonetheless rejecting an effort mounted largely on his behalf, and leaving Yuri and the programmers to decide and fend for themselves. One way or another the situation was hurtling toward catastrophe. As the train pulled into Victory Square station he also considered the ramifications for his stock options, now just 60-percent vested. Crowder was a volatile, uncompromising entrepreneur, prone to extremes. One who'd expended hundreds of thousands of dollars of corporate and personal funds on this undertaking, if not more, and was unlikely to sympathize with his decision. The outcome could be costly.

He glanced at Grinevicius, eyes concentrated from his lanky height. The lawyer sensed his gaze.

"I anticipated challenges when I came here," he said. "But nothing like this."

"Tell me about it. We were just sitting in a restaurant having dinner a couple of hours ago."

"What's next?"

Morris looked back at him and didn't answer. The evening had acquired momentum all its own.

The train pulled into Oktyabraska station, and about half the passengers in the car exited onto the platform. Morris re-grasped the support bar and stayed in rooted in place. He also pushed the stock options from his mind. He'd made that kind of mistake before.

The doors closed. Next stop was the train station.

*   *   *

For Lena the Minsk Metro constituted a lifelong fixture and diagram of reference, one she'd employed regularly since childhood. Now, after the novelty and hazards of the rooftop, its bland interior and familiar vibrations provided a semblance of normalcy---a connection with her life prior to this evening. Victory Square station disappeared behind them as the train resumed trajectory. How many times had she passed along this line, entered or exited along these platforms? Hundreds? Thousands?

However tonight's progression felt definitive and irrevocable. As though she was embarking along a new continuum. She presumed they were taking a train out of the country: overnight, like most of the international rail departures from Minsk. But to where? Given U.S. involvement, most likely to a NATO country. Poland? Lithuania? Latvia? Whatever the destination, this journey had no easy reverse direction.

There was another unmistakable aspect to this new pathway---Russell Piper's central position. He'd become an undeniable agent of change.

She reached into the pocket of her jeans. Then looked up at him and held out her aunt's keys.

"You should take these now, Mr. Piper. In case we're distracted later."

"Russell."

She nodded and felt a shot of electricity as she transferred the key-ring into his palm. The fact that he was married didn't subdue it.

The young male with the backpack moved down the train car to take a free seat, leaving no passengers in immediate earshot. At last her curiosity got the better of her. She lowered her voice and leaned closer to Piper, still speaking English.

"We're almost there. Can you tell me where we're going?"

After making another quick survey of nearby passengers, he angled his mouth toward the car windows.

"Ukraine," he said.

"The overnight train to Kiev?"

He nodded.

Lena had taken the same train before on numerous occasions. The journey was about nine-hours in duration. "It's not such a radical construct for me," she said. "My mother is from Ukraine. She's there now, visiting my grandmother."

"I admit...I was aware of that."

By now Morris and Grinevicius had dialed into their exchange. Piper leaned toward them and briefly communicated the same information. When he returned to his original position, Lena asked again in low voice if he'd been to Kiev before.

"I was based there for three years, in fact."

"So for you this is a return journey."

Her remark prompted a deep-seated reaction that she had trouble interpreting.

"Yes. You could say so."

CHAPTER 105

Most other passengers also exited at the Independence Square platform and streamed right: moving in groups of two, three or four, wielding luggage or carry-bags, intent on late-evening trains. Lena noted the contrast with her own unfettered hands, and general lack of accoutrements.

She really was making a profound break. Her new continuum started here.

Next to her, on the broad stairs leading up to the south entrance, Piper scanned the crowd, on the lookout for plainclothes operatives or militia checkpoints. She did likewise and detected no immediate danger signs, while her fellow citizens remained absorbed by life's conventional ebbs and flows. Probably indifferent to politics---resigned, like most Belarussians, to never-ending isolation and constraints...

She'd finally had enough. Enough of the KGB and their primitive threats...of detached Russian overlords like Mikhailov...of stifling state power and limited opportunities. Of the entire rubric of Belarussian life.

Her breakout was overdue. She, for one, was ready for a change.

Her liberation would occur only when she'd left the country.

After they passed the turnstiles she glanced back at Morris and Grinevicius, who kept pace less than two meters behind, alert, intent on not losing contact in the crowd. A bank of doors loomed ahead, leading to the train station's underground passage. "Turn right," Piper said. "Stay cool if we encounter any militia." The passage was thick with people, moving in both directions; he navigated out of the jumble and hewed to the near wall. About 30 meters ahead, in the center of the tunnel, Lena spotted a pair of blue-shirted militia standing near a pillar and felt her stomach tighten. As they drew closer Piper turned to her, composed and, by all appearances, completely unconcerned.

"Don't worry...we're on time," he said in unaccented Russian. "Your mother's train doesn't arrive for five minutes."

Lena looked back with theatric vexation, contriving behavior that was common to Russian wives in these situations. The militiamen glanced their way with slight amusement, quickly lost interest, and paid no attention whatsoever to Morris and Grinevicius, trailing behind.

She exhaled.

Twenty seconds later he pointed left across traffic, and they veered up a stairway marked "City." A tall young woman stood in the enclosure at the top. Behind her was a bank of glass doors through which the side of the train station was visible. When the woman spotted Piper she descended halfway down to meet them, out of direct sight from street level. Lena quickly recognized her as Piper's Russian cohort from the Embassy cocktail party. Piper greeted her by first name: Svetlana. When he asked her about the situation above ground, she answered in English, keeping her voice low.

"There are militia everywhere. Especially inside the main terminal. Also on certain platforms. From the upper waiting lobby I checked out the departing platforms. They seem to be focusing on Prague and Warsaw."

"Just as I expected. Did you get tickets?"

She held up a cloth attaché case.

"They're in here. Ten-twenty train to Kiev. Three compartments, just as you requested. All purchased with cash. Different windows."

"Perfect. Same wagon?"

"Yes, but spread apart. Lena is bunking with another passenger, a Belarussian woman, as far as I gathered. You have a full compartment to yourself, two doors down. Mr. Morris and Mr. Grinevicius are at the other end of the car."

Piper took the case from her, and extracted four passports. One of these he handed to Lena, bearing the color and emblem of Ukraine, along with the train ticket.

"You're a 25-year-old woman born in Kharkov, now living in Kiev," he said. "You can say you were here in Belarus, visiting relatives."

Lena was pleased about the age. She flipped open the front cover. Her photo was affixed, one she recognized from her old U.S. Embassy employee pass. Her name was Ekaterina Mironova, suggesting Russian rather than Ukrainian ethnicity.

"Anything else I should know?"

"You're an academic. I'll leave the rest to your imagination."

Next he turned to Morris and Grinevicius. "You're two Dutch businessmen. Making distribution arrangements in Eastern Europe for flowers, grown in Holland. In case you don't know, flowers are a major Dutch export here."

They took the documents, along with their tickets. Both reflected on their legends.

"What if someone speaks Dutch to us at the border?" Morris asked.

"Very unlikely. Anyway, just speak English. That's what an average Dutchman would do here."

"What about you?" Lena asked him. "Are you also travelling under a fictitious identity?"

"Yes. I happen to be a French businessman. I should also note that we'll all have luggage, so we won't look out of place." He checked his watch and glanced at Svetlana, who nodded, raised a cell-phone, and engaged a brief exchange in Russian.

"The driver will be here in two minutes with the bags," she said afterward.

While they waited Piper transferred the keys to Svetlana for the apartment. Just as Lena expected. He hadn't forgotten about Marta.

*   *   *

In keeping with Piper's instruction, Lena and Svetlana spearheaded their next procession: down the stairs, further along the underground passage, then up stairs again to Platform Three. Morris and Grinevicius followed at comfortable separation and Piper brought up the rear. In one hand Lena carried a medium-sized duffel-case, while her other remained free to accommodate a plastic bag---still for the moment in Svetlana's possession, which appeared to contain food items. Together they presented a familiar picture: perhaps two cousins, one seeing the other off after a family visit. Svetlana stayed alert for militia but also gave Lena several head-to-toe evaluations as they walked along. Lena sensed some parallel tension, of the type that marked female rivals. She wondered if Svetlana's connection to Piper veered outside proper rails.

She couldn't dwell on that now. At the top of the stairs she concentrated on more urgent matters.

"I gather we're supposed to be relatives," she said.

"First cousins, if anyone asks," Svetlana responded with forced pleasantness.

"Then we should probably embrace each other before I get on board. Say appropriate goodbyes."

Svetlana nodded and kept her focus, summoning a smile as they approached the train.

Two uniformed attendants were positioned by the boarding door, checking the tickets of other passengers. Lena and Svetlana stopped two meters away and hugged and kissed each other, while Morris and

Grinevicius hovered behind. Svetlana transferred the bag of food; for appearances' sake they had to run through suitable farewells.

"What's in it?" Lena asked.

"Cookies and chocolate. Also rolls and sausage for breakfast tomorrow morning."

"I appreciate that. Especially the cookies and chocolate. If there's a time to indulge, I suppose this is it. It's a long trip."

Svetlana re-encompassed Lena's figure and held her smile.

"You really shouldn't have to diet in the first place, Katya."

Lena caught quick sight again of Morris and Grinevicius several meters away, waiting their turn. She had to keep up the act for a moment longer. She lowered her voice so that it became indistinct to the attendants and other bystanders.

"...By the way, did you pack any food for the others?"

"Also rolls and sausage. And vodka, a bottle each for Evan and John. Standard prop for male travelers, you could say."

"Well...If we get over the border, we can even have a small celebration."

Svetlana considered the prospect for a moment, then signaled with her eyes that it was time to board. At the same time her expression became more sisterly than competitive. She rendered a final parting kiss.

"Three of you at least," she said. "When he's in working mode, Russell prefers to stay disciplined and under control."

CHAPTER 106

Piper had considered alternative guises. Among them: middle-aged foreigner and his younger Ukrainian wife---a template that was not uncommon and which also offered certain practical advantages, including ease of communication during the journey, quicker reaction time in the event of crisis, and a convenient milieu in which to debrief Lena over breakfast, before they reached Kiev. He was glad he'd rejected it. Given the extreme uncertainty and risk they faced over the next few hours, the prospect of a long night in the same compartment would have distracted them both. If they evaded detection at the border and successfully entered Ukraine, the hour would already be around one a.m. He would communicate the news to Langley, then seize some valuable sleep.

There would be plenty of time for debriefings in Kiev, not just for Lena, but for Morris and Grinevicius as well.

At the top of the stairs he inspected the platform. The only militiamen in view were one pair strolling along the glass panes of the main waiting area, suspended over the tracks, attention directed inward at waiting passengers rather than outward onto the platform.

Wagon 8 entered his sight-line as he rounded the corner, along with Morris and Grinevicius, showing their tickets at the entry door,

Grinevicius doing the talking. He placed down his suitcase and pretended to check his travel documents. Svetlana stood just three windows down, purporting to see off Lena, who was already inside. Her brief eye contact was alert but void of alarm signals.

A moment later the train attendant took his ticket as well.

"Nationality?" she asked in Russian.

"French."

After giving him quick scrutiny, followed by an unexpected welcome, she made corresponding notation on her passenger list and invited him to board. Once inside, he glanced into Lena's compartment from the aisle. Her travelling companion was a woman in her late 50s, average-looking in all respects, perhaps bound for vacation in the Crimea or on a visit to Ukrainian relatives. Unlikely to attract attention at the border, probably set to retire to her bunk soon afterward, if not before. Lena caught his eye before he moved on to his own cabin. Like Svetlana, she appeared alert but calm. He slid his suitcase under one of the lower bunks, opened the horizontal ventilation window, and settled into his seat. Next he took a deep breath, aware that their prospects would improve once they cleared the station.

Later, if they cleared the border and reached Kiev intact and unscathed, he guessed he'd have to contend with concerns of a different kind. Though this time around he was confident he could manage them.

He forced himself back to the moment.

Kiev remained far ahead. There were plenty of hurdles before that.

* * *

Grinevicius stepped back into the compartment and straightened on the opposite settee, his legs uncharacteristically jumpy with adrenaline. "Russell's boarded. He's about five doors down. Closer to Lena."

"No sign of trouble?" Morris asked.

"No. He nodded at me as if everything is okay."

Morris shot a quick glance out the window. Two militiamen strolled by on the next platform, but paid little heed to the Minsk-Kiev train. All the same he leaned back in his seat, in order to be less visible.

"Looks like we've evaded the dragnet."

"Looks that way." Grinevicius glanced at his watch. "Train leaves in three minutes."

"Gotten over your doubts about Russell?"

"Long time ago. Back on the rooftop, in fact." Grinevicius caught something in his query and examined him. "What about you?" I'm not talking about the Washington angle…I mean his escape plan."

Morris resisted another glance out the window, and a corresponding urge to close the curtains. He also suppressed the regrets and discomfort he'd experienced on the metro. "He's included Lena, even though she's not a U.S. citizen. He could have done otherwise. You have to give him credit for that."

"Agreed," the lawyer responded.

A slight shudder traveled through the train. They began moving along the track. Morris triangulated several city coordinates and confirmed their southward direction.

"Looks like we're bound for Ukraine," he said.

Grinevicius stretched out his long legs into his more typical posture.

"So far, so good," he answered. "Let's hope we get there without more mayhem."

CHAPTER 107

L andscapes melded together and skimmed by in the darkness, vague patchworks of thick forests and rolling farm fields---the contours of rural Belarus. Lena tried to draw comfort from the fertile topographies, abundant space, and prevalence of nature. The exercise was in vain.

In part because she wasn't sure when she'd see them again.

An analogous reflex prompted her to pull out the passport that Piper had supplied at the train station. She opened it and confronted her head-and-shoulders shot on the title page---the one taken during her summer employment at the Embassy seven years earlier. That summer now seemed part of another existence, innocent and irretrievable. She re-observed her assumed identity:

Ekaterina Mironova
Born 8 July 1983, Kharkov

Her assumed identity made her feel even more unfastened from previous coordinates.

While she contemplated the sensation, her compartment-mate, with whom she'd only exchanged brief greetings before departure---looked

up from her magazine and also took note of her passport. Lena automatically inverted herself to her legend.

"Where in Ukraine are you from?" the woman asked.

"I was born in Kharkov. I now live in Kiev."

"Visiting family in Belarus?"

"Yes, a cousin."

The woman nodded, as if this confirmed her assumptions. Perhaps
she'd seen Svetlana on the platform, bidding farewell and handing over
the bag of food. Lena asked the woman about her own provenance.

"I live in Minsk. My son married a woman from Yalta. Tomorrow
I'm continuing south from Kiev. Meeting them there."

"Nice destination in the summer, with the beaches and all."

"Yes…It's also a vacation. I try to go every year."

The woman looked out the darkened window for a moment, then
smiled and closed her magazine. "Well, the border's still about an
hour away…But I'm going to bed before that."

Lena recalled that border officers on the Minsk-Kiev line tended
to be perfunctory at late-night crossings, and were particularly
unlikely to linger in the compartment of two female passengers who'd
already bunked down for the duration. Being in bed could work to her
advantage.

"I guess I'll do likewise," she said.

They both stood and placed their hand luggage on overhead
shelves. Lena opened her overnight pack from the train service, spread
out the pressed sheets, and tucked them in as best she could. When
the beds were made the woman prepared to change into nightclothes.

"I'll step out into the corridor for a minute," Lena offered.

"You don't have to."

"It's all right. I don't mind."

She slid open the compartment door and startled when she saw
Morris just a few paces away, apparently returning from the restroom.
Also surprised, he collected himself, shortened his stride and made
eye contact as he attained her doorway, displaying the same resolve

he'd found on the rooftop. After he'd passed she stepped back out in the corridor and slid the door closed, glancing at his retreating form as he returned to the far end of the wagon. He shot her another steadfast glance up the aisle before disappearing into his own compartment.

She was relieved he'd re-gained his usual unflappability. This wasn't yet over.

Several ventilation panes were open up and down the aisle, sending a slight, invigorating breeze through her hair, which swept away some of the evening's stresses and cleared her head. She leaned against the handrail to maximize the sensation, and a moment later, heard a door slide open several compartments down.

Her clarity evacuated when Piper stepped into the aisle, several meters down. The first thing she noticed was that he'd changed his shirt. Unlike Morris he evinced no surprise, and held her gaze for several firm beats while also clasping the handrail. The voice of Lena's compartment-mate sounded through the closed door.

"I'm ready. You can come back in."

She grasped the aluminum lever. No other passengers were present in the aisle, and she paused to give Piper one more extended look. He reciprocated until she clicked the latch and went back inside. The woman, already in bed, bid Lena good night and turned off the lamp over her pillow. Instead of undressing as well, Lena lay down on top her sheets, fully-clothed. At this point there were too many pending, high-stakes events and open-ended concerns to think about disrobing.

She turned off her own reading lamp. It didn't matter. She was in no condition to sleep.

And she had to clear her thoughts again before they reached the border.

CHAPTER 108

Prior to 2004 the demarcation between Belarus and Ukraine had been symbolic---a cursory formality between two kindred ex-satellites. However during the intervening four years it had devolved into a political fault line---albeit not quite as pronounced as the one between Belarus and the EU. So Piper was not surprised by the stark illumination and imposing fences. These signaled the approach.

He leaned closer to the glass and peered up the left-side barrier, alert to trouble. Seeing none, he then stepped out of his compartment and made similar assessment along the right. Same: for all the bright lights, no foot patrols, attack dogs or other special measures. At the Belarussian checkpoint the train slowed and stopped. From back in his seat, he observed half a dozen customs and border control agents congregated on the platform outside, pale-faced and austere under the flood-lamps. The outer door to their wagon opened and the group entered, wasting little time.

Lena's compartment was first in line. He slid closer to his door and listened.

Customs, as usual, came first. A female officer issued inquiries to Lena and her compartment-mate, in perfunctory tones. Lena, at least, was traveling with minimal luggage.

"*Spasibo,*" the officer said.

He heard Lena answer in kind.

Minutes later the officer presented herself at his door. Piper summoned his best French accent and slipped into rudimentary Russian. After several routine questions and a visual check of storage spaces under the seats, she gave him a polite nod and proceeded on her way, moving along toward Morris and Grinevicius.

Next came the more hazardous part. Piper looked down at his false passport and forged migration card; he often operated incognito, but always *in country,* and had never crossed a border without the backstop of diplomatic immunity. He waited a moment, tilted again toward the door, and re-tuned down the aisle. Two passport-control officers had attained Lena's cabin. Their questions were more numerous and impatient than those from customs. He heard Lena's responses; most queries seemed directed at her.

Seconds intervened. At last he heard two *chi-chunks.* Both passports stamped. Lena was cleared. They were almost halfway there. Their escape was in full consummation.

The two officers appeared at his door. The taller and more senior-looking of the two scrutinized his face and took in his cabin.

"Passport."

Piper handed it over, saying nothing.

The officer pulled out the registration card, examined it, and ran the passport through a portable scanner, hanging at waist-level. Next he flipped through the pages. Forgers at Langley had created one prior Belarussian business visa in addition to the current one. Other pages included several stamps from Ukraine, a prior visa from Russia, and a conventional collection of EU and North American stamps.

"Business?"

"Da."

"*Kakoi* business...What business?"

The officer's English was obviously meager. Piper answered in both Russian and French, feigning awkwardness with the former.

"Oborudovanie...pitanie. *L'equipment traitant aliments.*"

The officer showed some irritation. Simultaneously a walkie-talkie came to life in the hand of his companion, who stepped away from the door. Crackle and indirection made the exchange hard to follow. Two minutes later, the issue, whatever it was, appeared resolved. The second officer re-opened Piper's visa-page, applied a stamp, and handed the passport back with a nod. Seven to eight minutes the officers reached the compartment of Morris and Grinevicius, where they proceeded with greater dispatch. In short order the officers retraced down the length of the wagon and de-boarded. The doors latched shut.

When the train re-started Piper rose from his seat and ventured back into the aisle. They would not be entirely in the clear until they crossed over the Ukrainian side, but he relaxed by several degrees as the train covered the final distance. Within 60 seconds later border posts came into view, in a clearing cut through the forest.

At last he could lower his guard.

At almost the same instant Lena emerged from her cabin and looked straight down the aisle. She stopped and grasped the rail with one hand, facing him. He noticed she'd remained fully clothed, just as he had.

For now there was no point in moving closer; the Ukrainian check-point lay less than 60 seconds away. He kept his voice just loud enough to he heard.

"Almost there," he said in Russian.

"I can hardly believe it."

He nodded and smiled. "Once we've formally entered Ukraine, the four of us should have a small celebration. Make a toast or two."

"Agreed. I'd say we deserve it."

"My cabin, then. I'll round up Evan and John."

As the train slowed again, Lena seemed to comprehend the full import of the threshold they were crossing, and raised her face upward with eyes half-closed. She drew an uninhibited breath, as if all the pressures and constraints she'd sustained over the previous hours and weeks---even years---were receding all at once.

He stared after her when she returned to her compartment, also releasing a long exhalation. He was feeling liberation of his own, a kind he'd felt before.

They'd sprung to freedom. All impediments were falling away.

CHAPTER 109

For almost five hours---from their would-be assassination all the way to the border---Grinevicius had faltered just once, when he'd tumbled into the *SAMSUNG* sign. Despite arriving in Minsk the night before on minimal sleep, under altogether different expectations, he'd never wavered in his focus or commitment to his client. And to Morris his stresses were evident, both in the circles under his eyes and the throatiness of his voice.

The lawyer's edge nonetheless receded when they crossed the checkpoint into Ukrainian territory---particularly when the Ukrainian border control officers stamped their passports. At last, through all his fatigue, he broke into an easy-going grin, the kind he'd displayed long ago in Vilnius.

"Well, looks like we're out," he said.

"Yes...incredible," Morris answered. "Without a hitch."

"Back in Lena's apartment, I would have said the odds were against us."

"And I would have agreed."

Grinevicius re-stretched his long legs, looked up at the ceiling and shook his head. Morris also leaned back and felt his tensions dissipate.

His first impulse was to seek out Lena. As the train left the platform, Piper appeared in their open doorway and pre-empted him.

"Congratulations," he said. "You made it."

"Thanks to you, Russell."

"The fact is, your plan worked," Grinevicius added. "Without it, we had nothing."

"Anyway...now that it's behind us, I propose a small celebration in my compartment. Lena has some snacks, ones which Svetlana packed."

"She also packed vodka, for each of us."

"I was going to mention that."

Grinevicius reached over into his bag, fished out his bottle, then looked over at Morris.

"Both of them?" Morris asked.

"Why not? Just in case."

With their bottles in hand they followed Piper down to his cabin, and upon entering, found Lena already sitting along the window. Four shot glasses were arrayed on the table, which Piper had secured from the attendant. He gestured for Morris to sit opposite Lena. "Please..." he insisted. "You and Lena have been at the epicenter of all this. By comparison John and I are the latecomers."

Morris relented as Grinevicius slid in next to Lena. For the first time since Minsk, he beheld her at length.

Much of the vigilance and skepticism she'd exhibited over the previous two weeks had slipped away. Once again he recognized the tribulations he'd visited upon her through his overreaching and miscalculation. But he also experienced an unburdening of his own. He'd done his part to get her out.

She looked back.

"This is a first," she said.

"You mean drinking vodka together?"

She nodded.

"We escaped the KGB," he responded. "I think that warrants at least one toast."

She smiled and looked up at Piper, who was opening a container of hors d'oeuvres. He remained standing and poured out the shot glasses. When he was done he took the free seat next to Morris and raised his glass.

"Here's to the three of you, and to the way you surmounted challenge and danger---the stuff of fiction."

Morris felt his throat burn and eyes water as the vodka went down. After Lena had taken a slice of bread and sausage, he grabbed one for himself.

Recapitulations ensued in short order, mostly on Grinevicius' initiative, going all the way back to dinner at *Zolotoi Vek*. Within seven or eight minutes, the lawyer proposed that Morris make a second toast. Morris felt the first already going to his head, and glanced at Lena to see how she was faring. Though she'd consumed hers in several doses, her face had flushed.

"Just half a portion for me," she said.

Piper obliged her, and filled the other three glasses to the brims without delay. Once he'd re-settled Morris took care with his phrasing, determined to strike the right tone. "To Lena…Who got involved in this through no fault of her own, ended up right in the middle of everything…And ultimately became the pivot of our escape."

Endorsements issued from Piper and Grinevicius, and the second shot went down smoothly, to immediate effect. After another round of compliments directed at Lena, Grinevicius expressed a desire to call his fiancé, and excused himself. As he did, Morris re-raised the subject of the Cognition Software rescue effort.

"I wouldn't worry so much about that," Piper explained. "While you were boarding in the train in Minsk, I called my Lithuanian counterpart, the CIA chief in Vilnius… not one of the operatives who were harassing John, it goes without saying…and advised him to stymie the whole thing. I even suggested he wait until the last minute, to keep the diversion in play for as long as possible. Who knows? It may have had the collateral effect of abetting our own escape."

Grinevicius returned to catch the gist, and proposed another toast, to Cognition Software. This time Lena deferred entirely, and the gathering began to wind down. Fifteen minutes later she served cookies and chocolate, and Grinevicius, partaking little of the dessert, finally seemed to hit a wall. The previous 48 hours had taken their toll. "We haven't even prepared our bunks," he said to Morris. "Are you going to stay up a while longer?"

Somewhat torn, Morris glanced across the table at Lena. His brain felt increasingly saturated by alcohol, and the last thing he wanted tonight, after his steps toward redemption, was to show himself half-drunk. He chose the safer course.

"Okay," he said, rising to his feet. "It's obviously been a draining day. I guess I should also get some sleep."

Piper stood to see them off, shaking hands, while Lena remained seated. Morris bid her good night, assuming she would retire soon herself.

However she exhibited no signs of movement.

At the door he re-registered the vibe that had been developing all evening between her and Piper. But it was too late now for regrets.

He could only hope it didn't lead anywhere. He really did want his chance in Kiev.

CHAPTER 110

During the pause Lena registered the vibrations and rhythm of the tracks. She remained too exhilarated to sleep.

Her brainwaves swung briefly onto Natasha---out of contact since the previous weekend, absorbed in her Italian visa application and upcoming travel plans. Natasha considered her gambit with Fabrizio daring and progressive, and while Lena still didn't approve, she had to admit that it did have a certain breakout quality to it. If Natasha only knew what had transpired with *her* during the past twenty-four hours...

The door to the compartment remained cracked open.

She recognized that she didn't really understand Russell Piper on a telling level, despite all they'd just been though. When he'd resettled on the opposite settee she beheld him across the table and recalled her initial, furtive observations at *Bagira*, some two weeks earlier. Morris was inscrutable and tightly demarcated, in his own way. But Piper---with his inhuman training routines and contained attractions---remained a true puzzle. This was her first opportunity, outside the bounds of crisis, to engage him one-on-one. To learn a little more. Maybe even refract some light onto some of the broader questions that had dogged her over previous weeks.

Conversely she felt awkward about lingering at such a late hour. By her standards, it could convey an unseemly impression.

Her sense of liberation offset her rectitude for a moment longer. Piper didn't appear keen to see her go, either. Just now she wished he would fill the void, preferably in Russian.

He obliged her.

"Three shots were more than I intended," he said. "But I think we all needed a release."

"I agree. It was a good idea."

He smiled at her across their separation.

"…I should admit," she added. "Those were my first toasts ever on a train."

"Mine too, come to think of it."

He made an addendum of his own.

"…We've experienced lots of firsts tonight."

The phrase hung in the enclosed space and for unknown reasons caused her to blush slightly. Surrounding pulsations re-asserted themselves. He cast a thoughtful look at the tabletop. "I wish it hadn't reached such extremes. For you especially, Lena. The other three of us are Americans. Washington escalated this crisis, and we suffered the consequences. You, by contrast, were forced to flee your own country."

"No need for regrets. Not on my behalf."

He examined her to make sure.

"…Really. The fact is, I'm glad to get out. The last couple of weeks underlined how repressive and constraining Belarus has become. You could even say the timing is good. My mother is in Ukraine now. She and I can stay with relatives, for as long as we need to."

"On that note, I should assure you. Regardless of what's just transpired in Washington, the U.S., government will take all possible measures to assist you in the way of material support. Your mother, too. I'll make sure of it."

"I appreciate that."

In complete contravention of her habitual self-reliance, his pledge of material underpinning, even on behalf of his government, gave her an odd quiver of pleasure. To counteract it she interlocked her fingers and placed them over her knee, inclining forward. This in turn produced an additional infusion of intimacy---the opposite of what she intended. Logic told her she should get up and go.

"Well," she said, uncrossing her legs. "I should probably also get to bed."

Piper's smile relaxed. "It has been a long night," he said, leaning forward from the backrest. "Though I can't go to sleep just yet. I've got to make a few phone calls."

Lena wondered if one of the calls would be to his wife. She also knew better than to ask. Meanwhile she remained poised on the edge of her settee. "Actually the same is true of me. My compartment-mate is pleasant enough. But she's a loud snorer. Normally I'd read in this situation. But I don't have a book."

Piper laughed. "One thing Svetlana forgot to pack."

She shared the quip, still in no rush to stand up. When the humor subsided his expression became more serious again. "Listen," he said. "Why don't you use my compartment? I can sleep with Evan and John. They have two empty bunks." Lena felt her nervousness re-surge. Also a new thrill, which she tried at once to suppress.

"It's probably not worth it. John in particular looked pretty tired."

"I'm sure they'll adapt."

"No...Really, it's not worth the trouble." Another pause drew her attention to the table, extending out from the side. "...However I will help you clean up after our party, so you won't have to deal with it later. Then I'll be on my way."

Piper pulled a deep breath and stood up. "Okay....Thanks, Lena, I appreciate it. Of course if you change your mind, the offer remains open." He retrieved his cell-phone from his briefcase and turned back toward her from the threshold, holding eye contact for a double-beat then stepping into the aisle and closing the door.

Before Lena stood to attend to the clean-up she noticed a bar of chocolate, half-finished, lying open on its wrapper. She reached across and broke off several squares.

Moderation and propriety had prevailed in one domain tonight. But limits had still been stripped away.

She required another indulgence before going to bed.

*   *   *

Piper held his alcohol well, but was nonetheless glad for the cake and chocolates afterward. Now he hewed to Agency protocol and gave precedence to his two operational calls: first to Svetlana, via scrambler on her end, informing her that he'd successfully escorted Lena, Morris and Grinevicius across the border; second to CIA station in Kiev. Stanley Davidson---Piper's successor as station chief---was indisposed, but Piper spoke to his deputy, conveying a brief summary of the operation and requirements for pickup at the train terminus in Kiev. His third call was to Caroline, by way of Kiev station's secure communications hub. Time in Rhode Island was now a little before 8:30 p.m. She didn't answer until the sixth ring, and sounded a little rushed. There was a hubbub of voices and miscellaneous noise in the background: a restaurant lobby. Her first reflex was to ask him if he was okay.

"Everything's fine, Caroline. Though I had to make an unexpected departure. I'm calling from the night train to Kiev."

"Emergency?"

"You could say that. But it's over now."

"I'm glad you called."

True to practice, they defaulted to the ordinary. Which meant she did most of the talking. A drive across the Newport Bridge for dinner. Table for five at a well-known restaurant on the waterfront. Piper could visualize both the dock-front patio and the interior lobby from which she was now speaking.

"I hope you've all finished your main course," he said.

"Not to worry."

"Swordfish, in your case?"

"You guessed it."

"Then I won't detain you. Give my love to Nick, Melanie, and your parents."

"And our love to you. Mine especially…You know we miss you. Will you call me tomorrow from Kiev?"

"Of course."

When they signed off, he held the phone in his hand for a moment and stared at the display screen. After a deep breath he glanced back at the closed door to the compartment, just three meters down the aisle. Lena was still inside, still tidying up.

His third call had mattered most. But he wished it had lasted a little longer.

*   *   *

While stowing several food containers on an upper rack, Lena repositioned Piper's half-open travel bag and inadvertently shifted an already-worn item he'd stuffed in next to it, releasing an expulsion of embedded odors. Her nostrils engorged with the zing of dried perspiration, catching her off-guard. It was the same white dress shirt in which he'd raced across the city and materialized half-soaked at her door.

Once she'd put the containers and shirt in place, she sat down. His excretions hung in the enclosed air.

She braced her palms on her thighs and distended her nasal passages for a deeper, more deliberate pull, and in fuller measure the scent raced through her principal neurons, opening switches and synapses that were normally closed. It also induced a reconsideration of Piper's proposal, after all---to select one of the bunks and prepare a bed for herself. She looked up at the opposite rack, where sheets, blankets and pillows had been deposited by the attendant.

Instead she remained in place. Some opposing force prevented her from going that far.

From the settee she listened through the door, trying to make out if Piper remained occupied with his calls. Part of her wished he would return quickly...End the expectancy....That they'd at least have the chance to talk again before she retired to her cabin, even though sleep remained out of the question. Meanwhile she was anxious---near-terrified, really---that he would make an overture. Not that some earth-moving episode would happen right away...tonight, in this compartment...but that what came next might form a prelude, a harbinger of something novel and exciting...

She sensed that Piper could be a change agent in more ways than one. Also that she felt supremely alive, in a way she never had before. Tonight she had no urge to philosophize. For perhaps the first time in her life she felt inclined to let herself go. To stop thinking.

She listened through the door and waited.

CHAPTER 111

Most outward indicators were innocuous. Inviting quarters. Dedicated collaborator. Joint afterglow from a fruitful operation. Then some overdue hours of sleep, free of physical danger and political crisis. Piper glanced back at the door and visualized Lena, just meters away, her immaculate skin and swelling hips, gray eyes and emissions of understanding…

Outlines were familiar and undeniable. This was the repetition he'd taken such pains to avoid.

Additional minutes were slipping by, and she still hadn't made the move. Instead of turning toward the cabin he gripped the handrail with both hands and took in the darkened landscape, unfurling at full speed..

Tonight, for all the parallels, there was a critical difference. At his core, he remained calm, equilibrated, lucid…confident in his ability to evade lapses and transgressions for the remainder of the journey. Tonight he had the advantage of two cardio obliterations over the previous fifteen hours, culminating with his two-and-a-half-kilometer dash to Lena's building…He drew another glance at the door.

What worried him was Kiev.

There they'd be in close proximity for full, consecutive days, with schedules that would push training to the margins...Both still in the flush of liberation, his tableaus in full activation and his baselines elevated well beyond normal levels, with a risk, in the end, that his method could incite precisely the wrong result...But he couldn't reverse the dynamic now. He released one hand from the railing, blew an exhalation and stepped toward his compartment.

At almost the same instant another door slid open at the end of the wagon, making him stop. Morris emerged, clad in a white t-shirt and boxer shorts, and waved down the aisle. The boniness and pallor of his legs accentuated his bare feet as he drew closer.

"Still up?" he asked.

"I had to make some phone calls."

A somewhat awkward silence ensued, which Piper filled.

"You also, I see."

"Not for long. One final trip to the restroom."

The train swayed around a curve and Morris, still under effects of vodka, reached for the hand-rail. During the pause he glanced first at Piper's cabin, then over Piper's shoulder to the end of the wagon. It was clear what he wanted to ask, but on apparent second thought, refrained---as if employing his own methods of self-regulation.

Before he could resume progress, the train began to slow suddenly. Concerned, Piper looked forward out the windows. An instant later screeching emanated from the rails below, surprising both of them. Abruptly the train's speed began to decrease. There was little mistake; they were braking.

Morris peered out through a window himself. "Is there a stop scheduled?"

"Not to my knowledge."

Various scenarios presented themselves, mostly unfavorable. There were no towns in the vicinity. Only woods.

"Could this concern us?"

"It might."

Piper thought quickly.

"I suggest you go wake up John," he said. "I'll also warn Lena."

Morris nodded and headed back at once down the aisle, without venturing a glance back.

At last Piper reached for the door latch. This hadn't figured in his tableaus.

CHAPTER 112

With each passing minute Lena's misgivings multiplied. What would Piper think after such a long interlude? From her perch on the settee she couldn't make out what he was saying, but could hear his voice through the door. On what she took to be his third call, his intonations became more tender and informal. Perhaps his wife? That provided the punctuation she needed. Her head cleared, and at last she got up to leave, making one last survey of the cabin. Footfalls from the corridor made her pause, followed by the familiar modulations of Morris. What on earth could he and Piper be talking about, now that all hazards were behind them?

Her impatience was superseded by slowing of the train.

Based on previous journeys to Kiev, she didn't recall any stops along this segment. Perplexed, she stepped to the window, parted the curtains, and squinted out into pale moonlight. All that was visible was darkened forest. While she retraced again to the door, the latch clicked down; Piper slid open the panel and materialized at the threshold. His look gave her a jolt of apprehension.

"Why are we stopping?"

"I don't know, Lena. We should go back on alert."

"Any idea what it might be?"

"The most benign possibility? A mechanical problem. But that could be wishful thinking."

He brushed around her and looked out the window as well, craning toward the forward end of the train. "Looks like a road crossing. There are searchlights aimed at the train, along with several sets of headlights." He strained further and squinted. "...There's also a slight curve in the tracks. But I think I see a number of figures in uniform."

His concentrated expression sharpened as he pulled back from the window. An instant later Morris and Grinevicius entered the cabin, both buttoning their shirts. Grinevicius' belt was still unfastened and he appeared to have been roused from sleep.

"Could this be the Belarussian KGB?" he asked. "...In Ukraine?"

"Very unlikely," Piper answered, in clipped tones. "They simply don't have the resources or audacity for such an operation here. That leaves the Russians, who have both, in principle. But if they've become that desperate... that is, to snatch us off the train and expunge the whole episode...then this has gotten more serious than I ever imagined."

The word "expunge" had an immediate, frightening effect on Lena, and seemed to provoke similar reactions from Morris and Grinevicius. Hers ratcheted several rungs higher when Piper, with no forewarning, pulled down his pre-packed travel bag from the overhead shelf, opened some sort of interior compartment, and extracted an automatic pistol and unconventional-looking lightweight holster. Without pause he propped one foot on the edge of the settee, raised his pant leg, and strapped the latter accessory to his ankle. He then pulled out several clips of ammunition, putting one in each back pocket and pushing the third into the chamber of the weapon. The entire procedure took about fifteen seconds. Once it was accomplished he turned back to face them. Lena noted that the pistol was compact enough to be enveloped by his hand.

"The gun is only for extreme circumstances," he said. "Let's hope I don't have to use it." He checked the safety, leaned down, inserted the weapon in his ankle holster, and re-dropped his pant leg. "The first thing I've got to do is determine what's going on. Before I do, the three of you should probably move down to the end-compartment of the wagon, which has exits onto both sides of the tracks. John, can you give me your cell number, so I can communicate back instructions, if necessary?"

"Of course..." Grinevicius, back in full activation now, stood up and took Piper's phone. He punched in the number, ringing his own phone in his back pocket.

"Okay, let's go," Piper said.

The four of them filed out, Morris and Grinevicius first, followed by Lena. Piper brought up the rear, flicking off the light and closing the door on his way out. At his instruction they walked single-file toward the end furthest from the locomotive, past the attendant's cabin---where the slider was cracked open and interior still dark---and re-assembled in the end-compartment.

"As you can see, the exit-doors operate by means of hand-wheels," he said, gesturing to the heavy-steel apparati on each side. "They open counter-clockwise, and require a bit of physical effort. If we have to make an escape, I'll designate the appropriate side. One of you..." He gestured to Morris and Grinevicius. "Probably better you, Evan, since John is injured...should spin the wheel to open it as quickly as possible. Once the door is open climb out onto the embankment on the side of the track, help Lena dismount, and run for the forest as fast as you can. I'll then try to coordinate a rendezvous later, also by phone."

"Any questions?"

There were none.

"Remember: stay here unless I give word. Let's hope this is a false alarm."

He exited the compartment, closing the swinging door quietly as he did. Lena heard his footfalls recede quickly and disappear. She looked across at the dimmed, serious faces of Morris and Grinevicius, who examined her in turn. The party atmosphere was gone.

She'd been apprehensive before. But the reason had been altogether different.

*   *   *

Piper re-traced to the forward-end of the wagon and entered the
opposite boarding-compartment. First on the left, and then from the
right, he pressed his face to the window and re-surveyed the scene
ahead. Bright lights still pervaded the intersection, illumining the
locomotive and leading wagons. He spotted vehicles and figures on
the adjacent roadways, but detected no additional presences further
down the train.

Opting for the flank with lesser activity, he spun the hand-wheel
on the right, opened the mechanism as quietly as he could, and
jumped down onto the gravel side-bank. From a crouching position
he scanned up below the undercarriage, alert to approaching legs
and feet on the left. Seeing none, he retreated further down the right
incline to the level, grassy strip that paralleled the tracks. Confident
that he was undetected, he made cautious line forward.

He didn't get far. Flashlights shone 40 meters up the tracks.

CHAPTER 113

Before their lights revealed him, Piper drew his pistol and moved laterally into the forest, taking cover behind several low-hanging pine branches. From his darkened vantage he assessed the approaching figures. He also took hold of his cell-phone with his left hand--- ready to transmit the flee signal.

There were three men. What struck him first was their apparent lack of urgency, and that they had not drawn their weapons. Next, at closer range: that they spoke casual, genial-sounding Russian, with Ukrainian accents. As they drew up even, under the nearest carriage, he also spotted hand-held lighting and three additional pairs of legs, moving down the other side of the train in parallel.

In the group on his side one of the men's flashlights swung incidentally onto the back of another, illuminating his uniform. At once Piper recognized the medium-blue, decidedly un-Soviet attire of the Ukrainian National Police. He re-holstered his pistol under his pant-leg and stepped out of the shadows. The threesome didn't even take notice until he was halfway back to the train, when startled by his footfalls on the gravel embankment, they at last directed their beacons upon him. Piper stopped and spread his arms, to demonstrate lack of threat. "I mean no harm," he said. "I'm an American diplomat, assigned to the U.S. Embassy in Minsk."

One of the officers stepped out from the two others, shining his light straight in his face.

"Are you a passenger on the train?"

"Yes. I simply de-boarded to learn the nature of the problem."

A pause ensued, of unidentifiable cause.

"Are you Russell Piper?"

Piper couldn't see his interlocutor's face. But he could see that his pistol remained holstered. In any case it was too late to reverse course.

"Yes, I am."

The officer relaxed and lowered his flashlight toward the ground, rendering his face visible, as well as those of the other two. He reached to his vest and raised a radio microphone.

"We've found Piper," he said.

"And his three companions?" said a discombobulated voice on the other end.

The officer extended Piper a querulous look, waiting for an answer. Piper hesitated, keeping his cell-phone in hand, then gestured toward the closest wagon, two cars away from the wagon in which they'd actually traveled and where Lena, Morris and Grinevicius remained situated.

"On the train," he answered.

Showing no impulse to board, the officer engaged in another radio exchange. From it, Piper understood they were to await further instructions from headquarters, and conduct him forward in the meanwhile. The other contingent was directed to return up the train as well.

"Could you please come with us?" the officer said, gesturing toward the floodlit area around the locomotive.

"Can you tell me what this about?"

"Orders from Kiev. That's all we know." The officer gestured forward again, adopting a beleaguered affability. "Please..."

The other two policemen followed behind as Piper walked with the first, rather than staying behind to secure the middle wagons, from which he drew further encouragement. If this interception proved to be staged---an entrapment by one party or another---he was at least adding distance. More time to send the alert signal back to the others.

Their assemblage passed several wagons, subtracting half the length to the locomotive and enabling to make out five or six additional blue-uniformed figures milling around the illuminated clearing ahead, along with two police vehicles parked on the right-side roadway. Ten paces on, he also heard a helicopter, approaching from the south, coming in fast. Upon sighting its taillights and white fuselage in the night-sky, he couldn't make out the markings, but identified it as non-military.

"One of yours?" he asked the lead officer.

"Your guess is as good as mine," came the answer, along with a shrug.

Just before they attained the crossroad, the helicopter pulled up overhead. Piper was squinting up, still trying to identify it, when it turned on another powerful searchlight, blinding him.

Several seconds later his cell-phone chortled in his hand.

* * *

The voice, even against the thump of the rotors, conveyed the usual jocular tone and required only an instant to recognize. The speaker was Leonid Kravchuk. Piper hadn't seen him since the Embassy party.

"Good to see you're up, Russell. I thought I might have to wake you."

"Wake me? Are you kidding, Leonid? I was preparing for the worst. What the hell is going on?"

"Excuse the lack of warning..." Piper heard Kravchuk pause and issue instructions to the pilot. "...We're about to land. Better if I explain on the ground."

The helicopter exited its hover-position and swung sixty-seventy meters down the roadway, beyond the police vehicles. While touching down it kicked up a swirl of dust, causing Piper to turn back toward the train. An instant later a lone figure rounded the locomotive from the other side, stepping over the rails with a cell-phone to his ear. When he spotted Piper amid the policemen he closed the device and adjusted direction.

Piper made another instant recognition. This one came coupled with a jolt of confusion.

He raised his phone again, ready to sound the alarm. Just now Oleg Mikhailov was the last person he expected to see.

CHAPTER 114

The first variant to strike Piper---one that was automatic under the circumstances---was also the most outrageous. Collusion between Kravchuk and the FSB on such a large-stakes operation, with such sweeping ramifications, violated too many geo-political precepts to be believable.

But the Russians had already demolished plenty of precedents back in Minsk, vis-à-vis their Belarussian proxies. Tonight, nothing seemed off-bounds.

Moreover they'd recruited numerous other Ukrainian intelligence officials onto their payroll over the years; Kravchuk, if he was the latest, would be far from unique. And the Ukrainian policemen could still prove to imposters or stooges. He punched up Grinevicius' number on his screen and placed his thumb over the call button.

Then scrutinized Oleg as he drew closer. What he noticed first about the Russian was his expression. Tense. Frustrated. Worried. And when he locked eyes again, perhaps for the first time in his experience with FSB operatives: embarrassed. Second, that the Ukrainian policemen milling around the area showed no recognition and little interest in him.

Oleg was hardly the picture of command and triumph.

Piper glanced back at Kravchuk's helicopter. The blades were decelerating to idle-speed and the side door had yet to open. When he turned back toward the train the Russian closed the final distance

"The first thing I want to do is apologize," he said.

Piper scrutinized him and said nothing.

"…What happened back in Minsk was appalling. The situation spun completely out of control. And I can tell you, the people responsible didn't only endanger lives; they also broke compacts with us."

"The FSB had no prior knowledge of them?"

"None. Those actions…the assassination attempt, their efforts to quarantine you within the city…were a panicked, primitive response to the signals they'd gotten out of Washington. Which perhaps is what your Vice-President Gallstone wanted in the first place."

"Perhaps," Piper conceded. "But that doesn't justify it."

"No, it doesn't."

Still wary, Piper shot another glance back at the helicopter. Kravchuk was descending the steps. Upon attaining hard ground, the Ukrainian looked over and waved, evidently not the least bit surprised to see Oleg. Puzzled, Piper turned back again and addressed the Russian.

"What I still can't understand is what you're doing here."

"Call it my last-ditch effort to avert disaster," he answered. "As the situation deteriorated I instructed a couple of our operatives to trail Svetlana Ivanova from your Embassy, rather than trying to follow you. I figured she'd provide the key to what came next, and I was right. I barely managed to buy a ticket and board the train."

Piper was about to ask the next obvious question when he sensed Kravchuk closing in behind him. Twisting around, he encountered the Ukrainian's customary easy grin and fleshy handshake. "Sorry about the lack of warning," he said. "Intercepting a train in the countryside in the middle of the night isn't as easy as it seems."

Just as notable as Kravchuk's manner was his order of greeting. The Ukrainian glanced at Oleg but didn't hasten to shake his hand. Instead he continued to address Piper:

"...I was back in Kiev for consultations, as you may recall, about to leave on vacation. We got the request from your James Stapleton to pull you and your three travelling companions off the train, before you reached destination. Due, as I understood, to urging from an unlikely source." At this he took a half-step to the side and finally extended his hand to Oleg. "I admit," he said as his gesture was reciprocated. "I haven't cooperated with the FSB like this for quite a while."

The Russian nodded an acknowledgement, taking the loaded compliment with evenness. When Kravchuk stepped back again Piper didn't relent.

"What you still haven't told me, Leonid," he said. "...Is the reason. Why are we being pulled off?"

"Looks like you're in for a detour," the Ukrainian answered. "According to latest instructions I'm to transport you to a military airfield about 20 kilometers from here. But let me confirm that..." He reached into the pocket of his windbreaker and pulled out a cell-phone. He engaged a brief conversation in Russian with a superior in Kiev, paused during an interregnum, then switched to English. "Yes, we did it," he said. "In fact Russell is standing here right in front of me."

With this he transferred the phone to Piper. Piper's last stores of wariness dissolved when Stapleton's voice issued over the connection. The first information the Deputy Director conveyed was where they were going, and what awaited them when they reached their new destination. As he proceeded to other details Piper glanced up at Kravchuk with a nod, then at Oleg, also still standing close-by.

He still didn't understand what Oleg was doing on the train.

CHAPTER 115

Since the border crossing Piper recognized that he'd projected him-self onto different premises and shorter timelines, ones that no lon-ger applied. The first and most essential adjustment was the nine-hour direct flight to Dulles. Subsequent tableaus emanated from there.

He wasn't returning to Kiev after all.

Once Stapleton had conveyed the new itinerary, and probable tem-plates for debriefings at Langley, he proceeded to explain how the changes had transpired, and how Oleg had indeed constituted their point of origin.

From the train, Oleg had alerted his superiors in Moscow to the assassination attempt and Piper's escape route. He'd then suggested further measures. Most important: a channel of communication with Stapleton, to assure Langley that the FSB had not authorized or condoned the assassination attempt, and was endeavoring to avert full-blown catastrophe. His biggest worry, as the train moved south, was that the Belarussian KGB would run data scans of all international passenger lists, make proper identification, and undertake additional extreme measures at the border.

"Moscow told me Oleg was ready to intervene directly with the border guards," Stapleton related. "At least to the extent he could, invoking wider interests from Moscow. Thankfully it never came to that."

Piper began to assemble the pieces. As he did, he also retreated five meters toward the forest line.

"I see," he said, once he'd distanced himself from Oleg and Kravchuk. "That explains why he was on the train."

"Yes. His next advice, also conveyed through Moscow, was along the same lines. That was to get you off the train before you reached Kiev. Even though you'd crossed the border, he figured there was a chance the KGB could make the match before the journey was complete. Kiev Central Station is a big, chaotic environment, and Belarus has at least some operatives in the city. A couple of snipers, some surgical shots...The way the situation had degraded, nothing seemed out of the question."

"In other words, better safe than sorry."

"Exactly. I didn't need a lot of convincing, and connected straightaway with the Ukrainian SVR, to orchestrate the interception. And given the severity of what happened, unwinding the whole episode at Langley seemed better all the way around."

Piper couldn't argue with the logic, even though it wasn't the end-point he'd envisioned.

"...However along with this suggestion the Russians made one firm request," Stapleton added.

"What was that?"

"That both sides permanently bury this episode...as if it never happened. Given Gallstone's role in inciting it, the proposal made sense. I acceded."

Piper couldn't fault that logic, either.

"Speaking of unwinding..." he said. "Where do we stand now on this with the Russians? Specifically, what's next with Oleg?"

"The first question remains open. Belarus is their de facto domain. As for Oleg, I have no idea. You're there in the field, and best able to ascertain that yourself."

"Agreed."

Piper closed Kravchuk's phone and opened his own, hitting the speed-dial button that he'd been on the verge of pressing moments earlier. Grinevicius answered at once, still tense. "You can relax," Piper told him. "Tell Lena and Evan that everything is fine. Go back to the cabins and gather your bags, and mine as well, if you don't mind. I'll send some Ukrainian policemen back in a few minutes to conduct you forward."

"Where are we going?"

"Change in plans. We're bound for Washington."

Despite his travails there the previous week, Grinevicius didn't balk. He sounded more than ready to return.

*　　*　　*

When Piper retraced to Oleg and Kravchuk, the former was on his phone and latter was conversing with a police captain. His first interaction was with Kravchuk, to request the pickup of Lena and the others. He then re-addressed Oleg, who had just concluded his call.

"I guess some measure of appreciation is in order."

"Not really," the Russian responded, still showing frustration. "The fact is, I simply backstopped your escape plan."

Piper nodded. He refrained from extending his hand.

"What would you have done if the KGB had found us out, and pulled us off the train?"

"Improvise. Thank God, I didn't have to. All the most destabilizing outcomes, it seems, will remain forever hypothetical."

"Yes, it seems so."

This latter component drew a sardonic look from Kravchuk, who detached himself from the police captain. An instant later, a second helicopter sounded in the night sky, approaching from the East. He also addressed Oleg.

"Yours?" he said.

The Russian nodded.

"Where to?" Piper asked.

"Back to Minsk. This isn't the first problem of this variety, but it's certainly the most serious. First item of business: relocate al-Tikriti to Russia…Get that issue off the table once and for all. Then some house-cleaning is in order, especially in the KGB. Some heads are going to roll. If not, then we have other levers to pull."

"Ones you should pull, in my opinion. And then?"

"If all goes well, Belarus will return to state of quiet. One which I should have ensured in the first place."

"I wish you luck with the first part." Piper observed. "As for the second…"

His pause prompted a slight smile from the Russian, Kravchuk also.

"…I doubt you can keep Belarus isolated and subservient forever."

"We'll see…. And what's next for you, Russell?"

"I'll be back in Minsk soon enough."

Further conversation was pre-empted by the approaching chop-per, whose lights drew up overhead, brightening the sky and augment-ing the stage-like atmosphere. After hovering a moment, it swung down the road and descended on the other side of Kravchuk's larger, military-style aircraft.

Oleg's helicopter, with Russian markings, looked newer and faster. He wouldn't take long to re-attain Minsk. At last Piper offered a hand-shake, which Oleg reciprocated.

"Well…good luck with the first part, then," he said.

"Thank you. I'll need it."

At last Piper shook his hand. After bidding corresponding farewell to Kravchuk Oleg turned and walked down the road. En route, he shifted his gaze to the pavement, as if already contemplating the tasks ahead. Piper and Kravchuk watched him go.

"Think there's a chance this will induce a new dynamic?" Piper asked.

"Who knows?" Kravchuk answered, reflecting for a moment. "It might be just the catalyst Belarus needs."

CHAPTER 116

From the helicopter they traversed 50 meters of flood-lit tarmac, which afforded an exterior view of the aircraft before they mounted the gangway. Once on-board Morris found its interior well-appointed, if not quite elegant, with space for 10-12 passengers, not including a communications cubicle which he glimpsed through a half-opened partition in the rear. A female attendant ushered them to four leather-upholstered seats in the main section: he and Lena in the first row, Piper and Grinevicius in the second. Before taxiing the pilot welcomed them for the flight and indicated that the jet was a Gulfstream GV. Minutes later they were airborne and climbing into the night sky.

Even during his period of riches, years of habitual first class, Morris realized he'd never traveled this well. And for the first time since, he felt thoroughly unburdened. Moreover it had nothing to do with money.

This time round, he'd confronted his misjudgments. Taken corrective action before it was too late. Not in front of a trading screen. But under mortal duress, in flesh-and-blood reality.

Halfway through their short journey by helicopter, Piper had raised his voice to above the din of the blades to address broader events. He'd characterized Grinevicius' recent travails in Washington as an "unconscionable transgression of U.S. legal norms…one that will not be repeated", and implied that the factions responsible, in the Pentagon and the Vice President's Office, were already marginalized and discredited. "In addition," he said, divulging his own leanings, "A new Administration will be elected in three months. If the outcome is as I hope, we won't experience these kinds of fiascoes and misadventures any longer."

To Morris' relief, he'd also relayed news that Yuri and the programmers had eschewed the Cognition Software rescue operation, displaying the discernment and good sense for which he'd hired them in the first place. The undertaking had fizzled to inconsequence, pre-empted at the Lithuanian border by both sides. That left some hope, based on declarations from Oleg, that the lab might even continue operation, given that none of the Belarussian personnel knew about al-Tikriti or were implicated in any way.

At 45,000 feet cruising altitude, the pilot predicted clear skies for the duration of the flight, and Piper retreated to the communications compartment. The attendant served herbal tea, and distributed blankets. Afterward she dimmed the cabin lights, and a moment later Grinevicius leaned back and fell asleep, with a tranquil expression on his face.

Morris next ventured a glance at Lena across the aisle, observing her profile: still in heightened activation, her thoughts elsewhere. She noticed him only after several seconds. Through the soft light she transmitted a slight smile…one of appreciation. If she was displeased about the outcome, or uneasy about the future, it didn't show. From her, just now, that was all he wished.

His frame of reference was different now.

He responded in kind, and faced forward again. Piper had obviously commandeered her main attentions, which he supposed was natural given the events of recent days. But his own life---while still in flux---seemed suddenly to be looking up. In Washington and beyond, who knew?

He laid the blanket over his legs, placed a pillow behind his head, and reclined his seat to near-horizontal. At one time he'd been able to sleep easily on planes, as he had in general. Though recently the skill had eluded him.

He closed his eyes imagined himself streaming through space. Within 30 seconds he slid into deep, untroubled slumber.

*   *   *

Lena watched Morris tilt back and levitate into sleep. Over their entire acquaintance, including the long months of language tutoring before this had all started, she'd never seen him so serene...as if he'd at last gained release from whatever gnawed him. If so, she was glad. His actions over the past few days, particularly tonight, had earned him extra esteem in her eyes, coupled with new strains of affection. He deserved any and all reprieve.

And to emerge, at last, from his shutdown. The thought occurred to her that there was potential between her and Morris after all.

She twisted slightly and glanced back down the aisle. The rear cubicle remained closed off, Piper out of sight---quite possibly talking to his wife, she supposed, along with other interlocutors. The recognition didn't bother her. Instead she turned and gazed again out the window, onto the flowing mosaic of moon and star-light, and reacquired the perspective she'd first gained on the rooftop.

Even if she came to know Piper somewhat better in Washington, she expected she'd never really learn what drove him, any more than when she'd first glimpsed him in the health club. And that the desires he'd felt for her but stifled, together with the spontaneous, wild, and altogether ill-considered longings she herself had experienced on the roof and the train, would recede forever into a hypothetical past. Very much for the better, for both of them.

All the same she waited for him to reappear. Until then she doubted she could fall asleep herself. She heard the partition slide open at the rear of the fuselage.

Piper stood in the opening, back-lit by screens and pulsing LEDs, shoulders squared and arms extended loosely against two rear seats. After an elongated look, he drew several even, intrinsic breaths and walked toward her down the aisle, bending his head forward to avoid brushing the ceiling. His movements appeared more lithe and economical than ever.

He settled into the opposite seat, buckled himself in, and looked over at her again, full of clarity and self-direction. Whatever he was thinking, he'd been just the sort of change agent she'd needed.

She was hurtling along a fresh trajectory. For now, that was all she wanted.

ACKNOWLEDGMENTS
BY THE AUTHOR

I took more risks with this novel than my first. So when I distributed initial drafts to a small circle of friends and diligent first-line readers, perhaps unsurprisingly, I received some forceful reactions. These were also invaluable; considerable honing and adjustment were still required to make the themes, story and characters cohere and work. The upfront commentary and criticism of these readers enabled me to make vital and necessary improvements before I moved to publication.

This capable and dedicated circle comprised: Ann Johnson, Chris DiNapoli, Dave Johnson, Marina Mishuk, Roger Moore, Stephanie Weaver and Thibaut Behaghel. Two additional readers, both citizens and current residents of Belarus, should also be included in this list, but in light of current political circumstances in the country I am compelled for now to leave them anonymous. I hope I am able to name them openly in future editions.

Both within Belarus and without, all devoted untold hours to this book, and I salute their willingness to participate in my creative process, if for no other reasons than their affinity for fiction and general good will. I am grateful to each and every one.

That said, I hold none of them responsible for the outcome. I alone am answerable for that.

Finally, on more sublime note, I wish to recognize the inestimable contribution of my cat Cleopatra, who was at my side through the writing of every page of this book, across multiple countries on two continents, and who passed away unexpectedly as I prepared for release. I dedicate *Minsk Rises* to her memory.

NOTES BY THE AUTHOR

R eaders unacquainted with Belarus may notice that I employ the labels "Russian" and "Belarussian" somewhat interchangeably for characters that live within its borders. This reflects general attitudes among Belarussians themselves, many of whom have ancestors from Russia or relatives that still reside there. Indeed, modern Belarus has existed as an independent state only since the break-up of the Soviet Union in 1991, and although the Belarussian language is today one of the two official state languages, 98 percent of the population employs Russian for everyday communication, both in the workplace and at home. The cultural, ethnic and linguistic lines between Belarus and Russia, at least for now, remain blurred.

I have likewise hewed to the physical realities of present-day Minsk. Those readers who have visited or lived in the city will recognize many streets, parks, buildings and even commercial establishments that appear in the narrative, which I have for the most part rendered with accuracy. I have taken similar approaches with Vilnius and Kiev.

With the characters, by contrast, I have given complete reign to my imagination. This holds for all the nationalities represented. Any resemblance among them to specific individuals, living or deceased, is incidental. Same for the storyline; while rooted in current events, it is also entirely my own creation.

In personal vein, I should add that I have a longstanding association with Belarus, have worked and resided there off and on for many years, and have developed great fondness for Belarussian people and for the city of Minsk in particular. Quirks of history and inopportune political developments since independence have however saddled the country with a repressive, dictatorial government---one that stifles the aspirations and potential of the population and largely excludes it from the contemporary Western world. Very soon, I hope, the people of Belarus will at last gain the freedom and democracy to which they have a deserving and long-overdue claim.

Kiev, July 2011

ABOUT THE AUTHOR

Eric Almeida was born in Ithaca, New York in 1962 and raised in Rhode Island. He attended Tabor Academy and majored in History at Brown University, where he also competed on the rowing team. Upon graduation in 1984 he worked as a Sports Writer at *The Providence Journal* for one year, then resumed his education at The School of Advanced International Studies (SAIS) of Johns Hopkins University, receiving an M.A. in International Affairs in 1987.

From graduate school he detoured into business, working as international sales manager for an American high-technology company for five years, primarily in Europe. He proceeded to co-found a software-development venture based in Belarus and Paris, for which he also served as President from 1996-2001.

Soon thereafter he returned to writing, his core interest. He currently divides his time between Ukraine and the New England coastline.

More information about Eric Almeida and his books is available at http://www.ericalmeida.com.